Praise for H

'Irresistible love stories in gorgeous ⸏ ⸏ ⸏ ⸏ ⸏ ⸏
feel like friends. A Holly Hepburn ⸏ ⸏ ⸏ ⸏ ⸏
Miranda Dic⸏ ⸏ ⸏

'Like a ray of sunshine on a cloudy ⸏ ⸏ ⸏ ⸏ sparkling story
will sweep you away and leave your heart full of love'
Cathy Bramley

'Losing yourself in a Holly Hepburn book is one of
life's pleasures – they're the perfect escape'
Milly Johnson

'Wholly satisfying reads – a warm glow is guaranteed
when you snuggle up with a Holly Hepburn book!'
Heidi Swain

'I devoured this gorgeous book as quickly as a tin of Scottish
shortbread. You'll be on the first train to Edinburgh after reading.
Cosy, comforting, escapist and romantic, and in the most wonderful
setting, this is the perfect way to start the New Year. Delightful!'
Veronica Henry

'A feel-good story that captured me – then
held me until the last page'
Sue Moorcroft

'An uplifting, indulgent treat of a romance, perfect to curl up with
on sunny days or cold winter nights. I loved everything about it!'
Cressida McLaughlin

'The perfect cosy romance, I loved hanging out with Fraser
and Maura in Edinburgh – a gorgeous celebration of love
and the magical city that brought them together'
Laura Wood

'A Holly Hepburn novel is guaranteed to fill your heart with joy'
Isabelle Broom

Holly Hepburn is the author of many novels including, *Escape to Darling Cove*, *Return to Half Moon Farm* and *Healing Hearts on Thistledown Lane*. Follow her on Instagram at @HollyH_Author and Bluesky at @hollyhauthor.

Also by Holly Hepburn

A Year at the Star and Sixpence
The Picture House by the Sea
A Year at Castle Court
Last Orders at the Star and Sixpence
Coming Home to Brightwater Bay
The Little Shop of Hidden Treasures
Escape to Darling Cove
Return to Half Moon Farm

Holly Hepburn

Healing Hearts on Thistledown Lane

**SIMON &
SCHUSTER**

London · New York · Amsterdam/Antwerp · Sydney/Melbourne · Toronto · New Delhi

First published in Great Britain by Simon & Schuster UK Ltd, 2026

Copyright © Tamsyn Murray, 2026

The right of Tamsyn Murray to be identified as author of this work has been asserted in accordance with the Copyright, Designs and Patents Act, 1988.

1 3 5 7 9 10 8 6 4 2

Simon & Schuster UK Ltd, 1st Floor
222 Gray's Inn Road, London WC1X 8HB

Simon & Schuster Australia, Sydney
Simon & Schuster India, New Delhi

www.simonandschuster.co.uk
www.simonandschuster.com.au
www.simonandschuster.co.in

The authorised representative in the EEA is Simon & Schuster Netherlands BV, Herculesplein 96, 3584 AA Utrecht, Netherlands. info@simonandschuster.nl

Simon & Schuster strongly believes in freedom of expression and stands against censorship in all its forms. For more information, visit BooksBelong.com

A CIP catalogue record for this book is available from the British Library

Paperback ISBN: 978-1-3985-1204-7
eBook ISBN: 978-1-3985-1205-4
Audio ISBN: 978-1-3985-5665-2

Typeset in Bembo by M Rules
Printed and Bound in the UK using 100% Renewable Electricity at CPI Group (UK) Ltd

FSC
www.fsc.org

MIX
Paper | Supporting
responsible forestry
FSC® C013604

For Charlotte,
who has held me up more times than I can count.

PART ONE

PROLOGUE

The pub was standing room only. Maura stood with one arm uncomfortably pinned to her side, the other bent at the elbow so she could take the occasional sip of her drink, nodding along to what her friend Ruth was half-shouting over the remake of 'Do They Know It's Christmas?' that was belting from wall-mounted speakers.

'I can't believe how many people from school are here. It's like a six-month reunion.'

Maura couldn't argue. The Strawberry in Edinburgh's New Town had always been the preferred pub for the St Ignatius School students who were old enough to drink, as well as plenty who were not, so perhaps it wasn't a surprise that so many had been lured back for the first Christmas after leaving. For some, it was a return home from their first term at university or college, and for others, it was simply an opportunity to catch up with friends. Maura had decidedly mixed feelings about being this close to so many of her old classmates, some of whom she'd be quite happy never to see again. But it was almost Christmas – what else had she expected? 'It's mobbed,' she bellowed in Ruth's direction, waving away a plume of cigarette smoke from the man next to her. 'Even Queen Sarah is here.'

Her friend craned her head to follow the direction of Maura's gaze, then scowled. 'Of course she is. Holding court, as usual.'

Sarah Grant had been the most popular girl in their year – the one who seemed to sail through puberty without a single spot, the one who'd got top marks without apparently ever revising, the one most likely to marry a footballer and live in an ostentatious mansion with a Chihuahua called Gucci. Maura hadn't held any of that against her; it would have been like blaming the sun for shining, and it helped that she'd occupied a completely different sphere of school life. Maura had been quiet, unshowy and had generally hidden away in the art block. She doubted Queen Sarah even knew they'd been in the same year.

Another puff of grey smoke curled around them and Maura suddenly became aware of how thick the air was. So many bodies created warmth, which enhanced the hops and apple aroma from the alcohol being consumed. The combination of music, the bombardment of other conversations with their abrupt bursts of laughter, and the smothering second-hand smoke made Maura's head swim. 'I'm going outside for a minute,' she told Ruth. 'Are you coming?'

Ruth downed the last of her pint and shook her head. 'I'll get us another drink. Might take me ten minutes to reach the bar.'

Outside, the night was cool and considerably less overwhelming. The moon skimmed in and out of clouds overhead, playing hide and seek with the stars, but the temperature was mild for December. The cobbled street was empty. A glance at her watch told her it was just before ten-thirty, meaning the night was still young. Most of the city's drinkers would be inside one of its many pubs, making the most of the festive vibe before hitting a club around midnight. Maura had no intention of joining them. Leaning against the wall of the pub, she took in several lungfuls of blessedly clean air as the bass vibrated through the bricks against her shoulder blades, wishing her ears would stop buzzing. She just needed a minute to ease the ache in her temples, she told herself as she closed her eyes. Then she'd go back in to find Ruth.

Her peace was shattered by the door of the pub slamming back to hit the wall just inches from her head. Maura jumped and squeaked, her eyes snapping open to take in a lone figure stumbling out into the glow of the streetlamp. 'Oof,' it said as the door closed, muting the burst of music and conversation and leaving Maura to survey the newcomer, who had straightened up to stare unsteadily around. 'Urgh.'

'Are you okay?' she asked warily.

With erratic, almost cartoonish wobbliness the figure turned to blink at her. Maura recognised the face. It was Fraser Bell, another of the popular gang from school. He looked more than a little the worse for wear; his usually pristine hair was ruffled and his black leather jacket hung from one shoulder, as though pulling it on properly had been a step too far. He gazed at Maura in bleary curiosity and took a couple of steps towards her. 'M'fine. How are you?'

His lack of coordination produced an alarming lurch that Maura feared would end in a collision with the cobblestones. Automatically, she reached out to steady him. 'Here,' she said, drawing him to the wall. 'Lean against this.'

He did as she suggested, heaving in the night air much as she had done a few moments earlier. His eyes closed. Maura waited, hoping against hope that he was not going to be sick. But the seconds ticked by with nothing more than the steady rise and fall of his chest, and Maura began to relax. After almost a minute, she gave in to curiosity and risked a glance at his face. She'd watched him often enough from a distance, making his way to and from the drama studio at school, and had stolen looks in some of the other classes they'd shared; she knew the set of his shoulders, the grace with which he moved and the flash of his smile that could light up the dourest day. If Sarah Grant was a queen, then Fraser Bell was a king. He had the same irresistible ability to draw the eye, something she supposed might be called 'presence', that made him stand out, even at eighteen. And now that Maura was close, she could appreciate the perfection of his bone structure – the high cheekbones, the straight nose, the firm chin. His eyelashes were a darker blond than his hair, longer than they had any right to be, matching the fine feathering of his eyebrows. His lips were full, if a little slack with drink at that precise moment. Maura felt her hands twitch, the familiar pottery student's desire to capture what she saw in clay. And then Fraser opened his eyes and stared straight into hers. 'Hello.'

His gaze was unexpectedly clear for someone so unsteady on his feet. Maura pulled back hurriedly, caught out. 'Hello. I thought you might have passed out.'

Fraser puffed out another long breath that misted in the chilly air. 'No. I'm definitely still conscious.' The words were only slightly slurred as his gaze roved across her face. 'Although you might be a dream.'

Maura eyed him in slight confusion. 'No, I'm real enough. Do you want me to get your friends? Malky or someone?'

'No, m'okay. Just need some fresh air.' His eyes remained fixed on her and a moment passed before his forehead crinkled. 'Wait – I know you. You're Laura. No, Morag.' His frown deepened. 'No. *Maura.*'

She stared at him. 'That's right.'

He nodded, the gesture comical in its enthusiasm. 'I'm Fraser. From school.'

The idea that she wouldn't know who he was almost made her smile. 'I know.'

'You were always so mysterious,' he said, studying her with an intent, if slightly unsteady gaze. 'Mysterious Maura.'

She didn't know what to say to that, because she hadn't been mysterious in the least, she'd just occupied a different part of the school ecosystem. As highlighted by the fact that it had taken him three attempts to get her name right. But she didn't blame him for that, not when he'd clearly had a skinful. 'I'm not at all myster—'

'Yes, you are,' he interrupted, raising an unsteady finger. His voice dropped for dramatic emphasis. 'An angel is like you and you are like an angel.'

Maura felt her jaw drop. 'Sorry?'

He tapped the side of his nose, or at least tried to. 'That's Shakespeare. *Henry V.*'

'Oh,' Maura managed, hoping her face wasn't as pink as it felt. He'd always been into drama – perhaps he was studying it at university. 'Look, I should probably go back inside. Will you be okay on your own?'

'I'll be fine. Absolutely fine.' He took a breath, made a conspicuous effort to straighten up and slid gently sideways across the brickwork to lean against her.

She pushed him upright again, regarding him doubtfully. 'I don't think you will be. Why don't I go and get someone?'

'You really are an angel,' he murmured, and turned his head, his blue eyes fixing on her with such focus that he suddenly didn't seem drunk at all. 'Can I kiss you?'

'What?' The question was so out of left field that her reply came out as a yelp. 'No!'

His gaze didn't waver. 'Why not?'

Maura took a deep breath, willing her heart to stop thumping. 'Because – because we hardly know each other. And you're drunk.'

Fraser paused, as though considering. 'Both true.' He brightened. 'But we'll know each other better afterwards.'

The words were delivered with such conviction that she had to bite her cheek to stop herself laughing. 'You'll still be drunk.'

He frowned, opened his mouth to argue and then sighed. 'You have me there.' His gaze grew sorrowful. 'Is there no hope?'

Maura blinked, unsure whether to take him seriously. 'Why do you want to?'

His eyes did not leave hers. 'Because you're a heavenly mirage that will probably vanish at any moment, and I'll always regret it if we don't.'

No one had ever described her as a mirage, let alone a heavenly one, Maura thought faintly. It was so absurdly poetic that it made her head whirl. And that was not the only thing that was stirring; deep in the pit of her stomach, a whisper of warmth was beginning to swirl. He was so good looking, a treacherous part of her brain observed, practically an angel in his own right. More importantly, his logic somehow mirrored her own. He was Fraser Bell, the boy she'd subconsciously fancied for years, and he was asking to kiss her. Wouldn't she regret the missed opportunity too? She pushed logic aside. 'Okay.'

He stared quizzically at her for a long moment, as though making sure she really had agreed. Then, slowly, gently, he leaned in to press his lips against hers.

For Maura, the pub and the street and the city vanished, eclipsed by an aching sweetness that began at his touch and suffused her entirely. She floated, cocooned in its bliss, aware only of him. She did not dare open her eyes, afraid she would wake up and discover she was the one dreaming.

'Bloody hell, Fraser, I can't leave you alone for a minute.'

The voice, female and flat with amusement, was accompanied by a burst of noise from inside the pub. The intrusion sliced through Maura like a knife. She pulled back sharply, eliciting a huff of surprise from Fraser, and saw Sarah Grant watching them with a narrowed gaze that belied the amusement of her tone. Fraser turned his head. 'Oh, it's you. This is Maura. You remember Maura, don't you? From school.'

Favouring her with a cursory up and down, Sarah pursed her lips. 'No, I can't say that I do. I thought she was just some random who'd happened upon you.'

A hot gush of mortification washed through Maura. 'I didn't— He—'

'Look, whatever,' Sarah cut in, folding her arms. 'You can put him down now. I'll take it from here.'

Indignation wrestled with embarrassment as Maura glanced at Fraser. Should she back down? Or explain that Fraser had kissed her, not the other way round? He caught her look, apparently oblivious to the battle-lines being drawn around him, and smiled. 'Thank you. That was lovely.'

The intimacy of his smile nearly drew her back in. It *had* been lovely – a heavenly stolen moment neither of them had anticipated and yet both had recognised. But Sarah's sneering tone had brought her back down to earth with an emphatic bump and now reality was asserting itself once more. He was Fraser Bell. What had she been thinking? Had she been thinking? It appeared not. Face burning, Maura stepped away from Fraser and hurried, without a word, into the safety of the pub.

CHAPTER ONE

Eighteen Years Later

Maura was not entirely sure about Hogmanay.

Her reservations weren't something she ever admitted, of course – as Scottishness went, bringing in the bells was up there with tartan, haggis and Irn-Bru, and anything less than total enthusiasm felt like a betrayal of her country. But she did sometimes wonder, as the clock struck twelve and her fellow Scots swelled into 'Auld Lang Syne', whether the time-honoured tradition of grabbing the new year with both hands and dousing it liberally with drink was the best way to wipe the slate clean.

She knew she was very much in the minority – thousands descended on Edinburgh to join the famous Hogmanay street parties and admire the magnificent firework display that lit up the sky over the castle – but given any choice in the matter, Maura would secretly prefer to spend the final few hours of December in bed with a mug of cocoa and a good book, the better to greet January with a clear head and no hazy regrets about the night before. It was, she suspected, a symptom of reaching her late thirties. And it was absolutely not an option with a boyfriend like Jamie, who never missed an excuse for a big night.

Which was why Maura was currently squashed into the corner of a white leather sofa, at the house party of one of Jamie's rugby mates, watching a group of grown men down shots like they were teenagers. It wasn't that she disapproved – she'd done her fair share of drinking in her youth – but nothing could have induced her to join them now. *Each to their own*, she thought, watching them grimace as they bit into wedges of lemon.

On the sofa beside Maura, her friend Zoe raised two elegant eyebrows and leaned closer, her Home Counties accent cutting through the thumping music. 'Are you thinking what I'm thinking?'

Maura glanced at the clock on the wall, which showed 10.15pm, and then back at the drinkers, who were enthusiastically setting up another round of shots. 'Is Archie going to make it until midnight?'

Originally from Dunfermline, Archie was a new recruit to the rugby club, a fresh-faced university student who was doing his best to keep up with his more seasoned teammates but inevitably starting to look a little green around the gills. Zoe followed Maura's gaze and narrowed her eyes in appraisal. 'Absolutely no chance,' she said firmly. 'But I doubt he'll be the only one, unless someone hides the tequila.'

That was a mission Maura had no intention of accepting. If five years of hanging around with Jamie's friends had taught her anything, it was that the Fun Police were never well-received. And while Zoe was a relative newcomer to the group, having only dated her boyfriend, Liam, for ten months or so, Maura knew she wasn't about to intervene either. 'They'd only open a bottle of something else,' she said pragmatically. 'Best to let them get on with it.'

Zoe nodded her agreement. 'Good advice. Never get between a scrum half and the bar.'

Maura laughed. 'Or a fly-half. Or any of them, to be honest.' She eyed her friend curiously. 'So what were you thinking, if it wasn't "how long before Archie passes out"?'

The other woman looked momentarily perplexed, then her expression cleared. 'Oh, I was looking at the guy who just arrived – the one in the hallway.' She gave Maura a mischievous look. 'And what I was thinking was, *HELLO.*'

Automatically, Maura glanced across the crowded room but her view of the hall was obscured by a couple standing in the doorway. 'Someone you know?'

'Someone I'd like to know,' Zoe said, then gave a little shrug. 'If I wasn't with Liam, obviously.'

Maura craned her head, her curiosity piqued. The party was at a house in Edinburgh's New Town – a stone's throw from the rugby club that formed a significant part of her social life – and she'd thought she knew everyone there. 'A player?' she asked Zoe, who shook her head.

'Too pretty.'

Maura raised her eyebrows. 'Some of our boys are good-looking.'

'You know what I mean,' Zoe said. 'The kind of face that has never been on the wrong end of a crunching tackle.'

And Maura did know what she meant. Jamie was rugged and handsome but his nose had been broken more than once and there was a faded silvery line on his forehead from a collision that had resulted in hospital treatment for concussion. Every rugby player she knew had similar battle scars that they wore with immense pride. 'I wonder who he is,' she said, glancing towards the hall again in case the view had cleared and noting with mild disappointment that it had not.

'Only one way to find out,' Zoe said decisively, and levered herself off the sofa. 'Can I get you another drink?'

Maura considered the dregs of lukewarm Prosecco in the bottom of her glass. 'Maybe just a Coke.'

'Sensible,' Zoe replied, 'if just a tiny bit boring. Wait here – I'll report back with the gossip.'

A moment later, she was weaving her way through the crush, trading smiles and nods. Maura watched her go, noting the appreciative looks from some of the guests as the slender blonde passed by. She hadn't known Zoe long, only for the months she'd been dating Liam, but they'd quickly become friends; she made Maura feel less out of place among the often-raucous rugby crowd. There were other wives and girlfriends, of course, many of whom had been part of the group much longer than Maura, and she liked them too. But Zoe had a sparkle that had drawn Maura in from the first moment they met. Hogmanay might not be so bad with a partner in crime, she decided.

A roar from the hardened drinkers made her look over to see Jamie holding a tray of lime-green jelly shots aloft. These were quickly snatched up. Jamie glanced Maura's way, raising an enquiring eyebrow. She shook her head. Shrugging, he offered one of the two he held to Archie, who hesitated for only a fraction of a second before tipping it into his mouth. Maura's lips twisted in wry amusement. It wouldn't be long before that was coming back up, if she was any judge. Jamie, on the other hand, would be fine. His tolerance for alcohol had been finely honed by years amid the play-hard, party-hard environment of the rugby crowd.

Not for the first time, Maura reflected how different she and Jamie were. He was gregarious and immensely likeable, with a charm few could resist once it was turned their way. It was that charm that had first ensnared Maura, at a ceramics gallery viewing sponsored by the bank Jamie worked for. He'd made a beeline for her, hiding in the corner while people studied and discussed her creations, and kept a respectful distance even as he fixed her with a sympathetic smile. 'You look like you'd rather be anywhere but here.'

She had hesitated, because it wasn't strictly true. The people in the gallery were here to view the pieces she had made – bowls and vases she had worked on for months – and there was a part of her that wanted to see them admired and appreciated, not to mention bought. But she'd be lying if she pretended she found prestigious events like this easy, even though she knew most potters would kill to be in her shoes. A down-to-earth pottery show was more her thing, in a chilly marquee or village hall, full of ceramics enthusiasts with wide-ranging, quirky tastes and fellow potters to chat with. A show that wasn't exclusively about her. 'Not at all,' she'd replied as she looked up at him, hoping the lie wasn't too transparent, and held out her hand. 'I'm Maura.'

'I know,' he said, encompassing her fingers completely with his own large hand. 'You're the talent behind all of this beauty.' He waved a hand at the spotlit gallery, with its pedestals and tables of gleaming blue and green and turquoise ceramics. 'I feel as though I'm on a desert island, surrounded by gently lapping waves. You must really love the sea.'

'I do,' Maura said, gratified. 'Although I'm not sure I came anywhere close to capturing its true depth or beauty.'

He eyed her quizzically, black brows beetling. 'Seriously?' Turning, he studied a wide, wavy-edged bowl glazed in a delicate sea-green. 'I can almost hear the crash of the surf when I look at this piece. And the way the glass shimmers at the bottom, half-covering the anemones and leaf patterns underneath – it's like peeping into a rock pool once the tide has gone out.'

Maura felt her cheeks grow warm, partly in pleasure that he'd understood what she'd been trying to achieve, but mostly in shame because she had totally judged this stranger by his appearance – tall, well-built and with a jaw that looked like it could crack boulders, let alone walnuts. He was immaculately dressed – his suit was expensive and well-fitted – and his thick dark hair was tamed into submission by liberally applied gel, all of which had led her to automatically label him as a typical city banker. Not the type to appreciate art, she had decided, without even realising she'd done so. And now he was forcing her to reappraise her initial assessment, and her own preconceptions along with it. 'Thank you,' she said, praying her face wasn't as crimson as it felt.

He smiled then, his blue eyes crinkling at the edges in a way that somehow eased her discomfort and made her feel worse. 'You're welcome. But where are my manners? I haven't even introduced myself. I'm Jamie Wallace. I work for Castle Finance, and I can tell you on behalf of all my colleagues how honoured we are to be sponsoring this exhibition.'

'Oh.' Maura heard the faint squeak in her voice and took a deep breath. It was time to take control of herself and act like a professional. 'It's nice to meet you, Jamie.'

'I hope so,' he said, a smile curving the corners of his mouth again. 'Even though you're secretly hoping I'm going to leave you alone soon.'

'I am not,' she protested and was startled to realise she meant it. 'I have a tendency to hide away at these things and then be annoyed at myself afterwards for not speaking to anyone,' she admitted. 'At least I can congratulate myself later on talking to you.'

Jamie laughed, a deep, warm sound that Maura found made her want to laugh too. 'I'm not sure anyone has ever congratulated themselves for being cornered by me. But you're very kind to say so.'

His wry self-deprecation was as charming as it was misplaced. Maura raised her eyebrows. 'I don't believe that for a second.'

'You don't?' His blue eyes rested on her with interest. 'Then have dinner with me. Tonight, when the gallery closes.'

She gaped at him, wrongfooted again. 'I – uh –'

'But I'm an idiot,' he said, slapping his forehead. 'You must have plans – a glittering celebration with your friends and family. Your boyfriend.'

Maura pressed her lips together. She did indeed have plans, and they involved a hot-water bottle, pyjamas and her sofa. But Jamie didn't need to know that. He was giving her a way out, an excuse to turn him down without either of them losing face, and she was very much surprised to realise she didn't want to. 'No,' she said, before she could change her mind. 'I don't have anything planned. Dinner sounds good.'

To her mild amusement, he looked momentarily nonplussed, as though taken aback by her assent. 'So it's a date, then?'

Maura gazed up at him, noticing all over again how broad he was, so that he almost towered over her, even though he had taken care to keep some distance between them. He must work out, a distracted part of her brain observed, even as she smiled in acceptance. 'Yes. It's a date.'

That had been more than five years ago, Maura reminded herself as she was roused from her memories by another enthusiastic roar, and it had been a long time since Jamie had shown such interest in her work. These days he left her to it in the pottery studio below the Dean Village flat they shared, and she couldn't remember the last time he'd come to one of her shows, although it had been years since she'd had a glitzy solo exhibition like the one where they'd met. It was the way all couples went, she knew – familiarity led to comfort, which eventually bred a benign lack of curiosity in even the most loving relationships. Truth be told, she wasn't sure she'd be able to explain exactly what Jamie did for a living, beyond 'something clever in investment banking'. It didn't mean anything. And yet there were times when Maura couldn't help feeling a little wistful for the man who had wooed her so determinedly when they'd first met.

Zoe materialised in front of her, a glass of Coke in one hand and a red wine in the other. 'Mission accomplished,' she announced as she sat beside Maura once more. 'He's an actor, which explains the pretty face, but he's taking a break at the moment.'

'An actor,' Maura echoed. 'Is he famous?'

Zoe took a swig of wine. 'He says not but I suppose that's what he would say. I didn't recognise his name so he can't have been in any big films or done much TV.'

Maura took a sip of her own drink. 'He could be a stage actor. What's he called?'

'Fraser Bell,' Zoe said, and Maura felt a clang in the pit of her stomach. That was a name she knew, although she hadn't heard it for years. It couldn't be the same person, could it? There had to be more than one Fraser Bell in Edinburgh. But an actor . . . that was harder to write off as a coincidence. 'Was he – is he Scottish?' she managed, after a few seconds had ticked by.

'Yes,' Zoe said. 'He could hardly be anything else, with a name like that.'

'No, I suppose not,' Maura said faintly, suddenly transported to the crowded, chaotic corridors of school, where she'd admired Fraser Bell from afar. And then the Spirit of Christmas Past raised its head, reminding her of a stolen kiss one winter's night after they'd left school. She tried to sound casual. 'What's he doing here?'

'Hoping to get blind drunk, like the rest of us,' Zoe replied with a snort, then eyed Maura's Coke. 'Well, apart from you. Or do you mean why is he in Edinburgh?'

'The second part.'

Zoe shrugged. 'I didn't ask. He just said he was taking a break from acting and I assumed he must have family here.' She eyed Maura closely. 'Are you okay? You look like you've seen a ghost. You don't know him, do you?'

'I might,' Maura admitted, although she had no intention of saying any more than that. Zoe definitely didn't need to know she and Fraser had been anything more than schoolmates. 'We might have gone to school together. How old would you say he was?'

'Mid-to-late-thirties,' her friend said, without hesitation. 'Around your age.'

Which meant it could be him, Maura reasoned. But guessing someone's age was tricky, especially with men, who didn't have the benefit of make-up to disguise the passing of the years. It was so easy to get it wrong.

It seemed Zoe had arrived at a decision while Maura dithered. 'Go and say hello,' she demanded, her eyes wide. 'Go on. And if it is him, you can have a mini reunion in the kitchen. Bond over the teachers you hated, get sentimental over the old days – it's practically the law at Hogmanay, anyway.'

Maura couldn't argue with that – teary-eyed reminiscences were very much part of the New Year celebrations. Except that if this was the Fraser she'd known from school, there was a very real possibility he wouldn't remember her, let alone the drunken kiss they'd shared. And then Maura would wish she'd left well enough alone. Maybe it was better to try to catch a glimpse of him first, she thought, her gaze sliding towards the doorway once more. But Zoe had the bit firmly between her teeth. 'Go and say hello,' she repeated, her tone gently insistent. 'What have you got to lose?'

The question made Maura feel as though she was nineteen again, awkward and shy and with all the social skills of a mouse. She'd changed over the years – art school in London had helped with that, and the need to develop some confidence to sell her work – but she'd never lost her shyness. And Zoe only knew the bare facts – she had no idea Maura had nursed a crush on Fraser at school, much less snogged him once. But both of those things had happened a long time ago and she hadn't thought of Fraser for years. Would it really cost her anything to see if it was him? It didn't need to be anything more than a fleeting conversation. Especially if he failed to recognise her.

'Okay,' she said at last, unsure whether the sudden flutter in her stomach was caused by nervousness or anticipation. 'I'll go.'

'Excellent,' Zoe said, and Maura thought she might actually clap her hands. 'I'll come too.'

'No.' The word was out before Maura could stop it; she didn't need a witness to the humiliation she felt sure was coming. 'Let me see if it's him first.'

Zoe sighed. 'Fine. I'll give you five minutes and then I'm coming in.'

There was a strong possibility Maura would have fled by then but she kept that to herself. 'Okay. Wish me luck.'

'You're going into the kitchen at a party,' Zoe observed with a grin. 'Not storming the Bastille. You don't need luck.'

If only she knew, Maura thought as she made her way across the room. Then again, it was much better that she didn't.

CHAPTER TWO

Fraser Bell had always loved Hogmanay. He loved the enduring traditions, passed from one generation to the next and maintained with steadfast enthusiasm. No one knew why the first person to cross the threshold of a home after the bells had struck twelve should be a dark-haired man, just as nobody remembered why the crossing of hands when singing 'Auld Lang Syne' was important, but everyone observed the rituals all the same. He loved the defiance with which they set the sky aglow, an 'up yours' gesture to winter and a welcome reminder that the light would return soon. Perhaps most of all, he appreciated the almost palpable sense of renewal, that the dying year passed the baton to a fresh new year on the stroke of midnight and everything began anew, although he imagined most people simply saw it as an excuse for a good drink.

That was the thing with being an actor; everything became a story. Logically, he knew Hogmanay was no different from any other night but, deep in his soul, something resonated. Especially in Edinburgh. It had been years since he'd greeted the new year in the city of his birth and he was determined to soak it up. Although not as determined as some of the revellers in the living room, if the noise they were making was anything to go by. Rugby players, he guessed, knowing his host was an enthusiastic member of the Inverleith Warriors. It wasn't a sport he'd ever wanted to play, although he enjoyed cheering on his national team as much as anyone.

'So is this a temporary homecoming?' The host of the party, Pete, glanced at Fraser as he reached past him for the bottle of Highland Park whisky on the worktop. 'Or are you back for good?'

Fraser glanced across the kitchen to where his girlfriend, Naomi, stood chatting to Pete's wife. 'I've been back for a while,' he said. 'Since September. I started a ghost tour business in the city centre.'

Pete snorted. 'Fleecing gullible tourists, is it? Plenty of those around, I bet you're doing a roaring trade.'

Fraser tried not to take offence. The truth was the majority of his customers were tourists. 'I keep my prices competitive. And there's a lot of genuine city history mixed in. It's not all woo-woo, Scooby-Doo stuff.'

Pete laughed. 'Who needs Scooby-Doo when you have Greyfriars Bobby?'

Fraser couldn't argue; the story of Greyfriars Bobby was world-famous – a faithful terrier who was so heartbroken when his owner died that he refused to leave his grave for years. There were several ghost tours that visited the gravestone in Greyfriars Kirkyard and claimed the howls of the dog could be heard even now but Fraser tried to avoid the more well-beaten tourist trails. He smiled at Pete. 'My ghosts are generally less sentimental. The butcher of Fleshmarket Close, the plague doctor of Auld Reekie. You get the idea.'

'I do,' Pete said, nodding approvingly. 'It sounds like you're well settled then.'

Again, Fraser glanced at Naomi, who had only agreed to relocate from London on the basis that the move was temporary while he recharged his creative batteries. 'For now,' he said easily. 'But enough about me – what have you been up to? Still playing rugby, I assume?'

'Still playing,' Pete agreed. 'Although things creak a lot more than they used to. I'm in the veterans team now, which makes me feel older than the gods.'

Fraser eyed him with some sympathy. 'I know the feeling. But I prefer to think we're seasoned rather than old.'

'Seasoned,' Pete repeated thoughtfully. 'I like that.'

'Or maturing, like a fine whisky,' Fraser went on, tapping the top of the bottle beside him. 'We haven't reached our smoky, delicious best yet.'

Pete sighed. 'The only time I'm ever smoky is when we've had a barbecue.' He stared into his glass and took a long swig. 'But there's no use in moaning; we might as well enjoy the time we have. Can I get you another drink?'

'That's the spirit,' Fraser replied, his lips quirking. 'I'll have a beer, thanks.'

As his host made for the garden, where the crates of beer were stashed, Fraser took the opportunity to check his phone. Four more bookings had come in for the next day's tour, meaning it was very nearly at capacity. He'd better take it easy on the alcohol – performing with a hangover was definitely not his idea of fun.

'Excuse me.'

He looked up to see an attractive, dark-haired woman before him, her brown eyes quizzical. She was frowning slightly, as though she was trying to work something out. It was a look Fraser had seen before, usually on the face of someone who had seen him in an advert or in a TV show but couldn't quite place him. 'Hello,' he said easily. 'Can I help you with something?'

She hesitated, studying him as if unsure how to begin. 'Are you Fraser Bell?'

He nodded, wondering what she was going to ask him to autograph. He'd once signed a paper coffee cup, in lieu of anything better, although that particular fan hadn't been nearly as pretty as this one. 'I am. What can I do for you?'

The woman puffed out her cheeks and looked oddly reluctant. 'This is going to sound really random but you didn't used to go to St Ignatius School, by any chance, did you?'

It was the last thing Fraser had expected her to say. His eyebrows shot up. 'I did. Why do you ask?'

'Because I did too,' she said. 'We were in the same year.'

She stopped talking, a little abruptly. He studied her more closely, taking in the glossy dark hair that fell in waves to her shoulders, the lively brown eyes and the roses in her cheeks that contrasted so perfectly with the paleness of her skin. It was as though Snow White had stepped out of the pages of a storybook to stand before him, although she was wearing a much better dress than her fictional counterpart. And then a memory stirred, of a quiet, dark-haired girl who was always on the periphery, never really part of the bubbling teenage maelstrom around her. Fraser followed the breadcrumb trail further into the past, trying to get a better hold on the elusive recollection. What had she been called? Laura? No, that wasn't it . . . 'Maura!' he exclaimed with a triumphant snap of his fingers, only realising how loudly he'd spoken when she visibly recoiled. 'Sorry, it just came to me. Maura McKenzie. You did something creative, didn't you? Not drawing or painting – something else.'

'Pottery,' she supplied.

'Of course,' Fraser said, looking back across the years and remembering more. 'I used to see you in the art block, on my way to the drama studio.'

An inscrutable look flashed across her face as she studied him. 'That's right. I was in a lot of your other classes, though.'

'Of course,' Fraser said, and now he could picture her sitting in the corner, rarely raising her hand. 'Well, it's good to see you after all these years. How have you been keeping?'

She tilted her head, sending a lock of black hair cascading over her eyes and he watched as she self-consciously tucked it behind one ear. 'I'm well, thanks. How about you?'

'I'm really well too,' he said. 'Back in the old place after a few years in London. You know how it is.'

Maura nodded. 'I do. I spent a few years in London after we left school, then went to study in Glasgow for a while. But I always knew I'd come back to Edinburgh eventually. There's something about the city that draws you back.'

'Don't I know it,' Fraser agreed. 'So what did you study? I assume that's why you went to London.'

'Ceramic design at St Martin's College,' she said. 'And then a master's degree at Glasgow School of Art.'

He blinked, impressed. They were both prestigious institutions and not easy to get into. 'Very nice. Have you managed to make a living out of it?'

'I get by,' she said. 'I've got a studio at home, and I teach a few days a week. But tell me about you – what have you been doing all these years?'

Fraser wasn't arrogant enough to be upset that she had no idea he was an actor. He wasn't especially famous, although several of the adverts he'd starred in had been very successful and he'd enjoyed a number of smaller roles both in TV and on stage, enough to pay the bills and give him a comfortable enough lifestyle. But if he was honest, most of his career had been spent waiting for his big break – the role that would open the door to real success and acclaim – and it was that relentless, never quite satisfied anticipation that had eventually propelled him to try something else. 'I went to drama school – we must have been in London at the same time. Anyway, I spent a few years as a jobbing actor, auditioning for pretty much anything my agent threw my way, and that led to a few good roles.'

She threw him an enquiring look. 'Anything I would have seen?'

It was the question most actors dreaded, in the same way that writers hated to be asked whether they'd written anything the other might have read, but Fraser accepted her curiosity as natural. 'Let's see now,' he said, stroking his beard as though pondering. 'Do you remember the toilet bleach advert a few years back – the one with the man who proposes to a human-sized, cuddly duck?'

There was a brief silence, during which Maura seemed to be trying to work out whether he was being serious. 'Yes. Did you play the man?'

'No, I was the duck,' Fraser said solemnly. 'Then there were the fast-food adverts starring Louis the chicken, but I doubt you'd have recognised me under all the feathers.'

She shook her head, and Fraser thought she was definitely trying not to laugh. 'Um, I don't think I remember—'

'Or, if you're into soap operas, I played Marion's bit on the side in *Broadoaks* for a few months. And – my personal favourite – I was once horribly poisoned by Penelope Keith in an episode of *Death in Dorset*.'

That did it – a snort of laughter escaped Maura's best efforts to hold it in. 'You're not serious,' she said, mirth dancing in her eyes.

'Oh, but I am,' he assured her gravely. 'One of my finest performances. I guarantee you'll never see anyone faceplant into a bowl of broccoli and stilton soup with more perfectly encapsulated astonishment and regret.'

Maura laughed outright then, just as the blonde woman Fraser recalled introducing herself as Zoe materialised at her shoulder. 'What's the joke?' she asked, glancing from Maura to Fraser with undisguised interest.

Maura grinned. 'Fraser was just describing some of his favourite acting jobs.'

'Was he?' Zoe said, studying him. 'So did you find out if you were at school together?'

'We were,' Fraser confirmed, smiling at Maura. 'It's a small world, apparently.'

'Or Edinburgh is a small city,' she countered. 'Although I don't run into many old St Ignatius students, it has to be said.'

Fraser was about to respond when he saw Naomi making her way across the kitchen to where he stood. Her porcelain features were impassive as she joined the group. 'Are you keeping these ladies entertained, darling?' she asked, slipping her arm through his. Her head tilted indulgently towards Maura and Zoe. 'He's always the life and soul of the party. Can't take my eyes off him for a second.'

Fraser cleared his throat. 'Naomi, this is Zoe, who I've just met, and Maura, who I went to school with.'

Was it his imagination or was Maura's smile a little strained? 'Pleased to meet you,' she said.

'Likewise,' Naomi offered. 'It's so nice to get these little glimpses into Fraser's past. Edinburgh seems to be full of people he used to know.' She broke off to glance meaningfully at the expensive-looking watch that decorated her wrist. 'Speaking of which, we really ought to get going if we're going to catch the fireworks from the Balmoral.'

'Already?' Fraser said, checking the time for himself and seeing it was almost 11.15pm. 'Hell's bells, you're right.' He threw Maura an apologetic look. 'Sorry, I'm afraid I've got to go.'

She waved a hand. 'I'd be going as well, if I had a ticket to the Balmoral.' A smile pulled at the corners of her mouth. 'But it was good to catch up.'

Fraser had to agree. Up until half an hour ago, he'd forgotten Maura McKenzie even existed but now he was surprised to find himself more than a little intrigued. It was a shame he had to leave. 'It was good,' he said. 'Really good. I'm glad you're doing well.'

Whatever Maura had been about to say in reply was interrupted by a commotion in the hallway. A young man stumbled into the kitchen, his face an unhealthy shade of green. He took several uncertain steps forward and then stopped dead in front of the group. Out of the corner of his eye, Fraser saw Naomi move hurriedly back and he did the same, just as the youth let out a strangled moan and bent double. With a yelp, Zoe jumped out of the way but Maura was not so lucky. Trapped by the edge

of the table, there was nothing she could do to avoid the contents of his stomach. It landed with a splatter all over her feet.

'Well,' Naomi said brightly in the silence that followed. 'I
think that's our cue to leave. So lovely to meet you both.'

Fraser caught sight of Maura's horrified expression. 'Shall I
get you some kitchen roll?'

'No,' she croaked, lifting one foot to create an unpleasant
squelching sound. 'You head off to your party.'

'But—'

'Really,' Maura said, with determined jollity. 'Off you go. It
was great to see you again. Happy New Year.'

He hesitated, caught between the desire to help and the
realisation he was somehow only making her feel worse. 'Um –
Happy New Year to you too,' he said finally. 'And to you, Zoe.
Things can only get better.'

A drunken roar erupted from the living room, causing Zoe
to shake her head and wince. 'I'm afraid it sounds as though
things are going to get very much worse.'

CHAPTER THREE

Jamie was still snoring when Maura woke up the next morning. She lay there for a moment, listening as each breath reached an impressive crescendo, and then rolled carefully out of bed. The floor was cold, so she rummaged under the bed for her slippers before she padded out of the bedroom and into the decidedly fresher air of the hallway. A pair of jogging bottoms lay neatly folded across the back of the sofa in the living room, loaned to Maura by Pete's wife after Archie had thoughtfully covered her shoes and the hem of her dress in regurgitated tequila. The dress had gone straight into the washing machine the moment Maura got home. The shoes were wrapped in a bin liner outside the front door until Maura could decide how to dispose of them.

She stood in the half-light, weak morning sun creeping around the edges of the blinds at the windows, and considered the events of the night before. The party had continued in full swing, although Archie had curled up on the sofa to sleep it off. A few minutes before midnight, Jamie had been ushered outside, a box of finest Scottish shortbread in one hand and a bottle of whisky in the other, to re-enter the house once the clock had struck twelve and let the New Year in. There had been a moment or two when Maura had wondered if he might drink the whisky while he waited in the cold but her fears were unfounded. He barrelled through the door, food and drink held triumphantly aloft, and bellowed New Year greetings to everyone. When he reached Maura, he had swept her into his arms and swung her round, indifferent to her squeaks of alarm, before planting an enthusiastic kiss on her lips. And then the celebrations had begun in earnest. No one else had gone as far as Archie but Maura was sure there would be plenty of sore heads among the partygoers when they eventually woke up.

After making herself a mug of coffee, she pulled on some clean clothes and made her way down the stairs to the door that opened onto the street. Thistledown Lane was empty, the terraced apartments as silent as the cobbles gleaming under a sheen of frost. If Maura listened hard, she could hear the babbling Water of Leith, the river that flowed from the Pentland Hills to the southwest of Edinburgh, through the heart of Dean Village and finally reached the coast through the city's port. She stood for a moment, absorbing the peace and quiet. Then, with barely a glance at the sad black bin liner that contained her shoes from the night before, she closed the front door of the flat and turned to let herself into the studio that occupied the ground floor.

The space had begun its life as a garage, with arched double doors at one end and windows overlooking the river at the other, but Maura had known the moment she saw it that it would be perfect as a potter's studio. Workbenches lined one gloss-painted wall, with tall black seats underneath, and a white butler sink stood at the end. Floor to ceiling wooden shelves ran along the other wall. These were filled with pots and other projects in all stages of the creative process: some were recently made, air-drying before being fired for the first time; others were fired but awaiting glaze or decoration and more still were glazed and awaiting their second, final firing. In one corner, there was a potter's wheel, clean and ready to be used. Sunlight settled in pools on the linoleum floor, creating bright puddles that stretched to the far end, where the hulking steel cylinders of the kilns sat. The air at that end of the room was noticeably warmer, heated by the firings that had run a day or so before.

Maura took a sip of coffee, wrapping her hands around the mug with an unadulterated sense of anticipation. This was her favourite part of the making process – the moment of lifting the heavy lid to see how the intense heat of the firing had transformed the glazed treasures within. She felt the way she had on so many Christmas mornings, when the miraculous hoard of unopened presents under the tree had promised so much. Yet at the same time, there was the risk that something unexpected might unfold – a longed-for present might turn out to be a disappointing pair of socks, a carefully crafted plate might have cracked, or worse, stuck to the kiln.

When she'd first been learning her craft, Maura had raged at the unpredictability of her work – too often the glazes did not turn out the way she anticipated, or a shape she had created many times before bubbled and warped. As she'd grown more adept, she'd learned to accept the variations and appreciate that they often helped to create something unique, if not always what she'd had in mind. Many of her best, most ambitious pieces were one-offs for that precise reason. She could never guarantee being able to replicate exactly what she had made before.

Warm air engulfed her as soon as she lifted the lid of the kiln. She held her breath as she peeped at the top shelf; an intricate seascape bowl she had made appeared to have turned out perfectly and various mugs and pots made by the students who shared her studio for a few hours each week had survived. Carefully, she lifted each piece out, still warm, and carried it to the shelves to finish cooling. She wasn't expecting any students until the following week – plenty of time for their work to release the heat of the firing and return to room temperature.

The bottom shelf of the kiln revealed a delicate porcelain plate made by one of her students, a black clay vase Maura had been experimenting with, and a set of four soup bowls she'd thrown on the wheel at the request of her sister and glazed with a combination of greys and greens. The effect was pleasing; the colours had merged in places to create a whole new shade and she thought Kirsty would like them, although she wouldn't like the fact that they were best handwashed. She'd asked for something no one else would have and Maura thought she'd fulfilled that brief rather nicely.

Once the kiln was empty, she stood in front of the shelves and surveyed the morning's treasure. There were no breakages and nothing had fused to the kiln, which was a relief. No matter how many times she reminded people to wipe the glaze from the base of their pots and leave a gap around the bottom, there was almost always one who forgot. The handle on one of the mugs was wonky, but she knew Effie wouldn't mind. *As long as it doesn't leak*, she would say with a satisfied nod.

Maura checked the time – almost ten o'clock. Jamie would still be asleep – perhaps wouldn't stir until the afternoon, and even then he would likely be groggy and not inclined to do much. At some point today Maura needed to load the kiln again, this time for a bisque firing that would transform the recently made, unfired pieces into something much more robust, ready for glazing. But before that, she had time to get her hands dirty.

Pulling a clay-dusted apron over her head, Maura tied it hurriedly behind her back and turned her attention to the wheel. It wasn't heavy – made from plastic and metal, with a turntable that was controlled by a foot pedal. She filled up a broad plastic jug with water and placed it within arm's reach, then cut a wedge of clay from the black plastic bag it was stored in. There wasn't anything in particular she planned to make, she just wanted to mould the clay beneath her hands and let it become what it would. And afterwards, if it wasn't a shape she was happy with, she could simply squash it up and start again. *If only everything in life was so simple*, she thought as she settled on the stool and pressed her elbows against her knees.

The clay spun slowly on the wheel. With care, Maura forced her hands to smooth it into a round shape. It always surprised new students that it took such force to control the clay, and how much water was needed to prevent friction and heat from building up – she'd watched more than one potter send their would-be creation flying off the wheel because they hadn't planted it well enough in place, or had failed to control the speed of the wheel. It might even have happened to her, back when she was just starting out at school, although she couldn't remember enduring such a humiliation. The process was second nature to her now, which was probably why she found it so soothing, and it wasn't long before she had coaxed the dull brown clay into a thin, elegant and perfectly round bowl.

Dipping her fingers into the water, she wet the base and sliced neatly through it with a cheese wire, releasing the bowl from the wheel. Inspecting it with a critical eye, Maura decided it was good enough and reached for more clay.

Her nerves were still jangled from the party the night before, she thought, as she worked the wheel and allowed muscle memory to take over the task of shaping the bowl. Most of that was due to the unfortunate incident with Archie, which Jamie and the rest of the rugby crowd had found funny, but Maura also found her thoughts coming to rest upon her unexpected encounter with Fraser Bell.

That hadn't been stressful, unless she included the mortifying moment Archie had thrown up on her, but she'd be lying if she said meeting him again hadn't unsettled her a bit. She had enjoyed talking to him, once the initial stomach twist of recognition had died away; she'd found him funny and self-deprecating in a way that made her wonder whether he'd been that way at school, although he clearly had no memory of the kiss they'd shared. *But why should he remember?* she asked herself sternly. Almost two decades had passed since then – she'd barely thought of it herself until Zoe dropped his name into conversation.

Maura had managed to resist her friend's insistence that they Google *Fraser Bell* at the party but the temptation had been too strong to resist once she was at home in the early hours. He hadn't lied about the duck advert, nor about *Death in Dorset*; both were listed on his IMDb page, along with a number of more substantial roles. There was nothing to suggest he'd come close to the heady heights of Hollywood, but he appeared to have built the kind of steady, successful career that most actors could only dream of. So why had he decided to take a break? Was it really simple disillusionment with the roles he'd been offered, as he'd hinted?

Distracted, Maura let the tension in her hands lessen and the bowl on the wheel wobbled in protest. Digging her elbows into the soft tissue just above her knees, she concentrated on correcting the problem, smoothing the clay upwards and outwards with her hands until she had a decent sized plant pot. Judging the piece to be ready, she removed it from the wheel and arched her back, stretching her tensed muscles. Hours of standing around at the party had done her no favours, she realised, wincing. She wasn't in her twenties anymore, when she could sit at the wheel for hours. It was time to do something else.

It took her another thirty minutes to solve the Tetris puzzle that was loading the kiln for the next firing. By the time she locked the studio and went back upstairs for a shower, it was nearly midday. She wasn't expecting Jamie to have surfaced and was therefore surprised to see him watching her from the sofa as she rounded the top of the stairs and entered the living room. 'You've been working,' he said flatly.

'I needed to unload the kiln, put it on for another firing,' she said, frowning at the irritation in his tone. 'You were sleeping, I didn't think you'd mind.'

'Most people take New Year's Day off,' he said. 'Have breakfast with their loved ones, go for a walk. They don't go to work.'

Maura stared at him. 'Some people do. Doctors and bus drivers and people in hospitality. They all work on the holidays.'

Jamie shook his head. 'You're self-employed, Maura. You don't have to work. It would have been nice to wake up to find you next to me this morning.'

She felt a stab of disbelief. He'd been out for the count, sleeping off the excesses of the night before and snoring loud enough to wake the dead. It wasn't unreasonable of her to assume he'd stay that way for a few hours more. She took a deep breath. 'I'm here now,' she said, trying to sound calm. 'Do you want to go for brunch?'

He huffed out a breath. 'It's too late now. I've made plans to meet a few of the boys – go for a run to chase the cobwebs away.'

Maura counted slowly to five. 'Then there's no problem.'

'No, there's no problem,' Jamie said. 'Except it would have been nice if you'd at least thought about us doing something together, instead of sneaking off to the studio as soon as the sun came up.'

Briefly, Maura closed her eyes. 'I didn't,' she explained, as patiently as she could. 'You were asleep. I didn't expect you to have woken up yet but I can see I was wrong, and for that I apologise. Do you want to do something after your run?'

'The football is on later. We'll be going to the pub.' He paused. 'You can join us if you want.'

So much for spending some quality time together, Maura thought but did not say. Ordinarily, she might have agreed to meeting them at the pub but, after a heavy night, the last thing she wanted to do was watch Jamie and his friends drink. 'I might go to the beach, since you're not using the car.'

He slumped back against the sofa. 'Fine.'

When it became clear he had nothing more to say, Maura turned and headed for the bathroom, allowing the hot water to soothe her. Perhaps she should have waited for Jamie to wake up before going to the studio, she thought as she studied her wavy reflection in the steamed-up mirror. It wouldn't have killed her to unload the kiln in the afternoon, and then they could have spent the morning together. Although in her defence, she'd had no idea whether he'd be in any fit state to do more than groan and beg for coffee. Even so, she was willing to concede she might have been wrong. But Jamie was gone by the time she went back to the living room, prepared to kiss and make up.

With a sigh, Maura trudged back to the bedroom to dry her hair. Maybe she would join him at the pub after all.

The morning frost had burned off by the time Maura pulled into a parking space alongside Portobello Beach. She took a deep breath of bracing sea air, her eyes watering in the chill wind that whipped across the golden sand. Pulling her bobble hat down further around her ears, she zipped up her coat and collected her tote bag from the boot of the car. There wasn't usually much in the way of sea-glass washed up on the beach here, but she could live in hope, and she much preferred to use glass she had found in her work, rather than buy a bag from a seller on the internet. It mattered to her that she tried to recycle locally sourced sea-glass – somehow, it increased the sense of connection she felt with each piece.

There were plenty of others enjoying the beach. The tide was out, leaving a wide expanse of dark wet sand before a distant shimmer of silvery blue. Maura watched a beautiful red vizsla chase a ball across the flat expanse, returning to a woman with two children muffled up against the cold. There were other families too, taking advantage of the day off to get some fresh air, and plenty of couples. Maura tried not to look at them.

Earlier in the day, the sands would have been graced by Loony Dookers – foolhardy souls who banded together to brave the freezing waters of the Forth for a restorative New Year's Day dip. It wasn't something that had ever appealed to Maura but she saluted anyone who could bear it. Another Hogmanay tradition she'd prefer to avoid. Sometimes she wondered if she was even Scottish at all, although she suspected most Scots considered the Loony Dook a step towards insanity.

Maura skimmed the shoreline for the best part of an hour, picking up the odd jewel of sea-glass but mostly just enjoying the wide-open space and sound of children playing. Seagulls whirled overhead, ever vigilant for dropped chips or an unwary tourist, and their cries were snatched away by the wind.

Eventually, Maura realised she could not feel her fingers and she was forced to concede it might be time to go home. She pulled her phone from her pocket, flexing her fingers to get the blood flowing again, and checked for messages from Jamie. There were none. She did have one from Kirsty, reminding her of the family lunch they had planned for the next day.

Tapping out a reply, she was about to put the phone away when it flashed up a notification from Artsy, the website she used to list some of her pottery, indicating she had made a sale. She swiped on it, opening the email, and was pleased to see it was a large piece that had sold, one that had turned out better than she'd hoped and had consequently demanded a large price tag. She scanned the words, checking to see the buyer had understood they would need to collect and stopped dead when she saw the purchaser's name.

Puffing out a disbelieving breath that plumed in the freezing mid-afternoon air, Maura skimmed the message he'd added.

Hi Maura,

As you've probably guessed, I couldn't resist looking you up after running into you last night and WOW – you are amazing! If this bowl is even half as beautiful as it looks on the website then I'm going to be a very happy man.

Let me know what the arrangements are for collection. I'm free most days up until around five in the evening – hopefully we can find a date that works so I can claim my prize and I can tell you how talented you are in person.

All the best,

Fraser

She read it three times before it sank in. It had been clear he remembered her from school when they met the night before but she'd assumed the ensuing party at the Balmoral would have chased the encounter from his head. That did not appear to be the case. Instead, he'd looked her up *and* bought one of her pots, for a considerable amount of money. Which meant she was going to have to see him again – soon – and she wasn't at all sure how she felt about that. If the mere act of seeing him again had transported her nineteen years into the past, what could she expect when he was standing in her studio?

Walking slowly, Maura made her way back to the car and sat behind the wheel for several long minutes, blowing on her fingers and waiting for the feeling to return.

That she had to see Fraser again was not in question – he needed to collect the piece and she wouldn't entrust anyone else to wrap it. She would simply have to tell herself he was just another customer. Which, to all intents and purposes, he was.

Puffing out her cheeks, she began to type a reply.

Dear Fraser

No, that was a bit too personal, wasn't it? He wasn't her dear, any more than she was his. How had he started his message?

Hi Fraser,

Thanks so much for buying the bowl. I had no idea you'd look me up, much less buy one of my pieces. Thank you for your kind words.

I'm not around tomorrow but could do the following day or, failing that, one afternoon next week. Let me know what suits you and we can settle on a date.

Best wishes,

Maura

She read it over, agonising about every word, and then decided she was being ridiculous and hit send. Putting her phone away, she started the car and slotted it into gear.

Her response had been courteous and professional, the way she would be with any customer, and there was no need to second-guess herself just because it was Fraser she was emailing. All the same, she decided she wouldn't mention Fraser's visit to Zoe. She wouldn't put it past her friend to engineer an excuse to turn up, just for the chance to ogle him again, and then his high opinion of Maura's professionalism would be gone. No, she wouldn't mention their meeting to anyone, unless it came up in conversation – and the likelihood of that happening was remote.

Once the bowl had been collected, she would have no reason to think of Fraser Bell ever again.

CHAPTER FOUR

Fraser checked the address on the email twice once he arrived at 6 Thistledown Lane on Thursday afternoon.

He hadn't spent much time in Dean Village since returning to Edinburgh, although he knew its picture postcard prettiness had made the area an Instagram sensation and a must-visit for tourists. Certainly, he'd seen plenty of fashionably dressed teenagers posing for pictures on the bridges that spanned the canal on his journey from the eastern side of the city.

Leith, the part of the city where he now lived, was a world away from the old-world quaintness of the village – new developments seemed to be springing up every day and the docks were surrounded by glitzy new shops that felt slightly at odds with the traditional, centuries-old tenement buildings that had been home to the dockers and their families. On one hand, Fraser could see the developers were trying to appeal to a different demographic, with fancy penthouse apartments and enviable views over the Firth of Forth, but they had also created family-friendly homes and the area was very sought-after. For the time being, he and Naomi were renting, but he could imagine himself living there full time, if they decided to make the break from London permanent. Although Naomi was going to take some persuading. Her work as a model hadn't suffered with the move but her social life had. As she'd observed on more than one occasion, Fraser had a ready-made network of old friends to fall back on in Edinburgh whereas she was starting over. He couldn't really argue with that but he was quietly confident she would come round, in time.

Parking on the narrow-cobbled street, Fraser took a moment to study the property before him. It was one of several terraced houses, all dressed in the distinctive red sandstone that graced the nearby splendour of Well Court. Each property had a garage on the ground floor and a front door to the right, which Fraser guessed led up to an apartment. Number 6 had vibrant green double doors on the garage that matched the front door and a cluster of terracotta pots that suggested flowers in the warmer months.

Maura's instructions told him to ring the bell beside the garage and wait for her to answer. After a few moments, a smaller door cut into the middle of the left-hand side of the garage opened and Maura's glossy black head appeared. She had her hair tied back today, although several strands had escaped the ponytail and were coated with white. 'Hello,' she said, smiling at him. 'Come on in.'

She pushed the door wide and Fraser climbed through. The studio was long and narrow, which made sense considering it was situated in a garage. The walls had been lined with board – presumably for insulation in the colder months – and a number of strip lights were attached to the ceiling. Two electric heaters stood sentry at either end of the workbench and he spotted three or four portable heat guns dotted around. But it was the shelves along the right-hand wall that caught his eye the most. The range of pots was surprising – everything from slightly misshapen mugs to jugs and vases, small pottery animals to soap dishes, and one or two items that Fraser was at a loss to describe.

One set of shelves stood out from the general mismatch and clutter of items, however, and Fraser immediately understood that this was where Maura stored her own pieces. It wasn't that the work on the other shelves was bad; on the contrary, much of it looked very accomplished and it was certainly better than anything Fraser could have produced. He'd seen some of Maura's creations on Artsy, had found more when he'd searched further online, but he felt he would have recognised the supreme technical and artistic skill involved in producing these elegant pieces as belonging to a master potter even if he hadn't known who made them.

'I must say, your order came as a huge surprise,' Maura said, heading to the sink to wash her hands. 'To be perfectly honest, I didn't realise I'd made quite such an impression. Or did you just feel sorry for me after Archie kindly redecorated my shoes?'

Fraser grinned. 'I thought you could do with the cash to replace them,' he said. 'But seriously, I was intrigued. Who wouldn't be, upon discovering they went to school with someone so talented?'

She turned round, rubbing her hands on a faded scrap of towel, and he saw she was blushing. 'You're very kind,' she replied. 'I haven't wrapped the bowl yet – thought I'd let you see it up close and give you the opportunity to change your mind.'

He raised both eyebrows. 'I'm not going to change my mind. If anything, I'll be lucky to get out of here without buying more.' His eyes flickered back to the shelves and came to rest on an oversized pale green platter carved with swirling fronds of seaweed. 'How much is that?'

She threw him an apologetic look. 'That one's not for sale, I'm afraid. At least, not at the moment – it's for a gallery show I'm doing next month.'

Fraser's gaze lingered on the dish. 'It's a real beauty,' he said. 'But perhaps no bad thing that it's not available. Naomi would kill me if I came home laden with pottery, no matter how amazing it was.'

Maura watched him curiously. 'She doesn't like pots?'

'She doesn't like *stuff*,' he explained, looking rueful. 'Which makes life a bit tricky sometimes because I do like stuff. Especially beautiful stuff.'

'Ah,' Maura said with understanding. 'I can see how that might be a problem. Have you been together a long time?'

Fraser considered. How long was it since he'd been at the TV Soapstars awards and met Naomi at the crowded afterparty? Two years? Three? 'A while,' he said. 'Long enough to appreciate we're fundamentally unsuited to each other.'

Maura laughed, as he'd meant her to. It wasn't until he'd said the words that he realised how they might sound to someone who didn't know him very well. He and Naomi had got along fine back in London, spending time at each other's flats without actually living together. It was only now that they were occupying the same space twenty-four seven that their differences were coming to the fore. But that was relationships for you, he thought. Differences in taste and opinions were to be expected. No one wanted to date themselves, did they? 'Does she know you've bought this piece?' Maura asked. 'It's not small.'

'I showed her the pictures on Artsy,' he said, and decided not to mention Naomi's arched eyebrows when he'd told her who had made the bowl. 'She loves it.'

'That's good,' Maura said, moving towards a large box stashed beneath the workbench. 'I'd hate to think of you buying it only to keep it in a cupboard or under the bed.' She paused to throw him a mischievous look. 'Or worse still, the loft. I think there's probably a mountain of my efforts from school and college in my parents' attic, gathering dust and wondering what they did wrong.'

He smiled at the thought of a cluster of abandoned pots holding a meeting about how they could improve their languishing fortunes. 'We don't have a loft. We're renting a brand-new apartment over by Leith Docks – they don't come with much storage space. But don't worry, I already know where your bowl is going to go. It's going to have pride of place in the living room.'

Maura lifted the box and placed it on the bench. 'There you go. Take a look, check you're happy and then I can wrap it for you, to make sure it survives the journey.'

Reaching into the layers of cushioning newspaper, Fraser carefully lifted the bowl free so that the glaze caught the light. If anything, it was more beautiful in real life than it had looked on the website. The rim had been carved to represent the rise and fall of waves, smooth but somehow hinting at texture. It seemed to his uneducated eye that more than one glaze had been used; a dark, almost midnight blue had mingled with its azure and forget-me-not siblings to settle in the dimples of the inlaid sea-inspired design. They looked like tiny puddles of liquid but, when he tilted the bowl, they did not move. He brushed a wondering finger across the surface, half-expecting his skin to come away wet. 'How did you do this?'

'Trial and error, mostly,' she admitted, without embarrassment. 'I have an idea of what I want to achieve, obviously, but
I've found it doesn't do to get too attached to an outcome in
pottery. This one turned out well.'

The implication was that there were other pieces that hadn't
passed muster – he wondered what she did with them. 'Recycle
them, if they've cracked or warped,' she said when he voiced
the question. 'Or give them to my mother.'

Fraser laughed. 'If I had to present my mother with every
project I've starred in that didn't turn out the way I expected, she
wouldn't be able to move for evidence.' He stared at the bowl in
rapt admiration. 'Thank you for this. Will you wrap it for me?'

'Of course,' she said, lifting the bowl back into its box. After
a moment or two of rustling paper, she glanced up at him. 'I
should probably admit I looked you up too. You've been in
some really successful shows.'

He supposed he should have expected as much – his on-
screen murder at the hands of national treasure Penelope Keith
was enough to tempt anyone into a Google search – but the idea
that Maura had been as curious about him as he'd been about
her came as a pleasant surprise. 'With more than a few I'd rather
forget,' he said, even as he processed the fact of her interest.
'But I learned something from all of them, so I can't complain.'

'Even the chicken advert?'

'Especially the chicken advert,' he replied gravely. 'What I
learned from that was to ask for more details when my agent
said she had a juicy audition for me.'

She snorted then, which pleased him more. Naomi disapproved of his tendency to laugh at himself, although his time
as Louis the Chicken had been long before he met her and he

knew she pretended not to know about his less illustrious roles. She had suggested more than once that casting directors would take him more seriously if he took himself more seriously and Fraser had to admit that she might have a point. But Maura wasn't someone he needed to impress with his acting credits. He could be himself around her.

'Still, I bet it was a role you could really sink your teeth into,' she said, and now it was Fraser's turn to grin.

'Literally,' he said. 'They treated me to a full Big Bang Bucket when we'd finished filming. I definitely got my teeth into that.'

Again, Maura laughed. 'Sounds like it was worth the feather costume, then.'

He nodded. 'It was. I still get the occasional royalty payment.'

Maura finished wrapping the bowl and folded the lid of the box closed. 'That should be secure enough, as long as you don't throw it down any stairs.'

'I'll do my best,' Fraser said, and when she looked a little alarmed, he went on. 'It's going in the car, and then into the flat. It should be safe enough.'

She relinquished her hold on the box. 'Great. I'm sure I don't need to tell you this but the bowl shouldn't be used for food – the glaze is earthenware and purely decorative. And don't put it in the dishwasher or the microwave.'

Fraser tried to imagine a situation when he might be tempted to put such a beautiful thing into the dishwasher and failed. But he supposed it was a fair enough warning; Maura didn't really know him, after all. He might be a total heathen. 'Noted,' he said, and glanced around again. His eyes came to rest upon the shelves. 'This isn't all your work, is it? Some of it looks like your style but the rest . . .'

He trailed off, aware that there was a strong chance he might somehow insult her if he continued. What if he was wrong and the wonky mugs were hers? But thankfully, she understood what he was getting at. 'No, it's not all mine. I have a few amateur potters who come in and work in the studio each week. They tell me what they want to make, I give them a bit of advice – if they need it – and then I fire the pieces once they're ready.'

He frowned. 'Doesn't that interfere with your own creative process?'

'Not really,' she replied with a shrug. 'Most of them have been coming for years; they don't really need much from me but I like helping them. Occasionally it's a bit of a juggling act to fit everything in the kilns but we manage. And it helps to have a regular income.'

That was something Fraser totally understood; despite his relative success, he'd occasionally gone months with no earnings and he knew a lot of the creative industries were the same. He drifted closer to the assortment of pottery. Now that he was paying attention, he could see that some were quite accomplished, with decoration that suggested a lot of effort had gone into them. And all of them were more than he could achieve. 'Do you ever accept commissions?'

She blinked. 'Sometimes. It depends on who's asking and what they want.' There was a pause. 'And maybe how much they're paying.'

'Sensible,' he said approvingly, then hesitated, unsure whether to voice the proposal that had been swirling around his head from the moment he'd woken up on New Year's Day. Perhaps Maura would think it was a terrible idea, or even beneath her, given her evident talent. But in either eventuality, she might be able to recommend someone else who could help him, although he'd much prefer to work with her. 'Listen, after we met at the party, I had this idea that I wanted to sound you out about. Have you got a few minutes now?'

Maura eyed him curiously. He had her attention, at least. 'I've got time. What's on your mind?'

Fraser took a breath. 'I don't think I mentioned my new business venture when we talked the other night. I mean, it's not that new – I started it in September, when we came back to Edinburgh – but it's new in that I haven't done it before.' He stopped, aware that he was babbling, but she was watching him with a patient expression. 'What I'm trying to say is that I wanted to do something different, something that wasn't acting but that still made use of those skills because I'm sort of a one-trick pony in that regard.'

And now Maura was biting her lip. 'You're a chicken and a pony? Impressive.'

The gentle ribbing caused some of his apprehension to lift. 'I told you, I'm an actor with *range*. Anyway, I was looking around for the right opportunity and a friend of a friend told me about a ghost walk business that was up for sale. To cut a long story short, I bought it and I've been running it for the past four months.'

Her jaw dropped a little. 'Ghosts,' she repeated. 'Do you mean those walks around the city that revel in all the horrible things that have happened here?'

'Exactly,' Fraser said. 'People love a supernatural story – the more terrifyingly bloodthirsty the better. I was in a stage production of *The Highgate Hauntings* and you wouldn't believe how fast it sold out. Some people came two or three times.'

'So you've been doing the walks yourself?' Maura asked, her forehead crinkling. 'Or do you pay people to do them?'

'There's two of us,' he replied. 'Me and another guy called Tom. We split the walks between us – he does the stories he's always done and I researched a few others for my own route, to mix things up and offer something a bit different.'

'Go you,' Maura said, shaking her head. 'I hope you've got a big umbrella. You must be out in all weathers.'

'I have. It's got our logo on it. In fact, I'm thinking about adding them to the website so people can buy them.' He shifted his weight and studied her hopefully. 'Which sort of brings me to the point. When I was looking into taking on the business, I investigated a few other ghost-themed companies, to see what seemed to be doing well. And I found a company in York that really trades on their reputation as the most haunted city in England. They don't just tell stories – they sell the ghosts to go with them.'

She stared at him for a long moment. 'Erm . . .'

Reaching into his pocket, Fraser pulled out a small black and white box. He held it out to Maura. 'Here. Take a look.'

With an expression of bemusement, she took the box and examined the ornate decoration. A few seconds later, she flipped the lid back and slid the contents into the palm of her hand. 'It's an old map of York,' she said, examining the fine print on the tissue paper bundle.

'Uh-huh,' Fraser said. 'Their overall aesthetic is really great. Peel back the paper.'

She did as he suggested and revealed a slender ceramic ghost, no more than ten or eleven centimetres high. It was matte black, with two oval holes for eyes and a cluster of greenish-yellow powder where a face might have been. Its robes trailed behind it as though made of silk, with fine lines hinting at folds in the material. Maura turned it over in her hands, examining it with professional interest before glancing up at him. 'It's lovely – really well made. They've used a slip case so they can produce in bulk and each one looks the same. But the decoration is applied by hand. It's a really original idea.'

He nodded. 'That's what I thought. They have a shop on The Shambles but seem to do a lot of business through their website, with limited editions that sell out in minutes. It's crazy – a real battle to nab one. Anyway, what I was wondering was whether you'd be able to do something similar for me.'

Her gaze jerked up from the ghost in her hand. 'Copy it? Sorry, I don't think that's—'

'Not copy it,' he said quickly. 'I'd like to commission you to design a uniquely Scottish version. An Edinburgh ghost that I can sell on my tours.'

She looked far from convinced. 'I don't use slip cases. I hand build or throw everything I make here.'

'That's okay,' he said. 'It would be up to you how you make them and I wouldn't need a huge number. In fact, I'd want them to be completely different to the York ghosts.'

'I don't know,' she said, shaking her head. 'It's not really my thing. My work is all about the sea and nature, not the supernatural.'

Fraser could see he was losing her. 'So create a sea-themed ghost – I don't know, like a pirate or a siren. I can come up with a story to go with it.'

She was turning the black figure over and over in her hands, frowning down at it. 'A sea ghost,' she said. 'Maybe.'

'Or maybe a sea witch,' Fraser offered. 'Sadly, there's no shortage of Scottish women who were persecuted for witch-craft back in the day. I talk about them on one of the tours.' He fixed an earnest gaze on her. 'But you don't have to decide now. Think it over and let me know. You could even come on one of my walks, if you like. Get a feel for the stories I'm telling.'

She was silent for so long that he was certain she was going to say no. But she surprised him. 'I'll think about it.'

'Great,' he said. 'And if you did fancy coming on one of the tours, they start at 7.30pm from the Mercat Cross by St Giles' cathedral on the Royal Mile. I do Wednesday to Sundays – no need to book, in your case. Just turn up.'

Maura offered him the ghost but he didn't take it. 'Why don't you hang on to it for now? Just don't keep it beside your bed. The face glows in the dark – gave Naomi quite a scare when she woke up for a wee.'

'I can imagine,' Maura said wryly.

Fraser lifted the box containing the bowl. 'I'll be on my way then. Thanks for this, I can't wait to get it home.'

She saw him through the door and back onto the street, and Fraser got the impression she was checking to make sure he stowed the box securely in his car. Evidently satisfied, she stepped back into the studio and leaned against the open door. 'Drive carefully,' she called as he climbed behind the wheel.

'I will.' As he drove away, he couldn't resist glancing in the rearview mirror for a final glimpse of her. He wasn't sure whether it was Maura's connection to his school days or the business opportunity she represented but he found himself very much hoping that he'd see her on one of his ghost walks.

CHAPTER FIVE

'A ghost tour?' Kirsty said doubtfully, when Maura rang her on Friday morning. 'Why on earth would I want to go on a ghost tour?'

Maura considered how much information to share and decided on full disclosure. 'I ran into someone I went to school with and he told me he owns a walking business here in Edinburgh. So I thought I'd go along and wondered if you fancied it too.'

Her sister was quiet for a moment. 'Why don't you go with Zoe?'

Zoe had been Maura's first thought too, but she wasn't entirely sure she could trust her not to spend the entire tour whispering inappropriate comments. She'd asked all the same, and been slightly relieved when Zoe had said no. 'She's away this weekend.'

'Jamie?'

Maura sighed. Jamie had been her second thought, and her contemplation had lasted all of fifteen seconds. 'Because he'd hate it. You know how he feels about tourists at the best of times – imagine if I forced him to rub shoulders with them.'

Kirsty couldn't argue with that. 'There'd probably be a murder,' she acknowledged. 'But at least your school friend would have another grisly crime to talk about.'

'Jamie has a game on Saturday anyway, so he won't want to spend his Friday evening traipsing around town chasing spirits,' Maura added. 'Not that kind of spirit, at any rate.'

'No,' Kirsty conceded and Maura thought she almost had her. 'What's he like, this old school friend? Am I going to be bored to tears?'

Maura pictured him as she'd seen him the day before, illuminated by a shaft of sunlight, all golden haired and bearded and radiating a charm she wasn't even sure he knew he had. Kirsty had been four years above them at school. There was little chance she would remember Fraser, so she wouldn't be swayed by nostalgia, but she appreciated an attractive man when she saw one. 'I think it's safe to say you won't be bored,' Maura said, crossing her fingers and hoping she wasn't overestimating his charisma.

'Okay, I'll come,' Kirsty grudgingly agreed. 'But you owe me.'

'Of course,' Maura said, and smiled. 'Hey, you can collect those soup bowls I slaved over for you.'

'Point taken,' Kirsty grumbled. 'But I'll get the bowls another day. I'm not going to risk them getting smashed by some malevolent spook.'

Maura hesitated. Should she tell her sister about the proposal Fraser had put forward? She hadn't mentioned it to Jamie – in fact, she hadn't mentioned Fraser at all. The York ghost he had given her was tucked away in a bedside drawer, where its glow-in-the-dark face could not trouble her. It wasn't that she was keeping the visit from Jamie, more that she was sure he'd dismiss the whole ghost idea out of hand, would tell her it was beneath her and then she'd find it hard to justify spending any more time thinking about it. In actual fact, she could see the appeal of themed ghosts made to order for the tour. The York company might be well established and very successful but that didn't mean they had a monopoly on highly desirable, limited edition ceramic ghosts. And as she'd already told Fraser, she couldn't match their slick production methods; anything she made would be considerably less polished and therefore could not be seen as trespassing on their patch. She was more than two hundred miles away, for a start. 'I'll bring the bowls over on Sunday instead,' she said.

'Thanks. Do you want to meet for food tomorrow?' Kirsty asked. 'I can get Doug to collect the kids and put them to bed.'

'Sounds like a plan,' Maura said. Her niece and nephew were adorable but both were picky eaters and she suspected Kirsty would be glad of a night off. 'My treat.'

'I'll book Georgie's,' her sister said. 'Is five-thirty too early?'

The restaurant was one of Maura's favourites, off the beaten track and serving delicious food made with locally sourced produce. It was not cheap. 'Perfect,' she replied, trying not to wince. 'See you then.'

'Great,' Kirsty said, her tone much more enthusiastic. 'Always best to hunt ghosts on a full stomach.'

Maura rang off and checked her banking app, pleased to see Fraser's payment for the bowl had been deposited in her account, boosting her balance. That meant she could afford to take her sister to Georgie's without dipping into the account she and Jamie shared. It wouldn't have been a problem if she had – Jamie was used to her fluctuating income and never questioned anything she paid for from the joint account. But it was nice to be able to treat Kirsty all on her own, and somehow it seemed fitting that it was Fraser's purchase that enabled her to do it.

It wasn't raining as Maura and Kirsty arrived at the Mercat Cross around quarter past seven that evening but the air was cold and laced with fog. The pavements around St Giles' cathedral were slick with moisture and it was impossible to see further than ten metres along the Royal Mile. Perfect weather for a ghost hunt, Maura decided as she wrapped her scarf more securely around her neck. On a night like this it was easy to believe claims that Edinburgh was the most haunted city in the world; Maura could certainly imagine a sinister spirit or two clustered in the deep shadows around the cathedral.

Fraser looked pleased when he caught sight of her. She hadn't contacted him to say she was coming and if he was surprised that she'd brought a guest, he didn't show it. Instead, he gave a little wave to show he'd seen them, and returned his attention to the couple before him, whose tickets he had been checking. Waving them past to stand beside the towering stone monument, he moved on to the next people in the queue. She was a little taken aback to see him turning a few people away. 'I'm sorry but we're completely sold out this evening,' she heard him say. 'Our numbers are limited to twenty, to ensure I can keep everyone safe in the event of paranormal attack.'

The deadly earnest with which he spoke made Maura smile and, beside her, she knew Kirsty would have raised eyebrows, but the couple lapped up the excuse and eagerly pulled out their phones to book for the following evening.

'You're popular,' she said admiringly, when Fraser eventually made his way across to them to say hello.

'We sell out most evenings,' he said, without even a hint of self-satisfaction. 'But it's great to see you both. Nice to meet you, Kirsty.'

'And you,' Kirsty said, offering what Maura knew to be her most charming smile. 'Maura has told me all about you.'

Fraser turned faintly reproachful eyes towards Maura. 'You didn't tell her about Louis, did you?'

Maura laughed. 'I didn't realise it was a secret. But no – I hadn't mentioned it, although I'm obviously going to have to tell her now.' She glanced across at the tree that stood a little distance away, where another tour guide was gathering his group around him. 'I thought you might be dressed up,' she said, nodding towards the man with his ghostly white face and heavy black cloak.

'No need,' he said easily. 'Each to their own but I prefer a simple lantern and the power of the imagination to bring my ghosts to life. And speaking of which, we should probably get started.' He waved them both towards the rest of the group and raised his voice. 'Please, huddle close together. You'll be safer that way.'

'No wonder you were so keen to come,' Kirsty murmured as they joined the edge of the small crowd. 'Did he look like that at school?'

'No,' Maura lied, grateful when Fraser began to speak and saved her from the full force of her sister's disbelieving look.

'Ladies and gentlemen, welcome to the Dead Famous Ghost Tour. This evening, we will be exploring some of Edinburgh's most haunted streets and, along the way, I'll introduce you to some of her most infamous spirits. You'll hear about Stuart the Slice, the grisly butcher who wasn't too fussy about where he got his meat. You'll learn about Dr George Rae, who stalked the city's plague-stricken streets in a hook-nosed mask with his rusty knife, ready to lance the boils of the poor.' He paused to let an ominous silence spread. 'We'll pass over long-abandoned streets that run beneath the city and maybe, if you listen, you'll hear the screams of those who were walled in down there and left to die. But what you won't hear about is any kind of cute little ghost dog. This is not that kind of tour.'

Maura listened, spellbound in spite of herself. He had the entire audience in the palm of his hand, plus a few more bystanders who had stopped to listen. No wonder he hadn't bothered with a costume, she thought with a sideways glance at Kirsty. He didn't need one.

'I must warn you that this walking tour takes in some of the city's darkest wynds and most twisted alleyways,' he went on solemnly. 'You may be required to run at any moment. It is not a tour for the faint-hearted, nor for the afflicted of limb. If either description applies to you then tell me now, because I must warn you, in the event of a supernatural assault, we may not be able to come back for you if you fall behind.'

'Bloody hell, I'm almost scared,' Kirsty whispered in Maura's ear. 'Should I tell him about my dodgy knee?'

Maura hid a smile. Growing up, Kirsty had always acted as though being the eldest gave her the right to boss her younger sister around. As they'd reached adulthood, it had morphed into a conviction that she was always right. It was quite enjoyable to see her out of her comfort zone for once. 'Don't worry,' Maura whispered back. 'I'll protect you.'

'Brilliant,' Kirsty muttered. 'We're both doomed.'

Turning her attention back to Fraser, Maura saw him raise the lantern. 'Now, if you're ready, we'll go to meet our first spirit on the aptly named Fleshmarket Close. Stay together and get to know the stranger beside you. There's a chance you may need them before our journey is complete.'

He set off down the Royal Mile, his light bobbing as he held it high. The rest of the group broke into excited murmuring. Some hurried forward to speak to Fraser; Maura guessed they were real ghost aficionados who wanted the inside scoop on the stories Fraser was going to share. Maura had to admit she was impressed by what she'd seen so far. She'd known he must be good but she hadn't expected to feel a tiny shiver of apprehension as they entered the narrow alleyway of Fleshmarket Close.

It wasn't possible to walk side by side – by necessity, they moved in single file through the shadows. At the top of the stone steps, beside the Halfway House pub, Fraser paused and gathered his audience in close. 'The year is 1842 and we find ourselves on Fleshmarket Close, in the heart of the city's meat market. Times are hard, especially for those with little money but one butcher in particular could always be relied upon to find a decent cut of meat for a good price. His name was Stuart MacBinnie, also known as Stuart the Slice.' He gazed around soberly. 'Now, some of Stuart's neighbours are becoming resentful of his success. They want to know how it is he can undercut their prices and supply his meat so cheaply, when the slaughterhouse dictates the price they all pay. Around the same time, a number of mysterious disappearances happen, mostly from the infamously licentious vaults beneath the South Bridge. It's not long before one of the butchers, Jack Furness,

starts to eye Stuart the Slice with suspicion. He breaks into
Stuart's backroom and makes a horrific discovery. Not only is
Stuart behind the disappearances, but he's also disposing of the
evidence by passing it on to his unsuspecting customers to eat.'

A faint moan escaped the woman beside Maura but Fraser
didn't stop. 'But just as Jack is about to make his way to the
authorities, Stuart comes back and finds him. A desperate fight
follows, during which Jack is mortally wounded. He manages
to drag himself out here, where Stuart catches up with him.
Just as he's about to strike the blow that will finish Jack off, a
pistol shot rings out. The bullet pierces Stuart's heart and he
tumbles to the ground, dead before he even hits the pavement.

'Who killed him, you may ask?' Fraser went on, gazing
around at his rapt audience. 'No one ever knew. Rumours flew
that it was the lover of a missing woman from the vaults, who
had deduced Stuart's guilt and had come to take his revenge. It
must be said that the authorities did not waste much time trying
to catch the mystery sniper. But the other butchers began to
report an unnatural icy chill around the spot where Stuart had
died. Others felt a malevolent presence they couldn't explain,
as though an evil spirit watched them.'

'My money's on Stuart,' Kirsty whispered to Maura. 'But I
suppose it could have been Jack.'

Maura tipped her head. 'Or it could have just been winter,
combined with some overactive imaginations.'

'Spoil-sport,' Kirsty said, rolling her eyes.

'Whatever the truth, visitors lingering in Fleshmarket Close
have been known to experience the same phenomenon,' Fraser
said, as several members of the crowd began to glance uneasily
around. One or two rubbed their arms, as though suddenly

cold. 'Perhaps we shouldn't linger, either. Come, let's continue on our way and leave these dark deeds behind.'

It didn't matter how much Maura reminded herself that the story could not be true, she was still glad to reach the bustle of Cockburn Street and she suspected the rest of the group felt the same. Conversations broke out as Fraser led them up the hill and then took a sharp left down Warriston's Close stairs. 'He wasn't joking about the afflicted of limb bit,' Kirsty said as they traversed the steep stone steps. 'My Fitbit is going to love me.'

Back in the shadow of St Giles' cathedral, at the site of the Old Tolbooth, long since demolished, Fraser regaled them with tales of the truly terrifying plague doctor who had undertaken the grim task of caring for Edinburgh's many sick and dying during the 1600s. Amazingly, he had survived the plague but when he approached the city councilmen for the handsome payment they had promised him, they had refused to pay. He battled for years but eventually died penniless. Legend had it that he had haunted the council's offices at the Old Tolbooth, demanding fair payment for his services. 'He might be there even now, had the building not been turned to rubble.'

They passed by Mary King's Close, where those suffering from the plague were said to have been walled in and abandoned for fear of spreading the infection. On the corner of Lawnmarket, Fraser pointed out the gold symbol in the pavement that marked the site of the old gallows, where one half of the infamous Resurrection Men, William Burke, had met his end after being found guilty of murder and grave robbing. The last stop was in Greyfriars Kirkyard, but Fraser was true to his word and it was not the grave of the little dog that he took them to. Instead, he led them to the Covenanters' Prison, where Bloody George Mackenzie maltreated and executed over a thousand prisoners for their religious beliefs.

'I hope we're not related,' Maura murmured to her sister as the story unfolded and Fraser described some of the terrifying poltergeist activity that had been experienced on the site ever since.

'So do I,' Kirsty said. 'The ghost might pick on us first.'

It seemed some of the other audience members harboured similar concerns, judging from the way they huddled nearer. But Maura could only applaud as the tour drew to its close. She had been entertained, frightened and altogether captivated by Fraser's storytelling and, from the rapt expressions on the faces of those around her, she guessed everyone else felt the same. 'You were brilliant,' she said, when Fraser had at last finished accepting thanks and made his way over to where Maura and Kirsty waited. 'Completely monstrous, of course, but also brilliant.'

'Thank you,' he said, grinning with delight. 'I'm glad you enjoyed it.'

'We did,' Kirsty said fervently. 'Even if I will struggle to sleep tonight.'

He laughed. 'Then my work here is done.'

'Maura tells me you're an actor,' Kirsty went on. 'It really shows. At one point, I thought you actually were William Burke.'

Fraser looked gratified. 'Thank you again.'

'It really was great,' Maura said. 'Thanks for inviting me – us – to join you.'

'My pleasure,' he replied warmly. 'No need to ask if you know your way home. Will you be okay getting out of here? I can walk with you if you'd like?'

Maura thought Kirsty might accept so she shook her head fast. 'No, don't trouble yourself. Get away home – Naomi will be wondering where you've got to.'

He laughed. 'She's in Paris. I don't think she'll be missing me.'

'Oh. Well, thanks again,' Maura said, feeling awkward without knowing why. 'See you, Fraser.'

'Who's Naomi?' Kirsty asked as they made their way out of the graveyard. 'An impossibly beautiful girlfriend, I suppose.'

'Got it in one,' Maura confirmed. 'You didn't think he'd be single, did you?'

'No,' Kirsty said with a sigh. 'And you went to school with him? How come I never heard you talk about him?'

Maura shrugged, hoping her suddenly too-warm cheeks didn't give her away. She'd never told anyone what happened the last time she saw Fraser, outside the Strawberry Arms, least of all Kirsty, who had been away at university herself by then. 'We weren't friends.'

Her sister eyed her. 'But you are now.'

'Not exactly.' Maura wasn't sure she could describe Fraser as a friend – if anything he was a customer, albeit one who had put forward a business proposal. If she agreed to work with him, she would certainly see more of him and it was possible friendship would follow. Was that something she wanted? 'I think I'd call us acquaintances.'

'Well, he certainly knows how to make an impression,' Kirsty declared. 'He's got presence, which I suppose is quite handy for an actor.'

Maura smiled. 'Probably. Have you got time for a drink before you head off?'

Kirsty lived in a small village across the Firth of Forth, near their parents' house, which was convenient for babysitting but less so for nights on the town. She checked her watch and nodded. 'I'm not ready to go home yet. It turns out being terrorised by the dead actually makes you feel alive.'

'Who knew?' Maura said, laughing. 'Come on. It's your round.'

'What on earth are you making?'

The question came from Cordelia, a silver-haired sixty-something with a penchant for blood red glazes. She was gazing at the board in front of Maura with something approaching horrified fascination and Maura supposed she could hardly blame her. The prototype ghost she was currently working on was just as tall and slender as the ghost Fraser had given her as a reference point, with a rounded head and scored lines to suggest folds of fabric, but that was where the similarity ended. In trying to make something the same but different, Maura had only succeeded in moulding the clay into a shape that was vaguely ghost-like, if she squinted a bit, but also undeniably . . . well, phallic.

The other students abandoned their work to come and take a look. 'Is there something you want to tell us?' Effie said, tilting her head to one side. 'A new direction your work is taking?'

Sharon giggled and immediately clapped a hand over her mouth. 'Sorry,' she said. 'It's just such a departure from what you usually make.'

Maura couldn't argue with that. She puffed out a long breath and sat back on her chair. 'It's meant to be a ghost.'

'Oh,' Cordelia said, taking a step back to get a clearer

perspective. 'I thought perhaps a disembodied finger – wondered if you'd gone all Tate Modern on us.'

'I'm thinking of a completely different body part,' Effie declared. 'It reminds me of my ex-husband. He leaned to the left as well.'

'Too much information, Effie,' Sharon said, wincing.

Maura groaned. She had over twenty years' experience of working with clay, had made everything from an espresso cup to an intricate glazed sculpture that was currently on display in the Royal Botanic Garden. Surely she could design a ghost for Fraser that didn't look as though it had escaped from a Soho sex shop. 'Back to the drawing board,' she said, reaching for more clay.

'Is this your model?' Effie asked, picking up the black ghost and smoothing her fingers across its matte surface.

'That's my starting point,' Maura said. 'A friend wants something he can sell on his ghost tour but obviously I don't want to copy someone else's idea.'

Cordelia looked thoughtful. 'What about a different shape?' she suggested. 'More *Scooby-Doo*, less Wyrd Willy.'

Sharon let out a snort of laughter and Maura couldn't help grinning. She liked the name Wyrd Willy. Perhaps she wouldn't squash her first effort flat and recycle the clay after all. 'More *Scooby-Doo*,' she repeated, trying to recall the cartoon ghosts and monsters that had featured on the TV show. Without fail, they turned out to be crooks in complicated disguises, attempting to draw attention away from their dastardly schemes, but there had definitely been one or two villains who had favoured the simple sheet-over-the-head trick. Perhaps that was what Cordelia meant – a more obviously cartoonish ghost. Could that work? Would Fraser find it too childish? She could only try. Her plan had been to create a few prototypes to see which worked and which didn't. At least she had eliminated one potential design early on.

Effie was studying her thoughtfully. 'If your friend is planning to sell the ghosts, does that mean you're going to be paid?'

'Yes,' Maura said. Although now she came to think of it, Fraser hadn't actually mentioned money. 'Maybe not for the initial models – these are just for me to establish the right shape and design.'

'So you're doing him a favour?' Cordelia's pale blue eyes were sharp, reminding Maura that she had been a highly successful CEO before a bout of ill health forced an early retirement. 'I hope this friend is trustworthy.'

'Of course he is,' Maura replied, then hesitated. She'd instinctively liked Fraser. It hadn't occurred to her that he might not be someone she could trust. 'We went to the same school. And he bought one of my bowls. The most expensive one.'

Effie let out an impressed whistle but Cordelia pursed her lips. 'Not exactly a watertight character reference but at least he's splashed the cash. Does he have any idea whether this new product will actually sell?'

Here, Maura felt she was on firmer ground. She still remembered the rapt expressions of the audience as Fraser had woven his uncanny magic, and the way they'd hung around afterwards, like superfans at the stage door. She was sure she'd overheard one of the women asking for his autograph. When she'd got home, Maura had taken a look at the Dead Famous Tour website and had noted there was already a well-established online shop, although the merchandise was limited. If Fraser's market research was to be believed, and the York ghost seller was as successful as he suggested, then there was no reason to think a range of Edinburgh ghosts would not sell, she had concluded. If she could settle on a design that both she and Fraser were happy with, that was. 'He's following a business model that has worked elsewhere and I think he has his head screwed on,' Maura said, her doubts fading. She stood up and stretched. 'Who'd like a cup of tea?'

By the time the kettle had boiled and tea was brewed to each student's liking, they had all gone back to their places on the workbench, allowing Maura to consider her problem anew. The simplicity of a blatantly draped sheet intrigued her – instantly recognisable as a ghost but with a childlike appeal that belied its supernatural essence. Her thoughts circled back to the gruesome nature of the stories Fraser had told; she'd have to be careful not to make the design too cute. Absently, she reached for the clay and pulled some free, rolling it into a ball. Perhaps if she used something as a support, she might be able to drape the clay over the top to look like cloth . . .

Twenty minutes later, Maura had a shape she was not unhappy with. It wasn't as elegant as the York phantom – the folds of clay were thick rather than emulating the clean flowing lines moulded by the slip case – but it was recognisably a ghost and substantially different from her reference point. Using a damp sponge, she smoothed the edges, flicking some into soft upward curves to create the illusion that the figure was hovering just above the ground. When at last she was satisfied, she used the end of a wooden paintbrush to create two empty eye sockets and sat back to admire her work.

'Very nice,' Effie said, glancing across from the jug she was coiling. 'Not a hint of the erotic about that one.'

'Thanks,' Maura said. 'I quite like him.'

'Make sure you put your mark on it,' Effie said, peering over the top of her glasses. 'I know it's only a prototype but it's still your work.'

It was a good point, Maura thought. She had a specially designed stamp with her signature embossed upon it for her larger pieces but that wouldn't work here. Lifting the ghost with care, she scratched her initials into the underside of a fold of clay. 'Done,' she said with satisfaction. 'What else can I try?'

Sharon frowned thoughtfully. 'What about adding some hands? Hidden underneath the sheet, I mean. A bit like the one from that kids' film back in the day.'

'Casper the Friendly Ghost,' Effie supplied. 'My daughter loved him.'

Immediately, Maura could picture the cheery cartoon character. It would mean a more rigid structure, she mused, taking up another ball of clay. And perhaps she could add a hidden foot beneath the folds of clay, to raise the figure up and enhance the impression that it was floating. She kept the rounded head but added a protruding bump to the right and left, as though the draped cloth was concealing two outstretched arms. The overall effect was different, perhaps a little too cutesy, but she had to concede it was also recognisably a ghost.

'They're great,' Sharon said, when Maura placed them side by side on the shelf to dry. 'I'd buy one.'

Effie winked. 'You could use Wyrd Willy to tap into the hen do market. I bet he'd be popular – the ghost of boyfriends past.'

It was probably a genius idea but Maura doubted it would fit in with the overall Dead Famous vibe. 'I don't think I'll suggest that to Fraser. That particular prototype is never leaving this studio.'

It wasn't until her students were gone that Maura felt the inevitable creep of creative doubt. The ghosts were very different from the pieces she usually produced. What would Fraser think of them? Would he be offended that she'd listened to his spine-chilling tales and produced something less threatening, quite unlike the slip cast model he had given her? She supposed only time would tell; her efforts needed to dry, to be fired and glazed before they could be presented to Fraser, and that would take a few weeks. There was no point in fretting about his reaction until then. In fact, she told herself sternly as she wiped the workbench with a damp yellow sponge, there was no point in fretting at all. If the ghosts weren't what Fraser wanted, then she would simply go back to her usual work and have no reason to stay in touch with him. Given how much he seemed to be occupying her thoughts recently, perhaps that would be no bad thing.

Maura was weary by the time she locked the door to the studio and trudged upstairs to the flat that evening. She'd spent the afternoon working on a few pieces for the gallery show she was taking part in the following month, finishing up a leaf-shaped bowl inspired by a copper beech tree that grew in her parents' garden. It wouldn't be exclusively her work on display – the space would be shared with three other potters – but she wanted to supply the gallery with some larger items that would show her range, as well as hopefully tempt one or two buyers. The plant pot she'd made on New Year's Day also needed to be glazed; it had sat on the bottom shelf in mute accusation for weeks and Maura found she couldn't bear to neglect it any longer. On a whim, she decided to use a stencil and underglazes in various shades of green to create a rainforest effect. The finished design was bold and different but she liked it and she thought the gallery would too.

The apartment was dark and empty, as it often was when Maura finished work. Jamie rarely made it home before six-thirty, and was much later on the evenings he had rugby training or after-work drinks. On those nights, Maura usually made whatever she wanted to eat and curled up on the sofa to watch the television. But tonight, he'd messaged to say he was picking up a curry from their favourite takeaway and she was glad she wouldn't have to cook. Her work was not especially physical, unless she was manhandling a delivery of clay from the wholesaler or emptying out the clay trap from beneath the sink in the studio, but it did take concentration and she was often tired when Jamie arrived home. It was an occasional source of friction between them but, this evening, he seemed to have read her mind.

'I've got a dopiaza, a jalfrezi, sag aloo, onion bhajis and more poppadoms than we can possibly eat,' he called as he climbed the stairs, bringing with him the delicious smell of hot, mingling spices. 'Did you remember to warm the plates?'

'I did,' Maura said, taking the bag from him and heading for the kitchen to start unpacking. 'Did you get mango chutney?'

He nodded, stripping off his suit jacket and loosening his tie. 'Of course. But we've been going to the same takeaway for the last five years. If they don't know our standard order by now then they never will.'

Maura smiled. 'Great. I'll serve up.'

She expected him to leave her to it, as he usually did. Instead, he stood in the doorway, watching her open containers and spoon the contents onto the plates she'd taken from the oven. 'This kitchen is too small,' he said, after a few moments spent observing her moving things around to accommodate the lack of space.

'Small but perfectly formed,' she said, reaching into a drawer for knives and forks. 'It has everything we need.'

Jamie wrinkled his nose. 'Apart from enough worktops, a bigger fridge-freezer and a dishwasher that takes more than four dinner plates.'

Maura frowned as she opened the brown paper bags that held the poppadoms. It was true that the kitchen was smaller than either of them would like but that was because the flat also held two double bedrooms and a decent-sized living room. She'd inherited it from her aunt, who had died childless ten years earlier and left it to Kirsty and Maura. It was a kindness Maura appreciated every day – she would never have been able to buy a property in Dean Village on the money she made from her business. One day, she hoped to buy her sister's share and own the apartment outright but she would need to sell a lot more pots for that to happen. Or perhaps she would give in to Jamie's increasingly more frequent suggestion that she and Kirsty sell the flat, which would provide Maura with enough equity to put into buying somewhere with him. The difficulty there was finding a property with a garden big enough to add a studio; those were few and far between in Edinburgh and she liked living in the heart of the city. 'Luckily, there are only two of us,' she reminded Jamie. 'We don't need more than four plates.'

He didn't laugh. 'I'm being serious. There are new developments springing up all over the city. We could move into one of those.'

It wasn't the first time Jamie had mentioned them – he'd left brochures on the coffee table too. But now she was reminded of Fraser, and his assertion that he didn't have much space in the shiny new flat he shared with Naomi. 'We've been over this,' she replied, holding out a laden tray to Jamie. 'None of them have space for a studio.'

'You can rent somewhere nearby to work in.' His tone was as reasonable as ever. The suggestion wasn't a terrible one, but they'd had this conversation before and she'd had to remind him that her work needed a very specific environment to operate safely and efficiently. Kilns needed ventilation, she needed space to store the pots she made, and she needed enough workbenches to give her students room to work. And that was before she considered the convenience of having her studio right downstairs. Why would she go searching for somewhere new when she had everything she needed here? But she also knew from experience that Jamie failed to appreciate how much more difficult her life would be if they moved to the wrong place, and she wasn't about to ruin her favourite takeaway with another argument. 'I'll look at the brochures,' she said, hoping that would be enough to placate him.

Jamie beamed at her. 'Thanks. I brought some new ones home with me. John at work went to a viewing and said they're really nice. We could arrange to have a look, if you like.'

She'd met John a number of times; he'd once suggested she give up pottery and get a proper job, so she wasn't convinced their tastes would align on much, let alone on living space.

But she was probably being unfair. A brand-new home had its appeal, even if the apartments she'd seen going up around the city seemed a little soulless. It was not an observation she was about to share with Jamie, however. 'Maybe,' she said, and picked up her own tray. 'Come on, let's enjoy this before it gets cold.'

CHAPTER SIX

It took the best part of a week for Naomi to stop scowling when she caught sight of the bowl on the coffee table. Fraser explained who had made it, which she greeted with an indifferent sniff, and he'd even shown her Maura's sculpture on display in the Royal Botanic Garden. 'Yes, but what is the bowl for?' Naomi had asked when he'd finished. 'It's just going to sit there and gather dust.'

'It won't, because we'll dust it,' Fraser had replied. 'And it doesn't have to have a purpose. It's a thing of beauty – isn't that enough?'

She'd opened her mouth to object and then closed it again, being self-aware enough to recognise that to most people, her own job involved looking beautiful and not much else. 'Isn't there somewhere else it can go?' she went on, changing tack. 'It might get broken there.'

'Not if we're careful,' he said reasonably. 'Besides, I want it somewhere I can see it.'

She'd given in eventually, not with good grace but with a mutinous muttering that Fraser had decided it was best to ignore. He hadn't told her about the ghosts Maura was making for him; anything that hinted he was putting down roots, making their move to Edinburgh more long-term, would elicit an even more stormy response. It was something he was going to have to face head-on at some point, and decisions would have to be made about their future together, but he didn't think either of them were ready for the difficult conversations that would inevitably follow. For now, he was content to fine-tune the Dead Famous tours, test out new content when he could and build the business into the most sought-after tour in Edinburgh.

It was all he could do not to contact Maura to ask how she was getting on with the designs, however. He hadn't heard from her since the morning after the tour, when he'd emailed to thank her for coming and she'd agreed to come up with a couple of prototype ghosts. He knew the process took time but he couldn't help feeling a tickle of impatience as the days slid by. Creativity couldn't be rushed, he reminded himself. When Maura had something to show him, she would let him know.

In the meantime, he'd kept himself busy during the last few days of January by catching up with the friends he'd lost touch with during his long absence. Two of his oldest friends had been in the same year at St Ignatius – one, Malcolm, had stayed in Edinburgh, building a property portfolio, but Graeme had travelled. Like Fraser, he'd recently returned to his old stomping ground but his circumstances were different, having just finished with a messy divorce. The three of them had seen each other sporadically over the years but had slipped back into friendship as though no time at all had passed, and tried to meet once a month for a pint and a chat.

'You'll never guess who I ran into on New Year's Eve,'

Fraser said as they settled down with their pints in the World's End pub.

'Taylor Swift,' Graeme suggested, taking a sip of his beer.

'George Clooney,' Malcolm put in, equally deadpan. 'I hear he loves Hogmanay in Edinburgh.'

'Ha ha,' Fraser said, without rancour. 'You should both be at the Fringe, you're so funny.'

He waited, sipping his own pint and knowing they would not be able to resist the bait for long.

'So?' Malcolm demanded after a short, impatient silence. 'Are you going to wait until next Hogmanay to tell us?'

Fraser hid a smile. 'Someone you might know, although I'm not sure you'll remember her. Maura McKenzie. She was in our year at school.'

Malcolm's face wrinkled in thought. 'Nope. I've got nothing.'

'I do,' Graeme said slowly. 'Dark-haired girl. Never spoke much.'

'That's her,' Fraser said. 'She spent most of her time in the art block.'

Malcolm nodded sagely. 'That's why I don't remember her. The art teacher hated me – in fact, I was banned from the art block for knocking over someone's GCSE project.'

Fraser felt his eyebrows shoot up. 'I don't remember that.'

His friend shrugged. 'You were too busy playing at Shakespeare in the drama studio.' He gave Fraser a sidelong look. 'I always reckoned you fancied the teacher, that's why you were so keen.'

Fraser cast his mind back. The drama teacher had been en-couraging and he had liked her, but she had been old, or at least the age he was now, and that wasn't what had kept him coming back to the drama studio. It had been his love of performing, the feeling he got when he slipped into someone else's skin and stepped into the limelight. That had been what drove him to work as hard as he had on passing his exams and winning a coveted place at drama school. It was perhaps a little ironic that he had fallen so badly out of love with the thing that had once meant everything to him.

'So what's Maura been up to since school?' Graeme asked. 'Have the years been as cruel to her as the rest of us?'

'Speak for yourself,' Fraser said mildly. 'And no, the years have not been cruel to her. The opposite, in fact. She's doing very well for herself.'

Graeme perked up. 'Is she single? Can you get me her number?'

He shook his head. 'Sadly not single. She has a strapping great rugby player of a boyfriend.'

'Shame,' Graeme said, subsiding into his pint. 'I was hoping you were about to offer me an excuse to get off the dating apps. They're driving me to drink.'

Fraser felt a stab of sympathy for him. It couldn't be easy to start over, especially when your ex-wife was happily coupled up with a new man. But Maura was so far out of Graeme's league that there was no way he stood a chance of a date with her, even if she had been single. Fraser wasn't about to dent his friend's already fragile ego any further, however, so he said nothing.

Malcolm had been tapping at his phone. 'Maura McKenzie,' he said, holding out the screen to show a Google page filled with hits. 'Bloody hell, she can't have looked like that at school.'

It was exactly what Fraser had thought when she'd first

introduced herself, although he wasn't about to admit that now. 'She's a really talented potter, makes some incredible things. I'm hoping she'll make some ghosts for the tour website – I think the tourists will snap them up.'

'Good plan,' Malcolm said, still scrolling through the search hits. 'And I suppose the fact that she's so easy to look at helps too, right?'

Fraser sighed. 'Not everything is about looks, Malky.'

The other man grunted. 'Says the man with the model for a girlfriend.'

'What's your point?' Fraser asked, raising an eyebrow.

Malcolm looked up. 'No point, Fraser. I'm just saying you always were a sucker for a pretty face.'

Graeme looked from one friend to the other. 'Ignore him, Fraser. He's just jealous because he looks like a bull's arse.' He paused to stare at the multiple pictures of Maura currently adorning Malcolm's phone. 'Although she is fine, I'll grant you that. I don't blame you for sniffing around.'

Fraser put down his pint. 'I'm not sniffing around. It's a business arrangement, one that hasn't even been finalised. if you must know. And I believe I mentioned the fact that she has a boyfriend – just as I have Naomi.' He bristled across the table at them. 'I wish I'd never told you now.'

To their credit, both his friends looked shamefaced. 'Sorry,' Malcolm said.

'Aye, and I'm sorry too,' Graeme admitted. 'I don't get out much these days.'

Sitting back in his seat, Fraser felt his irritation drain away. Wouldn't his friends in London have reacted in similar ways? And the truth was that Maura was very attractive – if he was brutally honest with himself then he had to admit he would have been interested, had they both been single. But perhaps it was better not to think about that. 'It's okay,' he said, and glanced up at the big screen in one corner of the bar, where a football match was playing in silence. It was time to change the subject. 'So, what do you reckon? Have Dundee got any chance this season?'

The message he'd been anticipating arrived a few days later.

Hi Fraser,
    I've got a couple of sample ghosts for you to look at. Do you want to drop by the studio or would you prefer to meet somewhere?
    All best,
    Maura

Fingers stumbling with enthusiasm, it took him three attempts to type something that made sense.

Whatever suits you. Less hassle for me to come to you?
When works?

Her suggestion of the following morning pleased him and, since February had decided it was time to roll out a perfect blue sky, he decided to take the tram to the West End and stroll through Dean Village.

As before, there were plenty of tourists out and about, as well as dog walkers and joggers. The sunshine seemed to have brought everyone out of hibernation, although there was still

a chill in the air that made Fraser glad of his coat. Having arrived early, he took a deliberately circuitous route through the
winding streets, crossing Bell's Brae Bridge to wander past the
red sandstone turrets and spires of Well Court. The village had
been a thriving milling community for centuries, with no fewer
than eleven working mills at one point, and Well Court had
originally been built to house workers and their families. These
days it was a UNESCO World Heritage site but its purpose
hadn't changed, although Fraser suspected it cost an awful lot
more to live there now.

Fraser stood for a moment on the Water of Leith Walkway,
gazing along the river as it babbled beneath the houses on either
side of its banks. In some ways, it was like stepping back in time;
there was evidence of the area's industrial past everywhere he
looked. Tall warehouses that once stored grain and flour had
been converted into apartments, but it was the smaller houses
that had been home to the millers that gave the place its village feel, even though it was merely a stone's throw from the
bustling city. There were stories here, he thought as he gazed
around, perhaps even ghost stories that he could use if he ever
wanted to add to the Dead Famous repertoire. From its nearby
location, he guessed Thistledown Lane must overlook the river,
but he had no way of knowing which window belonged to
Maura's apartment.

He loved the mingling of old and new at the Port of Leith
but he had to admit he felt a tiny stab of regret that he didn't
live here. Maybe, if he did decide against going back to London,
he could look into buying a property nearby.

A quick glance at his watch told him it was time to meet
Maura. Following the winding path, he made his way along the

picturesque Hawthornbank Lane and into Thistledown Lane. Maura opened the door almost immediately, as though she'd been waiting just behind it for him to arrive. As before, her hair was tied back in a ponytail. There was no streak of clay in it this time. She was wearing a clean apron today, although he saw the potter's wheel was out. 'Oh, have I interrupted you?'

She shook her head. 'I have a student coming over for a throwing lesson at midday. I'm trying to be organised.'

'Lucky them,' he said. 'Having someone so well qualified to teach them.'

Her cheeks grew pink. 'It's more practice than anything else,' she said modestly. 'Once you've explained the basics of throwing, the rest is just dedication and hard work to improve.'

Fraser tipped his head. 'Like most things, then.'

'Like most things,' she agreed wryly. 'So, would you like to meet the ghosts?'

He couldn't resist looking around, as though they might come floating towards him. 'Very much.'

She waved him towards the shelves. 'I experimented with a few different shapes and sizes,' she explained as she moved various pots out of the way. 'Some worked well, others not so well. I'm afraid I couldn't get anywhere near the perfection of the ghost you gave me – he's here too, by the way; don't forget to take him home – so I went for a less elegant look.' She hesitated and he realised she sounded more than a little nervous. 'Anyway, here they are. See what you think.'

She presented him with a shelf containing six or seven ghosts. Some were plain white, a couple were an aged cream colour, and others were bright, with speckles of glaze that shone under the lights. One had an elegant swirling pattern painted in black down the back of his robe. A few appeared to be holding their sheet aloft with unseen hands. They all stared at him with oval eyes that somehow contrived to look anxious and perhaps even mournful, as though they knew they were awaiting his judgement. Fraser studied them in silence, taking in the care and attention to detail that had gone into each of them. Maura had not lied when she'd said they were not like the York ghost but, in Fraser's eyes, they were vastly superior. He'd wanted something that represented the ghosts at the heart of the grim stories he told, while also being unique to Edinburgh and highly collectible, but he hadn't dreamed Maura would also manage to imbue them with a sense of melancholy.

'I love them,' he said, reaching out to pick up the black painted ghost and inspect the intricate pattern. Turning it over, he saw the initials *MM* marked on the base. Replacing it, he took another ghost. This one was a pale green, with wispy strands of a darker green twisting through it. 'Seaweed,' he said, recognising the delicate fronds. 'This is the sea witch, isn't it?'

She nodded. 'I based the design on Agnes Sampson, who was tortured and executed during the North Berwick witch trials. They said she raised a tempest to sink the fleet of James VI while at sea.'

Fraser shook his head, impressed that she'd taken the time to do some research of her own. 'I cover those trials on my other tour. Not the city's finest moment.'

Maura shuddered. 'I know. The stories you tell are scary and gruesome but afterwards, it struck me how terribly sad they were too.'

He knew what she meant. When he'd begun negotiations

with the previous owner of the tour business, the man had outlined what worked well with audiences and what didn't. 'Focus on the supernatural – that's what they want,' he'd advised, with grim practicality. 'If you dwell too much on the awfulness of human nature then you won't survive a month, financially or emotionally.'

And once Fraser had read the background behind each story for himself, he understood. His acting experience helped – he was playing a role, just like any other job he'd undertaken. Once the patter of the stories had become familiar, he'd been able to square the horror of the real-life events with the importance of reminding people they had happened. And the advice he'd been given was sound. The job of a tour guide might be to educate and encourage remembrance, but the goal of a ghost tour guide was to bypass the natural scepticism and logic of the audience to invoke their oldest fear – that something malevolent lurked in the dark. Fraser took pride in giving his customers exactly that experience, but he also hoped that at least some went away a little more thoughtful than they had been before.

'The stories are sad,' he said to Maura. 'And you've somehow managed to capture that in your design.'

'They're just prototypes,' she said, although he thought she looked gratified. 'Obviously, you'd want to give me instructions on each theme and I'd need plenty of time to make them – the process isn't quick.'

'I don't want you to change a thing.' He touched the sea witch again, marvelling at how exquisite she was. 'But I think this shape, rather than the one with hands. How many can you make for the first batch? Is twenty too many?'

She blinked, and let out a surprised laugh. 'Whoa there, slow down a bit. We need to think this through. You haven't told me how you see this partnership working – is it a fifty-fifty split in terms of money?'

His eyes slid to the ghosts once more as he ran some rapid calculations. The figures he'd come up with had been mostly based on the prices he'd taken from the York ghost website but he could see now he had been way off. Their ghosts were desirable and appealing to collectors, but even the limited editions were mass-produced compared to Maura's work. Her ghosts were all one-offs, and that made them more valuable. They also came with her mark, claiming them as hers. The last thing Fraser wanted to do was price the ordinary punter out of the market but he was looking at something special and he would be a fool not to price it accordingly. 'Given the amount of work you've put in, I don't think fifty-fifty is a fair split,' he said, his eyes coming to rest on her. 'I propose sixty-forty in your favour, payable on delivery of the first batch. Does that sound fair?'

She nodded. 'More than fair. Do you know how you're going to price them yet?'

'I need to do some more research,' he said. 'Obviously, I've got a rough idea but I don't want to undersell them.'

'Okay, that makes sense. When do you want the batch of twenty by?'

Fraser shrugged, even as his thoughts whirred. 'You tell me when you can deliver them. You're the one doing the hard work – all I have to do is add them to the website.'

'Hardly,' she observed. 'You'll be the one out in all weathers, telling the stories behind them and generating the sales.'

She had a point, Fraser had to concede. But the storytelling came naturally to him, as he supposed creating the ghosts did to her. 'Why don't we just agree we're both brilliant and leave it at that?'

She laughed. 'Deal. As for when you can have them, they don't take long to make but the firing and glazing process takes a while. How does four weeks sound for the first batch?'

Fraser puffed out his cheeks. 'It sounds brilliant. Why don't we go with Agnes the sea witch for our first design? I can take this one away with me, get some photos done and start taking pre-orders.'

'Sure,' Maura said, and lowered her voice. 'Don't tell the others I said this, but she's my favourite.'

'Mine too,' Fraser replied. 'Although I'm sure they're all excellent at haunting.'

She smiled. 'I'll wrap Agnes up for you.'

Moving away, she rummaged under the bench to retrieve some old newspaper. Fraser took the opportunity to study the other ghosts, admiring the workmanship. 'How do you get them all the same size? I know you said the York ghosts used some kind of mould but you don't, do you?'

'No,' she said as she wrapped up the sea witch. 'Hand building is often a bit hit and miss, but I'll create a basic template so they're as similar as possible. Then it's just a case of arranging the folds into the right shape.'

Fraser eyed her with some scepticism. 'You make it sound so easy.'

'It is,' she said, shrugging. 'Here, I'll show you.'

She pulled a black polythene bag across the worktop and reached inside to pull out some clay. With brisk, sure movements, she kneaded it into an even shape and placed it onto a board. 'The clay shrinks in the kiln, so it's important not to roll it too thin,' she said, taking a rolling pin and flattening the shape into a wide circle. 'Then you use your template to cut the shape you want.'

Her hands moved quickly, manipulating the clay so that it transformed into a ghost before Fraser's eyes. 'There,' she said, and pulled more clay from the bag to place before him. 'Why don't you have a go?'

He felt his eyebrows shoot up in alarm. 'Oh no. I couldn't.'

'Yes, you could,' Maura encouraged. 'Roll your sleeves up and give it a go.'

Fraser's gaze slid from the well-crafted, sightless ghost she had created in just a few minutes to the glistening grey blob in front of him. 'Erm . . .'

'Here,' Maura said, offering him an apron. 'What's the worst that can happen?'

He blinked. 'You'll see how utterly devoid of artistic talent I am and decide not to work with me?'

'Unlikely,' she replied firmly. 'Roll out the clay. I'll help you with the rest.'

There was, he knew, no way he could refuse. The clay was cold and softer than he'd expected; his fingers sank clumsily into its smoothness as he picked it up. With tentative movements, he ran the rolling pin across the surface, applying what he hoped was an even pressure to flatten the clay to the right thickness. Maura watched, then crossed to another bench to retrieve what looked to Fraser like two long rulers. 'Use these as guides,' she said, placing one on either side of the rolled clay. 'They'll stop you taking it too thin.'

The guides helped; before long, Fraser had a flat expanse of clay. Maura handed him a stubby, angled knife and the bowl she had used as a template. 'Now cut around that and peel the excess away.'

He did as she instructed and gave her an enquiring look.

'That's great. Next, you'll need to make something for the clay to drape around. Roll some of the spare clay into a ball around the size of a large marble.'

The next part was where he felt it all went wrong. The circle of clay stuck together once it was arranged across the top of the ball, creating thick clumps that thrust out in odd directions rather than lying in ethereal folds. 'Ease them apart,' Maura advised. 'Use your fingers to create the shape you want.'

But it was no good. No matter what Fraser tried, the clay stubbornly refused to do his bidding. He fired a pleading glance at Maura. 'Help.'

'Like this,' she said, moving nearer. Her deft fingers teased and tugged at the ghost, smoothing out the damage he'd in-flicted and shaping it into something that resembled the one she had made. 'See?'

'What I see is that I could fiddle with that lump of clay all day and not make it look like yours,' Fraser said. 'I think I'll stick to acting.'

'You're not done yet,' Maura said. 'Your ghost needs eyes or he won't be able to see.'

Fraser sighed. 'I think mine might be blind, actually. Haven't you ever heard of Sightless Sam?'

'Nope.' She created two small ovals in her ghost's face, and then offered Fraser the thin paintbrush handle she'd used. 'Your turn.'

He would have been happier if the eyes had been level but at least they were broadly the same size. Maura didn't comment. Instead, she handed him a sliver of damp sponge. 'Smooth away any bobbles or creases, or they'll turn hard in the kiln and catch on things.' She leaned past him to run the sponge over the clay. 'See?'

Obediently, Fraser bent for a better view, just as Maura turned her face towards him and, for a moment, they were no more than a few centimetres apart. The breath froze in his chest as her gaze met his. Several startled observations collided in his brain at once. The first was how dark her eyes were, framed by thick black lashes that shimmered as he stared at her. The second was the faint dusting of freckles across the bridge of her nose that he had never noticed before. And the third observation was that this was not the first time he had been this close to her. A memory surfaced, of another time and place when she'd been so near, perhaps even closer. Near enough for him to lean in and kiss her. Just as she was now.

Maura cleared her throat and the memory vanished. Blinking, Fraser straightened. 'Sorry,' he croaked, still reeling with the implications of the shocking recollection. 'Yes, I see. You smooth out the rough bits. Got it.'

She had turned her attention back to the ghost and was methodically tidying the edges. 'I'll carve your initials into one of the folds, so we know which one is yours.'

He took several breaths in and out, forcing his bewilderment aside. Maura's voice was utterly matter of fact, perfectly normal. With a bit of luck she hadn't noticed him staring at her like a lovestruck fool. 'Thanks,' he said, swallowing a hot rush of embarrassment. 'Although I think it's pretty clear which is mine.'

Gathering up the tools they had used, she carried them to

the sink. 'You should wash the clay off your hands before you go. It gets everywhere if you don't.'

He untied the apron he wore and laid it on the workbench. 'Occupational hazard, right?'

She smiled. 'You have no idea.'

Taking refuge in the act of washing the dust from his hands, he waited until he was sure he could meet her gaze before he looked up again. 'I'll have my solicitor draw up the paperwork and send it over to you before you start work,' he said. 'Make sure you're happy with the financial details. Obviously, you'll retain the rights over everything you make.'

She pursed her lips. 'I hadn't even thought about that. Thanks.'

Fraser nodded. 'Let me know if you have any questions.'

If Maura thought his suddenly formal tone was strange, she didn't say so. 'I will. And don't forget to take Agnes,' she said, holding out the wrapped ghost. 'I'm looking forward to seeing how she looks in her photos.'

He took the package. 'Great. Well, I'll be in touch over the next few days.'

'Okay,' she said, following him to the door and pulling it open. 'Speak soon.'

Fraser was glad of the cool fresh air as he closed the door behind him and made his way along the cobbled street. His forehead felt feverish, his thoughts hot and jumbled as he made for the bridge, but he knew his discomfort had nothing to do with the temperature inside the studio and everything to do with Maura herself. Now that he was outside, the flash of memory had crystallized into something more tangible, an insistent recollection of pressing his lips to Maura's, of cupping her cheek and sinking his fingers into her hair. It had happened, he was sure of it. The question was when, and why hadn't he remembered it before now? Did Maura remember? Why hadn't she mentioned it? Although she'd probably realised he didn't remember and that was why she'd kept quiet. It wasn't exactly the kind of thing old schoolmates dropped into conversation, after all.

With a heartfelt groan, Fraser let his eyes drift briefly shut. In the space of a few seconds, his life and his new business partnership had both become considerably more complicated. The problem was not the realisation that he had once kissed Maura McKenzie. It was the fact that he very much wanted to do it again.

PART TWO

PROLOGUE

Fraser Bell remembered with absolute clarity the first time he noticed – *really* noticed – Maura McKenzie. School had finished for the day, although parts of the building still hummed with the chatter of students engaged in various after-school clubs, and the chill of autumn hung in the air as Fraser hurried to the drama studio on the far side of the playground. He was late, held up by an uncomfortable conversation with his maths teacher about some uncompleted homework, and his friends had all gone on ahead.

Muttering under his breath, he was intent on reaching the studio; they were supposed to be reading through *Romeo and Juliet* and he knew the juiciest parts would have been given to those who'd arrived on time. But he was a favourite of Miss Laing – with a bit of luck, she'd have kept something for him, despite his being ten minutes late.

His gaze was caught by the glow of the art room windows as he passed, cheerfully yellow against the darkening sky. There were students inside, some seated at tables, others standing at the sinks as they washed brushes or filled water pots. A teacher was talking to a small group, waving at a Van Gogh print on an easel as she spoke.

Fraser slowed, in spite of his lateness. He'd never been able to resist peeking into the windows of houses as he walked along the street, wondering what stories were unfolding within, and the art block was not a part of school he had any reason to enter. Paintings and drawings adorned the walls, a metal sculpture of a horse reared up in one corner. It was like a mini gallery and he was impressed at the talent it showcased.

And then one of the students sitting at a table directly opposite Fraser raised her head to stare out of the window.

He froze, paralysed by the guilt of being caught. But she wasn't looking at him, he realised after a moment of panic, as his thudding heart began to beat more normally. She probably had no idea anyone was even there – the bright lights inside the room would ensure dusk turned into darkness, cloaking him in its shadows.

She was clear enough to him, however; her name was Maura and they were in the same year, although he couldn't remember them ever having spoken. Her face was pale, framed by a riot of dark curls that most girls Fraser knew would have straightened into submission every morning. Their exuberance made him smile a little – she must keep all that hair tied back during the school day; he would definitely have noticed such glorious abundance otherwise.

The expression she wore was far away, as though she saw past her own reflection in the glass. Perhaps she was considering what to draw, although there was no paper in front of her and no pencil in her hand. Instead, Fraser saw a square board with a blob of something grey resting in the centre. Not an artist, he corrected himself with a curious frown. Was it clay? And then the teacher approached, her lips moving in silent enquiry.

The girl's daydream was broken – her eyes came into focus and she half-turned to answer. The teacher paused at her shoulder, spoke again, and this time she smiled. It wasn't the kind of sunny smile that dazzled, Fraser thought, but it transformed her even so. It was moonlight peeping out from behind a midnight cloud, soft and ethereal, slowly gaining in luminosity to bathe the beholder in its gentle glow. He watched as she gathered her hair into a ponytail, snaring it with a band so that its wildness was subdued. With a word to the teacher, she reached for the clay and Fraser found himself fascinated by what she would do with it. But a sudden spatter of rain pulled him out of the classroom, an unwelcome reminder of where he was – or, more importantly, where he was not.

'Crap,' he muttered and ducked his head to hurry for the safety of the drama studio. With a bit of luck he might still be in time for the fight scene.

CHAPTER SEVEN

Twenty-One Years Later

On a clear day, the view across Edinburgh from Calton Hill was unbeatable. Rising steeply at the eastern end of Princes Street, it was not as tall as the neighbouring Arthur's Seat, but it was home to a charming hodge-podge of centuries-old structures.

Maura had fond memories of childhood picnics where she and her sister had chased each other through the Doric columns of the unfinished National Monument, and around the upside-down telescope tower that commemorated Lord Nelson, but her favourite had been the green-domed observatory, which she imagined held all the stars during the day, to be released like twinkling fireflies after dark.

In the distance, the castle crouched on its craggy outcrop, part of a panorama that was especially spectacular around sunset. It was early evening now, and the gentle April sunshine had enticed plenty of people to take in the views.

'I can't believe I've lived in Edinburgh for over a year and never been up here,' Zoe said, slightly out of breath as she gazed around. 'Although that climb nearly finished me off. You'd think my legs would be used to it by now, wouldn't you?'

She meant the city's infamously up and down topography, criss-crossed by countless vertigo-inducing staircases that made navigating the city quicker, if not necessarily easier. Many a tourist could be spotted taking a breather halfway up Granny's Green Steps while attempting a shortcut to the castle from Grassmarket, as the locals trotted by with all the stamina and sure-footedness of mountain goats. 'You should try running up Jacob's Ladder, over by Waverley Station,' Maura said dryly. 'Jamie sometimes does it for training and made me try it once. I thought I was actually going to die.'

Zoe looked faintly horrified. 'You train with the rugby team?'

'Not anymore,' Maura hurriedly assured her. 'This was back in the early days of our relationship. When I was trying to impress him.'

Her friend grimaced. 'I'm not sure I've ever fancied anyone enough for that. But it obviously did the trick with Jamie.'

'I think he mostly felt sorry for me,' Maura admitted, re-calling the consternation in Jamie's eyes as she'd puffed and wheezed. 'We don't exercise together now.'

'Liam's never suggested it,' Zoe said, referring to her own boyfriend, who played at the same rugby club as Jamie. 'He prefers a different type of workout where I'm concerned.'

She raised her eyebrows, leaving Maura in no doubt exactly what kind of exercise she meant. That was something else she and Jamie didn't do as much anymore, although perhaps it was to be expected after five years together. 'Things are going well, then?'

Zoe shrugged as they began to amble along the path that wound around the top of the hill. 'Sure. There are times I wish Liam was a bit less devoted to the club, but I imagine all the other wives and girlfriends feel the same.'

After only a fractional hesitation, Maura nodded. She'd never begrudged Jamie the considerable time he spent training, playing and socialising with his Inverleith Warriors teammates, mostly because it allowed her the freedom to pursue her own interests, which had mostly involved hanging out in her studio, coaxing reluctant clay into something more beautiful. 'It's part of who they are,' she said. 'And there are upsides.'

'Totally,' Zoe responded, her eyes lighting up. 'A ready-made social life, for a start. Very helpful when you've just changed jobs and moved more than halfway across the country.'

That was certainly true. Maura had never felt anything less than welcome at the rugby club, despite preferring to hang out on the fringes of the social scene. It must have been perfect for someone like Zoe, who was bubbly and keen on joining in. 'They're a decent bunch.'

'I know,' Zoe said. 'I fell on my feet when I met Liam. But how about you and Jamie – any chance of a Warriors wedding soon?'

It wasn't the first time Maura had been asked that question – her own family, or at least her sister, Kirsty, had been demanding to know when there might be wedding bells for at least the past two years – but she could honestly say it wasn't something she'd given much thought to. Apart from anything else, getting married was notoriously expensive and there always seemed to be something else to save for. It helped that Jamie had never shown any inclination to propose, in spite of a steady stream of invitations to friends' weddings ... but Maura had no plans to rock the boat.

She shook her head. 'Jamie has his eye on a fancy new apartment,' she said, feeling like a politician dodging an awkward question. 'We went to see a couple at the weekend.'

Zoe could not resist the bait. 'Are you selling your place, then?' she asked, her eyes widening. 'You'll make a fortune if you do, Dean Village is very sought-after.'

She sounded like an estate agent, Maura thought, but it wasn't anything she didn't already know. Jamie had repeatedly tried to draw her attention to Edinburgh's soaring property values but she had so far resisted his encouragement to have the apartment valued, pointing out that half the money would go to Kirsty, since their late aunt had left it to both of them. The subject had caused several heated disagreements in recent weeks.

'We haven't decided yet. It's early days.'

'You could always rent it out,' Zoe suggested as they reached the crest of the hill. 'You'd get good money that way too.'

It wasn't the worst idea, Maura had to admit. The thought of a regular income was appealing; being a ceramic artist was not a career that lent itself to predictable earnings, although her weekly pottery classes helped. But the thought of anyone else living in the flat above her studio made her stomach clench. 'Maybe. Jamie wanted to see what was out there.'

Zoe nodded. 'There are some really nice developments over Leith way. Is that where you looked?'

Maura knew all about the redevelopment of Leith, the port area out towards the eastern side of the city, because her new business partner, Fraser, had told her about it, but she knew

Jamie wanted to stay near the city centre. 'No, in New Town,' she told Zoe. 'Those high-rise developments.'

Just saying the words made her spirits droop. Jamie had wanted to see the penthouse, of course, and Maura would be the first to concede the show flat had been luxurious, with enviable views over Edinburgh. But as the estate agent had waxed lyrical about the virtues of the modern building, she'd allowed her gaze to roam around the fresh white walls and across the sparkling black tiled floor. With the blinds closed, they might have been anywhere, in any city. There was no quirky Edinburgh architecture, no sense of the city's rich history and importance across the centuries. She couldn't help feeling it was all a bit soulless.

'Very nice,' Zoe said, looking impressed. 'Jamie's got great taste.'

Maura dredged up a smile, just as she had when he asked her what she'd thought as they strolled back to the cobbled streets of Dean Village. 'He'd be delighted to hear you say so.'

'Exciting, too,' Zoe said, and sighed. 'I'm a tiny bit jealous.'

If only she knew, Maura thought but didn't say. 'Mmmm.'

But it seemed Zoe picked up on her lack of enthusiasm, because she gave her a sidelong look. 'So what else have you been up to? How's the new business venture going? Enjoying working with Fraser?'

Maura's gaze settled on a small child clambering onto the Portuguese cannon to the left of the path, with the help of her mother. Running into her old schoolmate, Fraser Bell, on New Year's Eve had led to him getting in touch with a business proposition. But after the initial flurry of communication that had surrounded the design of a prototype ceramic ghost to go

with his Dead Famous walking tour, and signing the agreement he'd sent over, she hadn't heard anything from Fraser for
almost four weeks now. It wasn't necessarily a surprise – she'd
told him it would take that long to produce the twenty ghosts
he'd ordered and she assumed he was giving her the space to do
the work – but there was a part of her that expected he might
check in to see how things were going. As the days passed, she
began to worry that his silence meant the pre-orders he had
been so confident about generating had not materialised. The
price he'd set seemed a lot for something so small, even though
she knew exactly how much work had gone into producing
Agnes the Sea Witch. She'd had to give herself more than one
stern talking to as the weeks went by; her job was to make the
ghosts. It was up to Fraser to sell them.

'I've almost finished the batch,' she said cautiously. 'They've
been fun to make.'

'It's such a clever idea,' Zoe enthused. 'I might have to buy
one myself, and try one of his ghost walks around the city. How
was the one you went on – any good?'

'Oh, it was great,' Maura replied warmly, because Fraser's
storytelling had been impressive, skilfully drawing his audience
in with a delicious blend of history and the macabre. 'He was
turning people away.'

'I suppose it helps that he looks like he does,' Zoe observed.
'He could probably sell pebbles to Brighton beach with that
face.'

There was no denying Fraser's good looks; tall, blond-
haired and bearded, he exuded an easy self-confidence that
drew people in. He'd been much the same at school, as Maura
recalled only too well, and it hadn't been much of a surprise

to discover he'd gone on to become an actor. She'd looked up some of his television work and it had been clear the camera loved him. He had something about him – more than great bone structure and a dazzling smile – and Maura could easily imagine that it might contribute to the success of the ghost tours too. She certainly hadn't been immune to that charisma at school, despite the fact that they'd hardly ever spoken. And then there'd been a single chance encounter outside an Edinburgh pub when they'd both been back from university for Christmas, a drunken kiss that Fraser had no idea had even happened. The memory had come flooding back to Maura the moment she'd heard his name and she'd spent no small amount of energy trying to forget it since.

'As long as he sells the ghosts to Edinburgh's tourists first,' she told Zoe dryly.

'It doesn't sound like that's going to be a problem, if he's as good at telling stories as you say,' Zoe said. 'You're a perfect match.'

She meant in business – Maura knew she meant in business – but it didn't stop an uncomfortable surge of warmth from rising in her cheeks. 'We'll see,' she said, a touch more abruptly than she intended, and decided it was time to change the subject. She pointed to the Dugald Stewart monument, a gothic confection of a bandstand framed against the start of a promising sunset. 'That's the shot you want for Instagram. Let's grab it now before the influencers notice.'

Jamie hadn't returned from training by the time Maura got home, just before ten o'clock. She'd introduced Zoe to Café St Honoré, her favourite French bistro tucked away on Thistle

Street, and they'd stayed later than she'd expected, due in no small part to the irresistible dessert menu. Afterwards, she'd caught the bus back to Dean Village, too full of excellent food and a decent bottle of red to feel like walking, and had stood for a moment in the silent apartment, before retracing her steps down the stairs and letting herself into her studio.

The kiln had been cooling for more than twenty-four hours. The items within would be ready to remove but Maura had no intention of emptying it after a glass or two of wine – that kind of recklessness could easily lead to disaster. But she couldn't resist lifting the lid to check on the final cluster of glazed ghosts. They were mixed in with pieces made by her students, dotted among the mugs, jugs, and tealight holders.

She'd used a template to make them the same size but each one was subtly different; some had floatier folds, others had barnacles between the painted fronds of seaweed decoration. One or two had mournful green eyes. All were marked with her initials.

She surveyed them for a moment, her fingers itching to lift them out for a proper look, but she resisted the urge. If she dropped one, she wouldn't have enough to deliver to Fraser, and she was conscious she had kept him waiting already. Worse still, she might drop something made by one of her students and would have to endure their disappointment when she explained what had happened. For now, it was enough to look upon the treasures inside the kiln and know that she could examine each one in detail the following morning with sober hands.

Once she was sure these last ghosts hadn't cracked or failed in the firing, she could message Fraser and let him know his order was complete and ready for collection. The thought made her nerves thrum with excitement and trepidation at the same time, but she felt that way whenever she delivered commissioned work to a client – there was always a chance it wasn't quite what they'd had in mind. But she doubted that would be the case with Fraser. The ghosts were different in subtle ways, with an individuality that only came from being handmade, but they were all recognisably Agnes the Sea Witch and, despite her misgivings, Maura found she was very much looking forward to seeing Fraser's reaction to the finished pieces. She could only hope he'd managed to sell some.

CHAPTER EIGHT

It wasn't unusual for Fraser to receive an email from his agent, although they were significantly less frequent than when he'd lived in London, searching for the role that would make his career. Recent communications tended to relate to royalty payments due for past roles, so he wasn't surprised to see Sam's name in his inbox. But the subject line was unexpected: MAJOR AUDITION.

Fraser sat back on the sofa, staring at the screen. In his younger days, he wouldn't have been able to open the message fast enough, eagerly scanning the contents and prepared to drop everything to attend, regardless of whether he had any chance of landing the role. Over time, he'd learned to be more discerning, although he'd never quite managed to escape the nagging fear that one of those unsuitable jobs might have led to his big break. And as his acting resumé had grown, his agent had sent better roles, some of which led to opportunities and friendships Fraser might not have had otherwise.

But he'd been clear when he'd told Sam he was taking an extended break – unless Spielberg came calling, he wasn't taking any new roles. And since there was zero chance of that happening, Fraser felt confident in assuming Sam had forgotten he was out of the game.

Even so, Fraser was almost tempted to open the email, but the urge was only fleeting. Attending an audition now would be difficult; it would involve travel, quite probably an overnight stay, and that was before he factored in any preparation. He had sold-out ghost walks most evenings over the coming weeks, with a small number of allowances for walk-ups on the night which would put the tour at capacity – he couldn't just disappear to London, or wherever the audition was being held. But over and above any practical obstacles, Fraser found himself baulking at the prospect of putting himself through the stress of auditioning, of waiting anxiously for news and the all too frequent swoop of disappointment when he discovered the role had gone to someone else. That part of his life was over and he didn't miss it in the slightest. With a decisive stab of his finger, he relegated Sam's email to the trash folder and put his phone on the coffee table.

The door to the hallway opened and Naomi came into the room. She detoured to the fridge, collecting a wheatgrass shot before turning back to survey Fraser. 'I thought you might like to take me out for lunch today.'

Fraser hid a smile. It was typical of Naomi to assume he had no plans of his own. 'I can't. I'm collecting the ghosts from Maura at one o'clock.'

Naomi shrugged. 'That won't take long, will it? We can meet afterwards.'

In theory, she was right – he could be in and out of Maura's studio within minutes if needed. But he had no intention of being so disrespectful. The time had been arranged around

Maura's teaching commitments, to give him the opportunity to check how the process of making them had been for her, and reveal how the ghosts had been received. He wanted to make sure she knew how much he appreciated the work she had put in, to bask in the shy smile he knew the words would elicit, and sound her out about producing a second batch. It was not a question he planned to hurl over one shoulder as he raced out of the door. 'I'm not picking up a curry, Naomi,' he said. 'This is a business meeting – we have things to discuss.'

Her eyes narrowed slightly. 'Surely you don't have that much to talk about. In case you've forgotten, I'm leaving for London tomorrow and it would be nice to spend some time together before I go. It's not as though we can make dinner plans, is it?'

The fact that he worked most evenings was a source of increasing friction between them. When they had first moved to Edinburgh, she had been understanding of the need to build the ghost walk business and establish his brand of storytelling, but her patience had worn thin over the following eight months. He didn't work every night – Mondays and Tuesdays were covered by a freelance tour guide – but Naomi had grown tired of trying to manage their social life around so short a window and Fraser supposed he could understand her frustration.

'Of course I haven't forgotten,' he said. 'I'll be finished by nine o'clock tonight. Why don't we grab a late dinner?'

'Because I've got an early flight in the morning,' Naomi objected. 'Can't you move your meeting? Maura works from home, doesn't she? I'm sure she won't mind if you pop round later in the day.'

Again, he marvelled at her apparent incomprehension that other people might have things to do. 'I mind,' he said. 'Apart from anything else, it's unprofessional.' He took a breath and checked the time. It was almost ten o'clock. 'How about brunch instead? We could go to that new place overlooking the docks.'

She sighed. 'I'm not hungry now.'

'A late lunch, then. Two-thirty in New Town. You can choose the restaurant.'

Her eyes flashed. 'That's too late.'

Fraser felt his temper start to slip. 'So basically what you're saying is, we do it your way or not at all.'

Naomi folded her arms. 'I don't think I'm being unreasonable.'

And that was part of the problem, Fraser thought. But he didn't want another argument — there had been too many of those lately and a disagreement now was likely to fester while she was away. He rubbed his brow. 'Okay,' he said, in what he hoped was a conciliatory tone. 'Let me see what I can do.'

'Great,' Naomi said, and beamed at him. 'I thought Henderson's at twelve-thirty. Will you book?'

He gritted his teeth slightly. 'I don't know if Maura will agree to move the meeting yet.'

Naomi shrugged and tossed back the wheatgrass shot. 'I'm sure she will. Mention my name when you ring the restaurant. The owner is a friend — he'll give us a nicer table.'

She was moving before Fraser could frame a reply, disappearing back through the door to the hallway, and he decided in the silence that followed that it was probably for the best. Just as it wasn't such a bad thing that she was going to London in the morning. A break might be just what they needed to reignite their spark.

*

It was just before three o'clock when Fraser parked outside Maura's studio on Thistledown Lane.

Lunch with Naomi had been pleasant, although he sensed they'd both been taking care to avoid anything that might trigger a disagreement. They'd been given a prominent table in the window and the restaurant owner came out to greet them personally. The food had been faultless. It would have been perfectly enjoyable had it not been for Naomi's insistence on having her own way. Fraser had tried to let that go, especially since Maura had reassured him it was no problem and suggested a time later in the afternoon, just as Naomi had predicted she would, but there was a stubborn kernel of irritation that no amount of conversation and good food could remove. He couldn't shake the feeling that they had both been playing a role.

His irritation melted away when Maura presented him with the ghosts, however. They sat in solemn rows on the workbench, their empty eye sockets wide and somehow soulful. All were the same shape and size but no two were identical – delicate green strands swirled over the smooth white clay of each in ever-changing patterns, as though abandoned by the ebbing tide. Some were encrusted with barnacles. One gave the definite impression it was winking at Fraser. And yet they were clearly, recognisably, by the same potter. He was no expert but he would have known who made them even without checking for the MM mark Maura had inscribed on the back of each ghost.

'They're amazing,' he said, after staring at them for several long seconds. 'What's the collective noun for a group of ghosts?'

Maura's lips quirked in amusement. 'I have no idea. A spookiness? No, wait, that's too cute. How about a haunt?'

'Sounds good to me,' Fraser said, nodding. 'I might even use it on the tour.'

'If it helps to sell them, I'm all for it,' Maura replied.

He glanced at her in surprise. 'They don't need any help. This batch sold out in a few days.'

'Oh!' Her eyes widened in what appeared to be genuine surprise. 'But I thought . . . Why didn't you tell me?'

Fraser tipped his head. 'You said you needed four weeks. I didn't want to put any pressure on you so I thought I'd talk to you when the ghosts were ready.' He regarded her steadily. 'Did you think I hadn't been able to sell any?'

Maura's cheeks turned pink. 'Well . . . yes. I've been to plenty of pottery shows where people have walked past my stand all day without buying anything. It can be hard to know what will sell.'

Fraser found that hard to believe. Maura was so talented – surely there was a queue of people waiting to snap up her work. 'I have a captive audience, don't forget. Most of the people who come on the tours jump at the chance to own their very own Edinburgh ghost.' He paused, wondering whether to reveal just how many people had wanted to buy the Sea Witch. 'In fact, there's a bit of a waiting list. I'd like you to make some more, if you can fit them in.'

'Oh,' she said again, as her gaze dropped to the ghosts. 'More of this design?'

He nodded. 'Agnes is popular so it makes sense to stick with her for now. How long would it take you to make another forty?'

Blinking, she puffed out her cheeks. 'Around six weeks, I think. But I could deliver the order in two batches, if you have people waiting. So the first twenty or so in three weeks, and then the rest by six weeks.'

Fraser did some rapid calculations. 'That could work,' he agreed. 'And in the meantime, I'll get these ones packaged up and sent off to their new owners.' He picked up the nearest ghost and examined it, delighted all over again by its mournful brilliance. 'You're about to make a lot of people very happy.'

'I hope so,' Maura said, and he thought the praise pleased her. 'I must admit, I have a soft spot for them myself.'

'Me too.' Fraser's gaze travelled around the studio, taking in the full shelves. 'Those are new, aren't they?' He indicated a pair of round plant pots embossed with a delicate leaf design.

'They're an experiment,' she explained. 'I'm exhibiting at ScotPot at the start of June and the theme is "season's greetings", which is supposed to be a celebration of nature throughout the year. So I thought I'd make four plant pots – one for each season. That one is spring.'

He could see the appeal immediately. Who wouldn't want the whole set? 'ScotPot,' he repeated. 'Is that in Edinburgh?'

She nodded. 'It's been held in the grounds of Craigmillar Castle for as long as I can remember. Quite a lot of people go along.'

Fraser pictured the dramatic ruins to the south-east of the city, the roofless medieval tower and crumbling walls standing tall amid lush parkland and ancient woods. It had been used as a location for the TV series *Outlander*, which had only added to its appeal. 'Great venue,' he observed as he studied the plant pot, admiring the perfect shape and intricate decoration. 'What else will you take?'

'Mugs, mostly.' Maura reached to the back of the uppermost

shelf and withdrew an exquisitely rounded cup that Fraser felt was far too elegant to be referred to as a mug. It was made of a darker clay than the ghosts and was glazed a deep shimmering blue. 'I'll make some plates to go with them. People seem to like matching sets.'

Fraser took the mug, turning it over in his fingers. 'I bet they do. Can I buy this one? It's perfect for my morning coffee.'

'Of course,' Maura said, sounding both surprised and pleased. 'But you don't have to buy it – take it as a gift from me.'

'Absolutely not,' Fraser replied firmly. 'It's a beautiful cup and worth paying for.'

'But—'

He held up a hand. 'I'm afraid I have to insist, Maura. It's very kind of you but I won't get the same enjoyment if I'm reminded I manoeuvred you into a freebie every time I use it. How much would it be if I bought it at a show?'

Her expression remained reluctant and he suspected she wanted to argue. But he'd played his trump card by explaining it would diminish his enjoyment if he didn't pay and, after a moment, she nodded. 'The mugs are twenty pounds. Thank you. I'll wrap it up with the ghosts.'

'I don't know how you find time to make such lovely things, the ghosts, and still manage to teach,' Fraser observed as she pulled out a sheaf of old newspaper and began to package everything. 'When do you sleep?'

'It's mostly about juggling,' she replied, flashing him a rueful smile. 'Making sure the kiln is fully loaded before it runs, so that things get fired in a timely way. My regular students have all been coming for a while, so they don't need to be taught that much but they do make a lot of pieces that I fire on their behalf. It can be a bit of a balancing act to make sure their work doesn't get pushed out by my own.'

Fraser felt himself frowning. 'I don't suppose the ghosts help with that. Are you sure I'm not asking too much of you?'

'No, it's fine. I'm glad people like them.' She tipped her head and offered a wry smile. 'It makes a change from mugs.'

Fraser's gaze travelled to the shelves where Maura's other pieces nestled together. Now that he understood how long the process of ceramics took, he appreciated Maura's skill and dedication even more. How many people truly understood the hard work and time that went into her work? But perhaps that wasn't the re-action she was striving for; in the performing arts, the goal was to transport the audience and make them forget they were watching a performance at all. The visual arts were all about emotional connection too – the almost instant, unconscious response that led to someone deciding whether they liked, or didn't like, what they saw. In Fraser's case, every piece on Maura's shelves made him want to smile. But if he was honest, Maura made him smile more. It was a realisation that had troubled him the last time he'd seen her, when the long-forgotten memory of a school-days kiss had surfaced, stirring up some confusing feelings. He'd been glad then that the ghosts would take several weeks to make – it had given him time to put things into perspective.

Bumping into old school friends famously made people nostalgic, maybe even led them to rue missed chances, but in Fraser's case, those feelings had passed and he'd been able to see Maura as a business partner once more. The fact that he found he liked and admired her just as much as her work was neither here nor there.

'Okay,' he said, forcing his thoughts back to the task at hand.

'I'll send payment for this batch. Will you let me know when the next twenty are ready?'

Picking up a small box, Maura began placing the wrapped ghosts inside. 'Of course. I'll get started on them as soon as I can.'

He reached into his pocket and pulled out his wallet. 'And here's the money for the mug,' he said, laying a twenty pound note on the workbench. 'Although I have a feeling you've un-dercharged me.'

Her impish smile told him he'd guessed right. 'Mates' rates,' she said. 'And don't even think about asking the non-mates' rate.'

With a shake of his head, Fraser accepted the compromise. 'I wouldn't dream of it.'

Naomi's lips thinned when she came back to the apartment around five o'clock and found the living room was strewn with flat-packed cardboard boxes. 'What's this?'

'Boxes,' Fraser said, frowning as he concentrated on slotting a sturdy flap into place without acquiring yet another paper cut. 'For the ghosts.'

She glanced at the cream carpet, which was dotted with a number of small rectangular boxes embossed with the words *The Edinburgh Ghost Company*. The sofa was covered with sheets of artistically aged tissue paper, a bag of shredded paper was overflowing across one arm and the coffee table was strewn with the larger boxes Fraser was intent on putting together before he left for his evening tour. With luck, he'd get the pre-ordered ghosts packaged up and in the post the following day, once he'd taken Naomi to the airport.

'I can see they're boxes,' she said pointedly. 'What are they doing all over our living room?'

He looked at her in mild surprise. 'I'd have thought it was obvious. I'm putting the orders together ready for posting. To do that, I need to wrap the ghosts in tissue paper and pop them in here.' He held up one of the small rectangular boxes. 'And then put that box into this larger box, with a packing note and some shredded paper to protect everything.'

Her nose wrinkled. 'I see. Is this going to happen every time you get a delivery from Laura?'

'Maura,' he corrected, then nodded. 'Possibly. But I'll make sure I get them out of the way as soon as I can.'

Naomi did not appear to be reassured. 'I don't want to live in a sorting office, Fraser.'

He opened his mouth to object but then glanced around and saw that the room was rather more untidy than he'd realised. Every surface was covered and the armchair beside the sofa was taken up by the box containing the ghosts. It would all be gone by midday tomorrow but Naomi wouldn't be around to see that. He checked the time. 'Let me just finish folding these and I'll move everything to the bedroom.'

She looked even less impressed. 'I don't want to sleep in a sorting office, either. Can't you find somewhere else to do all this?'

Perhaps he could, Fraser thought, if demand for the ghosts grew. But he absolutely could not find an alternative space that evening. 'I'll put them in the hall cupboard,' he said. 'There'll be room in there once you take your suitcase out.'

It was clear from the frosty silence that this solution was not acceptable either.

Fraser sighed. 'It's just for tonight, Naomi. By the time you get back from London, they'll all be delivered and I'll look for a lock up or a garage nearby to store things in the future. Happy?'

She looked, he thought, a long way from happy but she did at least manage a short nod. 'I don't have a lot of choice.'

With hindsight, he should have known she would react like this. Naomi was a neat freak who liked clear, clutter-free surfaces. She did not cope well with chaos, no matter how short-lived he promised it would be. 'Sorry,' he said. 'I'll put everything out of sight until tomorrow. What time do you need to be at the airport?'

'By six-thirty,' she said coolly. 'But don't worry about giving me a lift. I've booked a cab to pick me up.'

Fraser had to admit he was a little relieved. He was not a morning person and hadn't been looking forward to getting up before dawn. 'Oh. Okay. Will you be awake when I get home later?'

'At eleven o'clock? I doubt it.'

He got to his feet and crossed the room to pull her into a hug. 'I'll try not to wake you when I come in, then. Have a good trip.'

For a moment, he thought she would remain stiff and un-yielding in his arms, but then she softened. 'I will.'

He breathed in her perfume, a sharp lemony scent he'd never really warmed to. 'I know it's a work trip but I think the change of scene will do you good.'

'Me too,' she said, and disentangled herself to head for the door to the hall. 'Enjoy playing postman.'

True to his word, Fraser transported the ghosts and their packaging to the hall cupboard before he left to meet that evening's audience beside the Mercat Cross on the Royal Mile. When he returned home, a little after ten-thirty, he found a note from Naomi next to the kettle.

I've checked into the Hilton so I don't wake you in the morning. Speak soon, N x

He stared at it for a few seconds, then reached out to flick the kettle on.

It wasn't the first time she'd stayed at the hotel beside the airport before an early flight, but it was the first time she'd done so without telling him in advance and he couldn't help feeling the business with the boxes had driven her to go tonight. Perhaps he had been unfair in expecting her to put up with the mess, he thought, as he dropped a herbal teabag into a mug. And she'd had a point about the likelihood of the situation happening again – in three weeks, he would have another batch of ghosts from Maura and there was a strong probability of another disagreement.

Fraser lifted the kettle and poured the boiling water over the teabag.

The sooner he found somewhere else to process the orders, the better.

CHAPTER NINE

The rugby club bar was full, the crowd spilling outside onto the paved area that overlooked the pitch. A DJ was diligently working his way through the standard list of classic hits, guaranteed to appeal to most of the guests at a fortieth birthday party; Maura suspected 'Sweet Caroline' and 'Come On Eileen' were in her imminent future. But it wasn't even nine o'clock yet – a little early for the dance floor to be filling up. It was currently occupied by various clusters of cavorting children, some of whom were starting to flag, if Maura was any judge. She watched them for a few seconds, smiling at their antics, and then turned back to Polly, who was seated next to her. 'So how is Matt coping with the big four-O?' she asked. 'Jamie says he's been in denial about it for the past year.'

The other woman rolled her eyes. 'Don't. You'd think he's turning seventy, to hear him go on about it.'

Maura grimaced in sympathy. 'It doesn't really mean anything, though. It's just a number.'

'You know that and I know that,' Polly said dryly. 'But Matt doesn't agree. I caught him googling convertibles the other day – can you imagine? He says he doesn't want to wake up one morning and find he's turned into his dad.'

Maura couldn't help glancing at Jamie, who was roaring with laughter on the other side of the bar. He was still three years away from his fortieth birthday but had started to make noises about trading in their perfectly blameless Volvo for something faster, despite the fact it could comfortably accommodate all Maura's pots and accessories when she went to pottery shows. When viewed alongside his newfound interest in penthouse apartments, Maura wondered whether Jamie was contemplating the approach of middle age with every bit as much trepidation as Matt. 'He still wanted a party, though,' she observed to Polly, who snorted.

'Of course he did. He's been planning this since his last birthday. Any excuse for a session, right?'

But her tone was indulgent, if a little resigned, and Maura understood where she was coming from. Inverleith Warriors had three squads, all of which played hard and partied equally fiercely. Anyone who fell in love with one of their players quickly learned not to get in the way of that. 'You're only forty once,' she said. 'Even if Matt would rather stick with thirty-nine.'

'He'll get over it,' Polly said, with the easy dismissiveness of someone who was still five or so years away from that particular milestone birthday. 'Like you say, it's just a number.'

Time seemed to speed up after the buffet had been consumed and cleared away. The number of children dropped, as parents took their sleepy-eyed little ones home. The dancefloor filled up as the DJ moved seamlessly into higher tempo crowd pleasers.

Maura found herself in among the dancers more often than usual, pulled into the throng first by Zoe and later by Jamie, who was clearly the worse for wear but on good form.

As the bar staff served the final drinks and the DJ finished his set with The Killers, a bright-eyed but slightly unsteady Zoe appeared before Maura. 'Some of us are going into town. Say you'll come!'

She'd barely finished the last sentence before Maura was shaking her head. 'Absolutely not,' she said. 'Apart from anything else, my feet are killing me. They're not used to all this dancing.'

Zoe pouted, as though 'no' was a word she didn't hear often. 'Oh, go on. It'll be fun. Jamie wants you to.'

Maura glanced across at her boyfriend, who was lustily singing a famously unsuitable rugby song with his teammates. 'Jamie knows very well how boring I am,' she replied. 'But thank you for asking. Tell him I'll see him when he gets home.'

It wasn't unusual for Maura to wake up and find Jamie's side of the bed empty after a night out. Occasionally, she'd discovered him asleep on the sofa or, once or twice, on the floor beside the sofa.

The morning after Matt's party, however, he was not snoring in the living room. He was not at home at all. Instead, he materialised at one-thirty that afternoon, rumpled and bleary-eyed and smelling like an explosion in a tequila distillery.

'There you are,' Maura exclaimed, caught between relief that he was okay and exasperation that he hadn't bothered to respond to her text messages. 'Where have you been?'

He ran a hand over his chin. 'At Liam's. It got a bit messy once we hit the town.'

'So I see,' Maura said, unsure whether to laugh or feel aggrieved. 'Is his shower broken?'

'Someone threw up in it,' Jamie admitted, and paused. 'I think it might have been me.'

'Lovely,' Maura said faintly, when it became clear he wasn't making a joke. Liam was in his twenties – she expected such things from the younger members of the rugby club. But surely Jamie should know better. Perhaps she should have gone along, if only to curb the worst of his excesses. 'And how do you feel now?'

'Tired,' he said. 'Hungover. And not in the mood for one of your lectures.'

That stung, because she had no intention of lecturing him. Apart from anything else, it looked as though he was suffering enough. 'I was worried. You could have let me know where you were.'

Jamie's expression darkened. 'Like I said, it got messy. Bloody hell, Maura, lighten up a bit.'

She stared at him. 'Lighten up? I don't think it's unreasonable of me to expect a message when you haven't come home after a night out.'

He scowled. 'Of course you don't think you're being unreasonable. You're Saint Maura, after all.'

The words hung between them for a moment, as brittle as shattered glass. She cleared her throat. 'I assume you've forgotten we're due at my parents' house for lunch in thirty minutes. I'll make your excuses, shall I?'

It was clear from the startled look on his face that he had indeed forgotten. 'Shit.'

For some reason, that was the thing that annoyed her the most. 'If you're planning on going to bed, can I suggest you take a shower first?' she said, reaching for her bag. 'Try not to be sick in this one.'

*

It was Kirsty who met Maura at the door of their parents' house. 'You're late,' she grumbled, as she stood back to let her sister into the hallway.

'I know,' Maura said with a sigh. The journey to the village on the north side of the Firth of Forth should have taken forty minutes. 'There was an accident just after the bridge. Nobody moved for an hour.'

Kirsty peered over her shoulder. 'No Jamie?'

Maura fought to keep her tone light. 'Nope. He's sleeping off a heavy night.'

'Ah,' Kirsty said, and adopted an innocent expression. 'Another one?'

Maura's first instinct was to spring to Jamie's defence and gloss over the fact that he hadn't managed to make it home. But Kirsty had a point – last night was the latest in a long line of heavy nights and Maura was beginning to feel weary of making excuses. Even so, she wasn't sure she was ready to share all the details of Jamie's behaviour with her sister. 'I'll tell you later,' she said. 'Let me go and say hello to Mum and Dad first.'

If her parents were surprised at Jamie's absence, they didn't show it, and Maura was glad of their unquestioning acceptance. Lunch around the crowded kitchen table was the usual comforting mix of good food, laughter and mild chaos. Kirsty's husband, Dougal, was on cheerful form and their two children, Ciara and Teddy, endeavoured to outdo each other in their efforts to impress their grandparents and Aunt Maura. Conversation ranged from the up and down fortunes of the local football club to an intricate but mysterious collection of knitted decorations that had sprung up around the village.

'No one knows who made them,' Maura's mum Judith

said, her expression intrigued. 'The one on top of the postbox appeared in the dead of night last Tuesday and there's knitted bunting wrapped around the doorposts of the pub too. They left a woollen poppy wreath at the war memorial, even though it's only April.'

'Maybe there's a secret society of yarn bombers in the village, communicating through the medium of knitting,' Kirsty suggested. 'You should investigate.'

Dougal sat forward, his eyes twinkling. 'This has all the makings of a smash hit Netflix series. I'd watch it.'

'Maybe Fraser could star in it,' Kirsty said, turning to Maura. 'I know you said he's taking a break from acting but I bet he'd come back for something like this.'

'Fraser?' Maura's mum repeated. 'Who's he?'

Maura opened her mouth to answer but Kirsty beat her to it. 'Maura's new friend.'

'My new business partner,' Maura corrected. 'I told you about this ages ago, Mum. We were in the same year at St Ignatius. I've been making a few ceramics for him.'

'You didn't tell me he was an actor,' Judith grumbled. 'Is he one of those pretty types or does he do characters?'

'His name is Fraser Bell,' Kirsty supplied, once again before Maura could speak. 'And he's definitely pretty.'

Dougal threw her a mildly affronted look. 'Oh, aye? You kept that quiet when you came home after the ghost tour.'

Maura's father, Grant, who had been following the conversation like a tennis match, looked confused. 'I thought you said he's an actor. Was he dressed up as a ghost?'

'Woooooo!' Ciara intoned around a mouthful of roast potato, wiggling her fingers to emphasise her spookiness. Teddy joined in, several decibels louder, sending a spoonful of carrot flying through the air.

'No, he runs the tour,' Maura said over the din, wishing Kirsty hadn't mentioned Fraser at all. 'He's a really gifted storyteller. The business is doing well.'

'I'm not surprised, if he's good looking,' Judith said. 'How exciting. I'll have to look him up – find out if he's been in anything I've seen.'

Maura didn't mention *Death in Dorset*, or any of the other roles she'd discovered Fraser had played. With a bit of luck, her mother would have forgotten his name by the end of the meal. 'It's no big deal. Like I said, he's taking a break from acting.'

Kirsty gave her a mischievous grin as she got up to retrieve the airborne carrot. 'I'll send you a link, Mum.'

After lunch, they took a stroll around the village, ostensibly to allow Ciara and Teddy to get some fresh air but Maura and Kirsty privately agreed that it was really an excuse for their mother to check whether any more yarn bombing had been perpetrated.

'So what's the story with Jamie?' Kirsty asked as they ambled along behind their parents and Dougal with Teddy in the buggy.

Maura glanced down at four-year-old Ciara, who was clinging onto her hand with a limpet-like grip and humming to herself. 'Oh, you know. The usual.'

Her sister nodded.

'What time did he get home?'

Maura sighed. 'About half past one.'

'In the morning?' Her sister glanced at her. 'That's not so bad.'

'In the afternoon.'

'Ouch.' Kirsty winced. 'No wonder he needed to sleep it off. Did he tell you where he'd been?'

'He crashed on someone's sofa,' Maura said, deciding to keep the shower fiasco to herself.

Kirsty shook her head. 'Which is fine when you're in your twenties, but less so in your mid-thirties. Was he embarrassed?'

She thought back to Jamie's churlishness when she'd confronted him. Part of it was probably due to shame at the state he was in but he hadn't done much to defuse the situation. 'Hard to say. He didn't seem to think he should have let me know where he was.'

Her sister stared. 'He went radio silent?'

'Yeah,' Maura said. 'I'm not sure he did it on purpose but that's not really the point. I was still starting to worry.'

'I bet.' Kirsty puffed out her cheeks. 'I'd kill Dougal if he tried that.'

Maura scuffed at a pebble on the path. No sheepish messages from Jamie had popped up on her phone; just like the night before, there had been no communication at all. 'I'll see what he has to say when I get home.'

'He needs to be waiting on the doorstep with chocolates and flowers,' Kirsty said. 'It's a bit lacking in imagination but at least it would be a good start.'

'I'd settle for an apology,' Maura replied, not at all certain she would get one.

But Jamie surprised her. He wasn't waiting at the door but he was at the top of the stairs when she came home just after eight o'clock. 'I'm sorry,' he said, before she was even halfway up. 'I'm a total idiot. Can you forgive me?'

Maura swallowed a sigh, because although it was an apology, she couldn't help feeling it was one designed to manoeuvre her into making him feel better about his behaviour. She continued to trudge upwards until she reached the top and met his gaze with frank honesty. 'I suppose it all depends on what you're sorry for.'

'All of it,' Jamie said, eyes wide and beseeching like a naughty schoolchild. 'I shouldn't have drunk as much as I did and I should have messaged you to let you know what was going on.'

There wasn't much Maura could say – he was right on both counts. But she was tired of arguing, weary of the sullen anger and resentment that had burned all afternoon. Her beloved and much-missed aunt had often advised her never to let the sun set on a disagreement and it was advice Maura had always tried to follow. 'Don't ever do it again. I mean it, Jamie.'

He shook his head. 'Believe me, I won't. I'm not sure I ever want to drink again.'

The pained fervour in his voice elicited a smile from her, even though it was a sentiment she'd heard before. 'I'm sure that will pass.'

'Possibly,' Jamie conceded. 'But all I care about now is making up for my stupidity.' He took her hand and drew her gently nearer. 'So what do you think? Can you forgive me?'

She glanced past him then to the living room, where a bouquet of red roses and something that looked like a large box of expensive chocolates lay upon the coffee table. The sight was so close to Kirsty's prediction that Maura half-wondered whether her sister had messaged Jamie to tell him what he needed to do. She would doubtless advise Maura to make him sweat but she'd never been interested in playing relationship games and wasn't about to start now. She didn't resist when Jamie wrapped his arms around her, although she did not hug him back. 'Why didn't you message me – let me know where you were?'

He sighed and buried his face in her hair. 'My phone battery died. By the time I realised and found a charger, I knew it was going to take more than a text message to clear things up. So I came home to face the music.'

And promptly accused her of being unreasonable, Maura recalled. 'Didn't it occur to you that I'd be worried?'

'Not until I turned my phone on and saw all the missed calls,' he said. 'That's when I knew I was in trouble.'

'In trouble?' she echoed and drew back to stare at him. 'Was that really your first thought?'

A faint pink flush appeared on his cheeks. 'No,' he said, and ran a hand through his hair. 'I meant that I knew I'd messed up and you were upset.' He planted a kiss on the top of her head. 'I'm sorry, Maura. I don't know what else to say.'

She stood rigid for a moment, wondering if she was imagining the veiled implication that she was somehow being unreasonable again. But she'd told Kirsty that she would settle for an apology and Jamie had offered that. Was there really anything to be gained by holding onto her anger and disappointment? With an inward sigh, she shook the negative emotions away. 'Okay.'

'That's my girl,' Jamie said. He ushered her towards the sofa. 'Now, why don't you make a start on those chocolates and I'll bring you a cup of tea?'

'More ghosts?' Effie peered over Maura's shoulder at the pale cluster on the workbench in front of her. 'Your friend must have liked what he saw if he's put in another order.'

It was a week after Fraser had collected the first batch of

ghosts and Maura had wasted no time in getting to work on the next order. Fifteen had been dried and fired, with another five cooling in the kiln as they spoke. She nodded at Effie. 'He wants forty more.'

Cordelia paused in the act of removing her coat. 'Forty?' she repeated, eyebrows raised. 'That makes sixty in total. Is he sure he can shift that many?'

'He certainly thinks so,' Maura said, picking up the under-glaze she used to add the seaweed effect to Agnes. 'In fact, he says there's a waiting list for more, which is why I've had to rush to make these.'

'If there's one thing I've learned about pottery, it's that it is never a good idea to rush it,' Cordelia said with a sniff. She eyed the ghosts suspiciously, as though she expected them to show signs of their hurried creation. 'But I suppose you know what you're doing.'

Behind Cordelia's back, Effie pulled a face and Maura had to fight a sudden desire to giggle. 'You're right, of course,' she said. 'But making the ghosts is the simple bit. It's the decoration that takes the time.'

'Hmmm,' Cordelia said. She crossed to the shelves to peer at the assembled pieces. 'Do I have a mug ready to be glazed? I made it last week.'

Maura frowned in thought. 'I think it's in the kiln now. It won't be cool enough to glaze today, sorry.'

Effie looked up. 'Is my plate in there too? I can't see it on the shelf.'

'I'm afraid so,' Maura said apologetically. 'Between the ghosts and the pieces I need for ScotPot, there hasn't been much space in the kiln. They'll be ready next week.'

'Okay,' Effie said cheerfully, and pulled open the bag of clay. 'In that case, I'm going to get started on a jug. That should keep me busy for a few hours.'

Cordelia arched an eyebrow. 'Didn't the last one take you four weeks?'

Effie gave her a grave look. 'If there's one thing I've learned about pottery, it's that it is never a good idea to rush it.' She reached for the cutting wire. 'That's my excuse, anyway.'

Maura allowed their chatter to wash over her as she turned her attention to her own work. The ghosts needed to be painted with underglaze and then coated with a clear glaze before being fired again. Even allowing time for the current kiln load to cool before she could open it up and add the ghosts, she thought the first batch she had promised Fraser would be ready in two weeks rather than three. Should she message him and suggest he collect them early? Or was that setting up a dangerous expectation that she might be able to deliver the rest of the order more quickly too? She didn't want her students' work to take a backseat because she had to prioritise the ghosts but, at the same time, she wanted to do what she could to help the joint venture succeed. And, if she was honest, she enjoyed seeing Fraser's pleasure when she showed him her work. His praise made her feel as though she was doing something right, even if other parts of her life were a little bumpy.

'Maura.' Sharon had been quietly working away at the furthest end of the studio but was now gazing plaintively across the room, a lopsided vase on the workbench in front of her. 'I think I need some help to rescue this. It's on the wonk.'

Setting down the paintbrush she'd been about to dip into

the dark green underglaze, Maura made her way towards her. 'It's not too bad,' she said after a quick assessment. 'All you need to do is take a bit off the top and then smooth the sides. Here, I'll show you.'

CHAPTER TEN

On Saturdays, there was a market at Dock Place and the square was filled with cheerful yellow and white canopies as the stall-holders tried to tempt the locals to part with their hard-earned cash. It was mostly food, as far as Fraser could tell – fresh bread, seafood, cheese and meat seemed to do especially well, but he saw the occasional craft stall selling handmade cards and other arty goods. It drew a good crowd, even on the days when the weather did not cooperate. Fraser liked to wander through in the morning, when Naomi was still asleep, and pick up something tempting for breakfast. But since she was still in London, he had no one to please but himself and bought a sweet and buttery crepe to eat as he browsed, and a smoky fish pie for lunch. He passed a pottery stall and lingered to study the pieces offered for sale. There was nothing wrong with them – the mugs looked perfectly serviceable and the tealight holders were cute – but Fraser couldn't help comparing them to Maura's work and finding them wanting. He moved on without buying anything, then guiltily remembered Maura's description of watching people pass her own stand without buying. He doubled back then and bought a small wax melt burner that he thought his mum would like.

He spent the afternoon on paperwork, catching up on some admin that was long overdue and drafting the latest edition of the Dead Famous walking tour newsletter for distribution. The next batch of ghosts from Maura would clear the waiting list and leave a handful for general sale – he was tempted to promote the ones that remained to his subscribers. But Maura had made it clear that the full order would take six weeks to fulfil and Fraser was reluctant to take orders so far in advance. He settled for advising Edinburgh Ghost fans to keep an eye on the Dead Famous social media channels for news of upcoming sales.

When his phone rang around four o'clock, he was surprised to see Naomi's number on the screen. They'd last spoken on Thursday, when she told him she was staying in London for the weekend. Perhaps her plans had changed, he thought as he accepted the call. 'Hey,' he said. 'How's life in the big city?'

'It's good,' she said. 'I ran into your agent last night, at the Ivy. He asked me to check whether you'd seen his email last week. He said it was important. Do you have any idea what he's talking about?'

Fraser thought guiltily about the email he'd deleted without opening. 'Something about an audition,' he said. 'I need to remind him not to bother sending those through. Apart from anything else, I don't have time.'

'But what if it's a big role?' Naomi asked, and Fraser thought he detected a faint undercurrent of horror in her voice. 'You'll miss out.'

'Then I'll miss out,' Fraser replied firmly. 'Besides, how would I spare the time? The tours are selling out every night – Tom says he had to turn people away all week and I've been the same. I'm starting to think I should recruit another guide – the demand seems to be there.'

'That's an excellent idea,' Naomi said, noticeably more enthusiastic. 'Another guide could take over some of your walks and give you more freedom. That way, you could go to auditions, if the right role came up.'

Fraser scratched his beard. 'That's not what I meant. I'm talking about expanding Dead Famous, not stepping back. If I take on someone in addition to Tom and me, they could start an hour later or cover another route. There's no shortage of stories to tell, that's for sure.'

There was a long silence. 'Expanding,' she said at length. 'Right.'

'It makes perfect sense,' Fraser went on. 'And if the sales of Maura's ghosts really take off, we could easily become Edinburgh's number one walking tour.'

This time, the pause was so long that he thought the line must have gone dead. 'Are you still there?' he asked, glancing at the screen.

'Yes, I'm here,' she said, although she sounded strangely muted. 'It's just . . .'

Fraser frowned as her voice trailed off. 'Hello? Naomi, I can't hear you. Have you got signal where you are?'

The line crackled. 'It's not the signal that's the problem,' she said. 'Look, Fraser, I've been thinking. Maybe we should take a break.'

'A break?' Fraser repeated with a burst of incredulity. 'I've just told you how busy I am. I can't spare the time for a holiday right now.'

'That's not what I meant.' He heard her take a deep breath.

'I mean a break from us. I'm not coming back to Edinburgh next week. I'm going to stay in London.'

Fraser sat back against the sofa. 'Oh.'

'I've been offered several jobs while I've been here – photoshoots I want to take. And, well, the truth is I haven't been very happy in Edinburgh. It's okay for you – you've got all your friends and the business, but I don't. So I think a break would do us both good, while we think about what we want.'

He closed his eyes. Now that the initial shock of the suggestion was fading, he wasn't entirely surprised. If he was honest, they'd been growing apart for months, ever since leaving London, and he'd had doubts of his own. But it still hurt. 'I didn't realise you'd been so unhappy,' he said quietly.

'Of course you didn't,' she said, suddenly sharp. 'You've barely noticed me at all since the start of the year.'

'That's not true,' he countered, stung. 'I've been working hard, that's all. It takes a lot of time and effort to run a successful business.'

'Believe me, I know,' Naomi snapped. 'That's my point, in fact. You don't have time for a relationship right now. You don't have time for me.'

Even as she said it, he knew she had a point. He sighed and ran a hand over his eyes. 'So what happens now?'

Naomi puffed out a breath. 'Nothing happens. I'll stay here and we'll give each other some space.'

Fraser shook his head. He'd seen friends do the same thing when their relationships were faltering. It had rarely resulted in them getting back together. 'How long do you propose we give it?'

'Two months,' she said, with such alacrity that he knew she'd decided on the timeframe in advance. 'That should give us both time to decide if we want to be together.'

Two months of uncertainty, he thought doubtfully. Two months where neither of them would be able to lick their wounds and heal, or start to move on. And at the end of the two months, one of them might choose to end the relationship for good, leaving the other to relive the pain of the break-up, knowing it was permanent this time. 'No,' he said. 'If this is what you want then we end things here.'

'That's your pride talking,' she replied. 'When you've had time to think about things, you'll realise that isn't what you want.'

The trouble was, the more he thought about it, the more he realised it was exactly what he wanted. She was probably right, there was almost certainly some wounded pride colouring his feelings, but there was no use in prolonging the inevitable. 'You don't want to live here, and I'm not moving back to London. That seems to be a pretty insurmountable problem.'

'Which is why I suggested we take a break,' Naomi said. 'A few months apart might help us see what's really important.'

The light dawned on Fraser. She anticipated that he would be unable to live without her and would agree to return to London. If that was the case, she had underestimated how deeply he had reestablished his roots in the city. Things were going well in Edinburgh. If Naomi intended to make him choose between her and the new life he had begun to build, she was going to be sorely disappointed. And it was better that it happened now than in two months' time. 'Neither of us deserves to be kept dangling, Naomi. I'm sorry it's ended this way but I agree it's for the best.'

When she spoke, her voice was hard. 'You're going to regret this. I'm the best thing that ever happened to you.'

Wincing, Fraser summoned up an image of her face. Her claim wasn't entirely without merit – there'd been plenty of good times and he was going to miss her. But she could also be demanding and temperamental, meaning he had often found himself treading on eggshells around her, especially in recent months. It was something of a relief to know that he wouldn't have to deal with her self-absorption and tantrums anymore. 'Probably,' he said wearily. 'Take care of yourself, okay? And don't worry about the practicalities. We can sort everything out over the next few weeks.'

She didn't answer; a muted chime told him she had hung up.

Slumping back against the cushions, Fraser dropped his phone to his lap as doubts assailed him. Had he been too hasty? Should he have agreed to a break instead of hitting the self-destruct button? He let out a long slow breath and closed his eyes as he contemplated this sudden hole in his life. From the way Naomi had reacted, he knew one thing: there was no going back.

'Hello. You don't remember me, do you?'

The woman smiling at Fraser was faintly familiar, now he came to look at her more closely, but he had no idea why. She was standing a little apart from the small crowd that had assembled near the Mercat Cross on the Royal Mile, and he had the distinct impression she was not used to being forgotten. Perhaps she'd been on the tour before and expected him to remember her, or they might have chatted after a theatre performance years earlier.

He shook his head in polite apology. 'I'm afraid not,' he said. 'Have we met before?'

'At Hogmanay,' she said. 'I'm a friend of Maura's.'

And then he placed her, in Pete's kitchen on New Year's Eve, although her name still evaded him. 'Of course,' he said, nodding. 'It's good to see you again.'

'Maura hasn't stopped raving about how good your tour is so I thought I'd come and see for myself,' she said.

'Thank you,' Fraser said, trying to ignore the small flutter of pleasure at the thought of Maura's recommendation. He lifted his phone. 'What name did you book under?'

'Zoe Pieterson,' she said.

He scanned the screen until he found her. 'Got it,' he said, and checked the box beside her name. 'Welcome, Zoe. If you'll just wait here, the tour will get started shortly.'

She stayed close to him for the duration of the tour, listening with rapt attention when he spoke and falling into step as the group cut through the city's wynds and alleyways. He didn't mind, exactly – she was on her own, after all, and any friend of Maura's deserved special treatment – but it did leave him less time to chat with the other attendees. When Maura had come along on one of the tours with her sister, they'd both been un-obtrusive, indistinguishable from the paying customers. Zoe was different. If Fraser didn't know better, he might suspect she was flirting with him.

'That was great,' she gushed when the tour was over and the crowd had begun to disperse. 'Every bit as brilliant as Maura said it would be.'

'Thanks,' Fraser said, and nodded to a couple who were shyly smiling goodbye. 'Glad you enjoyed it.'

'It's obvious you've been professionally trained,' Zoe went on. 'You made everything seem so real.'

Fraser smiled. 'I try.'

'I'd love to hear more about the stories behind the ghosts,' she said, laying a hand on his arm. 'Have you got time to go for a drink? I'm buying.'

He looked at her then, because there was no doubt that she was interested in much more than his stories. For a nanosecond, he was tempted; she was blonde and attractive, if ten years too young for him, and her interest was flattering. But it wouldn't be fair to encourage her, no matter how much he could do with the ego boost. He shook his head. 'Not tonight, I'm afraid. But thanks for coming along. Hope to see you again soon.'

If she was disappointed, she didn't show it, which made Fraser wonder whether he'd got the wrong end of the stick. 'No problem,' she said, smiling. 'It was just an idea.'

Once Zoe had gone, Fraser turned his attention to the others who had hung around, obviously waiting for an opportunity to speak to him. He accepted their effusive praise with thanks, recommended the other Dead Famous tour run by Tom, and advised them to sign up for the newsletter for details of new tours and Edinburgh Ghost releases.

As the last stragglers began to drift away, Fraser found himself presented with a business card. 'My name is Alistair Caldwell. I work for Edinburgh City Council,' the man said.

'Hello,' Fraser said as he took the card, wondering uneasily if he had inadvertently broken one of the city's ordnances. 'Can I help you with something?'

The man smiled. 'I hope so. Part of my job is to support and encourage tourism in Edinburgh, and we hold occasional networking meetings to allow various stakeholders to meet up and swap ideas.'

Fraser eyed him warily. 'Who do you mean by stakeholders?'

Alistair Caldwell shrugged. 'Some are storytellers, like yourself, or in similarly creative industries. Others represent the city's larger tourist attractions, like the castle or Mary King's Close. It's all quite informal, with wine and nibbles. There's one in a few weeks, if you're interested in joining us. It's being held in the City Chambers, opposite where your tour starts.'

'I know it,' Fraser said as he studied the card. The City Chambers were housed in the old Royal Exchange, accessed through a series of ornate arches that led to a cobbled courtyard boasting a magnificent bronze statue of Alexander taming the warhorse Bucephalus. It was a splendidly elaborate building that Fraser imagined had plenty of stories to tell, and it wouldn't do his business any harm to network a little. If there was one thing he had learned from a hundred after-show parties, it was that opportunities sometimes came from the most unexpected places. 'Thanks, Mr Caldwell. I'll see what I can do.'

The man looked pleased. 'My email address is on the card. Drop me a line and I can send you more details. And thank you for the tour. It really was excellent.' With a final nod, he left Fraser alone.

Tucking the business card into his pocket, Fraser set off for Princes Street and the tram that would take him back to Leith. It had turned out to be an unexpectedly interesting evening.

CHAPTER ELEVEN

There were many things Maura loved about living in Edinburgh but the city centre traffic was not one of them. She was on her way to drop off a delivery of vases to Morningside Gallery, less than three miles away from Dean Village, but a journey that should have taken around ten minutes had lasted more than half an hour and she was still a few minutes away from Morningside Road. It was a good thing she wasn't in a hurry.

Eilish Swan, the gallery owner, spotted her through the wide bay windows and hurried to greet her. 'Let me get that for you,' she said, pulling the door back to allow Maura to edge inside with the box of ceramics. 'Did you manage to get parked or are you on the double yellows?'

'I'm in the bay by the florists,' Maura said.

Eilish smiled and took the box from her. 'Then let's see what you've brought me today.'

A flutter of nerves rippled through Maura as the gallery owner lifted the first vase out. She didn't know why she was worried – Eilish had never been anything other than thrilled with the ceramics Maura had brought to the gallery. This vase was asymmetric, with one curve swirling above the other like a wave. She'd glazed the inside a deep emerald green, like the depths of the ocean, while the outside was a speckled foam green with white flecks along the rim. Eilish looked up, her eyes shining. 'It's beautiful. Really stunning.'

The butterflies subsided. 'There's a companion piece – the same shape with a reversal of the colour scheme.'

Eilish set the first vase carefully to one side and dug into the box again. When she'd unwrapped the second piece, she put them next to each other. 'That's the new window display sorted,' she said with evident satisfaction. 'I've a couple of breathtaking seascapes by Juliana Cruickshank that will complement these perfectly.'

Maura smiled, pleased at the thought of being displayed alongside Juliana's paintings. 'Great. I popped another bowl in there as well, since you said you'd sold the last one.'

Eilish nodded as she unwound the protective packaging from the bowl. 'Business has been brisk and your work is always snapped up quickly. I could sell everything you bring me two or three times over.'

Maura thought of her packed kiln, and the shelves of unfired pieces that silently berated her every time she walked past them. 'If only I had a clone,' she said wryly. 'And a bigger kiln.'

But Eilish didn't seem to be listening. Instead, she was frowning down at the box. 'What's this?' she asked, pulling something small and pale from its depths. 'Have you picked up a hitchhiker?'

'Oh!' Maura exclaimed as she recognised one of the ghosts she had been packing for Fraser that morning. 'How did that get in there?'

'I don't know but I love it,' Eilish said. 'What's it for?'

Maura explained how she'd met Fraser and started to produce the ghosts.

'No wonder you need a bigger kiln,' Eilish said, when she'd finished. 'Edinburgh Ghosts, unique to the city and handmade by you. I bet they're selling like hot cakes.'

'They seem to be popular,' Maura agreed. 'But I think that's down to Fraser's brilliant storytelling. Anyone could make these.'

The gallery owner turned a surprised gaze upon her. 'I'm not sure about that. They're different from your other work but they're still Maura McKenzie originals.' She turned the ghost over in her fingers and shook her head. 'I hope this friend of yours appreciates how lucky he is.'

The words came back to Maura as she drove home. Cordelia had said something along the same lines when Maura had first begun to produce the ghosts and she supposed from the outside it did seem as though she was bringing more to the partnership than Fraser. But it had been his idea in the first place, inspired by his existing business, and Maura suspected that no one cared much who had made the ghosts. It was Fraser Bell they were buying, not Maura McKenzie.

She hadn't been back in the studio more than five minutes when there was a knock at the door. Frowning slightly, she rinsed the clay from her hands and peered out to see her elderly neighbour, Paolo, hovering on the cobbled street outside. She opened the door wide and smiled at him. 'Hello.'

He turned towards her and she had to stop herself from letting out a horrified gasp. The right-hand side of his face was a mass of purple bruising; his eye was swollen shut and there was a nasty graze on his cheek.

'Oh my goodness, Paolo, what have you done?'

'Just me and my two left feet,' he said, the words thickened a little by the visible bruising on his lip. 'I tripped over while I was walking Hubert yesterday. It looks worse than it is.'

'It looks really painful,' Maura said, eyeing the livid bruising with sympathy. Hubert was a cute but loudly opinionated dachshund with big dog energy, who ruled Paolo and the rest of Thistledown Lane with an iron paw. 'I'm sorry you're hurt. What can I do to help?'

Paolo looked wretched. 'I hate bothering you when you're working but I didn't know who else to ask. I haven't been able to take Hubert out today – my balance isn't so good because of this stupid eye. And as you've been kind enough to walk him once or twice in the past, I thought . . . well, I hoped you might take him out for a quick stroll.' He sighed. 'He gets a bit grumpy when he's cooped up, you see.'

'Don't we all?' Maura said, although she privately thought that Hubert had grumpy tendencies no matter how many walks he had. 'Of course I'll help. When does he need to go out?'

A volley of high-pitched barking split the air. Paolo winced. 'As soon as you can manage. He keeps catching sight of the cat from Number Three through the window and he won't stop shouting at it.'

Maura nodded gravely. She had walked Hubert several times over recent months and it was her experience that he barked at anything he perceived as infringing on his patch. Number Three's cat was an arch enemy. 'Of course. Just let me finish up what I was making and I'll take him out now.'

'Thank you,' Paolo said. 'I'm sorry to be such a nuisance.'

'Not at all,' Maura said. 'To tell the truth, I'm glad of an excuse to get some fresh air myself.'

Promising to knock as soon as she could, she closed the door of the studio and surveyed the half-thrown pot on the wheel. The clay would have dried by the time she'd given Hubert a good walk and she was anxious not to keep Paolo waiting. Reaching for the cheese wire, she sliced the pot from the wheel and squashed the clay back into a ball, returning it to the plastic bag she'd taken it from not ten minutes earlier. It wasn't much of a sacrifice – she could easily start again once she and Hubert were back from their walk.

Once she'd tidied up, she glanced around the studio to make sure there was nothing else that needed her attention. Her gaze came to rest on the box of ghosts for Fraser, carefully packed up for him to collect the following day. She planned to take Hubert to Portobello Beach, in the hope that the wide expanse of sand and sea air would wear him out enough to give Paolo some peace. Leith was only a few minutes' drive from Portobello. Should she offer to drop the ghosts off to Fraser, to save him the journey in the morning? Picking up her phone, she tapped out a message.

Hey, are you in Leith now? I'm heading to Porty Beach –
can drop the ghosts off on the way?

Her phone pinged almost immediately: I am! Are you sure it's no trouble?

She smiled. None at all, as long as you don't mind being told what's what by a bad-tempered sausage dog. I'm walking my neighbour's dog.

Once again, Fraser's reply was quick. My favourite kind of telling off. I could do with a walk myself – want some company?

Maura stared at the message for a few minutes, trying to

work out how to respond. She hadn't considered he might offer
to join her – all she'd wanted to do was save him a journey. But
now that the offer was there, she found herself tempted to say
yes. They didn't have much to discuss, business-wise, but that
didn't mean they wouldn't find other things to talk about. Sure,
she typed. Meet you in the car park at 2?

Perfect. See you there.

With Hubert in the back of the Volvo, and the ghosts safely in
the passenger footwell, Maura set off for Portobello Beach. The
morning clouds had cleared to reveal a blue sky dotted with
cotton wool but Maura knew the beach of old – even on sunny
days, the wind could cut in from the North Sea. Hubert had a
smart little coat to wear and so did Maura, as well as a bobble
hat. Jamie told her it made her look like a garden gnome but
she didn't care as long as her ears were warm.

She'd arrived a few minutes early, so had time to scan the
beach. It tended to be quieter on weekdays but there were still
a few young children skipping across the sand, and several dog
walkers. Maura made a mental note to avoid both; Hubert was
all bark but she'd learned from experience that it was easier to
maintain plenty of distance.

'Nice coat,' a male voice said, and Maura spun round to see
Fraser approaching.

'Oh,' she said, wrong-footed. 'Um, thanks.'

He smiled. 'I meant the dog's but yours is nice too. Goes
well with your hat.'

The words seemed sincerely meant but even so, Maura eyed
him with some suspicion. 'It's cold.'

'I know, that's why I've got hat envy,' he said, and looked at her appraisingly. 'It suits you. You look like—'

'If you're about to mention garden ornaments then don't,' Maura said sternly.

Fraser looked amused. 'I wouldn't dream of it. I was going to say you look like you've stepped out of a magazine spread extolling the virtues of life by the sea.' He glanced down at Hubert, whose thin tail was whipping back and forth in a frenzy of excitement. 'Is this the fearsome beastie you warned me about?'

She watched as he held out a hand to be sniffed and then crouched down to rub Hubert's ears. At least that meant she didn't have to acknowledge the compliment he'd just given her. 'Yes. He's usually much more growly with strangers.'

'Ah, but I'm not the least bit strange,' he said, and glanced up at her. 'Am I?'

Something odd happened in Maura's stomach then, a sort of lurching, twanging sensation that inexplicably made her feel sixteen again. 'He doesn't think so,' she said, fixing her attention on Hubert. 'I think he likes you.'

'Good to know someone does,' Fraser said cheerfully, which almost made Maura laugh because popularity had never been a problem for him. 'Shall we see if we can wear him out?'

They made their way onto the sand, with Hubert stopping to sniff at regular intervals.

'Do you walk him much?' Fraser asked.

'Not really,' Maura replied. 'My neighbour is elderly and had a fall so he asked me to help out today. It's no trouble really.'

Fraser nodded. 'I miss having a dog. We had a pair of German shepherds when I was growing up and I always thought I'd have one of my own, but I chose the wrong career for that.' He caught Maura's quizzical look. 'Unpredictable working patterns and long hours at rehearsals. Flying out the door at a moment's notice for an audition on the other side of London. Parties, if you're lucky, and travel. It didn't seem fair to get a dog when I didn't know how much time I'd have to spare.'

It made sense, Maura thought. 'Your working pattern is a lot steadier now. Does Naomi like dogs?'

There was a slight pause. 'No. She's not really an animal person.'

Maura had only met Naomi once but she couldn't say she was entirely surprised by the news. 'Jamie isn't either,' she said. 'Although his argument is that we don't have a garden, so it wouldn't be fair.'

Fraser pursed his lips. 'I can see his point. But plenty of people manage without. Your neighbour, for example.'

It was an argument Maura had tried herself but Jamie had refused to budge. And if they moved to the new apartment he wanted, that was the way it would stay. 'Do your parents keep dogs, at least?' She stopped. 'I mean, assuming they're still ... that they haven't ...' She trailed off, unable to finish the sentence in a way that didn't sound horribly unfeeling. She had no idea how old Fraser's parents were – her own were in their sixties – but it was quite possible he'd lost one or both.

'They're still going strong,' Fraser said, interpreting her meaning. 'They live near North Berwick now, with an extremely over-indulged cockapoo that thinks it's a human. I'm going to see them this weekend, as a matter of fact.'

Hubert tugged on the lead, pulling towards a small cluster of seaweed he clearly wanted to investigate. Maura allowed him to sniff at it, although she kept her gaze fixed upon him. The first time she'd brought him here, there had been an unfortunate incident with a dead seagull and it was an experience she had no intention of repeating. 'My folks are across the Firth, just past Aberdour. My sister too, with her husband and kids.'

'Kirsty, isn't it?' Fraser said. 'We met on the ghost tour.'

'That's right,' Maura replied, surprised he'd remembered her name. 'You made quite an impression, by the way. She was a little bit starstruck.'

Fraser sighed. 'It comes with the territory when you've played such a high-profile role as Louis the Chicken. People look at you differently.'

Maura couldn't contain a snort of laughter. She was developing a healthy appreciation for Fraser's dry self-deprecation. He had every right to be proud of his talent and achievements but he never missed an opportunity to downplay them, usually to elicit a laugh. 'Hungrily, I imagine,' she said.

He eyed her with mock severity. 'You may laugh, Maura McKenzie, but I have a Red Rooster card that entitles me to free fried chicken for the rest of my life. You can't buy perks like that.'

'Wow,' Maura said, grinning. 'Naomi is a very lucky girl.'

Fraser started to reply but Hubert chose that moment to let off a volley of ferocious barks in the direction of a swooping gull. By the time Maura had calmed the dog down, Fraser's gaze was fixed on the distant shoreline. They walked in amicable silence for a few moments, then Fraser glanced sideways at her. 'Do you ever wonder why we weren't friends at school?'

Maura blinked. Surely he had to know they had been as different as night and day back then. 'Erm, not really. We ... uh ... moved in different circles.'

'But we were both arty,' he said. 'I remember seeing you once, in the art block, and peering through the window to see what you were making. But I don't remember us talking much.'

The fact that he remembered her at all caught Maura off guard. When had he seen her in the art block? she wondered, and then decided it didn't matter. For the vast majority of their school days, she had swum beneath Fraser's notice. Although that wasn't strictly true, she recalled, because there had been that kiss, when he'd said such lovely things and it had been clear he'd been more aware of her than she'd realised. And here was a gilt-edged invitation to test her conviction that he had no idea it had happened. All she had to do was drop it into conversation now. *Oh, we did a little bit more than just talking, Fraser. Don't you remember?*

She cleared her throat. 'I'm not sure we did.'

'I wish we had,' he said, his gaze lingering on her.

For a moment, she was back outside the pub on a cold December night, staring into his blue eyes and wondering whether she was dreaming. 'Me too,' she said, before she could stop herself.

Fraser smiled. 'At least we're friends now.'

It was on the tip of her tongue to correct him, to remind him, the way she reminded everyone else, that they were business partners, not friends. But somewhere along the line the boundaries had blurred, and Maura found herself thinking of Fraser as more than someone she worked with. 'Yes,' she said, returning his smile. 'It might have taken nineteen years but I think we're finally friends.'

CHAPTER TWELVE

'Darling.' Fraser's mother pulled him into a hug before he'd even crossed the doorstep. 'How are you feeling?'

'Hello, Mum,' Fraser said, absorbing the comfort she always gave. 'I'm okay.'

Releasing him, she stood back to study him with a narrow-eyed gaze. 'You look like you've lost weight. Are you eating?'

He suppressed a smile, because she said the same thing every time he came to visit. 'It's all the walking I'm doing,' he said, as she stepped back to allow him into the house. 'Don't worry, I'm not pining away from a broken heart.'

'I should hope not,' she said briskly. 'Come on inside and see your father. Don't mention golf, whatever you do. He's got a new club he's desperate to bore you with.'

Pausing to ruffle the teddy bear ears of Elvis the cockapoo, Fraser followed her along the hall and into the kitchen, where his father was filling the teapot. 'Hullo, son. How was the journey?'

It was another time-honoured question. 'Not too bad,' Fraser replied, bending to give Elvis some more satisfactory attention. The dog rolled onto his back, legs waving comically. 'The road-works through Longniddry slowed me down a bit.'

His dad grunted. 'They're a real pain. Another two weeks of them, so they say, although I never see anyone doing any work there.'

Fraser nodded, because this was a well-worn grumble. Everything had been much faster in Micky Bell's day, because people knew the meaning of hard work then. It was not a lecture Fraser was in the mood to hear again so he decided to head it off. 'Mum says you've a new club to show me.'

'I do – a real beauty,' his father said, taking the bait. 'You'll have to come and play a round or two, see her in action.'

'What sort of club is it?' Fraser asked, avoiding the invitation because Micky had become ferociously competitive since taking up golf in retirement and Fraser had learned long ago it was not much fun to play with him.

'A seven-iron,' Micky said, his eyes gleaming. 'She's got me out of trouble a few times already, I can tell you.'

Roberta rolled her eyes as she filled a plate with shortbread. 'Don't encourage him, Fraser. Anyone would think he's Rory McIlroy, the way he goes on.'

'He asked,' Micky objected. 'What am I supposed to do, pretend I don't have a new club?'

'You're supposed to ask how he is,' Roberta said. 'He's just broken up with his girlfriend, remember?'

Fraser shook his head as he reluctantly straightened up. It was time to reassure both his parents that breaking up with Naomi had not been the emotional rollercoaster they were imagining. 'Really, there's no need. I'm fine.'

His mother sniffed. 'Putting on a brave face. You were the same as a boy – never let anyone see when you were hurting.'

There was a grain of truth in that but it wasn't a topic Fraser had any intention of discussing now. 'I promise you I'm okay, Mum,' he said. 'Obviously, I'm sorry things turned out the way they did but neither of us was very happy. It's probably all for the best.'

His dad clapped him on the shoulder. 'That's the spirit, lad. Plenty more fish in the sea.'

'Micky!' Roberta snapped. 'It's only been a week. I'm sure Fraser isn't thinking about that now.'

'I'm just saying,' Micky said, raising his hands in a semblance of injured reasonableness. 'He's got a lot to offer the right woman.'

'I know that,' Roberta said. 'But the boy's had his heart trampled. He needs time to heal.'

Fraser shifted uncomfortably. He'd been low in the days after the break-up with Naomi but, once the sadness had passed, he had begun to see how inevitable it had been and a burgeoning sense of relief had replaced any melancholy he felt. He hadn't tried to contact her and she hadn't been in touch, which led him to suspect she was feeling the same liberation he was. 'I'm really not heartbroken.'

His mother looked at him askance but didn't press the point. 'I'm glad,' she said, and busied herself with loading the tea and biscuits onto a tray. 'What else is new? Are you keeping busy with work?'

'Very,' Fraser said, following her out to the table and chairs on the patio. 'I've started advertising for another tour guide.'

'That's good news,' she said, nodding her approval. 'Isn't it, Micky?'

'Aye,' his dad said. 'Great stuff.'

Roberta settled into a chair and began to pour the tea. 'And how are things going with the wee ghosties? Are they still selling well?'

Fraser thought of the new orders that had landed overnight. 'You could say that. I took delivery of another twenty this week and I still need forty more. Maura can't make them fast enough.'

'Is this the girl you went to school with?' Micky asked.

He nodded. 'That's right. Maura McKenzie.'

'I still don't remember the name,' Roberta said, shaking her head. 'But I looked her up, when you said you'd be working together. She makes some lovely things.'

Fraser pictured the bowl on the coffee table in his apartment, and the mug he used for his morning coffee, both of which brightened his day with their elegance. 'She does. You'd love the ghosts too. I'll have to bring you one, when I've got some to spare.'

Or perhaps he might suggest she visit ScotPot, since Maura was one of the exhibitors. Was it too much, to introduce her to his parents? He'd met her sister, after all, and he had meant it when he said he thought of her as a friend. Even so, he was aware that their friendship was still very new. He'd held back from mentioning his split with Naomi during the walk on Portobello Beach but it wasn't something he wanted to hide. People broke up all the time, it was no big deal. When he judged the moment was right, he'd drop it casually into conversation. Until then, he'd keep it to himself.

The City Chambers were every bit as splendid as Fraser imagined they would be. Alistair Caldwell had been true to his word; he'd responded with prompt enthusiasm to the email Fraser had sent, giving the date and time of the networking session, and a rough outline of what to expect. Happily, the event had fallen on a Tuesday evening, one of the nights Fraser took off from his ghost walks, and he'd seen no reason not to go along. And now he was inside the magnificent European Room, with its fresco-painted walls, gilt-panelled ceiling and arched windows. The carpet beneath his feet was a plush royal blue and golden chandeliers glowed overhead. The room was perhaps three-quarters full, which allowed space to mingle, and there was a pleasing buzz of chatter over the discreet background music. So far, Fraser had sampled several excellent canapés, drunk a glass of Prosecco and swapped notes with two fellow tour guides. And now Alistair Caldwell was making a beeline for him, with another man in tow.

'Fraser, glad you could make it. Can I introduce you to Ewan McRae? He's in charge of visitor engagement at the castle.'

Fraser shook the man's outstretched hand. 'A pleasure to meet you.'

Ewan McRae nodded. 'And you. Alistair was just telling me about your ghost tour. He says it's the best in the city.'

Fraser smiled, flattered in spite of himself. 'That's very kind. I try my best.'

'And you're a professional actor, is that right?'

'Yes, that's right,' Fraser said. 'I trained at the Central School of Speech and Drama, quite a long time ago now, but my heart has always been in Edinburgh.'

'Very good,' Ewan said and eyed him speculatively. 'I'm organising an interactive storytelling night at the castle in July. As I'm sure you're aware, we have a reputation as being the most haunted place in Scotland. I'd be interested in booking you to bring some of our ghost stories to life. Is that something you might consider?'

'Absolutely,' Fraser said, without hesitation. 'It sounds like just my kind of thing.'

The other man nodded. 'Excellent. Perhaps you'd like to come along for an informal chat in the next few weeks – I can give you a tour and explain what we're looking for.'

'I'd love to,' Fraser said, hardly able to believe his luck. 'Thanks.'

Ewan looked pleased. 'I understand you also sell ceramic ghosts to go with your tour. Who makes those?'

'An Edinburgh-based potter called Maura McKenzie,' Fraser replied. He took a breath and launched his sales pitch. 'Each one is handmade and unique, taken from the stories I tell and representing part of the city's history. They've been very popular so far.'

'I can imagine,' Ewan said, his expression intrigued. 'I'd be interested in seeing them too. Could you bring one along when you come in?'

'Of course,' Fraser said, crossing his fingers that Maura would deliver the next batch of ghosts before the meeting took place. 'I'd be happy to.'

Ewan smiled. 'Perfect. Alistair can give me your details and I'll be in touch with some dates.'

Alistair stepped forward, rubbing his hands briskly. 'That's all sorted, then. Now, if you'll excuse us, Fraser, there are a few other business owners Ewan needs to meet.'

With a further round of handshakes, they parted company, leaving Fraser to reflect on his unexpected good fortune. An event at Edinburgh Castle would almost certainly boost the reputation of Dead Famous, as well as being a feather in Fraser's own storytelling cap. He glanced across the room, to where Ewan was now talking to one of the storytellers Fraser had met earlier. It might all come to nothing, of course, but it was starting to look as though he might owe Alistair Caldwell a very large drink.

Fraser had visited Edinburgh Castle a number of times while growing up but its grandeur never failed to impress him. Built on an outcrop of volcanic rock, it had kept watch over the city in one form or another for thousands of years and had seen more than its fair share of bloodshed, which he supposed was only to be expected when it had been home to so many of Scotland's kings and queens. The hair on the back of his neck rose as he made his way up Castlehill, passing through the arched gatehouse and beneath the iron portcullis to follow the curving path into the castle beyond. If he closed his eyes, he could almost hear the tramp of soldiers' boots on the cobbles, the cries of alarm as the walls were besieged or the triumphant procession of a royal coronation. This had always been the thing Fraser loved most about visiting places steeped in history – the way countless stories reached across the ages and came alive in his head. He sometimes thought if he hadn't been an actor, he might have been a writer.

Ewan McRae's office was tucked away in the uppermost reaches of the castle, far from the bustling tourist areas. It was small and wood-panelled, with a stone fireplace that boasted carved lions on either side, and latticed windows hung with heavy velvet drapes; in fact, if it hadn't been for the laptop and telephone on the desk, Fraser might have been fooled into thinking he had somehow stepped back in time.

'Did you enjoy the tour?' Ewan asked from his seat across the desk. 'I'm sorry I wasn't able to escort you personally, but the truth is Catriona knows much more about the castle and its secrets than I do. You were in safe hands.'

'I was,' Fraser agreed. His guide had been both friendly and knowledgeable. She'd pointed out the ramparts where the legendary headless drummer was said to beat out his mournful warning of attack, led him through the dungeons thought to be haunted by Napoleonic prisoners of war and shown him the tower room the Earl of Argyll was alleged to haunt after his gruesome beheading. 'I especially liked the ghostly dog.'

Ewan smiled. 'Ah, yes. I've never seen him myself, or any of our other apparitions, but they certainly capture the imagination of our visitors. Which is where you come in. Did you have time to read the event brief I sent?'

'Yes, I did. It sounds like a great idea.'

'I certainly hope so,' Ewan said. 'Guests will be welcomed into the gatehouse by a piper and led on a tour of the various supernatural hotspots around the castle, where their guide will thrill them with the stories behind the ghosts. At various points, there will be projections onto the walls, and some pre-recorded audio, but we won't have actors in character. It will be up to you as a storyteller to create the appropriate atmosphere and bring the ghosts to life, as it were.'

It was exactly as Fraser had envisaged when he'd read the brief. 'It would be helpful to see and hear the effects beforehand.'

'Of course,' Ewan said. 'We'll arrange an after-hours visit a week or so before the event for all the storytellers.'

Fraser thought back to the brief. 'And you're expecting two tours per guide, is that right?'

'Yes. At the end of your first tour, you'll leave your group in the Great Hall and take a break before your second group arrives. We'll make sure you have refreshments – whatever you need.'

Fraser nodded. It was going to be different to his nightly tour, where he could switch the route or timings if needed. With several other storytellers making their way around the castle, and special effects to factor in, he would need to keep to the schedule fairly closely. 'Okay.'

Ewan steepled his hands. 'We're planning to offer a press preview the night before the public opening and we'd like you to run that tour. Would that be possible?'

Fraser considered the question. It would mean finding someone to cover his usual tour, but the benefits of showcasing his talents to the press would far outweigh that small inconvenience. 'Very much so,' he said. 'I'd be honoured.'

'Then that's settled,' the other man said. 'I'll get the contracts drawn up and you can start working on your unique interpretation of the stories. Catriona will be your point of contact if you need to check anything factual – obviously we need to keep things historically accurate where we can.'

Fraser hid a smile. Several of the city's ghost tours had abandoned any attempt at accuracy in favour of spicing up their stories. Dead Famous was not one of those. 'Understood.'

Ewan got to his feet. 'You've got my email if you have any questions.'

'I have,' Fraser replied and stood up. As he did so, his hand brushed against his jacket pocket, and the box he'd tucked away before leaving his apartment. 'Oh, I nearly forgot. Here's an Edinburgh Ghost for you.'

'Ah, yes,' Ewan said, and took the box. Opening it, he teased the tissue paper apart and examined the contents. 'Very clever. Did you say it represents one of the stories you tell on your tour?'

'That's right,' Fraser said. 'This is Agnes the Sea Witch, inspired by Agnes Sampson, who was executed for sending a storm to drown King James, among other accusations.'

Ewan ran a finger over the feathery green strands that trailed across the ghost. 'I can see why they're popular. The design is excellent and it's exquisitely made.'

Fraser couldn't help feeling a swell of pride on Maura's behalf. 'I'll be sure to pass that along.'

'We might consider commissioning something like this for one of the castle ghosts in the future,' Ewan said thoughtfully. 'In partnership with your company, obviously.'

'I'm sure that could be arranged,' Fraser said cautiously, even as he contemplated how busy Maura was already. 'I'd have to consult my business partner.'

The other man nodded. 'Something to keep in mind,' he said, as he handed the ghost back to Fraser. He checked his watch and winced. 'I'd better show you out. I'm due at Holyrood Palace in thirty minutes and it doesn't do to keep the royal court waiting.'

On the tram back to Leith, Fraser found himself wondering how Maura would feel about a potential tie-in with the castle. She had delivered the second batch of the forty ghosts at the end of the previous week, just in time for his meeting with Ewan, and he'd asked her to repeat the order. The ghosts sold out almost as soon as he released each new batch and he knew a castle ghost would be popular too. He'd have to handle the supply carefully to keep things running smoothly. And in the meantime, it wouldn't hurt for him to make sure Maura knew how much he appreciated her hard work. It was time to fall back on his show business experience and apply a tiny bit of schmooze.

CHAPTER THIRTEEN

Maura read the message from Fraser three times before she got the better of her surprise. She looked up at Jamie, who was glued to a documentary at the other end of the sofa. 'We've been invited out for dinner.'

He didn't take his eyes from the television. 'By who?'

'Fraser,' she said. 'As a thank you for all the work I've put in making the ghosts.'

Jamie frowned. 'Why does he need to thank you? He's paying you, isn't he?'

'Yes,' Maura said patiently. 'But I suppose it's a bit like all those times you wine and dine clients on behalf of the bank. You want them to feel valued.'

'But they're multimillion-pound clients,' he objected. 'They're not pottery teachers knocking out a few bits and bobs on the side for some guy they went to school with.'

The words were casually uttered but they still felt like a kick to the stomach. Maura stared at him, wondering whether she could possibly have misheard. 'Sorry?'

He glanced at her. 'You have to admit, I'm right. You do

mostly teach these days, and the ghosts are hardly going to relaunch your career, are they?'

A roaring began in her ears. He'd always been so proud of her work – when had that changed? When the solo exhibitions began to dry up? 'I have work on display at several galleries,' she said, swallowing hard. 'I'm selected for ScotPot every year. I wasn't aware my career needed to be relaunched.'

'What I mean is that you don't seem to have the same ambition you did a few years ago.' He sighed. 'But you're obviously happy with what you're doing so it doesn't really matter. I'm just not sure it's appropriate for this guy to suggest selling a handful of trinkets to tourists is anything to celebrate.'

The worst of it was that his words echoed Maura's own early doubts, causing her to gnaw at her lip. It wasn't the first time she'd worried the ghosts weren't worth the price Fraser put on them. But the fact that they'd sold, and sold well, had proved her fears wrong, as had the reaction of Eilish at the gallery. And the additional income had been welcome. Jamie might think making the ghosts was somehow beneath her, but Maura had no intention of giving them up. Not while Fraser still wanted her to make them.

She took a deep, calming breath and let it out slowly. 'Firstly, his name is Fraser, and he's my business partner – you could try to be a bit more respectful. And secondly, I do enjoy teaching but it's only a small part of what I do. I'm sorry that my career isn't what you expected it to be but there's no need to belittle it.'

Jamie's eyes flashed. 'I didn't—'

'Yes, you did,' she cut in. 'Suggesting that I'm knocking out trinkets for tourists is belittling, Jamie, and I'd really appreciate it if you could avoid insulting Fraser in the same way.'

'If that's how you feel then maybe I'd better not come.'

'That's fine,' Maura fired back. 'I'll go on my own. But don't expect me to play the dutiful girlfriend at your next work party.'

He scowled. 'Now you're being ridiculous. It's hardly the same.'

Maura thought she might explode. Was he being deliberately obtuse? 'It's exactly the same! I go to your work things when you ask because I want to be supportive, but apparently that's not a two-way thing.' She raised her chin. 'When was the last time you came to a pottery show or exhibition of mine?'

'You can hardly expect me to turn up to every church hall craft fair.'

'ScotPot isn't a craft fair,' she cried, throwing her hands up. 'It's one of the most prestigious ceramics shows in Scotland.'

'But you've never asked me to go,' he growled.

'I don't ask my parents or Kirsty to go, either, but they still turn up.' She took another breath and tried to get her temper under control. 'But I'm not even asking you to come to ScotPot. I'm asking you to come for dinner with my business partner and his girlfriend, to celebrate how well it's gone. Is that really too much to expect?'

His jaw bunched as he glared at her and she thought he was going to launch another furious objection. But he surprised her. 'No,' he muttered after several mutinous seconds had ticked by. 'I suppose not.'

The submission took the wind out of Maura's sails. 'Oh,' she said. 'Good.'

'Tell me where and when and I'll be there,' he said, although his tone wasn't entirely free from resentment.

She checked her phone. 'He's suggesting Monday evening, at The Witchery. Seven-thirty.'

'Fine,' Jamie said, and levered himself up from the sofa. 'I'm going to the rugby club.'

Maura watched him leave the room, her own anger and adrenaline seeping away. She'd had no idea he had such scant regard for her work, or so little interest in supporting her, but the way he had sneered about Fraser and the ghosts troubled her deeply. She might have won the battle in demanding that Jamie join them for dinner, but she was starting to suspect it was part of a war she'd had no idea she was fighting until now.

The Witchery by the Castle was an old-fashioned restaurant tucked away in the grand sandstone buildings at the very top of the Royal Mile. Maura had only eaten there once, for her parents' silver wedding anniversary, but the burnished oxblood leather seats and ornate oak-panelled ceiling had made an impression. It was often booked up for months in the evenings, especially when the city was thronging with visitors, and she thought Fraser must have pulled some strings or called in a favour to get a dinner reservation with barely a week's notice. But somehow he had managed it and he was already waiting for her beside the entrance to Boswell's Court when she arrived ten minutes early.

He was facing away from her, gazing up at the looming castle, and she took a moment to appreciate the smart grey suit he was wearing. She'd never seen him formally attired – school uniform definitely didn't count – but she wasn't surprised to note that it suited him. Then again, he was an actor, she reminded herself. He could probably carry off most things. The sight of him made her glad she'd made an effort too; her knee-length red woollen dress was understated but elegant, even if it did keep clinging to her tights.

'Hello,' she called as she approached.

He turned immediately, his expression lighting up. 'Hello yourself. How are you?'

'Hungry,' she said truthfully. 'I seem to remember some especially fine Orkney scallops last time I was here and I've been looking forward to them all day.'

Fraser tipped his head. 'Good recommendation.' He glanced enquiringly over her shoulder down Castlehill. 'Is Jamie on his way?'

'He is,' Maura said, hoping she was right. She hadn't heard from him since lunchtime, when she'd messaged to remind him not to be late and he'd responded with the eyeroll emoji. 'Has Naomi been held up?'

An uncomfortable expression flashed across Fraser's face, followed by a rueful smile. 'She won't be joining us, I'm afraid. We ... uh ... split up a few weeks ago.'

Maura stared at him in shocked sympathy. 'Oh, I'm sorry. I had no idea.'

'It's fine,' he said quickly. 'I meant to tell you but things have been so busy. She was finding it hard being so far from London and we agreed it was best if we went our separate ways. All quite amicable and grown-up.'

She eyed him suspiciously. He sounded matter of fact but she wondered if he was taking it as well as he seemed to be. 'Even so, a break-up takes its toll. Are you sure you're okay?'

He smiled. 'I'm sure. Things had been tricky for a while, to be honest. I think Edinburgh was a bit too melancholy for her.'

'Well, I'm still sorry,' Maura said. 'And I'm sure you have loads of friends, but if you ever need anyone to talk to—'

She broke off as his gaze met hers with frank honesty. 'That's kind of you, Maura. But really, I'm fine.'

'Okay,' she said, reassured that he didn't seem to be pining from a broken heart. 'So, just the three of us.'

Fraser nodded. 'I'm looking forward to meeting Jamie properly. I saw him at the New Year's Eve party, of course, but didn't get to say hello.'

'Probably a good thing,' Maura said, remembering how many shots Jamie and his rugby mates had downed. 'He'll be much better company this evening.'

But as her watch ticked round to seven-thirty, her faith in him began to wane. He couldn't have forgotten. She checked her phone. There was no text to say he was running late. There was nothing at all. She stabbed at the screen, calling him. Her cheeks grew hot as it went to answerphone. She hung up, not trusting herself to leave a jolly 'Where are you?' message.

Fraser cleared his throat. 'We should probably go in. They won't save the table for long.'

Maura peered down Castlehill, hoping to see Jamie's tall frame puffing towards them, and sighed. 'You're right. I'm sure he'll be here soon.'

The dining room was every bit as gothic as she remembered. The deep red seating was studded with brass. Each table was lit by flickering white candles in tall brass holders. Discreet wall lights added to their glow but the atmosphere was unquestionably intimate. Carved satyrs cavorted among curling leaves across the beams above their heads and tapestry drapes hung at intervals. Their waiter led them to their table, which had been laid for three, and Maura felt a small whoosh of relief at the detail. The Witchery had a romantic reputation. If it had been just her and Fraser, they might have been mistaken for a couple.

'So, what will you have to drink?' Fraser asked, offering her the menu. 'Champagne is definitely in order but we should wait for Jamie to get here.'

Maura nodded, turning her attention to the list of cocktails and trying to ignore the needle of misgiving in the pit of her stomach. Jamie would be here soon. He wouldn't let her down.

'How's the preparation for ScotPot coming along?' Fraser asked, when the waiter had taken their drinks order. 'It's soon, isn't it?'

'It opens on Friday 6th of June and runs over that weekend,' she said. 'I've still got a few things to finish off – a couple of my seasons pots cracked in the kiln – but as long as the next batch behaves then I should get everything done in time.'

Fraser looked surprised. 'Why did they crack?'

She shrugged. 'It could be anything – an issue with the clay, or how I've made the pot. They might have dried too quickly, or not quickly enough. The temperature in the kiln might have been off. Basically, it happens and there's nothing much you can do except try again.'

'Wow,' Fraser said. 'So every time you make something, there's a chance it might go catastrophically wrong.'

'Pretty much,' Maura said. 'It certainly encourages resilience.'

He laughed. 'And I thought acting was a brutal business.'

'At least with pots you know it's nothing personal,' Maura replied.

'It usually isn't with acting, although I admit it's hard to remember that when a casting director suggests you lose half a stone.'

Maura gaped at him. As far as she could tell, Fraser was in great shape. 'No. I thought it was only the women who got told that.'

He shook his head. 'Nope. But at least losing weight is achievable, if not always desirable. I've been told I'm too tall, too short, too old, not old enough. Too Scottish, too hairy and too ordinary.'

The last one almost made Maura sputter with indignation. Whatever else could be levelled at Fraser, he was most certainly not ordinary. 'How rude.'

'But that's just it – none of it was meant as a criticism,' he said equably. 'If you're not right for a role then you're not right, even if you think you're perfect for it. When I was fresh out of drama school, I auditioned for the role of Dexter in *One Day*. I hadn't read the book, had only glanced at my agent's email and thought they wanted an Edinburgh university student. It was only after that I realised he's not Scottish at all, and that the story spans decades.'

It still felt harsh, even though she accepted the explanation. 'I hated that film,' she said. 'The book was better.'

Fraser's lips quirked. 'Actors hear that a lot.'

She waved a hand as long-buried indignation rose inside her. 'And Dexter was an idiot, anyway. He didn't deserve Emma.'

'I've clearly touched a nerve,' Fraser said gravely, as their drinks arrived. 'I'm glad I didn't get the part now.'

Maura shook her head decisively. No matter how talented an actor Fraser was, she couldn't imagine him playing someone as infuriating as Dexter. 'You should be.'

He winked. 'I would never have got my Red Rooster card, for a start.'

Maura couldn't help laughing as the waiter respectfully cleared his throat. 'Are you ready to order?'

Instantly, Maura's good humour vanished. She checked the time again. It was almost eight o'clock – where was Jamie? She gave Fraser an embarrassed look. 'I have no idea how long he'll be. I think we'd better push on.'

Fraser nodded. 'He can order when he arrives. What are you going to have, apart from the scallops?'

She glanced at the menu, even though she knew exactly what she wanted. 'The burrata to start, please,' she said, and smiled at Fraser. 'Followed by the scallops in chorizo with potatoes as my main course.'

'I don't think I can wait until my main course to sample the scallops,' Fraser mused as he perused the menu. 'So I'll have them as a starter, with the grilled lemon sole to follow, please. Oh, and a bottle of the Bollinger Special Cuvée.'

'Very good, sir.'

Maura did her best to enjoy the splendid surroundings but it was hard when her insides seethed with stress and annoyance. Jamie hadn't returned her call, hadn't messaged. When the champagne arrived, and the waiter filled her glass with golden bubbles, she resolved to put Jamie out of her head entirely. Wherever he was, he wasn't thinking about her and she refused to let him spoil the evening.

Fraser raised his flute of fizz. 'To you,' he said, 'and your Edinburgh Ghosts. I'm so glad I went to Pete's party and met you again.'

His gaze was sincere and Maura felt warmth rising in her cheeks as a disconcerting tickle of something rippled out from her belly. She tapped her glass against his. 'And to you, for coming up with the ghosts in the first place.'

She took a sip, savouring the buttery crispness and trying

not to think about how Fraser's words had made her feel, or to wonder how much the bottle of Bollinger was costing him. A large chunk of his profits from the sale of the ghosts, if she was any judge. 'You know you didn't have to do this,' she said. 'Thank me, I mean.'

Fraser put his glass down and studied her. 'But I wanted to. I know you've had to work hard to make the ghosts, and that you've had to juggle everything to fit them in. This is my way of showing you how much I appreciate that.' He paused. 'And I wanted to suggest a slight change to the way we work. How would you feel about a minimum order of forty ghosts every month?'

It wasn't a change she'd been anticipating but, at the same time, it made sense. She did some rapid calculations, switching to business mode. Delivering forty ghosts in thirty days would mean a change to her working pattern but it could be done, if she made them all in one day and fired them over several weeks. She could make an early start one day a week to get the bulk of the decoration done while the studio was empty. A regular order would give her a guaranteed income too, providing she could meet the deadline. 'I think that might work,' she said cautiously. 'I don't suppose I need to ask whether you're confident you can sell them.'

'Easily,' Fraser said. 'More, in fact, but I know you have other commitments. I'd like to brainstorm a new design too, maybe after ScotPot. I think people are going to want more than one Edinburgh Ghost.'

It was something Maura had already thought about, although she hadn't got much further than acknowledging the need for a fresh design. The idea of coming up with a new ghost with

Fraser pleased her. 'Okay. We can definitely do that, once ScotPot is out of the way.'

Their starters arrived and Maura gave her full attention to the oozy perfection of the burrata, with its drizzle of piquant pesto to offset the creaminess of the cheese. Fraser pronounced the scallops delicious, easily as good as the ones he'd eaten on Orkney itself. The conversation flowed as freely as the champagne, so that by the time their main courses arrived, the bottle was empty and Maura was feeling more than a little tipsy. 'What next?' Fraser asked, as the waiter cleared the champagne bucket. 'Wine?'

'Water, for now,' Maura said, taking a long sip. 'But maybe a small glass of white to go with the scallops.'

He nodded. 'I had an interesting meeting last week. You remember I told you about the guy who turned up at one of my tours and invited me to a networking event at the council?'

'I remember,' she said. 'How did it go?'

'Really well,' Fraser said. 'I met someone from Edinburgh Castle who asked me to take part in a supernatural storytelling night in July.'

Maura beamed at him. 'That's excellent, although I'm not surprised they've snapped you up. Well done.'

He inclined his head. 'Thanks. But the reason I'm telling you about it is because the guy from the castle – Ewan McRae – was very impressed by your ghost. He went so far as to say that they might be interested in commissioning one especially for the castle.'

'What?' she said, blinking. 'But . . . that's—'

'I know, you're working flat out as it is,' he said, raising his hands. 'It's all just a thought at the moment, probably a long way down the road if it even happens. But what I did think was there might be scope to get you your own exhibition there.'

And now Maura's mouth fell open. Edinburgh Castle was the city's flagship tourist attraction – they did not allow just anyone space to exhibit there. 'But . . .' she began, and then marshalled her thoughts. 'What kind of exhibition?'

'That's up to you,' Fraser said. 'As I said, Ewan liked the ghost. If my storytelling event goes well, I don't see why we can't arrange for you to meet him. I get the feeling they're very keen to support local artists – you'd be perfect.'

She sat back in her seat, trying to take everything in. Her work was mostly inspired by nature and the sea. Could she produce something that would reflect the castle in some way?

Fraser sat forward to catch her eye. 'It's just an idea. You don't have to if you don't want to.'

Maura's thoughts flew back to Jamie's observations that her career had stalled. He couldn't level that accusation if she had an exhibition at the castle. But was it a coup Fraser could actually pull off? She met his gaze and managed a smile. 'It's definitely something I'd consider.'

He nodded. 'Good. Your work is so incredible. It deserves to be seen by loads more people.'

Blushing, she was saved from having to answer by the arrival of their main courses. Fraser ordered a bottle of Pouilly-Fumé, because it did not come by the glass. 'We don't have to drink it all,' he said.

Maura shook her head. Jamie was something of a wine buff and she knew Pouilly-Fumé was not the kind of wine to be left unfinished. 'You might have to roll me home but we're definitely drinking it all.'

Fraser laughed. 'Maybe we'll get you a cab.'

The scallops in Maura's main course were as exquisite as those in Fraser's starter, although she thought the chorizo enhanced their salty goodness. She savoured each mouthful, marvelling at how well they paired with the crisp dryness of the wine he had chosen. He offered her a taste of his lemon sole and that was delicious too, the white flakes melting into the beurre blanc sauce. He made her laugh with tales of his golf-mad father, and she countered with stories of her mother's obsession with uncovering the identity of the mystery yarn bombers. It wasn't until they had almost finished eating that Maura saw Fraser's expression shift. 'I think that's Jamie, isn't it?'

She followed his gaze to the entrance of the dining room and her good humour evaporated. It was Jamie, and she knew in an instant that he was drunk. The signs weren't obvious – a casual observer would have no idea – but there was a looseness about the way his arms hung by his side, a barely perceptible sway as he glanced around the room until he found her. He wasn't unsteady but she knew with cold certainty the reason he was so unforgivably late. 'Oh god.'

Fraser's eyes immediately returned to her. 'What's wrong?'

She ran a hand over her face and tried not to watch as the waiter led Jamie towards them. 'He's been drinking.'

Fraser smiled. 'That's okay. So have we. He can help us finish the wine.'

The smile she summoned up felt brittle. 'You don't understand. He can be a bit—'

And then Jamie was beside them, with the waiter hovering nearby, as though asking the unspoken question about whether they knew this man. 'Maura,' Jamie said, and bent down to kiss her. 'I'm so sorry. It was Richard's leaving drinks – I only meant to stay for one.'

A waft of fumes washed over Maura as she turned her cheek to divert the kiss. She detected hops and the sour scent of whisky. 'It's almost nine o'clock. You've missed the meal.'

Jamie looked down at the plates. 'Shit. Sorry.'

Fraser stood up and held out a hand. 'It's no bother. I'm Fraser Bell. Nice to meet you at last.'

For one awful moment, Maura thought Jamie would ignore him. Behind Jamie, the waiter also seemed to be holding his breath, although his face was implacable. But after several long seconds, Jamie took Fraser's hand. 'Good to meet you too. Maura's told me all about you.'

Fraser smiled. 'Will you have a seat? Join us for a glass of something?'

Jamie nodded. The waiter pulled back the chair and he sank into it, slumping against the back in a way that made Maura want to groan. 'Whisky, on the rocks. Make it a large one.'

'Thanks, that's all for now,' Fraser said, when the waiter turned a politely frozen look his way.

Once he'd gone, Jamie eyed the empty seat beside Fraser with a frown. 'Maura says you've got a girlfriend. Where is she?'

A sudden spike of anxiety stabbed through Maura. Most of the time, Jamie was an amiable drunk, but whisky sometimes brought out the meaner side of his personality. He'd never been the jealous type but she suddenly didn't want him to know that Fraser and Naomi were no longer together. Her eyes met Fraser's and she gave the faintest shake of her head, hoping he would get the message.

'At home with the flu,' Fraser said smoothly. 'She's spent most of the day asleep, poor thing.'

Jamie raised his eyebrows. 'And she doesn't mind that you're out wining and dining another woman? She sounds like a rare breed.'

'Jamie!' Maura objected, her face flushing as the couple at the neighbouring table turned to look. 'How many times do I have to remind you that this is a business meeting?'

His gaze came to rest on the bottle of wine. 'Looks like one.'

The waiter placed a tumbler of whisky on the table in front of Jamie, who snatched it up and took a large swig. 'Good stuff,' he said, baring his teeth. 'I'll have another.'

The waiter glanced at Fraser, who nodded. Maura felt her mortification rising. Other diners were glancing their way now and leaning towards each other to whisper.

'We were about to get the bill, actually.'

Jamie studied the plate in front of her. 'You haven't even finished your main course. You wanted me to come and support you, now stop being such a killjoy and eat your food.'

Out of the corner of her eye, she saw Fraser's expression harden. She picked up her cutlery and began to eat what remained of her now cold scallops. Thankfully, he took his cue from her and did the same with his fish. With a bit of luck, if they forewent dessert and coffee, they could leave before Jamie embarrassed her any further.

'I hear you used to be an actor,' Jamie said, after another gulp of whisky. 'Have you been in anything I would have seen?'

Fraser reached for his wine glass. 'No.'

'Nothing?' Jamie said. 'That explains why you're making a living peddling ghost stories to tourists.'

'Jamie,' Maura snapped.

'It's okay,' Fraser said with a bland smile. 'In fact, it's not a million miles from the truth. I fell out of love with the job, and it's not something you can do if your heart's not in it.'

Maura wasn't sure Jamie would understand what he meant – he was good at his job but she didn't think he loved it. For him, work was something he did to enable him to do the things he did love, like play rugby. But she also knew he viewed it as a way of establishing status. To Jamie, acting was a high-status career. Running a walking tour business was not, and the lazy smile he aimed Fraser's way told Maura that was exactly what he was thinking. 'Each to their own, I suppose,' he said, and drained his glass.

Forcing herself to swallow the last bite of scallop, Maura laid her cutlery upon her plate. 'That was delicious,' she told Fraser. 'Thank you.'

'You'll have to get yourself to Orkney sometime – taste them fresh from the sea,' he said. 'A friend of mine was filming up there a few years ago and he couldn't get enough of them.'

'I'll add it to my list,' Maura said.

A brief silence fell, during which she saw Jamie watching Fraser through narrowed eyes. 'How were the leaving drinks?' she asked, to head off any danger of another insulting insinuation. 'I'm not sure I know Richard.'

Jamie shrugged. 'He works in the compliance team. He's moving to the New York office, lucky sod.' He brightened as the waiter reappeared with his drink. 'I'll say one thing for this place; the service is fast.'

The briefest flicker of a smile crossed the waiter's face.

'Thank you, sir.' He turned to Fraser. 'Would you like to see the dessert menu?'

'No, thank you,' Fraser said, after a quick glance at Maura. 'Just the bill, when you're ready.'

Jamie huffed out a breath. 'Why do I feel like I've gate-crashed a private party?' His voice was too loud and once again, heads turned their way.

'You were invited,' Maura said pointedly. 'You just arrived too late to join in.'

He rolled his eyes. 'I said I was sorry. I couldn't get away.'

Maura pressed her lips together, determined not to be drawn.

Fraser cleared his throat. 'If you'll excuse me, I'll just be a minute.' Flashing Maura a sympathetic smile, he edged around the table and was gone.

Jamie leaned back in his chair. 'I hope you got your money's worth.' The words were slurred now, and he'd abandoned any attempt to keep the volume down.

Briefly, she closed her eyes. 'It was a very nice meal.'

He glanced around. 'The tour business must be doing all right if he can afford to bring you here. Shame his girlfriend couldn't make it. Or do you think he wanted you all to himself?'

'He would hardly have invited you, in that case.'

'No, I suppose not,' he rumbled. 'I'm not sure I trust him, though.'

'Mmmm,' Maura said vaguely, wishing the waiter would hurry up with the bill. The sooner it was paid, the sooner she could get Jamie outside – hopefully before they were politely asked to leave. But the bill did not appear and suddenly Fraser was back.

'I've taken the liberty of ordering you a cab,' he said. 'I hope you don't mind.'

Maura stared at him in consternation. 'But the bill—'

'All taken care of,' he said in a low voice. 'I settled up just now.'

She wanted to hug him. Instead, she offered him a grateful smile. 'Thank you.'

'No problem. We can all head out together, and then I'll jump on the tram back to Leith.'

Jamie looked up from his drink. 'What's this? The party's over already?'

Maura nodded. 'Time to go home.'

She half-expected him to argue but the sight of Fraser pulling on his jacket seemed to satisfy him that it was indeed time to go. Draining the rest of his drink, he stood up and swayed alarmingly. Maura clutched at his arm to steady him, as the couple at the table next to him leaned back. 'Let's go,' she said firmly.

It was a minor miracle that they reached the street without knocking into any tables or stumbling up the stairs. Out on Castlehill, night had fallen and the air was chilly. Maura wrapped her coat around herself as she peered along the street in search of the cab. Fraser caught the gesture. 'The maître d' said it was on its way.'

She nodded, watching Jamie carefully. The fresh air seemed to have hit him hard; he was much more unsteady than he had been inside the restaurant. She hoped he would straighten up when the taxi arrived. City centre cabbies were distinctly no-nonsense when it came to drunk passengers.

Fraser had also noticed Jamie's sudden deterioration. 'Are you going to be okay getting him home on your own?'

She puffed out her cheeks. 'As long as he can manage the stairs.'

A car drew slowly alongside them, the driver peering out at them. 'Cab for Fraser Bell?'

'That's us,' Fraser said, opening one of the rear doors. 'Hop in, Jamie.'

Maura tugged on his arm. 'Jamie. The taxi's here. Get in.'

He took two unsteady steps towards the car. The driver eyed him doubtfully. 'Is he fit to travel? It's a hundred quid if he throws up.'

'He'll be fine on the journey,' Maura said, guiding Jamie towards the open door. 'Getting him out at the other end might be trickier.'

The driver's eyebrows shot up. 'I cannae help with that, pal. I've got a bad back.'

Fraser shook his head. 'That settles it,' he said, as Maura slid onto the back seat beside Jamie. 'I'm coming with you.'

'You don't need to do that,' Maura objected, but it was too late. Fraser had opened the front passenger door and was climbing into the seat. 'Thistledown Lane in Dean Village.'

Muttering under his breath, the cabbie turned the car around and set off. The journey was not the most direct route but, late in the evening, it was mercifully quick. Once they had pulled up outside the flat, Fraser paid the driver and they set about easing Jamie out of the back seat. 'You keep him upright, I'll open the front door,' Maura panted to Fraser as the cab's tail-lights receded into the night.

Somehow, between them, they got him up the stairs. He staggered the few remaining steps to the living room and crashed down upon the sofa. A few seconds later, he began to snore. Maura stared at him, painfully aware of Fraser beside her, unsure whether to laugh or cry.

'Well,' he said, after a moment had passed. 'This wasn't how I expected the evening to finish. I had my eye on the sticky toffee pudding.'

It was enough to break Maura's fragile self-control. She let out a snort of laughter, which turned into a sob, and tears were tumbling down her cheeks before she could stop them. 'Hey,' Fraser said, frowning in concern. 'It's okay. No need for that.'

'I'm just so bloody embarrassed,' she said, between hiccups. 'What must you think of me?'

He watched her for a moment, then turned her gently to face him. 'I think the same as I always have. Your drunken lump of a boyfriend hasn't changed that.'

Misery flooded through her. He couldn't mean it. 'No, but—'

'I mean it,' he said. 'I have some doubts about your taste in men, but my basic opinion of you is the same as ever. You're a clever, generous, talented woman and I consider myself lucky to know and work with you.'

She sniffed and wiped her nose hurriedly, in case a snot bubble materialised to make her ruination complete. 'I'm sorry.'

Fraser smiled. 'You have nothing to apologise for. And I know it doesn't feel like it now, but one day, we'll look back on this and laugh.'

Jamie chose that moment to let out a particularly toe-curling snore.

Maura shook her head. 'I doubt that. But thank you for helping me get him home. And I'm sorry he was so ... well, so drunk.'

'Stop apologising,' Fraser said. 'It was the least I could do.

But I am going to get out of your way now. Is there anything you need before I go?'

She sighed. 'A memory-wiping device so I never have to think of tonight again?'

'Can't help with that,' Fraser said. 'And it wasn't all bad. We had a pretty good evening until Mr Whisky Pants here showed up.'

The sheer ridiculousness of the name coaxed a reluctant smile from Maura. 'We did. Thank you, for the meal and for everything you're doing to make the ghosts a success.'

He nodded. 'Like I said, it's no bother. I'll message you in the morning to check in.'

She followed him down the stairs and watched as he opened the door to step out into the night. 'Thanks, Fraser. I owe you one.'

'Don't be daft,' he said, and reached up to brush a stray curl from her forehead. 'That's what friends are for.'

The brush of his fingers only lasted a second but it felt to Maura as though her skin had been set alight, reminding her of another starlit night outside a different door. If she took a step towards Fraser, would he reciprocate? If she laid a hand on his arm, would his fingers wrap around hers? And if she closed her eyes and tipped her face to his, would he kiss her the way he had on that other velvet night? All of these thoughts spun through her mind in less time than it took for her to blink.

Above them, the stars held their breath. In the distance, the Water of Leith sang a love song as it burbled over its stony bed. Maura's heartbeat sped up and slowed, and it seemed, just for that moment, that she and Fraser were nineteen again, with their lives unravelled into glittering strands, waiting to be woven anew.

And then a car horn blared somewhere nearby, and reality reasserted itself with abrupt and painful force. They were not teenagers – what was done was done and she had no right to dream about kissing anyone except Jamie.

Afraid that Fraser might somehow divine her scandalous thoughts, Maura took a hurried step backwards and gripped the doorframe to anchor herself to the here and now. Squashing down an ache of regret, she took refuge in what she hoped was a friendly but business-like smile.

'Goodnight, Fraser,' she said, before her treacherous emotions could give her away, and closed the door.

PART THREE

PROLOGUE

'Settle down, 8B. Open your copy of *A Midsummer Night's Dream*, please.'

There was the usual murmur of conversation as the class did what their teacher demanded, the occasional groan that they were reading Shakespeare again.

'Can't we do something more interesting, sir?' Josh called out. He was instantly quelled by Mr Lacey's raised eyebrows.

'You can contemplate that in detention if you'd prefer, Joshua,' he said. 'Shall I add your name to the list?'

'No, sir,' Josh mumbled.

Maura didn't mind Shakespeare. She liked the way his characters spoke, the complex rhythms of the lines, even though she was hopeless at delivering them herself. She much preferred to listen to her classmates, who usually stumbled over the language just as she did but still couldn't erase the beauty of the words. And of course, Mr Lacey always called on Fraser Bell to read. Maura was sure he could make Shakespeare's shopping list sound like a sonnet if he tried.

'Let's see, where did we get to?' Mr Lacey muttered. 'Ah yes, act one, scene one – Athens. Josh, perhaps you'd like to read Egeus.'

'No,' Josh growled, too low for the teacher to hear but loud enough for those near him.

'Bethany, could you read Theseus? Kyle, please read Demetrius,' Mr Lacey went on, scanning the sea of heads for another victim. 'Fraser, you take Lysander, and Maura, you can be Hermia. Start at line twenty-three, *Enter Egeus, Hermia, Lysander and Demetrius*. That's your line, Josh.'

Maura didn't hear; she was too busy trying to control her suddenly flaming cheeks. She couldn't say the lines. What was the stupid teacher thinking? He never chose her. Never.

'Happy be Theseus, our renowned duke,' Josh said in a flat monotone.

'Thanks, good Egeus,' Bethany read, her voice perky. 'What's the news with thee?'

There was a heavy pause as Josh took in the length of the monologue he had to deliver next. 'Sir, there's like a hundred lines.'

'Just take them one at a time, Josh. You can do this.'

With a resentful glower, Josh stammered his way through. Bethany had a much smaller speech, and then Maura saw with horror that it was her line next. 'So – so is Lysander,' she managed. Her eyes fixed on the next chunk of Hermia's dialogue, which was at least ten lines. *Oh god*, she thought weakly as she listened to Josh and Bethany, *please let the fire alarm go off before I have to do this.*

But there was no divine intervention. Somehow, she stumbled through the words, sweat prickling her scalp. The others delivered their lines. And then Fraser was speaking, and it was as though all the awkwardness in the room was blotted out by his smoothness. The whispering behind hands stopped. Everyone watched him as he brought the words to life.

Maura was so transfixed that she forgot she was meant to be responding, until Mr Lacey reminded her. Flustered, she glanced down. The text swam before her eyes.

'Deliver your line again, Lysander,' the teacher told Fraser.

'How now, my love! Why is your cheek so pale?' he said, glancing over at Maura. 'How chance the roses there do fade so fast?'

She gulped in a breath, willed her heart to stop thumping in her chest. 'Belike for want of rain, which I could well be – beteem them from the tempest of my eyes.'

Fraser smiled encouragingly and kept his gaze fixed on hers. 'Ay me! For aught that I could ever read, could ever hear by tale or history, the course of true love never did run smooth.'

As the bell rang to save her from further humiliation, Maura understood two things. Firstly, that there was no one in the world who could say those words more perfectly than Fraser Bell. And secondly, she was utterly unworthy of being Hermia to his Lysander.

As her classmates slouched from the room, Maura hung back, hoping no one would notice her and take the mickey out of her terrible reading. But Fraser had stopped to speak to Mr Lacey – he was one of the last to leave too. 'Nice reading, Mary,' he said casually as she trailed reluctantly after him.

For a second, her brain froze. 'It's Maura, actually,' she managed. 'And you were good too.'

But she was too late – the moment had passed. Fraser was gone and she didn't think he'd even heard.

CHAPTER FOURTEEN

Twenty-Two Years Later

The last time Fraser Bell visited Craigmillar Castle, he'd been imprisoned for treason.

'Jacobite Prisoner #4' had been a blink-and-you'll-miss-it performance in the television series *Outlander*, although he'd enjoyed declaring one of the English soldiers 'a stinking stream o' pish'. The scenes at the fictional Ardsmuir Prison had taken several weeks to film, and he'd got to know the towering ruins of Edinburgh's other castle well; the pair of gnarled yew trees at the entrance of the courtyard had been a favourite spot to eat his lunch, when the area wasn't off-limits.

The atmosphere was very different today – no one had brandished an antiquated pistol in his direction, for a start, or called him Highlander scum. The lush lawns surrounding the ancient battlements were filled with large, open-sided marquees, and pastel-coloured bunting fluttered against the cornflower blue June sky. Banners announced that this was ScotPot, one of the biggest ceramics shows in Scotland, while visitors queued to pose for photographs between oversized sculpted letters spelling out SCOT and POT on either side of the iconic arched entrance. And somewhere inside the mêlée of tents and artists and eager pottery afficionados was Maura McKenzie, hopefully doing a roaring trade.

Fraser glanced at his parents. 'What shall we do first? Take a wander or grab a coffee?'

Roberta Bell pursed her lips. 'Let's get our bearings.' She held up the map they'd been given as they passed through the ticket booths. 'It says here your friend is in the Bothwell tent.'

There were eight marquees in total, each named after a Scottish family with links to the castle and surrounding area, as well as several food and drink areas with tables and chairs, although picnics were allowed. The idea was clearly to make sure the ScotPot punters had no reason to leave.

'Toilets first,' Micky Bell said, in a tone that brooked no argument. 'I hope they've laid on proper ones. The kind that flush.'

Fraser glanced at the crowd ambling past. It was a Friday morning, which he supposed might have some effect, but there was a definite skew towards middle age and older. There would be posh portable cabins with sinks and running water, he guessed, and plenty of them. ScotPot had been going for well over a decade and knew its audience – the organisers were unlikely to persuade people to stay all day if they had to take their chances in the kind of chemical loos found at music festivals. 'The castle toilets are here,' he said, pointing to the visitor centre on the map. 'But it looks like there are temporary ones in the east and west gardens.'

His father jiggled from one foot to the other like a toddler. 'Whichever is nearest.'

'The visitor centre, then,' Roberta said. 'Don't get distracted by the gift shop on the way back. We're here for the pottery, not the overpriced whisky and fudge.'

Looking faintly mutinous, Micky vanished wordlessly into the crowd, leaving Fraser and his mother to watch the tide of ceramics enthusiasts flow around them. 'I must say, I'm excited to meet Maura and see her work,' Roberta said. 'Does she know we're coming?'

Fraser nodded. It hadn't felt fair to spring the meeting on her unannounced. 'I said we'd pop in. We might need to pick our moment, though. She said something about offering demonstrations here and there throughout the day.'

'What a treat,' Roberta exclaimed. 'It'll be just like that television show, the one with the man who cries when he sees what the contestants have made.'

He raised his eyebrows. 'I didn't realise you were such a pottery lover.'

'I wasn't. Not until you told us Maura was making the ghosts to go with the stories on your walking tour,' she said. 'I watched an episode out of curiosity and, before I knew it, I'd binge-watched a whole series.'

'Maybe you should join a class,' he suggested, thinking back to the lesson Maura had given him a few months earlier, when she'd helped him to craft a ghost of his own, although it had been uneven and lumpish compared to hers. 'It's very therapeutic.'

'I expect it takes a long time to master,' his mother said practically. 'I'll stick to knitting. I know where I am with jumpers and scarves.'

She certainly did. Fraser still had the scarf she'd knitted for him to take to drama school in London, although it had been a newly adopted hobby back then. It seemed to Fraser that there was nothing she couldn't knit. 'Maybe something to keep in mind if you fancy a change.'

'Speaking of change, how's the new storyteller?' she asked. 'Settling in?'

She meant Rebecca, who had recently joined Dead Famous as a third tour guide. 'I think so,' Fraser said. 'She used to work on one of York's ghost walks so she's got plenty of experience, but she's spending a couple of weeks shadowing me and Tom while she learns the ropes here.'

His mother looked at him. 'I hope that means you won't have to work quite so hard.'

That was part of Fraser's overall plan but it wasn't why he'd expanded the Dead Famous team. 'I wanted another storyteller to try to meet demand,' he explained, 'especially now the tourist season is in full swing. I hate turning people away.'

'Yes, but all work and no play is a recipe for disaster,' she pointed out. 'And it's already cost you one relationship.'

Fraser tried not to grimace. There had been a number of factors involved in his break-up with Naomi and he couldn't deny that his change of career from actor to tour guide had been one of them, but perhaps not for the reasons his mum imagined. 'I'm fine. No need to worry.'

She sniffed. 'I'm your mother; it's my job to worry.'

'I know,' he said, smiling. 'But I'm enjoying the work, even if things are a bit hectic. At least it's keeping me out of trouble.'

'Hmmm,' she said, but thankfully the reappearance of Micky pre-empted whatever else she'd been about to say. She raised her arm to wave. 'Micky Bell – over here!'

'There was no need for the windmill impression,' he grumbled when he reached them. 'I knew exactly where I left you.'

Roberta rolled her eyes. 'This, from a man who got lost on a golf course last week.'

'I was hardly lost,' Micky protested.

Fraser hid a smile as his mother sighed.

'Did you, or did you not, take a wrong turn and complete hole fifteen before hole three?' she demanded.

'That could happen to anyone,' he said, waving an airy hand. 'Even the club secretary agreed.'

Roberta flashed Fraser a knowing look. 'So you say.'

'Shall we take a look around?' he cut in, before his father could launch into a more spirited defence and insist upon calling the club secretary as a witness. 'I could really do with a coffee.'

'Good idea,' Roberta said. 'We'll let you lead the way, won't we, Micky?'

Ten minutes later, Fraser was sipping a piping hot Americano from a cardboard cup and felt much better equipped to deal with both his parents and the crowds. There was a puzzling lack of signage to identify which tent was which, lending a slightly chaotic air to the flow of traffic. Fraser wondered whether it was to encourage visitors to browse, rather than make a beeline for their favourite potters. Whatever the intention, it meant he and his parents passed through three marquees before they found Maura. Her stand was made up of white shelves loaded with bowls, pots and plates, a few of which Fraser thought he recognised from her studio. A row of mugs hung from hooks suspended from a board, more delicate cups nestled on saucers, with matching plates nearby. An exquisitely hand-painted sign bore her name in iridescent blues and greens, putting Fraser in mind of waves and salty air.

Maura herself was barely visible behind a cluster of onlookers, some of whom were craning their necks for a better view. She must be demonstrating, Fraser realised as he and his parents drew nearer. Joining the back of the small group, he peered over the collection of heads to see what she was doing.

Her own head was bowed, dark hair pulled back in a messy bun as she focused on a thin sausage of clay on the table in front of her. 'You'll want to keep the coils as even as possible,' she said, expertly spreading her fingers as she worked the roll back and forth to increase its length. 'Once you're happy with the shape, add the coil to your base and start on the next. Make each one a little longer than the previous one if you're building up and out, and shorter as you come back in.'

Fraser watched her lay it on top of the base, cutting it to size and then repeating the action with the remaining snake of clay. He couldn't yet tell what the pot was destined to become – a jug, perhaps – but her mastery of her craft shone as she smoothed the layers into one with swift, assured thumb strokes. Evidently satisfied, she set about shaping another thread of clay.

'She's so fast,' a woman beside Fraser murmured. 'It takes me an age just to make decent coils, never mind build them up into something vaguely resembling a jug.'

Her friend nodded. 'You can tell she's a professional. I bet she's never made a wonky handle in her life.'

Fraser grinned, thinking back to Maura's confession about the pottery disasters hiding in her parents' loft. But the woman was right about one thing, he thought as Maura commanded the clay: she was most definitely a pro.

'How do you stop it from being too heavy?' a man at the front asked.

Maura held up a jagged-edged metal oval, no wider than the palm of her hand. 'With a serrated kidney. Once I've finished smoothing in the coils, I use this to remove the excess clay.' She pulled a wry face. 'It's best to be as brutal as you can bear, without weakening the structure.'

Other questions came and went – Maura answered them with infinite patience, even as her fingers worked the clay. Before long, she had a perfectly proportioned jug, albeit without a spout or handle. A moment later, she was wielding the serrated scraper, shearing off half the clay she'd applied with a ruthless efficiency that made Fraser wince. He'd expected some of the crowd to wander away, in particular his own father, but Micky seemed every bit as transfixed as the rest of the onlookers. Gathering the worms of discarded clay, Maura squeezed them together and reached for another kidney, this one rubbery and pliable. 'This will flatten out the ridges,' she said, working the jug with swift, curved strokes that transformed the clay into smoothness once more. She looked up with a smile. 'All I need to do now is add the spout and handle.'

'And hope it doesn't drip,' someone said, and everyone laughed.

Maura nodded. 'That too. If anyone has a foolproof method, I'm all ears.'

A few minutes later, she had crafted a spout, which she attached with practised expertise. She eyed the jug critically. 'What it needs now is a good smacking with a wooden paddle, to beat it into the right shape, but I'll spare you that and pop the handle on instead.'

It seemed she must have prepared it before Fraser and his parents arrived, because she reached for a curved strip of clay at the end of the board. The two women in front of Fraser leaned forwards, as if to get a better view. 'Handles are almost as tricky as spouts,' one murmured and the other nodded her agreement.

But of course, Maura had no issues. Once she was satisfied the handle was straight, she spun the turntable to show the finished jug to the audience, who broke into applause. 'Thank you,' Maura said, her cheeks reddening a little. 'There'll be another demonstration at three o'clock, if you missed any of this one.'

Most of the crowd began to drift away but several stopped to look at the items she had on display. Fraser's mother joined them, making a beeline for the rack of mugs. 'As if we don't have enough,' Micky complained. 'There's not enough room in the cupboard as it is.'

'You can never have too many mugs,' Roberta called over her shoulder, without turning round. 'Especially when they're as beautiful as these.'

There wasn't much his father could say to that, Fraser thought, least of all in a tent full of pottery lovers. Wisely, he kept his mouth closed. Fraser glanced across at Maura, who was chatting easily with a few members of the audience as she wrapped their purchases. Several more were waiting to pay. She needed an assistant, he thought. Someone to handle the mundane business of payment while she showcased her art. But he supposed part of the appeal of buying a Maura McKenzie original was the opportunity to talk to the artist herself. The people hovering nearby seemed happy enough to listen in as they waited their turn, at any rate.

As the crowd dispersed, he saw Maura look up and spot him. She gave a little wave and he thought she seemed pleased to see him, although that could have been due to the gratifying flow of customers. One woman appeared to want a full set of the four seasonal plant pots Fraser had admired when they'd been taking shape a few weeks earlier. 'Don't forget to come and collect them before you leave,' he heard Maura say as she stashed them safely under the cloth covering the bench.

Finally, it was Roberta's turn. She beamed at Maura like a long-lost friend, which prompted Fraser to step hurriedly forwards to introduce her. 'This is my mum. Roberta Bell, meet Maura McKenzie.'

'Hello, Roberta,' Maura said, her eyes crinkling into a warm smile. 'Although I should have guessed. He looks just like you.'

'Apart from the beard,' Fraser said gravely.

'He gets that from me,' Micky said, appearing from behind him to thrust out a hand. 'I'm Fraser's dad, Micky.'

Maura turned her radiance his way and Fraser was amused to see his father straighten his shoulders a little. 'Great to meet you,' she said. 'I hear you're quite the golfer.'

'I try,' Micky said, looking gratified.

'It keeps him out of the house, at least,' Roberta said. 'But it is so lovely to meet you at long last, Maura. Fraser has been singing your praises for months, with the ghosts and everything else you make.'

Maura's cheeks reddened slightly. 'He's very kind,' she said, and nodded at the mugs Roberta was holding. 'Would you like me to wrap those?'

'Yes, please. I can't wait to show them off when my friends come over for our weekly coffee morning.'

Fraser eyed the mugs she'd chosen. 'Aren't there matching plates to go with those?'

Roberta's eyes lit up. 'Are there? Where?'

'Here,' Maura said, stepping towards the shelves at the back of the stand.

'I'll take four,' Roberta said.

Beside him, Fraser heard the faintest of sighs from his father.

'There's a discount if you're buying the mug and plate set,' Maura said.

Roberta fired a triumphant look Micky's way. 'A bargain, then. Thank you.'

Fraser watched as Maura carefully wrapped the mugs and plates, and tucked them away for collection later. When it was time to pay, he stepped quickly forward, his card already in his hand. 'My treat, Mum. Let's call it an early birthday present.'

Roberta folded her arms. 'But it's not until September.'

'A very early present, then,' he said, smiling as he tapped the card on the reader. 'As long as you don't expect me to do the same at every stall.'

His mother enveloped him in a hug. 'You're a good lad, Fraser Bell. You'll make someone a wonderful husband one of these days. Naomi doesn't know what she's missing.'

From the corner of his eye, he saw Maura's expression soften and he wondered whether it was from pity or sympathy. He cleared his throat. 'Do you need anything, Maura? A cup of tea or a snack?'

She tapped the lid of a thermal mug on the stand. 'I've got one, thanks. Although it's probably lukewarm now.'

'Want me to bring you a fresh one?' he offered.

She shook her head, as he'd known she would. 'Don't worry.

With a bit of luck, I'll be too busy to drink it.' She paused for a moment, then her expression suddenly shifted. 'Oh, I almost forgot. Did you know there's a link between Agnes Sampson and this castle?'

He blinked. Agnes Sampson was a respected Scottish healer who had been burned as a witch after confessing to a plot against King James VI. She featured in the ghost stories Fraser told on his tour and was the inspiration for the first Edinburgh ghost Maura had created. 'Is there? She's meant to haunt the Palace of Holyroodhouse, not Craigmillar.'

'I know, but according to one of the guides I was chatting to, Agnes was accused of hiding a charmed wax image in one of the turrets here, to bring harm to the local laird's brother,' Maura said. 'Luckily for him, it didn't work.'

Fraser thought back to the historical records he'd read when he had first taken over Dead Famous. The sixteenth century witchcraft trials had begun in North Berwick and had made for grim reading, involving gruesome torture and unbearable humiliation for scores of men and women from Edinburgh and the surrounding area. Their supposed crimes seemed ridiculous to modern eyes – the summoning of contrary winds and consorting with the devil – but many had confessed, presumably to make the torture stop, and had been executed without mercy. It was not, he concluded, Scotland's finest moment.

'Not so lucky for poor Agnes,' he said, and raised an eyebrow. 'If she was truly guilty of everything they accused her of, she'd have met herself coming the other way.'

Maura offered a wry smile. 'As you'd expect from a witch.'

'Who will the next ghost be?' Roberta asked. 'Have you decided?'

'Not yet,' Fraser said. 'It's probably something we should start thinking about.'

Was it his imagination or was there a flicker of hesitation in Maura's eyes before she nodded?

'Sure.'

'It would be handy to pin it down before the storytelling night later this month,' Fraser said, thinking ahead to the prestigious event he'd been invited to at Edinburgh Castle. 'I might be able to sneak in a mention or two while I'm talking about the castle ghosts.'

Again, he caught a glimpse of something indecipherable in her expression. 'Good idea,' she said. 'Let's discuss it once the ScotPot dust has settled.'

She glanced at the crowds milling past as she spoke, and Fraser wondered if they were the reason for the slight reticence he'd detected; she was there to sell her work, after all. 'Okay. We'll stop by again before we go, to pick up the mugs Mum bought. You might be in need of a cuppa by then.'

Maura tipped her head, grimacing. 'I'll probably be in need of something stronger.'

'Just say the word,' Fraser said. 'There's a horse box decked out as a gin bar in the food area – message me and I'll bring you whatever you want.'

'I might just take you up on that,' Maura said, smiling. 'Thanks.'

A woman who had been examining the displays turned to look at Maura with an enquiring expression.

'Duty calls,' Fraser observed, even as Maura's smile became businesslike. 'We'll see you later.'

'Such a lovely girl,' Roberta said, as they joined the swell of pottery fans drifting through the tent. 'And so clever. I can see why you work well together.'

Micky nudged him. 'She's easy to look at too. I bet that helps.'

Fraser felt his stomach churn. His parents had no idea he had any history with Maura, other than attending the same school, and they couldn't know about the stirrings of attraction Fraser had fought when he'd first reconnected with her. But that was firmly in the past, along with the kiss they'd shared decades ago. He and Maura were business partners and that was all there was to it. He made a show of consulting the map. 'Shall we check out the Gilmour marquee next?'

'Excellent idea,' Roberta said. 'I think one of the potters from the TV show is in there.'

Micky held up a hand. 'I'll meet you there. That coffee's gone right through me – I need to use the facilities.'

'Again?' Roberta said.

'Yes, again,' Micky fired back. 'When you've got to go, you've got to go.'

Roberta thrust the map at him. 'You'd better take this. Not that I expect it will help.'

Snatching the paper, Micky executed an abrupt about-face and vanished into the crowd.

Roberta sighed. 'Honestly, he has a bladder the size of a thimble. It's a good thing we've got all day.'

Fraser managed a diplomatic smile. As much as he loved his parents, he was starting to wonder what he'd let himself in for.

CHAPTER FIFTEEN

The flat was quiet when Maura climbed the stairs and wearily dropped her bag onto the coffee table. When she and Jamie had first moved in together, Sunday evenings had been movie night, when they'd taken it in turns to choose a film to watch while snuggled on the sofa, and it had become one of their traditions. Over the years, other commitments had gradually crept in – an occasional football or rugby match in the pub, or a family Sunday roast – and now it felt rare for them both to be home. In fact, Maura couldn't remember the last time they'd watched anything together. Making the ghosts for Fraser meant she was in her studio more, and Jamie seemed to be spending more time at the office too.

She closed her eyes, laying a hand on the back of the sofa as guilt began to swirl. Was it terrible of her to be relieved he wasn't home this evening? She'd spent the past three days surrounded by people, chatting about pottery and answering questions, and while it had been wonderful to wallow in the enthusiasm of the ScotPot crowds, it had also been exhausting and now she wanted nothing more than a long soak in the bath and an early night. She didn't want to navigate the awkward silences and perfunctory exchanges that seemed to be all that passed for communication between them at present.

Nothing had been the same since the night Jamie had got so drunk over dinner that Maura had needed Fraser's help to get him home. It didn't matter that Jamie didn't appear to remember just how insulting he had been, nor that he'd offered an apology when she'd described his behaviour. Afterwards, the hairline cracks in their relationship had begun to widen and Maura had no idea how to fix them. But at least it wasn't a problem she had to face right now, she reminded herself. And with luck, she'd be asleep before Jamie came home.

She ran the bath as deep and hot as she dared, and sank into the steaming water with a blissful groan. The heat instantly began to soothe her aching legs and shoulders, easing the tiredness from her limbs, and she felt her forehead relax as a frown she hadn't even known she was wearing melted away. She closed her eyes, resting her head against the porcelain rim, and let the tension leach from her muscles. Jamie had never understood her inclination to linger in the water until her toes resembled prunes and the heat was gone but, for Maura, the bath was a cure-all that had never failed her yet. It was just a shame that its effects were only temporary.

After a few more moments of Radox-scented bliss, she edged her shoulders above the bubbles and reached for the hand towel she'd left folded neatly on a stool beside the bath. Beneath it lay her book – the latest historical novel by Merina Wilde, set on Orkney – and she opened it in eager anticipation of being whisked to the windswept beauty of Skara Brae. Reading was another of her tried-and-tested medicines, one that had comforted and thrilled her since childhood, but her eyelids felt heavy now and she struggled to focus on the words. She persevered for a few more minutes, then reluctantly set the book aside and instead took up her phone. If she couldn't read, perhaps her favourite podcast would do. But the chattering voices were too much, reminding her of the hubbub of conversation at ScotPot. She closed the app and sank back into the water once more. Maybe what she needed was to do nothing. With a slow breath in, and an even slower exhale, Maura let her thoughts drift.

At first, her mind rebelled. A list of jobs to do in the studio pushed its way to the fore. She stirred restlessly, her fingers twitching as though she was working a lump of clay. Clenching her hands tight, she kept them balled into fists for a moment, then relaxed, and a little more tension eased away. It had been a good weekend, she reminded herself – tiring but worthwhile. She had made a profit, which wasn't always the case, and several people had enquired about commissions. It remained to be seen whether any of those would amount to actual work but one – a restaurant owner in search of unique plates to showcase her chef's culinary brilliance – had seemed promising. Given the speed with which Fraser sold each batch of ghosts, it might be better if that was the only commission that came good. She wasn't sure she had the time or the kiln space to commit to more projects.

Fraser. Her thoughts snagged upon him, as they seemed to have done more often since the disastrous dinner at the Witchery. In the immediate aftermath of manhandling Jamie out of the taxi and up the stairs of the flat, Maura had been tempted to steal a kiss as she'd said goodnight to Fraser, and it had taken every bit of her willpower to resist. She'd awoken the next morning drowning in a hot swell of shame, hoping against hope that he hadn't noticed the split-second hesitation when she'd almost leaned in. But he'd checked in on her the next day, making sure she was okay, and he seemed the same as ever, leaving Maura to conclude that he was blissfully unaware of her momentary lapse of professionalism. And as her jumbled emotions settled, she'd begun to appreciate just how much the stress of the situation had affected her. The gratitude she'd felt towards Fraser for helping to get Jamie home had muddled her judgement, resurrecting her schoolgirl crush and creating a phantom attraction that had no more substance than the ghosts Fraser conjured up on the city streets every night. Thank goodness she hadn't ruined everything by giving in to the temptation his kindness had created. Thank goodness she could still look Fraser, and her own reflection, in the eye.

It had been lovely to see him in the crowd at ScotPot. Good to meet his parents too, even though they had been nothing like she'd imagined. Not that she had spent much time imagining them, of course, beyond wondering whether she'd ever encountered them at Parents' Evening. She'd liked them both, at any rate, and not simply because Roberta had bought two more mugs when she'd returned at the end of the day. The obvious affection between Fraser and his parents had made Maura smile, but meeting them had also allowed her a precious glimpse of who Fraser really was, beyond the talented actor and businessman she already knew.

With a wry little huff, Maura sank further into the water to drench her hair and reached for the shampoo bottle. She was beginning to suspect Fraser Bell was every bit as perfect as he had seemed at school.

*

The John Lewis store on Leith Street was not Maura's preferred lunchtime destination. If she was honest, lunch was usually a hastily thrown-together affair, eaten after her pottery students had left the studio but before she immersed herself fully in her own work, and she sometimes forgot to eat at all. But Kirsty had insisted they needed to start planning their parents' ruby wedding anniversary celebrations – still eight months away but looming on the family horizons – and Maura had put her off three times already. Apart from anything else, there was a very real danger that her sister might go rogue and book them all on a trip to Vegas if left to make the plans on her own.

Maura made her way along Princes Street as rain began to fall, causing a forest of umbrellas to bloom across the busy pavement. She navigated a cluster of wheelie cases and their owners on the corner of the North Bridge and stopped at the crossing, waiting impatiently for the lights to change. It wasn't that she was late – her phone told her she had seventeen minutes to spare – but she knew Kirsty would have arrived early at the fifth-floor café to nab a window table. Not that the view of the Firth of Forth would be particularly spectacular today, Maura thought as she glanced skyward at the heavy grey clouds – it was set to rain all afternoon – but Maura knew her sister. She would already be waiting.

The traffic slowed, allowing the pedestrians to cross the road. Maura picked her way through the milling tourists to Leith Street. As she approached the gleaming glass doors of the department store, she lowered her umbrella and shook the raindrops away. Head down, she slowed to wrestle with the mechanism, completely failing to notice the woman hurrying along the pavement, engrossed in her phone. They crashed into one another, each uttering a startled exclamation as they looked up. Maura had a jumbled impression of wide blue eyes and sleek blonde hair, then recognition dawned. 'Zoe!'

But instead of returning her surprised smile, the colour drained from her friend's cheeks. 'Maura. I—'

Her obvious consternation caused Maura to blink. 'Are you okay?'

Zoe's muscles moved, as though she was trying to smile. 'Yes. I'm just—' Her gaze skittered away. 'Sorry, I have to go.'

Ducking her head, she edged past and hastened along the rain-drenched flagstones, leaving Maura to stare after her in open-mouthed bewilderment.

'Wait!' she called, but Zoe showed no sign of having heard. A few moments later, she was gone, lost among the other pedestrians. 'Weird,' Maura muttered, turning to the shop doors once more. It was true that she hadn't spoken to Zoe much in recent weeks but she had assumed her friend was simply busy, much like she was. Now she wondered whether there was something more serious going on.

'Probably,' Kirsty said, when Maura had found her at the window table on the fifth floor and taken the empty seat opposite her. 'People are often fighting battles the rest of us don't know about. Maybe she was just surprised to see you.'

Maura toyed with the menu, replaying the encounter in her mind. 'No, it was more than that. She looked almost horrified.'

Her sister's gaze flickered upwards to her hair, which Maura knew was damp and frizzy from the rain. 'Well—'

'It wasn't my hair,' she said, raising her hand to her head in spite of herself. 'She barely even looked at me.'

Kirsty frowned. 'And you're sure you haven't inadvertently upset her in some way?'

'I don't see how,' Maura replied, after a moment's thought. 'I haven't seen her for weeks.'

'Then it's not you,' Kirsty said, shrugging. 'Maybe she's got work trouble. Or relationship problems.'

Either was possible, Maura thought. Hadn't Zoe hinted more than once that she was frustrated with Liam? 'I suppose I could ask Jamie,' she said slowly. 'If there's something going on, he might have heard about it.'

Kirsty raised her eyebrows. 'The rugby club jungle drums. But wouldn't he have mentioned it already? He knows Zoe is your friend.'

'He's been busy,' Maura said, not quite able to meet her sister's eyes. 'We both have.'

'I'm sure it's nothing,' Kirsty said, her tone pragmatic as she lifted the menu to study it. 'Why don't you drop her a message later to check in?'

Maura bit her lip. Whatever had caused Zoe's strange reaction was unlikely to be nothing, but that didn't mean it had anything to do with Maura herself. 'Good idea,' she conceded at length. 'Thanks.'

'I'm full of good ideas,' Kirsty said airily, and leaned back in her chair. 'Now, about Mum and Dad's anniversary. How do you feel about a Caribbean cruise?'

'Have you seen much of Zoe recently?'

Jamie looked up from the paperwork he'd been glued to since arriving home from work. 'Zoe?'

On the other side of the sofa, Maura nodded. 'Liam's girlfriend.'

'I know who she is,' Jamie replied, the beginning of a frown etching twin lines between his eyes. 'I'm just not sure why you're asking if I've seen her.'

'At the rugby club,' Maura said. 'I wondered whether she's been there lately.'

He shuffled the papers, selecting a new one from the pile and turning his gaze downwards again. 'I can't say I've noticed. Why?'

Maura shifted uneasily. 'I ran into her outside John Lewis on Tuesday, when I was having lunch with Kirsty. She seemed a bit off, so I sent her a text and she hasn't replied.' She waited but he didn't acknowledge her words. 'I'm a bit worried something's wrong.'

'No idea,' Jamie said, his tone preoccupied. 'Sorry.'

'How about Liam?' she persisted, because she knew he'd played at the weekend. 'Does he seem okay?'

A short huff escaped Jamie's lips. 'Again, no idea. I'm not the club's therapist, Maura. They don't confide in me when they have problems.'

The flatness behind his words made Maura pause. 'No, of course not,' she said, after a moment. 'I thought maybe you might have heard something, if he and Zoe weren't getting along or – or . . .' She trailed off, discouraged by the disengaged set of his shoulders. 'Look, it doesn't matter. Maybe I'll come to the club on Friday evening. See if I can catch Zoe for a chat.'

That did get Jamie's attention and this time his frown was full. 'You haven't done that for months.'

It wouldn't help to explain the reason for her absence, Maura thought – that she'd grown tired of watching Jamie get drunk with his teammates. 'All the more reason to come along,' she said, trying to sound jolly. 'They'll have forgotten I exist.'

'Hardly.'

There was something in his voice, a spark of irritation so fleeting that she wondered whether she'd imagined it. 'You don't mind, do you?'

Running a weary hand over his forehead, Jamie sighed. 'Obviously I don't mind. But I do need to make notes on this report before my meeting tomorrow morning.' He glanced up at her, a perfunctory smile flicking on and off. 'So if you're finished?'

It was the kind of dismissal she imagined he might use at work, to bat away an annoying colleague. Maura took a breath in, let it out, and smoothed the hurt away. 'I understand,' she said, getting to her feet. 'I'll go and put the kettle on.'

Jamie cocked his head. 'Not for me, thanks. But there's a decent Malbec I opened last night. I wouldn't say no to a glass of that.'

She nodded, knowing he hadn't left much more than that in the bottle. 'Sure. I'll bring it in.'

He didn't reply, his focus back on the papers in his hand.

Swallowing her misgivings, Maura set off for the kitchen.

The clubhouse hadn't changed much since Maura's last visit, although there were no birthday decorations in evidence this time. The crowd was smaller too, but she still saw the same familiar faces. Despite Jamie's initial diffidence at the suggestion she might join him for Friday evening drinks, she was greeted enthusiastically by the rest of his team. 'We thought you'd come to your senses and left the bugger,' Andy said, slapping Jamie cheerfully on the shoulder.

'Just busy with work,' Maura replied, smiling.

'Oh aye?' Andy said, looking interested. 'Are you still doing the pots?'

She nodded. 'That's right.'

'Maybe we'll see you on the telly one of these days,' he said with a wink.

'Maybe,' Maura said, smiling.

Jamie did not smile. 'I'm going to the bar,' he said, glancing at her. 'What do you want?'

'A Coke, please,' she replied. The rugby club was within walking distance of home so she hadn't needed to drive but she had a kiln full of ghosts to unload in the morning and she did not need a hangover to get in her way.

Jamie turned an enquiring gaze on Andy. 'Guinness?'

'You read my mind,' Andy replied. 'I'll come with you.'

Maura took advantage of their departure to seek out Zoe. She was not seated on the banquettes that lined the back wall, nor was she among the clusters of other wives and girlfriends gathered at the mismatched tables and chairs dotted around the room. There was no sign of her at the bar, although it was possible she was hidden by any one of several burly rugby players. Perhaps she and Liam hadn't arrived yet, Maura mused, scanning the room to see if there was anyone who might be able to shed some light on Zoe's odd behaviour. Georgie was a possibility – she'd seen the two of them chatting on a number of occasions and her husband was a Warriors old boy who might well be in the loop if the problem was Liam. But Maura could see Georgie was in the middle of a group, deep in conversation. Perhaps she'd be able to catch her on her own later, have a discreet word.

'Here's your Coke,' Andy said, offering her a pint glass bobbing with ice cubes and lemon.

A little miffed that Jamie hadn't brought it to her himself, Maura glanced towards the bar again to see him laughing with a few of the other rugby club stalwarts. She dredged up a smile for Andy. 'Thanks.'

Nodding, he was about to move away when Maura spoke again.

'No Liam this evening?'

He took a swig of Guinness. 'I'd be surprised.'

Maura raised her eyebrows. 'Oh? Why's that?'

Andy leaned closer. 'Rumour has it he's nursing a broken heart. The lovely Zoe dumped him.' He paused. 'Or maybe he dumped her, but I can't see that happening. He was always punching above with her if you ask me.'

That certainly explained Zoe's reluctance to speak to her, Maura thought, taking a sip from her own glass. But the fact that Andy knew suggested it was common knowledge, which begged the question, why hadn't Jamie heard the rumours? 'Are you sure?'

Andy waved a hand. 'He's not here, is he? First time I've known him to miss a Friday night social in years.'

'He might be ill,' Maura suggested.

'Except that he's confirmed to play in the match tomorrow,' Andy said. 'Nope, I reckon he's sat at home, feeling sorry for himself.'

With some justification if he and Zoe really had broken up, she thought but didn't say. 'Do you know if anyone has checked on him?'

'Malky messaged him, to make sure he was okay to play tomorrow.'

Not the most caring of approaches but better than nothing, Maura supposed. 'And Zoe?'

Andy shrugged. 'She's definitely not playing tomorrow.'

'I should hope not,' she said ruefully. 'Thanks, Andy. I hope Liam isn't too heartbroken.'

He took a long draught of his pint and smacked his lips. 'We'll take him under our wing, don't you fret.'

And they would, she knew. There was a real sense of community among the players, a camaraderie that meant they looked out for each other. Maura could only hope that Zoe had good friends of her own to support her, because it didn't seem she wanted anything from Maura. Perhaps she thought her loyalties would lie with Liam and the rugby club. Or perhaps she wanted a clean break, and that meant sacrificing Maura's friendship.

It seemed Kirsty had been right, which was annoying and reassuring in equal measure – whatever the reason for Zoe's odd behaviour outside the department store, and her subsequent silence, it had nothing to do with Maura.

CHAPTER SIXTEEN

There were any number of famous castles in the world – Neuschwanstein Castle in Germany with its fairy tale turrets, the gloriously Moorish Alhambra in Spain, or imposing Prague Castle overlooking the equally well-known Charles Bridge – but Fraser had always felt Edinburgh Castle to be the granddame of them all. It was not the oldest, although the rocky volcanic outcrop it occupied surely had a claim, but it was the most striking, especially when dressed in resplendent golden light and silhouetted against a dusky pink and blue twilight sky. If he'd been in charge of the set for that evening's ghostly storytelling press preview, he would have arranged a blood-red sunset, but the castle still looked suitably atmospheric as he strode up Castlehill. And if the rehearsal he'd attended was anything to go by, it was going to be an evening to remember, for Fraser and for the foolhardy journalists who were brave enough to attend.

He paused at the gatehouse, rummaging in his pocket for his pass and glancing down to make sure his kilt was straight. The Bell family tartan was the Bell of the Borders – light blue criss-crossed by a multitude of black, red and yellow stripes – but he'd felt the colours were too cheery for the evening's gore and instead, he'd opted for the more sombre darker blue and green of his grandfather's Murray clan. He'd broken with tradition in other ways, too; it might be summer in Edinburgh but he wasn't risking a chilly behind in the draughty castle vaults.

'Back again?' Callum said from behind the ticket booth window when Fraser showed his pass.

'No rest for the wicked,' Fraser replied. 'Especially not tonight.'

'I know.' Callum gave a delighted shiver. 'I'm off-duty soon and coming along to get scared half to death.'

Fraser smiled. There'd been a ballot among the staff to join the press evening – clearly Callum had been one of the lucky ones. 'I'll do my best.' His gaze travelled to the papers on the desk in front of Callum. 'Could you check my business partner is on the list, please? Her name is Maura McKenzie.'

'Absolutely,' Callum said as his finger trailed down the list. 'Here she is. Does she tell ghost stories too?'

'She's a ghost maker,' Fraser said, then saw the look of slight alarm on the other man's face. 'Small ones, from clay. She's a potter, not a serial killer.'

Understanding dawned on Callum's features. 'In Edinburgh, anything is possible. Just ask Ian Rankin.'

Rankin was perhaps the city's most prolific novelist, having written a plethora of books featuring his curmudgeonly detective, Rebus. Fraser had played the role of Thug #2 in the television adaptation of one of the books. It had indeed featured a serial killer who was stalking Edinburgh's shadows.

'Thanks for checking Maura's on the list,' he said to Callum. 'I guess I'll see you later, in the vaults.'

'Looking forward to it,' Callum said. 'Ewan is waiting for you in the Great Hall. I'm sure you know the way by now.'

'I do,' Fraser confirmed, and set off along the cobbles. For his own ghost tours around the city, Fraser did not wear a costume, but he'd contemplated adding a heavy black cloak for the castle event. In the end, though, he'd decided against it. The cloak was long, reaching almost to the floor, and a stumble on one of the unforgiving stone staircases might result in him becoming one of the castle's ghosts. With luck, the sight of his knees protruding from the tartan of his kilt would be just as terrifying as the cloak.

'You're looking splendidly Scottish,' Ewan McRae said as he greeted Fraser at the entrance of the Great Hall and took in his traditional garb. 'Ready to wow the esteemed members of the press?'

'Absolutely,' Fraser replied, glancing sideways at Catriona, who would be accompanying him around the castle, making sure he followed the agreed route and stuck to the schedule. She had gone for a dramatic black cloak, he observed, but had sensibly chosen one that posed no threat of tripping her up, and held an old-fashioned lantern on a pole.

'They'll congregate here for pre-tour drinks and canapés at seven o'clock,' Catriona said. 'The tour is due to start at seven forty-five and we'll return here afterwards for a short reception.'

'Where I'm sure you'll be roundly congratulated and lauded,' Ewan added. 'Doors close at ten, but of course you're free to leave once your storytelling duties are complete.'

Fraser nodded. He had no intention of passing up the opportunity to mingle with people who could help publicise Dead Famous, even if he wasn't representing the company that evening. And besides, Maura would be there. He wanted to introduce her to as many people as he could. 'Do you want me there for the pre-tour drinks? Or would you rather I made a grand entrance?'

Ewan gave a shrug. 'Up to you. For the public tour, we'll keep you out of sight, but this evening is more relaxed. It might be nice to mingle, if you're up for that?'

It was exactly what Fraser had been hoping for. 'Very much so.'

'Great,' Ewan said, rubbing his hands together. 'I'll leave you in Catriona's capable hands for now. See you here at seven.' With a final nod that encompassed them both, he strode across the room.

Catriona smiled at Fraser. 'I thought you might like some-where quiet to sit,' she said, ushering him towards a door that he knew led to a vaulted stone corridor. 'Can I get you a drink?'

He tapped a pocket. 'I've got some water, thanks. But it would be great to drop my coat off and run through the order one last time.'

She showed him to a small room, richly furnished as a bed-room. The four-poster bed and accompanying furniture were roped off but an incongruously modern table and chair sat just beyond the door. 'I hope this is okay,' she said apologetically. 'The offices are a bit too far away and I didn't want to wear you out before you'd even begun.'

'It's fine,' Fraser said, wondering who among the castle's illustrious residents might have slept here in the past. 'As long as it's not haunted.'

Her eyes twinkled as she surveyed him. 'Not as far as I know, but let me know if you meet anyone unexpected.' She cleared her throat. 'Any last-minute questions? Changes I need to be aware of?'

'None,' Fraser replied. 'It's all exactly as we rehearsed.'

'Good,' Catriona said, and checked the time. 'The guests should start arriving soon. I'll come and collect you just before seven, if that suits you?'

'Perfect,' Fraser said, and eased out of his coat. 'I'll be ready.'

He spent fifteen minutes or so checking the schedule and reading through the stories he was due to tell, even though he knew them by heart already. He'd done some research on the possible identities of the ghosts said to roam the castle and had plenty of grisly detail to bring their stories to life. The ghostly dog would undoubtedly be a favourite with the audience, but it was the mournful refrain of the lone piper that fascinated Fraser the most. He couldn't wait to see the reaction as he wove the sorry tale.

As seven o'clock approached, he began to feel a familiar buzz of energy build in the pit of his stomach. The thrill of live performance never got old, whether it was on the cobbled streets of Edinburgh or the venerated boards of London's oldest theatres. Becoming someone else was where he felt most alive, his most brilliant, and his own worries faded into insignificance. It was true that he didn't miss the insecurity and fear of chasing the Hollywood dream, but his love of performing burned as brightly as ever. He suspected it always would.

This evening, however, the familiar tingle of anticipation was underscored by a faint thrum of something else – a scratchy, needling sensation that prickled across his skin and made it hard to sit still. The feeling was so unexpected that it took Fraser a moment to identify it, and the realisation caused him to huff with disbelief. He couldn't be nervous. He never got nervous.

Getting to his feet, he prowled the room, trying to channel the almost palpable sense of history that laced the air. What was different about tonight compared to the countless other performances he'd delivered over the years? he wondered. It couldn't be the fact that it was a press evening – he'd done plenty of those in his time. He was well-rehearsed, knew the stories he had to tell were perfectly pitched and the setting spoke for itself. It was true that good reviews from the journalists in attendance would undoubtedly help to publicise Dead Famous, but the walking tours were doing very nicely on their own and Fraser didn't think that was the source of his sudden pre-show jitters.

He stopped beside the desk, frowning to himself. The only real difference he could pick out was that Maura would be in the audience – surely that couldn't be it? Yet even as he considered the possibility, he knew it was true. Performing in front of someone whose opinion really mattered changed things. He wanted to impress her – to show that she'd done the right thing by going into partnership with him, that he was capable of taking the Edinburgh Ghost Company to the next level. He suddenly felt the need to prove that he was good at what he did, despite the fact that she'd already attended one of his walking tours. For reasons he preferred not to examine, he wanted her approval. And that made his nerves sing with the kind of unwanted energy he'd only ever observed in other people. It made him feel slightly green.

Taking a swig of water, he shuffled his notes and tried to read them again but before he could focus, there was a gentle tap at the door, and Catriona was peering into the room. 'I've got a visitor for you. Is that okay?'

She pushed the door back to reveal Maura, still buttoned

up in her coat and eyeing him uncertainly. 'I don't want to disturb your preparation,' she said hurriedly. 'I just wanted to give you this.'

She stretched out her hand, offering him a small box. Fraser felt rooted to the spot, transfixed by her unexpected appearance, wondering whether he'd somehow summoned her. With fingers that seemed to belong to someone else, he took the package and fumbled the lid open. Nestled inside was a ceramic black hound, a miniature replica of the ghostly apparition that roamed the castle grounds, caught in the act of howling at the moon. The nose was tilted skyward, the eyes wide and sorrowful, the ears flattened against the head. The midnight clay had been artfully distressed to resemble fur; Fraser brushed it with the tip of one finger, half-expecting it to ripple at his touch. 'It's for luck,' Maura said, when he didn't speak. 'Not that you'll need it.'

He looked up then, touched by her thoughtfulness, and the sight of her soothed his jangling nerves. How had she known? 'Thank you,' he said. 'It's beautiful. I love it.'

A delicate pink flushed across her cheeks. 'Phew. I wanted to give you something to remind you of the castle, but I'm not sure any of the ghosts here are known for bringing good luck.'

Taking the figure from the box, Fraser examined it again.

Catriona stepped forward for a closer look and let out a little gasp of pleasure when she saw what he held. 'How wonderful.' She turned to Maura. 'You are so clever.'

Maura opened her mouth to reply and Fraser knew she was about to downplay the time and skill that had gone into the piece.

'She is,' he said quickly. 'You should see her studio – it's full of beautiful pots.'

'Oh, I'm not sure about that,' Maura said, and cleared her throat. 'Anyway, I should leave you to it. Break a leg, isn't that what I'm supposed to say?'

'Thank you,' Fraser replied gravely. 'With the unevenness of the castle floors, that's entirely possible.'

Catriona caught his eye. 'It's nearly show time,' she said. 'I'll escort Maura back to the hall, then come to collect you, if that's okay?'

He tucked the dog inside the leather sporran that hung from the strap around his waist. 'Perfect. I'll be ready.'

His eyes were drawn to Maura the moment he entered the Great Hall. She'd removed her coat and was wearing the same timeless red dress she'd had on when they'd gone to dinner at the Witchery. Her dark curls were loose, contrasting with her pale skin; she shone like a jewel among pebbles. The breath caught in Fraser's throat and he had to fight the urge to stop in the doorway to stare at her. Talented, beautiful and kind; Jamie was a lucky man, he mused to himself as he crossed the room, even if he seemed to have no idea of the fact.

Ewan materialised in front of him. 'Ah, Fraser. Could I introduce you to Deborah Jordan? Arts Correspondent at *The Scotsman*.'

The woman next to him held out her hand. 'Good to meet you,' she said. 'What have you got in store for us this evening?'

'An introduction to the castle's darkest secrets,' he replied, slipping seamlessly into his professional storyteller persona. 'You might think you already know them but there's no telling whose spirit we might disturb as we pass among the shadows. Death lurks around every corner.'

Deborah stared at him, her expression a mixture of startled

apprehension and delight, and for a moment he thought he'd overdone it. Then she smiled. 'Oh, you're good,' she said, and turned to Ewan. 'I'm going to enjoy this.'

It wasn't long before Ewan was introducing him to others. Fraser smiled and shook hands, committed their names to memory, and hoped Maura was okay. Their eyes met several times but no opportunity to speak presented itself and all too soon Ewan was tapping a wine glass and calling for quiet.

'Ladies and gentlemen of the press, thank you for joining us this evening for an evening of spine-chilling tales,' he said, his voice carrying effortlessly in the cavernous room. 'I hope you enjoy getting to know the castle's ghosts. I'm going to leave you in the very capable hands of our guides, Catriona and Fraser, for the tour. I hope you all survive.'

Laughter broke out as glasses were placed on the nearest available surfaces and an expectant hum filled the air. Fraser recognised his cue. Taking a moment to appreciate the weight of Maura's gift as it nestled against his kilt, he took a breath. 'Gather close, unhappy friends,' he began, in a low confiding tone that nevertheless commanded the attention of everyone in the room. 'No, closer than that. You do not know it yet but by the end of this evening, some of you may owe your lives to the person next to you.'

Again, there was laughter, but it was laced with the faintest edge of tension and some of them did shuffle nearer to each other. He raised his head, taking the measure of his audience the way he did every night. But these were not credulous visitors to the city, eager to drink in the stories he told. They were hard-bitten journalists, many of them born and bred in Edinburgh and well versed in the city's legends. If he wanted to impress them, he was going to have to up his game. 'You might think you know this castle. You might have walked her ramparts and heard the terrible events that have taken place over the centuries. You might tell yourself they're just words, stories to entertain fools, that the mournful sigh you hear is only the wind.' He paused, his stare deep and fathomless. 'We'll see if you still believe that by the end of the tour.'

Beside him, Catriona raised her lantern. 'Come with us now and be sure not to tarry. You never know who – or what – might be following.'

More nervous laughter. Fraser made a mental note to compliment Catriona later – her timing and wary tone had both been perfect. He couldn't see Maura, assumed she was loitering near the back of the group, where Ewan was bringing up the rear. But he couldn't fret about her now. Turning on his heel, he strode towards the door.

They began in the vaults, where Fraser told the story of Davey Bowen, apprentice to the castle's blacksmith. The armies of the English were terribly near, and the forge raged bright and hot, day and night, to provide weapons for the coming battle. 'The smith and his men were exhausted, suffocated by smoke and near the end of their strength,' Fraser said, as a hidden projector sent fiery red flames licking up the walls behind him. 'And still the army demanded more swords. When Davey cried out that he could do no more, one of the lords became enraged. He struck Davey across the head, sending him tumbling into the fire. Screaming in agony, his arms ablaze, he fell to the floor, but the lord drew his sword and struck at anyone who went to his aid.' Fraser gazed around at the silent faces. 'As he burned, Davey laid a terrible curse on the lord and all those present, that their deaths be as terrible and agonising as his own.' He paused, took a breath. 'Ever since, there have been reports of a leather-aproned man walking the corridors between vaults, weeping with pain. Some mention a tingling in their arms, as though seared by heat. Others report a malign presence watching them. I cannot say if what they feel is true. What is clear is that these vaults are not a place to linger.'

By the light of Catriona's raised lantern, Fraser saw Deborah Jordan clutch uneasily at her arm. Hiding a smile, he led the way towards their next location, the corridor where the Grey Lady was said to roam, railing against her tortured death. Lady Janet's was a grimly familiar tragedy – caught up in the intrigues of powerful men, she was accused and convicted of witchcraft and burned at the stake outside the castle. Visitors and staff members had reported seeing her shadowy figure walking throughout its walls, leaving a ferocious chill in her wake.

Outside, in the dimly lit garden where the bones of soldiers' beloved pets had been laid to rest over the centuries, Fraser described the ghostly black dog frequently seen stalking the battlements, imparting a sense of impending doom on all those who failed to look away. He was acutely aware of where Maura stood, silent and listening, and had to battle the temptation to let his gaze rest solely on her as he spoke. But the moment passed, and on the ramparts, he recounted the legend of the spectral drummer boy, who had appeared, headless and wraith-like on the battlements, to rattle out the same insistent rhythm as Oliver Cromwell's armies had laid siege to the castle.

By the time they reached the final location, Fraser judged his audience to have suspended all disbelief. Their expressions were rapt as he faced them beside the bars of the castle dungeons.

'Our final tale is perhaps the most poignant,' he warned. 'It concerns a network of secret tunnels that were uncovered beneath this very floor, leading under the Royal Mile and supposedly all the way to Holyroodhouse Palace. No one knows how the discovery came to be made but the entrance was very small, only wide enough to allow the slender figure of a young piper through. The boy was told to follow where the tunnel led, piping as he went so that the men above could trace his path. And for a while, the pipes could plainly be heard. Past St Giles' Cathedral, the wailing faint but unmistakable, and on to Tron Kirk. With chilling abruptness, the sound stopped and no amount of shouting could raise a reply from the piper.' Fraser paused, allowing the silence in the dungeon to deepen the atmosphere. 'When the men broke into the tunnel to look for the boy, they found it was empty. They searched for days without finding the slightest trace he had ever been there. Eventually, the city council ordered the tunnel sealed, which is how it remains to this day. Only sometimes, when the roar of traffic fades and modern life draws back, a plaintive sound can be heard drifting upwards along the Royal Mile. The mournful lament of a lone piper, desperate to be heard and remembered beneath the city streets.'

The light in the dungeon had been growing gradually dimmer as he told the tale. Now, a barely audible melody began to haunt the air, thin and wistful and somehow yearning. Fraser felt the hair on the back of his neck prickle and he had to fight the urge to glance behind him. He'd read the piper's story over and over in preparation, knew the music he was hearing was only a recording, being played as part of the event, just as the lights had grown dim on schedule. And yet it seemed to him that there was something more contributing to the atmosphere in the dungeon, an uneasiness he couldn't quite explain.

Catriona stepped forward, her lantern raised. 'Thank you, Fraser. I don't know about all of you but I'm in need of a glass of something fortifying. Shall we make our way to the Great Hall?'

Usually, Fraser's tours finished with a round of applause, but that wasn't what happened once Catriona finished speaking. Instead, a muted muttering began, as though those present were coming back to themselves. In fact, it wasn't until Ewan began to clap that the spell truly seemed to break. The applause felt too loud in the confines of the dungeon and Fraser was at pains to wave it away. 'Thank you. Now, let's head upstairs.'

Maura waited behind, beaming at him as the others filed along behind Catriona and her bobbing light. 'You were brilliant,' she said, squeezing his arm. 'I'm not sure I'll be able to sleep tonight but your storytelling was incredible.'

The warmth behind the words almost made Fraser flush. 'Thanks. That means a lot.'

'You had the whole room believing the ghost of that poor boy is still trapped under the Royal Mile,' she went on as they followed the others. 'Even though the story is so full of holes you could sieve flour through it.'

Fraser grimaced. 'You noticed that?'

'How did they know where the tunnel went if the entrance was too narrow for anyone but the piper to fit through?' she said. 'And if they could widen the entrance when the boy disappeared, why didn't they just do that in the first place?'

He raised his hands in mock surrender. 'Don't ask me. I wasn't there.'

'I think he realised it was a fool's errand and found another exit,' Maura went on. 'He probably lived a long and happy life somewhere a long way from Edinburgh.'

'I like that ending better,' Fraser said, smiling. 'Doesn't explain the ghostly piping, mind.'

'No,' she conceded. 'But if everything could be explained, you wouldn't have a job.'

Fraser inclined his head. 'And we wouldn't be working together, and I wouldn't have my very own Maura McKenzie original to remind me of this evening. Thank you again for that.'

She nodded. 'It's just a wee thing. Did it help?'

'More than you know,' he said honestly. 'Catriona was impressed too. I've got a feeling Ewan McRae is going to be even more interested in your work after tonight.'

CHAPTER SEVENTEEN

'Hello? Earth to Maura, are you receiving us?'

It took Maura several seconds to realise Effie was speaking to her. She looked up from the plate she was glazing to see all three pottery students observing her with varying degrees of subtlety. Cordelia was frowning down at the clay before her but darted a curious glance Maura's way. Sharon had stopped her habitual humming along to the radio, while Effie was staring with her head cocked, not in accusation but in mild concern. A bubble of consternation burst in Maura's stomach as she realised she'd missed Effie's question. 'Sorry,' she said, offering an apologetic smile. 'Did you need something?'

Effie pursed her lips. 'A winning lottery ticket, new knees and a husband who knows how to put the toilet seat down,' she said. 'But what I actually wanted to know is whether everything is okay. You're very quiet today.'

'Not that you're ever noisy,' Cordelia clarified. 'But you seem a bit preoccupied. Not quite with us.'

'You do keep sighing, though,' Sharon said.

Maura threw her a startled look. 'Do I?'

Effie nodded. 'I'm afraid so. And us mere mortals might be

prone to huffing and puffing when the clay won't do what we want, but you're a pro and that poor plate is starting to feel as though it's done something to upset you.' She eyed Maura levelly. 'Has it done something to upset you?'

The suggestion made Maura glance down to the workbench, where the plate sat in mute accusation beneath her dripping brush. It was possible she'd gone overboard with the blue-green glaze. 'It's not the plate,' she said, and sighed, the sound escaping her before she could catch it. 'I got an odd message through Artsy, that's all. From someone on Jamie's rugby team.'

'Not a pervy pic,' Effie groaned, rolling her eyes. 'What is wrong with people?'

'Nothing like that,' Maura said hastily, her cheeks tingling. 'But he did ask to meet up. For coffee.'

Sharon snorted. 'And the rest. What a chancer.'

But Cordelia was frowning. 'Did he say what he wanted?'

Maura thought back to the message that had arrived a few hours earlier. She hadn't been aware Liam knew about her pottery, much less where she sold it. Perhaps Andy had mentioned it, although she couldn't begin to imagine why. But somehow, Liam had found her Artsy page and had got in touch. 'Just that he wanted to talk, and that it needed to be face to face,' she said. 'He split up with his girlfriend a few weeks ago so I suppose it must be related to that. I'm friendly with her; maybe he thinks I'll be able to explain what went wrong or help change her mind.'

'Has he talked to you about relationship problems before?' Cordelia asked.

'No,' Maura conceded. 'We haven't spoken much, to be honest, beyond hello or goodbye at the clubhouse. That's what makes it so tricky – obviously my loyalties lie with Zoe but she's not answering my messages and I can't help wondering if Liam is looking for a sympathetic ear.'

Effie raised her eyebrows. 'I'm not sure it's your ear he's interested in.'

'What?' Maura stared at her. 'I don't think—'

'Stranger things have happened,' Effie said, shrugging. 'You're an attractive woman. His ego has taken a kicking. Maybe he sees an opportunity to make this Zoe jealous.'

Sharon tilted her head. 'Or maybe he's been in love with you this whole time and Zoe found out and that's the reason they split up. That's why she's cut you off.'

For a moment, Maura was speechless as a whole world of horrifying possibilities unfolded before her. She would have known, wouldn't she? There would have been clues – long, lingering looks and excuses to talk to her. Jamie might have noticed too; he'd been unreasonably suspicious of Fraser's motives and he spent a lot more time with Liam. And finally there was Zoe herself, who was younger, bubblier, blonder. Why on earth would any man fall for Maura when he had a woman like that in his arms? 'No,' she managed eventually, stinging from the act of comparing herself to Zoe. 'I'm pretty sure that's not it.'

Cordelia clicked her tongue. 'Stop it, you two. Can't you see you're not helping?'

To be fair to Effie and Sharon, they had the grace to look instantly shamefaced. 'Sorry,' Sharon said, turning red. 'I've been watching too much TV.'

Effie bobbed her head in apology, although the set of her shoulders remained faintly mutinous. 'I suppose it's possible he just wants to talk.'

'Exactly,' Cordelia said. She glanced at Maura. 'So what are you going to do?'

Gaze dropping once more to the unfortunate plate on the workbench, Maura tried to make sense of her jumbled thoughts. Effie and Sharon were wrong, she was sure about that, but she couldn't shake the faint whisper of doubt at the back of her mind, the niggling suspicion that there was more to Liam's message than a desire to pour his heart out. But she had no idea what it might be. 'I'm not sure Jamie would be happy if I met him.'

The three women exchanged glances. Sharon cleared her throat. 'From what you've said, I'm not sure he's ever happy.'

Which probably meant she was oversharing, Maura realised, making a mental note to watch what she said in the studio. It was easy to join in when her students bemoaned their relationships but it was perhaps not entirely professional. 'No, but—'

'He's a grown man,' Cordelia said, her tone a shade acerbic. 'Surely he's not so insecure that you can't meet someone for coffee.'

Maura shifted uneasily. When she put it like that, it did sound ridiculous. 'What about Zoe? She's my friend.'

'A friend who isn't answering your messages,' Effie pointed out. 'Has she done anything to reassure you she's okay?'

'No,' Maura admitted. 'I haven't heard from her for a while, actually. I thought perhaps she wanted a clean break.'

'There you are, then,' Effie said.

Cordelia gave Maura a knowing look. 'Is it going to bother you if you don't find out what he wants?'

Maura sighed. 'I hate the thought of him not having anyone to talk to. The rugby crowd aren't – well, let's just say some of them struggle to admit their feelings.'

'He must have other friends,' Effie said, folding her arms.

'I have no idea,' Maura said, and that was part of the problem. She couldn't be sure who else Liam had.

Cordelia turned her attention back to her clay. 'I'm afraid there's only one way to resolve this, Maura. And I think you know what that is.'

Conscious that Sharon and Effie were watching her, Maura swallowed the sigh that was threatening to escape her and dredged up a rueful smile. 'Yes,' she admitted, picking up her brush and dipping it into the glaze once more. 'I'm going to have meet him, aren't I?'

Despite reminding herself she had nothing to feel anxious about, Maura was still jittery and unsettled as she crossed Cockburn Street and pushed back the door of her favourite coffee shop. She'd chosen it as a comforting venue, one where she was on first name terms with most of the baristas, who served excellent coffee and the most melt-in-the-mouth *pain au chocolat* she'd ever tasted. Not that she expected to be eating while Liam confided in her, but there might be one or two left over that she could take home. She arrived ten minutes early, optimistic that four o'clock on a Wednesday might be a good time to snag one of the coveted window tables facing the Warriston steps, but a quick glance around told her she was out of luck. Both windows were occupied.

'There's a two-seater round the back,' Giulia the manager said when she spotted Maura peering past the counter. 'Any good?'

'Perfect,' Maura said, and placed an order for her usual hazelnut latte. 'I'm expecting a friend – tall, dark hair, rugbyish. Can you send him through if you see him before me?'

'Leave it with me,' Giulia said. 'Go and take a load off. I'll bring your coffee over.'

Smiling her thanks, Maura did as she suggested, casting a longing look at the remaining pastries as she passed the end of the counter. Right on cue, her stomach rumbled, reminding her of another missed lunch as she'd lost track of time in her studio. She'd buy one on the way out to eat as she strolled back to Dean Village.

The rear of the coffee shop did not get much natural light and felt a little cramped, although several strings of fairy lights did their best to make things cosy. Two of the three tables were empty, with the third being occupied by a young man wearing oversized headphones and staring at a laptop. He didn't look up as Maura chose the one furthest from the door to the toilets and hung her jacket across the back of the chair nearest the wall. No sooner had she settled into the seat than Liam materialised, his bulk blocking out the bright lights from the front of the café. She waved, relieved his timekeeping was better than Jamie's. 'Hello.'

Eyes downcast, he nodded in greeting and slid into the chair opposite her. 'Hello, Maura. How've you been?'

His gaze flicked up at the last moment and she took in the sallow tinge of his skin, the pinched unhappiness around his lips. But the thing that caught her attention most was the livid black and purple bruising that bloomed around his left eye and spread down his cheek to his jaw. The eye itself was bloodshot and still slightly swollen, although she'd seen enough of Jamie's rugby injuries to judge this one was a few days old. 'That's quite the shiner you've got there,' she said, shaking her head in rueful admonishment. Jamie's face had been badly bruised on Sunday morning, although the damage was nothing like as dramatic as Liam's. 'I gather the match got a bit feisty on Saturday – did you give as good as you got?'

To her surprise, Liam didn't seize the opportunity to denounce the opposing players. Instead, he picked up the menu. 'Have you ordered?'

'A latte,' she said. 'And here comes Giulia now, if you know what you want.'

The other woman placed Maura's drink on the table with a smile, before turning an enquiring glance upon Liam. 'Just a black coffee,' he said, dropping the menu onto the table so it made a flat, slapping sound. 'Thanks.'

Giulia retreated, leaving Maura to study Liam once more.

'So,' she said, when he didn't speak. 'Apart from the eye, how are you doing?'

His shoulders hunched as he looked first at the man on the neighbouring table, and then at the fairy lights shimmering overhead. 'I've been better.'

Maura felt a surge of sympathy. He looked terrible. She leaned forward. 'I'm so sorry about you and Zoe. Did you . . . Was it a huge shock?'

To her surprise, Liam let out a short bark of laughter. 'You could say that.' He glanced up, saw her expression and seemed to gather himself together. 'I had no idea she wasn't happy. The first I knew about it was when she told me it was over.'

'I'm sorry,' she said again. 'You seemed so well-suited.'

'I thought so too,' he said, and shrugged. 'Clearly, we were both wrong.'

Giulia reappeared, carrying a tray with a cup and saucer on it. 'Here you go,' she said, sliding it onto the table.

'Thanks,' Liam mumbled. Evidently picking up on his

tone, Giulia shot a covert look at Maura, who smiled in reassurance.

'No problem,' Giulia said, frowning slightly. 'Let me know if you need anything else.'

The barista retreated, leaving Maura to watch Liam stir his coffee without enthusiasm. She took a sip of her own drink, pausing to admire the rippled heart Giulia had created on the foam. 'I can't imagine how much you must be hurting,' she said quietly. 'Especially when you thought you were both happy. But what I will say is that it gets easier.'

Liam scowled. 'You'll be telling me next that time is a great healer.'

She dipped her head. 'No, although it is true. To be honest, I'm not sure there's anything I can offer that will help, but I'm here and I'm listening.'

He was silent for a long time, stirring his coffee until a miniature whirlpool grew in the blackness. 'That's really kind, Maura,' he said eventually. When he raised his eyes to meet hers, she almost flinched at the wretchedness she saw there. 'Which makes what I have to say next so much harder.'

A shiver of unease skated along Maura's spine. What did he mean by that? Could Effie's suspicions be right after all? She held up a hand to forestall him. 'Liam—'

'I did wonder if you might have worked it out for yourself,' he went on, as though he hadn't heard. 'Picked up on the signs, you know.'

Oh god, oh god, oh god. Maura's heart thudded as she eyed him in mute discomfort. What was the right course of action – to stop him before he embarrassed them both beyond repair, or wait until he'd got it all off his chest and let him down gently then? She had no idea which was best – kindest. What she actually wanted to do was run all the way home without a backward glance. She took a deep breath. 'Um ... I can honestly say—'

Once again, Liam didn't seem to register that she'd spoken. 'But Andy mentioned you'd been at the club on Friday night and I knew you'd never have turned up there if you'd known.' His mouth twisted into a grimace. 'Unless you were planning to knock Zoe out and that didn't seem like your style.'

Maura's brow wrinkled. 'What? Why would I—' She paused, replayed his last sentence over again in her head and still came up with nothing. 'Sorry, I don't understand. What is it I'm supposed to know or not know?'

He lifted his cup and lowered it again without drinking. 'That Zoe and Jamie are having an affair.'

It was such a preposterous idea that Maura felt sure she'd misheard. A bubble of laughter ballooned inside her but died before it could make a sound. She licked her lips. 'I beg your pardon?'

Liam regarded her with heavy eyes. 'I didn't want to believe it either. But it's true. Zoe admitted everything the night she dumped me.'

Blood roared in Maura's ears as she stared at him. It couldn't be true. He was lying. No, *Zoe* was lying. Maybe he'd refused to accept it was over and she'd needed a nuclear option, something there was no coming back from. 'You're wrong.'

'I wish I was,' he said flatly. 'From what she told me, it started the night of Matt's fortieth. She didn't go into detail, and I've probably blocked out some of it, but we'd all had a lot to drink. We got separated leaving the club – they ended up in a different taxi to the rest of us. Then, when everyone was back at mine, they disappeared for a bit.' Shaking his head, he took a swig of coffee. 'I remember wondering where they'd gone. Now I know.'

An awful image flashed into Maura's mind, of Jamie and Zoe entwined. She shook it away, heaving in a shuddering breath. 'You're wrong. Jamie wouldn't do that. He wouldn't.'

But even as she said the words, doubt was starting to creep in. She remembered his demeanour when he'd finally rolled home after Matt's party, defensive and ill-tempered and barely able to look at her. He'd blamed the argument that followed on a monster hangover and Maura had believed him – it was hardly an isolated incident, after all. But what if there had been more behind his snappiness than a thumping head and a roiling stomach? What if he'd also been weighed down by guilt?

Liam's gaze was troubled. 'Have you noticed his behaviour changing recently? Has he been working late more often?'

He had, Maura thought, her head spinning. She'd barely seen him since . . . since that night. And wasn't that when Zoe had become less chatty too? She fumbled in her bag, pulling out her phone and stabbing at the screen until her chat with Zoe appeared. Her last five messages stared accusingly back at her, not blocked but unread and unanswered. Maura scrolled backwards, noting how sparse Zoe's replies had grown. And then she reached it – the message she'd sent the day after Matt's party.

I hear it was a heavy night. Hope you behaved yourself.

Zoe's reply had seemed innocent enough at the time, but now it made Maura feel nauseous.

Ha ha. I promise I was a VERY good girl. Ask Jamie!

She stared at it, feeling her stomach churn. It had to be a coincidence. It couldn't be true.

'I found his wallet under my bed,' Liam said, and Maura dragged her eyes from her screen to his face. 'After the party, I mean. And I couldn't work out how it got there – he slept on the sofa. He laughed it off when I gave it back to him, said it must have been in his coat pocket and I didn't think there could be any other explanation, until Zoe came clean.' His lip curled. 'He wasn't laughing on Saturday after the match.'

'What?' The conversation spun off in another unexpected direction, taking Maura with it.

'We had a fight, on the pitch. I couldn't help it.' He touched the livid bruising around his eye. 'I'm currently suspended from the club.'

She gaped at him. 'Jamie said he took an elbow from the tighthead prop in the scrum.'

Liam shrugged. 'He lied.'

She wanted to deny it, to accuse Liam of lying rather than Jamie. The trouble was, she couldn't work out why Liam would. Or Zoe, for that matter. 'Why are you doing this?'

'Because you need to know what's going on behind your back,' he said, the words heavy. 'You seem like a good person, Maura. You deserve better.'

Maura threw up her hands. 'But you've only got Zoe's word that any of this is true. What if she's lying, to make sure you leave her alone or ... I don't know – to get her own back for something? Have you thought about that?'

He sighed. 'I've seen his messages. I'm sorry, Maura. She's not lying.'

The truth of it almost overwhelmed her then, the hideous realisation that brought with it hot tears that stung her eyes but did not spill onto her cheeks. She managed to stifle a groan, putting her hands over her face and willing the awfulness away. But the everyday sounds of the coffee house continued around her, anchoring her in the moment and somehow the darkness only made things worse. *Jamie and Zoe*, she thought dully, and the mere act of linking their names caused a wave of misery to course through her. She lowered her hands. 'Does everyone know?'

Liam's mouth twisted. 'No. They've been discreet, I'll give them that. But I imagine a few of the lads in the team might have put two and two together after I hit him.'

Her eyes burned with unshed tears; she could feel them hovering on her lashes, causing her vision to swim. She pressed the heels of her palms against her overheated eyelids. *Jamie and Zoe.* How could he? After five years together, how could he?

'Maura? Is everything okay?' The voice belonged to Giulia.

Maura moved her hands, blinking away black and white dots to see the barista standing nearby, watching her with a worried expression. The young man at the next table had stopped peering at his laptop and was now firing an accusatory glare Liam's way. Maura took a breath and let it out slowly before she felt capable of nodding to Giulia. 'I'm okay.'

'Sorry, but you're not.' That was the man at the neighbouring table. Maura saw his headphones were hooked around his neck; he'd probably heard everything.

'No,' she admitted, because there didn't seem to be any point in denying it.

Giulia's eyes narrowed as she surveyed Liam. 'Is this man responsible for upsetting you?'

'Yes.' The young man's glower intensified.

Liam straightened up in his seat. 'Hang on a minute, that's not true.'

The other man folded his arms. 'She wasn't crying before you got here.'

Maura dabbed at her face with her hands. 'It's not Liam's fault. I've had some bad news, that's all.'

'I know,' the stranger said. 'And his delivery of that news was terrible.'

Liam subsided, shoulders slumping as he glanced at Maura. 'Probably. I didn't want to be the one to tell you, but like I said, I thought you needed to know.'

Part of her wished he hadn't told her; an hour earlier she'd been . . . not *happy*, perhaps, but happily unaware. And now the rug had been yanked from beneath her feet and she felt as though she had broken on impact with the floor. In some far-off corner of her consciousness, she understood that this crash had been necessary, that in time she would be able to put herself back together, but right at that moment all she felt was pain. 'Thanks.' She didn't manage to imbue the word with much gratitude, but Liam seemed to take it at face value.

He pushed his chair back and got to his feet. 'You've got my number,' he said, nodding at her phone. 'Message me when you've had time to process this. If there's anything you want to know.'

To be perfectly honest, she couldn't imagine wanting to ask him anything. But even in her distress, she couldn't be so brutal. She nodded, not trusting herself to speak.

Liam ran a hand through his hair. 'What are you going to do?'

Mechanically, she reached for her bag. 'I'm going to the bathroom.'

'After that,' he said, with patience she wouldn't have suspected he possessed.

Her head dipped. 'I don't know.'

Clearing her throat, Giulia took a step towards them. 'We're closing now,' she told Liam, her frown no less severe than it had been a few minutes earlier. 'You need to settle your bill.'

Liam acknowledged the instruction with a nod. 'Okay,' he said, and glanced at Maura. 'Will you be all right?'

Would she? Maura wondered, and found she couldn't offer him any reassurance. 'I don't know. But I—' She made an effort to pull herself together. 'I'd rather you went.'

He hesitated for a moment, then stood. 'Sure, I understand. Take care, Maura.'

She said nothing as he left, kept her gaze trained on the dregs of cold coffee in the bottom of her cup, heard the bell jingle on the door and willed herself not to cry. After another minute, she rose and made for the bathroom, where she ran the cold tap to let the water run across her wrists. The chill barely registered. She splashed some on her face, noting her puffy eyelids and chalky skin with detached indifference. Her eyes had a glassy sheen, brought on by the threat of further tears, and her nose was red. She looked how she felt – a mess – but that was hardly a surprise when her life had been uprooted and tossed skyward with hurricane force. Some women exuded a fragile beauty in such circumstances. Maura had to concede she was not one of them.

'You want me to call someone?' Giulia asked when she finally emerged to an empty café and made her way to the counter. 'I don't like to think of you leaving on your own.'

'No,' Maura said quickly, because she could only think of Kirsty and facing her sister was the last thing she wanted. 'I'll be fine. Don't worry.'

'But I am worried,' Giulia said, frowning. 'You've had a terrible shock and you're clearly very upset. At least let me find you a taxi.'

A wave of shame engulfed Maura as she realised the other woman knew all about the grenade Liam had tossed her way. 'No, thank you. I don't want to go home yet. I need to walk a bit, try to clear my head.'

It looked for a moment as thought the barista might argue, but she sighed instead and pushed a white box tied with ribbon across the counter towards Maura. 'These are on the house. You're going to need them.'

Her compassion almost sent more tears cascading down Maura's cheeks but she dug deep for her self-control and managed a very wobbly, watery smile. 'Thank you. How much do I owe you for the coffee?'

'Nothing,' Guilia said. 'The young man at the table beside you paid for it when he left. He said he hopes it shows not all men are arseholes.'

Just my bloody boyfriend, Maura thought bitterly, but the small, unexpected generosity smoothed the edges of her distress. 'That was kind of him,' she said, blinking hard to retain what little composure she had left. 'Will – will you say thank you, if you see him again?'

'Already done,' Giulia said. 'But he's a regular, so I'll be sure to pass on your thanks the next time he comes in.' She paused, eyeing Maura with sympathy. 'What will you do?'

She meant about Jamie, Maura supposed, but it wasn't a question she could answer – not right at that moment. The bullet of his betrayal was too fresh; it lodged in her stomach, radiating cold and subjecting her to endless ripples of shock. She needed time to come to terms with this new reality, to absorb the damage, before she could even begin to fathom what came next. But before that, she had to make certain that what Liam had told her was true. 'Confront Jamie, I guess,' she said. 'Hear it from him.'

Giulia raised her eyebrows. 'Will he admit it?'

Maura thought back to the silent hours she'd spent in Jamie's company of late, the unmissable increase in his drinking, the sense that he was somehow elsewhere even when he was at home. She swallowed hard against the painful lump that rose in her throat. 'I think he wants to.'

'And you?' Giulia asked. 'What do you want?'

'I . . .' Maura looked down at the box of pastries, her eyes swimming. 'I don't think there's any coming back from this.'

The other woman reached out to squeeze her hand. 'Then do it tonight. Look him in the eye, hold firm and tell him it's over.'

The thought made Maura's head swirl but she managed to nod. 'Okay.'

Giulia took a notepad and pen from the pocket of her apron and scrawled a number on it. 'Call me if you need to. I'll bring more pastries.'

Again, Maura nodded, although it felt as though her head might fall off with the effort. 'I will. Thanks.'

She wasn't sure how she got home. She knew she'd walked – her aching muscles proved that – but she couldn't have told anyone where she went. For a time, she contemplated not going home at all. Catching a bus to her parents' house and immersing herself in their love and support. But Giulia's advice rang in her ears – *do it tonight* – and the small part of Maura's brain that was still functioning rationally knew she was right. Even so, when at last she opened the door to the flat and climbed the stairs, she found herself hoping Jamie was not there. But luck had deserted her, or perhaps it hadn't, because he was slouched in the furthest armchair, an open bottle of wine on the coffee table and an empty glass beside it.

He looked up from the papers in his hand, his expression irritated. 'You're back late. Where have you been?'

Heart thundering, she slid her bag from her shoulder and began fumbling with the zip of her coat. 'I went for coffee.'

'At this time of night?' His lip curled. 'I don't believe you.'

Maura shook her arms free of her coat. What was that saying about every accusation being a confession? 'I went for coffee,' she repeated and met his gaze with level frankness. 'With Liam.'

His expression was suddenly wary. 'With Liam? Why?'

'Because he wanted to tell me the reason Zoe broke up with him,' Maura said, maintaining eye contact. Now that the moment of confrontation was here, her head felt oddly clear of the cotton-wool fuzziness that had clouded her thoughts since leaving the coffee shop. It still hurt – really hurt – to look at Jamie, but her voice was steady. 'I think you know what I mean.'

He picked up the wine bottle, filled his glass, and leaned back in the chair. 'I know what he thinks happened. The bloody idiot got himself suspended for it at the weekend.'

'So he told me,' she said. 'Why didn't you tell me about the fight? Why did you say it was someone on the other team who gave you that bruise?'

Jamie shrugged. 'I didn't want to embarrass Liam. He's done a good enough job of that himself.' He eyed her over the top of the wine glass. 'So what exactly did he tell you? Some rubbish about me and Zoe, I suppose.'

Maura's stomach began to churn. She forced herself to stay calm. 'That's right. Except it's not rubbish.' She took a deep breath, reached inwards for her spine and gripped it hard. 'You and Zoe are having an affair.'

To his credit, he didn't summon up an expression of mock outrage or the blustering denial she was expecting. Instead, he simply stared at her, eyes glittering. 'That's not—'

'Don't bother, Jamie,' Maura said, moving forward to rest her hands wearily on the sofa. 'I know. What I don't understand is why.'

He opened his mouth to speak but she waved him into silence. 'Not why you did it – it's been obvious for a while that you're not happy with me, or our life together – but why you didn't do the right thing and tell me you wanted out.' She raised her chin. 'Honesty, Jamie. You owed me that, after all these years.'

'Honesty?' he echoed, his tone quietly incredulous. 'You're a fine one to talk. You can barely look at me, have no interest in what I want or how I feel. If we're being honest, Maura, how about admitting it's been a long time since you were in love with me?'

The words stung, slashed at her heart like shards of glass, but even as she flinched, she knew the truth. She wasn't in love with him, hadn't been for – well, she didn't know how long. But that didn't mean she deserved this betrayal. 'I'm not the one who slept with someone else.'

She saw him weighing his options. Would a denial now do him any good? Could he somehow talk her round? 'Maura—'

'Don't,' she said, running a hand over her suddenly too hot eyes. 'Don't try to make this my fault. I admit there have been problems – maybe I haven't tried as hard as I should have to put things right – but you're the one who's hit the self-destruct button. It's over.'

Jamie didn't move, didn't speak. He simply watched her until at last a sob escaped her iron determination not to cry in front of him. 'Okay,' he said.

His acceptance caught her off guard. She'd expected him to fight, to rail against Liam and accuse him of trying to blacken his name. She'd thought, even in the face of the affair, that he wouldn't just walk away. And for the first time, she got a sense of how unhappy he truly was. She took a breath to steady herself, gripped the cloth back of the sofa. 'Where will you go?'

He lifted one hand, pinched the bridge of his nose. 'Right now? To a hotel, probably. I'll sort something out.'

Maura's gut twisted at the speed with which the world was spinning. She supposed she should be grateful he hadn't said *Zoe's*, even though it was probably the truth. 'Obviously you can leave your stuff here,' she said, and her lips felt suddenly stiff, as though they belonged to someone else. 'Until you find somewhere more permanent.'

'Okay,' he said again. 'I'll pay you for the storage space.'

She shook her head. 'You don't have to.'

He sighed. 'Be sensible. You don't earn enough to pay the bills, Maura. You never have.'

'I'm earning more now,' she said, raising her chin. 'The ghosts are doing well.'

He glanced at her then and she knew he was about to say something poisonous about Fraser. But he seemed to think better of it. 'All the same, I'll pay you until I've moved everything out. Like you say, I owe you.'

Not money, she wanted to cry – he had always been more than fair on that score. But she didn't have the resilience to argue the point. Instead, she simply nodded.

Placing his half-full glass on the table, Jamie levered himself out of the armchair. 'I'll go and pack a bag.'

She watched him go, a sudden black hole of panic yawning where certainty had been only minutes before. Now that he was leaving, she wasn't sure it was the right thing. Perhaps his affair with Zoe was merely a symptom of his unhappiness, not the remedy. Maybe there was something she could do to put things right, get back to where they had once been. But even as dread tried to overwhelm her, she remembered Giulia's parting words. *Hold firm and tell him it's over.*

The sentiment kept her upright when Jamie came back with a black holdall in one hand and an armful of coat-hangered suits and shirts in the other. It sustained her as he passed by, not pausing to meet her gaze or speak, and swept down the stairs to the front door and the cobbled street beyond. It propelled her to the kitchen, albeit in stilted fashion, on legs that barely bent at the knees, and allowed her to fill the kettle, make a pot of tea. And it carried her back to the sofa with the tray, where she retrieved the box of pastries and stared down at it with dull, barely seeing eyes. Only then did it give way, taking with it the last remnants of Maura's brittle self-control. With an anguished sob, she dropped her head into her hands and let the pain pour out.

CHAPTER EIGHTEEN

There was no doubt about it, Fraser thought with a frown as he checked his calendar and compared it to the printed schedule on his desk. The ghosts were late. Maura was late, by more than a week, and the customers who had pre-ordered from the latest batch of Agnes were starting to ask when they could expect their delivery. And Maura herself had fallen uncharacteristically silent, failing to answer his previous four messages, which hadn't actually been about the missing ghosts. Two had been jaunty texts checking how she was doing, another had been letting her know Ewan McRae wanted a meeting to discuss a possible exhibition of her work at the castle, and the most recent had been a link to a funny Instagram video about a ninja penguin. As far as Fraser could tell, she hadn't read any of them. It was very unlike her. He was beginning to wonder if something was wrong.

'Maybe you should give her a call,' Tom, one of the other tour guides, said, when Fraser advised him not to mention the ghosts during his walks for the rest of the week.

'I'm sure she's just caught up with other projects,' Fraser replied. 'She said she'd taken on a couple of commissions after ScotPot – maybe they've taken longer than she anticipated.'

'That's not really our problem, though,' Tom said doubtfully. 'And if there is an issue, she should let you know. Ignoring your messages isn't exactly helpful.'

'It's only been a week,' Fraser pointed out, feeling the need to defend Maura. 'And I doubled the order last time round. She's told me before that pottery can be a slow business – it's probably my fault for demanding too much.'

Tom raised his hands. 'If you say so. There are bound to be people who ask about the ghosts, even if I don't push them. What do you want me to tell them?'

Fraser thought for a moment. Maybe there was a way to turn the lack of ghosts into an opportunity. 'Tell them pre-orders are closed at the moment but if they sign up to the newsletter, they'll get the details of an exclusive flash sale in the next month.'

'Risky,' Tom said. 'Didn't you say most of the orders come in directly after a tour finishes? What if they forget to sign up?'

'Then they miss out,' Fraser said, spreading his hands. 'But my gut feeling is that they won't forget. And at least this way, we won't be selling a product we don't actually have.'

'You're the boss,' Tom replied. 'I just do as I'm told. It's good things are going so well, though.'

And they were going well, Fraser knew. The ghost tours at the castle had been a roaring success, receiving glowing reviews in the press and ensuring Dead Famous had seen a corresponding upsurge in bookings that had stretched all three tour guides to full capacity. Each ran one tour per night, in different areas of the city, and all were fully booked for the next three weeks. July and August were the busiest months for the tourist trade, meaning the streets would be fuller than ever. The newest

Dead Famous guide, Rebecca, was already considering adding a second tour, starting at nine o'clock, to cope with demand. But what Fraser needed most was for Maura to deliver the overdue ghosts. He could only hope she wouldn't keep him waiting much longer.

Fraser would be lying if he said he wasn't curious about seeing Naomi again. They'd spoken once or twice since the break-up, mostly to discuss practicalities, and she'd messaged a week ago to ask whether it would be possible to collect some more of her things from the Leith apartment they'd shared. Fraser had readily agreed – there was no animosity between them, after all – but now that Naomi's arrival was imminent, he wondered how the sight of her might make him feel. He had no regrets about the end of their relationship, was sure she didn't either, but they'd had some good times together, admittedly mostly before he'd persuaded her to move from London to Edinburgh. And he had no doubt she would be as beautiful as ever. His heart might well offer a pang or two when she walked through the door.

What he wasn't prepared for was the effusiveness of her greeting. Naomi had always been impossibly cool, channelling more than a touch of Kate Moss at her most alluringly remote, and it was only the conviction that she was utterly out of reach that had given Fraser the confidence to flirt with her in the first place. That she'd deigned to flirt back had blown his mind and he'd been putty in her hands from that moment on. But she was not given to public displays of affection. And she was definitely not a hugger.

'It's so good to see you!' she declared when he opened the door to let her into the flat. She threw her arms around him almost before she was across the doorstep, enveloping him in a cloud of expensive perfume and cashmere. It was not, he had to admit, an unpleasant experience.

'Hi,' he said, his voice slightly muffled by the silky blonde tresses that hung loose around her shoulders. Gently, he disentangled himself and stepped back. 'Good to see you too. How was your journey?'

She pulled a face. 'The usual. A scrum at baggage reclaim.' Fraser's gaze slid to the corridor beyond her and saw a large suitcase. 'It's empty. I brought it to fill up with the clothes I left here.'

'Good idea,' Fraser said, picturing how empty the wardrobes would be once bereft of Naomi's many designer dresses and coats. He might be able to hang his own clothes up at long last. Reaching past her for the case, he wheeled it inside and closed the front door. 'How long are you here for?'

'One night,' she said, slipping her shoes off and padding through to the living room as though she still lived there. 'I've got a photoshoot in Cannes on Friday.'

Leaving the suitcase in the hall, Fraser followed Naomi. 'Sounds awful,' he said dryly. 'How will you cope?'

'Oh, stop it,' she said, pouting. 'It's work.'

'On the French Riviera,' he observed. 'There are worse places to do your job.'

She glanced out of the window then, at the leaden skies that hung over the grey North Sea beyond the docks, and he knew what she was thinking. As far as she was concerned, Edinburgh did not compare favourably to many places. 'Okay, you may have a point.' She stretched and sighed. 'It's been such a long day. I could murder a coffee.'

Fraser hid a smile. Naomi ran on coffee. 'Espresso, no sugar?'
She looked pleased. 'You remembered.'

'Of course I remembered,' he said, a little stung. 'My memory's not that bad.'

In the kitchen, he busied himself with the machine. Of all
the rooms in the apartment, this one had held the fewest traces
of Naomi. The juicer was hers but he assumed that was too
bulky to transport back to London. Apart from that, there were
some delicate crystal wine glasses he'd grown quite attached
to, plus a selection of herbal teas she'd tried and abandoned for
lack of caffeine. He didn't mind if she took those, although
he'd started to enjoy a camomile tea before bed. When had
he grown so middle-aged? he wondered ruefully as he carried
Naomi's coffee back through to the living room. He used to
drink whisky before bed.

'Have you missed me?' Naomi said as she curled her long legs
beneath her on the sofa. 'I've missed you.'

He sat beside her, taking care to maintain a discreet distance between them. The truth was that he hadn't missed her
much, once the initial shock of her absence had worn off, but
he didn't think honesty was the best policy. Not if he valued
his white carpet. 'Of course,' he murmured. 'But work has
been mad. I did some events at the castle and they really raised
our profile.'

'I saw,' she said. 'You made the papers. I'll even admit to
being a little impressed.'

'Really?' he said, glancing at her in surprise.

'Really,' she echoed, and wriggled a little closer. 'Although
a lack of talent was never your problem. Lack of ambition, on
the other hand . . .'

Fraser's mouth twisted in amusement as she trailed off. 'Thanks.'

She waved a hand. 'But that's all water under the bridge now. What's done is done.'

'True enough,' he agreed, relieved she didn't seem to be about to revisit that particularly well-worn path. 'So where are you staying tonight? Somewhere fancy, I hope.'

'The Balmoral,' she said carelessly. 'I haven't checked in yet.'

He frowned. 'You came straight here from the airport?'

'I wanted to see you,' she said, looking up through her lashes. 'Is that so surprising?'

'A bit,' he admitted. 'But I suppose it makes sense to collect your things first, give you time to enjoy the evening. Have you got plans?'

'No plans,' she said idly, and reached out to squeeze his bicep. 'I thought perhaps you might like to do something.'

A faint flicker of unease rippled through Fraser. 'I have to go to work, Naomi.'

She ran her fingers across his chest, walked them up to the soft hair of his beard. 'I thought you'd say that,' she said. 'So go to work. I'll be waiting here when you get back.'

He had to concede it was a tempting offer. Whatever the differences between him and Naomi, they had not manifested themselves in the bedroom and it would be no hardship to spend the night in her arms. But he'd never really been into one-night stands, and he knew from experience that he and Naomi couldn't offer each other more than that. 'And then what?'

She smiled, reaching up to caress his cheek. 'And then we enjoy each other's company. In the morning, I go back to London, and maybe next time you come down to visit me.'

Her face tilted towards his expectantly, and he knew she was waiting for him to kiss her. Gently, he removed her hand from his cheek. 'We both know that won't work.'

'Why not?' she asked. 'We were good together, before you made us come here. We could be good together again, without living in each other's pockets. Just think – all the fun of a relationship, with none of the hassle.'

It wasn't a terrible idea, Fraser thought. Plenty of people made long distance relationships work. The trouble was, the Fraser he was now wasn't the one Naomi wanted. She wanted the actor, the glamour that came with the party invitations and award ceremonies he'd always attended without a hope of being recognised for his work. She wanted who he had been five years ago. 'But what if a relationship is exactly what I want?'

She raised her eyebrows. 'Then come back to London. Move in with me and we'll make it work. Your agent has been trying to get hold of you – he says he's got the role of a lifetime to offer you. There's a future for you in acting, Fraser. All you have to do is take it.'

The mention of Sam caused a squirm of guilt; Fraser had ignored another email from him only last week. For a moment he wavered – his agent had frequently been known to exaggerate the importance of the roles he'd sent Fraser's way in the past, but he couldn't recall Sam ever describing one as 'the role of a lifetime', and he couldn't help wondering what it might be. But his curiosity didn't survive long, blown away by the bigger grenade Naomi had just lobbed his way.

He gazed at her for a long moment, taking in the perfect arch of her cheekbones, the flawless skin, the wide blue eyes that were virtually begging him to see sense. If his friends could see him now, they'd be roaring at him to do the obvious thing and take her up on her offer, both for the night and for the rest of his life. But he couldn't. To say yes now would be to turn his back on everything he'd built in Edinburgh – on Dead Famous, the other tour guides and on Maura, who was working so hard to help him make a go of things. As if summoned by the thought, a vision of her loomed into his mind, smiling as she showed him how to shape the clay, the tips of her dark hair speckled white as she brushed back a curl. He let out a slow breath. 'It's not what I want, Naomi. I'm sorry.'

Leaning back against the cushions, she sighed. 'I thought you'd say that.' Draining her coffee, she put the cup on the table and got to her feet. 'I'll never understand why you're so determined to waste your talents telling stories to tourists when your star could be on the rise. You're a bloody fool, Fraser Bell. Has anyone ever told you that?'

'Plenty of people,' he said, resisting the urge to point out that his star's failure to rise above the occasional recurring role in UK TV dramas was a big part of the reason he'd turned his back on acting. 'You're in great company.'

Her eyes flashed but he didn't think she was annoyed. Not by her usual standards, anyway. 'You'll change your mind,' she said with a confident toss of her head. 'Just don't leave it too long. I won't wait forever and nor will your agent.'

He nodded, relieved that she hadn't thrown the cup. 'Noted,' he said gravely. 'Now, do you want some help to fill that case or will I just get in your way?'

CHAPTER NINETEEN

'Oh no. No, no, no!'

Maura stared in dismay at the cluster of ghosts on the top shelf of her kiln. They'd been perfect when she closed the lid twenty-four hours earlier, delicately laced with fronds of green seaweed and dipped in a clear glaze to fix them. Now there was an indisputable pink tinge to each of their rounded heads and she knew without looking that the taint would have spread across the glaze. Sensing the attention of her students in the studio behind her, she resisted the urge to swear, but it was a hard-fought battle. She didn't have time to lose a whole batch of ghosts to a rogue pink tinge. She was behind enough as it was.

'Something wrong?' Nina asked.

Maura didn't turn around. This was her Thursday group, a frequently shifting selection of women who came in and out as their interest waxed and waned. They were not regulars, which resulted in a much less cosy teacher–student relationship than with Effie, Sharon and Cordelia on Tuesday mornings.

Nina had already complained that her dog sculpture from the week before had not been fired, despite Maura warning her that its size meant it might take longer to dry out. 'What about my plate, then?' she'd asked upon scanning the shelves. 'Surely that's not too big.'

'No,' Maura replied, 'but the kiln was full. I'm sorry, Nina. I'll try to run a stoneware firing before next week's session.'

Nina's mouth had turned down but she hadn't said anything further. Jude was similarly disgruntled at having to wait for her soap dish and tealight holder, and it had led to a rather sour start to the session. The atmosphere hadn't lightened much as the morning progressed and it did not encourage Maura to reveal the disaster that had occurred in the kiln overnight, but they had all heard her exclamations. She had no choice but to explain, especially as she had the sinking feeling Lisa had a cup on the bottom shelf that might very well have been affected. Nothing was guaranteed with pottery – the kiln could be an unpredictable mistress – but that didn't mean Lisa would accept the loss of her work with equanimity. Maura feared it was not going to go down well.

'Everything is pink,' she said, reaching down to pick up one of the ghosts. 'One of the glazes must have reacted badly with the heat and created a colour flash.'

Nina came to peer over her shoulder. 'I see what you mean. I'm quite glad I didn't have anything in there now.'

Maura refrained from pointing out that Nina hadn't had anything glazed to fire and turned the ghost over in her hands. The pink was delicate but unmistakable, an uneven bloom that made Agnes look as though she had spent too much time in the sun. The next was the same, although the blush was less pronounced. As Maura removed each ghost in turn, she saw that every single one had been tainted. All fifteen were pink. She wanted to cry.

'Do you know what causes it?' Jude asked, arriving to inspect the damage.

'It could be something organic in the clay that has oxidised but usually it's down to a chrome glaze,' Maura said. Her brow furrowed in confusion. 'The worst culprit is the tortured steel glaze but I put that away in the cupboard so no one would use it.'

'Oh.'

Maura turned to see Lisa staring at her in consternation, one hand over her mouth.

Her voice was small and uncertain. 'I think I might have used that on my cup. I did wonder why it wasn't with all the other glazes . . .' She trailed off, her expression sheepish.

Maura wanted to groan. She thought she'd added a label to the tub, warning her students to check with her before using it, but perhaps it had fallen off. Putting the last flamingo-tinted ghost down, she removed the now empty shelf from the kiln and peered down at the pottery below. And there, nestled among a further ten rosy ghosts, was Lisa's cup, beautifully shimmering in its metallic silver coat. Maura gazed at it for a long time before she sighed and picked it up. 'Well, the good news is that the glaze looks great.'

Lisa was beside her now, squinting into the kiln. 'I'm really sorry, Maura. I had no idea it would ruin your work.'

Maura pressed the heel of her hand hard against her head, willing a sudden swirl of anxiety to settle down. It would be okay – she had fifteen ghosts from an earlier batch and she could remake this batch in four or five days – but it would throw out her schedule and make her even later with delivery than she already was. It would also affect the plates commission she was working on, and mean juggling her students' work to accommodate the additional firings. But the ghosts had to take priority; Fraser had been patient enough, even though she knew he had orders to fulfil, and he was expecting another batch of forty in – she did a rapid calculation in her head – twelve days.

She would have to work harder, spend more evenings in the studio to get everything made and then hope she could somehow manage the kiln time. Her hand pressed harder against her forehead as she tried to mentally reschedule her workload. It was going to be very tight. But it wasn't as though she had anything else to occupy her time.

Jamie had moved out permanently, waiting until she had gone to her parents' house for the weekend to come in and empty his wardrobe and drawers, gather up the dusty trophies and medals from his sporting achievements. The bathroom was devoid of shaving equipment, the shower no longer cluttered with various gels and shampoo bottles. He'd also emptied the wine rack and taken all the expensive whisky from the cupboard, leaving her with a crusty bottle of Glenmorangie that looked as though it hadn't been sampled for years. She didn't begrudge him any of it, with the possible exception of vintage Taittinger he'd presented as a gift for her thirty-fifth birthday. Clearly he didn't expect her to have anything to celebrate in the immediate future.

Communication had been short and practical. There were no recriminations, no painful salvos back and forth in which they sought to hurt each other more. She carefully didn't ask where he was living, after establishing he'd arranged for his mail to be forwarded. It was as though someone had taken a sharp pair of scissors and neatly cut everything that bound them together.

He'd signed off his last message a week ago with 'Take care of yourself' and she did not expect to hear from him again.

Kirsty had been predictably incandescent. 'That toe-rag,' she had howled, when Maura broke the news. 'I never bloody liked him – he always had far too high an opinion of himself – but I thought at least he cared about you. And what kind of friend is this Zoe person, to go behind your back and steal your boyfriend?'

'She hardly stole him,' Maura had felt compelled to point out. 'He's not a car. It takes two to cheat and Jamie is just as guilty as Zoe.'

Kirsty stared at her. 'How can you be so reasonable? He's a toerag and she's a bitch, and I won't have it any other way. I'd be sewing prawns into the hem of his trousers, if I were you, and signing her up to every junk mail list I could find.'

Maura had almost managed a smile then. The prawn idea wasn't half bad. But what would be the point? Jamie had put his finger squarely on the problem when he'd asked her how long it had been since she'd loved him, and although her heart was still cut to ribbons by the betrayal, she was beginning to accept that breaking up was an inevitability. It just would have taken longer and worn them both down with a slow drip of misery instead of a deluge. 'I'm not being reasonable,' she'd told Kirsty. 'I've just got nothing left to spend on revenge.'

And the truth was she didn't mind the quiet evenings on her own. It was a relief to not be listening constantly for the sound of the front door opening, trying to judge from the tread of his feet on the stairs how much he'd had to drink. And work helped her too. In the days immediately after the break-up, she'd found it impossible to achieve anything – her fingers were slow and stupid, her eyes too often blurred by tears. But gradually, the smooth coolness of the clay had soothed her raging emotions and she'd felt her skill returning.

Effie had noticed her red-rimmed eyes, and all three women had gathered around, easing the facts out of her before clucking about men and insisting on making her a cup of tea. It wasn't fair of Maura to compare them to the students with her now but she couldn't help thinking that Effie, Sharon and Cordelia would never have taken the tortured steel glaze from the cupboard without asking.

'I'm really sorry,' Lisa repeated, and she looked it. 'I won't do it again.'

She wouldn't, Maura thought, because the tub of tortured steel was going in the bin as soon as the class was over. But she did her best to summon up a reassuring smile. 'These things happen,' she said, starting to remove the ruined ghosts from the kiln. 'And at least your cup looks good.'

She tried not to look at the forlorn pile of ghosts in the blue metal bin once she'd finished clearing the kiln, their eyes were too reproachful as she piled them on top of each other. Perhaps she would keep them as seconds, she thought, and instantly dismissed the idea. Agnes was a sea witch, mournful and tragic, and her story was a terrible one. Fraser would have no use for a patchy pink version.

Fraser. She ought to message him, explain that she could offer him fifteen but that the rest would be delayed by a week or more. He would understand. But she found herself strangely reluctant to contact him, a feeling that had begun the night she had confronted Jamie and had only grown since.

It made no sense – Fraser had started off as her business partner but she'd begun to think of him as a friend too, and she knew he would have nothing but sympathy for her situation. The trouble was that she didn't want to have to tell him. Didn't want to see the pitying look in his eyes when she explained what Jamie had done. The mere thought of it made her squirm and she couldn't bear the idea that Fraser might somehow think less of her as a result. And it didn't matter how many times she reminded herself that he wasn't like that, the seed was too firmly entrenched to root it out.

So she'd stayed silent and ignored his messages, especially the one about an exhibition at Edinburgh Castle; she had no bandwidth to even contemplate such a high-pressure commitment. Perhaps by the time she had remade the damaged ghosts, she might be in a better place emotionally. Perhaps.

'I hate to tell you this, Maura, but I think your clay trap might be full.'

It was Tuesday morning and Maura had spent a very long weekend firing and decorating and glazing another batch of ghosts, while simultaneously working on the set of thirty plates for the restaurant owner she'd met at ScotPot and trying not to test the already stretched patience of her students any further. The kiln had run three times, which had warmed the studio and helped the other pieces on the shelves to dry more quickly, but she dreaded to think what it had done to her electricity bill. She'd hidden the energy monitor in the kitchen cupboard and didn't dare look at the soaring cost.

'I know,' she said, glancing over to where Cordelia stood gazing at a sink full of greyish water. 'It'll go down eventually but there's a bucket on the floor you can use to wash things in the meantime.'

Nodding, Cordelia did as she suggested. At the workbench, Sharon was doing her best to manage in the little space she had. Most of the surface was taken up by plates in various stages of development – some were drying, others were waiting to be glazed and still more needed to be fired for the final time. Maura had done her best to stack them where she could but there was also the small matter of twenty-five Agnes ghosts.

'I thought you'd finished those,' Sharon said, as she squeezed a pot of slip into a tiny gap and began to dab it along the seam of her pot.

Maura rubbed her forehead wearily. 'I had,' she said, and explained about the disastrous glaze reaction the week before.

'Exactly what you didn't need,' Effie said sympathetically. 'How's Fraser been about it?'

'Fine, I think,' Maura said, and gnawed her lip. 'I – um – haven't actually told him what happened. I thought I'd explain when I delivered this batch.'

Effie regarded her levelly. 'But aren't you horribly late with them?'

'And don't you need to deliver forty more next week?' Sharon asked, looking up from her clay.

'Yes,' Maura exclaimed, her tone snappier than she intended. 'I know, all right? I'm doing the best I can. It's just . . .' Her gaze came to rest on the full sink, its unappealing depths a mute accusation. Emptying the clay trap beneath it was a dirty job that needed muscle power and patience and a pair of thick rubber gloves, followed by a slog to the tip to dispose of the discarded clay. It had always been something Jamie did. She sucked in a deep breath and tried to ignore the pressure building behind her eyes. 'With Jamie and the ghosts and the plates ... I feel like I'm failing at everything.'

Instantly, they were beside her. 'Absolutely not,' Cordelia said firmly, guiding her to the nearest chair. 'It's a wonder you're still standing upright – I'd have taken to my bed for a month if I'd been through half what you have.'

'She's right,' Sharon agreed. 'Although it seems you might have fallen into the classic trap of working too hard as a way to escape your problems. When was the last time you had a day off?'

'Um ...' Now that she came to think of it, Maura couldn't remember the last time there'd been a day when she hadn't set foot in the studio. 'A while. But there's so much to do – I can't afford to take time off.'

Effie glanced around, taking in the cluttered surfaces and half-completed work. 'You need help,' she said. 'Tell us what we can do.'

Maura was shaking her head even before Effie had finished speaking. 'No. It's very kind of you but I can't ask you to do anything. This is my mess; I'll find a way out of it.'

Cordelia was also looking around, her eyes narrowed in thought. 'Obviously, we can't do any of the plates – none of us have Maura's skill. But I'm up for sorting out the sink.'

'Didn't you hear me?' Maura said, looking from one woman to the other. 'I said no.'

Sharon puffed out her cheeks. 'No offence, Maura, but I don't think you're in a position to turn us down. Only an idiot would refuse help when it's so desperately needed, and I know you're not an idiot.'

'Well—' Maura began to answer, then broke off. Sharon was right. She wasn't stupid enough to ignore the fact that she needed help, but that didn't mean she was unprofessional enough to expect her students to bail her out. 'I can't let you do this.'

Effie had picked up one of the ghosts waiting to be painted and was studying it with a critical eye. 'This just needs a lick of green underglaze along the lines of the seaweed, right? And then dipping in clear glaze before you fire it?'

'That's right,' Maura said. 'But—'

'I can do that,' Effie said.

'So can I,' Sharon offered.

Cordelia planted her hands on her hips and fixed Maura with a determined stare. 'So that's sorted. Maura can concentrate on the plates, Effie and Sharon will finish the ghosts and I'll empty the trap.'

Their kindness was almost too much for Maura. She felt her eyes swim as she battled a sudden lump in her throat. 'But you're my students,' she said in a small voice. 'You pay me to learn. You shouldn't have to do this.'

Cordelia placed a hand on her shoulder and squeezed. 'We've all been coming here a long time. I like to think we're also your friends.'

'Besides, we will be learning,' Effie said. 'Cordelia is going to learn what it's like to be up to her elbows in cold, slimy clay, and Sharon and me will be learning what it's like to be Maura McKenzie.' She picked up a paintbrush and twirled it airily. 'I call that a win-win.'

'If you say so,' Maura said weakly, and once again felt the hot burn of tears. 'Thank you. It's too much to ask but thank you.'

'Rubbish,' Cordelia said. 'That's what friends are for. Now, where do you keep the gloves?'

CHAPTER TWENTY

The woman glowering at Fraser was familiar but he wasn't sure why. She hadn't been on the tour he'd just finished, he was certain of that – the scowl she wore would have scared his punters far more than any ghost story he could tell. But here she was, outside a darkened Greyfriars Kirk, glaring as though she had a king-size bone to pick with him. Perhaps she was one of a long list of unhappy customers who were waiting to receive the ghost they had ordered.

Maura had finally been in touch, sending him a one-line message to explain that there'd been a problem in the manufacturing process but she expected to deliver the batch by Monday. Relieved, Fraser had told her not to worry and sent out an update to the waiting customers. Most had been understanding but there was always one, he thought. Or perhaps she was simply a homicidal maniac determined to inflict a grisly death upon him. As Callum had suggested at the castle gates, in Edinburgh it could be hard to tell.

'Hello,' he said easily as the last of the ghost walkers drifted away. 'Can I help you with something?'

She folded her arms. 'Yes, as a matter of fact you can, Fraser Bell.'

The use of his full name almost made him wince. He straightened up. 'Obviously, I'm at a bit of a disadvantage. You know my name but I'm afraid I don't know yours.'

'Kirsty Black,' she snapped. 'Maura's sister.'

Fraser wanted to click his fingers. Of course, he should have known. She didn't have Maura's dark curls or ethereal beauty but there was enough of a family resemblance to make the relationship obvious. Perhaps the furious scowl had fooled him. 'I remember now. You came on the tour with Maura.'

She nodded. 'I did.' The ferocity of her expression lessened a bit. 'You were very good.'

'Thank you,' Fraser said gravely. 'So what brings you here this evening? Obviously you've missed tonight's tour.'

'I've come to find out what the bloody hell you think you're playing at,' Kirsty said. 'Do you have any idea how close to a breakdown Maura is?'

Fraser felt his jaw drop. Whatever he'd been expecting her to say, it wasn't this. 'What?'

Kirsty narrowed her eyes. 'All these ghosts you've asked her to make. She's working eighteen-hour days to fit them in. It's not healthy. You're taking advantage of her good nature to make a profit and it's about time someone told you where to get off.'

'What?' Fraser said again, but this time it was purely to buy himself a few seconds to process the accusation. Maura was putting in eighteen-hour days? It was news to him. 'But she hasn't said anything.'

'Of course she hasn't,' Kirsty replied, rolling her eyes. 'She's a people pleaser. She doesn't want to let anyone down, least of all you. But she's working herself into the ground and if someone doesn't stop her, she's going to make herself ill.' Her raised voice had begun to attract attention; passers-by were throwing curious looks their way.

'Sorry, can we backtrack a bit? I know she's had a problem delivering the latest batch of ghosts, but I thought it was fixed now.'

Kirsty let out a harsh laugh. 'Yeah, I suppose you could call being cheated on by her boyfriend a *problem*. Good of you to acknowledge that.'

And now Fraser could only stare at her in open-mouthed bewilderment. He shook his head, aware he was gaping like a stupefied carp. 'What?'

His obvious confusion made Kirsty study him more closely. 'Ah,' she said, her voice subsiding into a more neutral tone. 'That explains one or two things. You don't know.'

'Jamie cheated on Maura?' he managed, slowly making sense of her words. 'When?'

Kirsty waved a hand. 'A few months ago. With one of her friends, to make things worse. A girl called Zoe.'

Fraser blinked. 'I know her. She came on one of my tours, tried to get me to go for a drink with her afterwards. But I thought she had a boyfriend.'

'She did,' Kirsty said. 'But it doesn't seem like that meant much to her, nor did the fact that Jamie was living with Maura. Evidently, she set her sights on him and spilled the beans about the affair when she ditched the boyfriend, presumably to force Jamie's hand and get Maura out of the picture.'

Fraser swore. He'd never thought much of Jamie – had always

felt Maura was far too good for him – but he'd known better than to air his views, even after Jamie's drunken performance at the Witchery. She'd always been so forgiving – so understanding – of his poor behaviour and now he'd betrayed her in the worst way; Fraser couldn't bear the idea that she'd been put through such hell. His hands curled into involuntary fists and he had to take several deep breaths to loosen them. 'How's Maura?' He shook the question away, irritated by his own insensitivity. 'Sorry, that's stupid of me. She must be devastated.'

Kirsty paused to consider. 'She was hurt, obviously. But it hasn't been one of those long, drawn-out breakups. Jamie didn't try to deny it, which I suppose he deserves a sliver of credit for – he packed a bag and left the same evening.'

An image of Maura swam into Fraser's head, her eyes red from crying. Fury bubbled up inside him. He wanted to swear again. 'Why didn't she tell me? I could have helped or – or something.'

'I don't know,' Kirsty said, and eyed him speculatively. 'I assumed she had.'

'Which is why you were furious with me for not offering her any support,' Fraser observed grimly. He ran a hand through his hair and stared at her. 'So now what? Obviously, I want her to take all the time she needs but I don't know whether she'll be happy that you've told me what's going on.'

Kirsty shrugged. 'As an older sister, there are times when you have to take matters into your own hands, regardless of what your sibling wants. You needed to know.'

Fraser took a breath, willing his indignation and anger to lessen so that he could think rationally. 'I did. Thank you for telling me.' He paused, remembering something else Kirsty had said. 'Is she really on the verge of a breakdown? Because of me?'

'Not solely because of you, you numpty,' Kirsty said, eyeing him with no small amount of scorn. 'Get over yourself. Obviously, the break-up is the biggest factor – that's a life-changing event. But pressure from you to deliver the ghosts among all the other work she has going on isn't helping. So maybe take a step back, let her know that pressure is off. That should ease things a bit.'

'I can do that,' Fraser said, relieved he'd told Tom and Rebecca he was changing the way they sold the ghosts. 'No problem.' He eyed Kirsty with some trepidation as another thought occurred to him. 'Should I go and see her?'

'That's up to you,' she said. 'She needs friends right now, just as much as family. Can you be a friend to her, Fraser?'

'I hope I already am,' he said, remembering the conversation he and Maura had shared on Portobello Beach. But the fact remained that when she'd needed support, she hadn't turned to him. 'But maybe I need to try harder.'

'That's the spirit,' Kirsty said. 'Just tread carefully. And be patient. I'm not sure she's really dealt with the fallout from Jamie's affair.'

He nodded. 'Of course. I'll do whatever I can to help.'

She sighed as she turned to leave. 'I can see you've got good intentions, Fraser. Just try not to make things worse.'

Fraser wasn't surprised to observe a little thrum of anxiety dancing along his nerves as he waited outside Maura's studio on Monday evening.

After his disconcerting conversation with Kirsty the

previous week, he'd messaged Maura to ask if she needed more time to deliver the ghosts. She'd come back with a suggestion that he call round to collect them in the evening rather than the afternoon and, since Monday was his night off from Dead Famous, he'd been happy to agree. He didn't like the idea that she was still working at seven o'clock but Kirsty had made it clear how much pressure her sister was under and Fraser was all too aware he wasn't in a position to lecture anyone about working too hard. From what Kirsty had said, Maura might be using her work as a means to avoid facing up to the end of her relationship and Fraser had no idea what to expect when she opened the door. He'd been through a painful break-up or two of his own over the years and there had been days when he had struggled to get out of bed, let alone shower and take care of himself. He could only hope she wasn't falling apart that badly.

'Hello,' she said, poking her head out of the smaller door that sat in the middle of the left-hand side of the garage doors. 'Come on in.'

Fraser ducked inside. The studio was warm and brightly lit, much the same as it had been during his previous visits. The shelves were loaded with the usual assortment of pots, some more finished than others, but he thought he could easily pick out those made by Maura. Several boxes sat at the base of the shelves; he saw the edge of a wide plate poking out of the crumpled paper packaging of one. More plates covered the workbenches, white glaze on black clay in a striking pattern that he imagined would look great in a restaurant setting. An open tub of glaze stood at one end of the bench, a paintbrush submerged in its depths, suggesting he'd interrupted her in the midst of decorating something. There wasn't much unused space. He had no idea how she fitted her students in.

'You're still hard at work,' he said, nodding towards the telltale brush.

'No rest for the wicked,' she said, and as she turned round, Fraser was able to observe her properly for the first time.

The changes were subtle but undeniable. She was thinner, for a start, and it showed in her face. The delicate roses had gone from her cheeks, leaving her porcelain skin pallid against the faint bluish tinges beneath her eyes. Her hair was scraped back in a severe ponytail – no unruly curls escaped to soften the style. She looked exhausted, causing him to wonder how well she'd been sleeping. Nowhere near enough if she'd been working eighteen-hour days, he thought, and had to battle a sudden urge to wrap her in a duvet.

Uncomfortably aware that he was scrutinising her, he forced the notion away and waved a hand at the crowded workbench. 'No rest for the good, either, from the looks of things.'

She pulled a wry face. 'I'm not sure about that. But it does mean I owe you an apology.'

'You really don't,' he said. 'I remember you told me at the start that pottery is never an exact science. A little delay hasn't caused any problems.'

Maura appeared unconvinced. 'Sorry, but I doubt that's true – you have customers waiting and I let you down. I took on too much work and it all got on top of me.' She took a breath, offering him a mechanical smile that flashed on and off like a light bulb, with no trace of its usual warmth. 'It won't happen again.'

She wrapped her arms around herself and Fraser was struck all over again by the desire to cocoon her in blankets.

'Honestly, it's all fine,' he said gently. 'There's nothing to be sorry for, especially after everything you've been through.' She glanced sharply at him then, her weary gaze suddenly questioning. He tipped his head in acknowledgement. 'I know about Jamie.'

For a moment, she simply stared at him, then her shoulders slumped. 'How?'

'Your sister. She came to see me last week, mostly to shout at me for being a lousy business partner, I might add, but she also told me what had happened.' He pressed his lips together in sympathy. 'I'm sorry, Maura. It sounds horrific.'

Her gaze settled on the half-finished plate. 'Relationships end all the time,' she said. 'Life goes on.'

'Yes, but—' He took in the mulish tilt of her chin and tried again. 'You've lost something that mattered, Maura. It's okay to take time to adjust, to mourn its loss.'

'That's the thing,' she said, the words slow. 'I've come to realise that whatever Jamie and I had died a long time ago. You saw us together – did we seem happy?'

Instinct prevented Fraser from giving his honest opinion of the relationship. 'I know he didn't treat you very well,' he replied warily, watching her as she moved towards the bench and bent to retrieve a small box that he guessed contained the ghosts. 'And for what it's worth, I don't think he made you happy.'

'Exactly,' she said. 'So there's nothing to mourn. You might even say he's done me a favour.'

Her voice shook a little, in spite of her best efforts to disguise it. Fraser wasn't sure whether it was caused by the pain of talking about the break-up or tiredness brought on by overwork, but Kirsty's parting comment was fresh in his mind; he wasn't about to worsen a bad situation.

'Look, I know you're in the middle of glazing that plate, and I'm only supposed to be picking up the ghosts, but do you fancy sharing a takeaway?'

'Sorry?' she said, blinking in surprise.

'I haven't eaten yet and I'm starving,' he said, deciding it was a necessary lie. 'We can get whatever you want. I'm buying.'

He thought she was going to refuse. She stood with the box in her hands, staring down at it as though it could tell her what to do, and he saw her lips begin to frame the rejection. But then a long, ragged sigh juddered through her, and when she looked up, he saw the shadow of a smile. 'I'm not going to lie, I could murder a crispy chilli beef. There's a decent Chinese not far from here – I've got a menu upstairs.'

Nearly two hours later, they were sitting side by side on the sofa in her apartment, crumbs of prawn crackers and spring rolls strewn across the coffee table in front of them. The last time Fraser had been inside was to deposit an inebriated Jamie, but that memory had been pushed aside as he'd helped Maura pull out plates and cutlery for the food that was already on its way.

He half-expected her to pick at the dishes, and she had been listless at first, but then her appetite had seemed to return and she'd eaten with gusto. She'd offered to open a bottle of wine, which he'd declined, and had found a bottle of sparkling water instead.

Fraser had done his best to make her laugh with stories from his acting days and slowly, some of the stress and exhaustion had slipped from her shoulders. She relaxed against the cushions, one leg tucked underneath her, and listened with rapt attention as he talked.

He wasn't sure when her eyes began to droop — sometime around ten o'clock, he supposed — but he didn't stop talking. At one point in his career, he'd had a job narrating sleep stories for a popular mindfulness app, and he knew all about levelling his cadence and tone to encourage an overwhelmed mind to let go and rest. When he was sure she was asleep, he got soundlessly to his feet and retrieved a hand-knitted blanket from the armchair to spread across Maura's legs. Then he gathered up the takeaway containers and dirty plates, taking them to the kitchen and rinsing them. He couldn't see a recycling box, assumed she kept it downstairs, so he stacked the clean plastic tubs neatly on the draining board and loaded the plates into the dishwasher. Satisfied he hadn't left any cleaning up for Maura to do, he padded softly back to the living room.

She'd nestled deeper into the cushions in his absence and the blanket had fallen to the floor. He stood for a moment, watching her sleep, glad to see a bloom of colour had crept into her pale cheeks. Then he collected the blanket and draped it over her once more, leaning down to tuck the edges around her more firmly so it wouldn't fall again.

The action broke her sleep. Her eyes opened just as he finished tucking in the blanket. 'Fraser,' she murmured as he began to straighten up. Her face tilted towards him, eyes widening as she took in his nearness. She reached up to lay a hand on his chest. 'Don't go.'

Those two words caused the air to freeze in Fraser's chest. Around him, time seemed to expand and contract, fracturing into a kaleidoscope of nanoseconds that danced before him in rainbow colours before melting away, leaving him unsure just how long he'd been staring at Maura.

The need in her eyes was palpable and he understood exactly why she'd spoken. Her self-confidence was in shreds, driving her to seek out reassurance and comfort. And he was right there, a mere breath away. It would be the most natural thing in the world to dip his head and soothe away all her doubt and pain for a few hours, to make her feel loved. But it would also be wrong, no matter how tempted he was. No matter how much she thought this was what she wanted. He cared about her too much to do anything that risked making her feel worse.

Easing back was the hardest thing Fraser had ever done. Maura's expression crumpled as she absorbed the rejection, making him feel wretched. Her eyes filled with tears and, for a moment, his self-control wavered. But he pressed his lips together and inched further back. Her hand dropped to her lap as she turned her face away. 'Don't think for a minute I don't want to,' he said, his voice low. 'But you're hurt and unhappy and I'd be no better than Jamie if I took advantage of that.'

Maura said nothing and her silence wrenched at him. She sniffed, her face still towards the sofa.

He waited in steady silence until at last she turned to look at him. 'You've been through enough and I want you to know I'm here whenever you need me, only a text or a call away. But as a friend, not as a mistake you'll only regret in the morning.'

He thought she might break then. She certainly had the right to. But instead she managed to soften the thin white line of her lips to let out a barely audible reply. 'Okay.'

Fraser took in the dark circles beneath her eyes, somehow

made more pronounced by the glitter of unshed tears. 'Will you sleep, do you think? You look exhausted.'

Again, it took her a little time to summon enough composure to answer. 'The nights have been rough. I haven't slept much.' A sudden yawn seemed to catch her by surprise, appearing to lessen the misery that had been gripping her. 'But maybe tonight will be different.'

He offered a smile. 'Want me to make you some warm milk? Camomile tea does the job for me but I haven't reached the point of middle age when I carry it around with me.'

It wasn't much of a joke but it raised the ghost of a smile at least.

'I can make my own milk,' she said, rubbing her hands over her face. 'Thanks for coming over and making me eat. I think I needed it.'

'Like I said, I'm here whenever you need me.'

She sighed. 'And I'm sorry to put you in such an awkward position. Thank you for turning me down.'

At this, his mouth quirked. 'Oh. Any time, I guess.'

She pulled the blanket across her lap and leaned back against the sofa. 'Trust me, it won't happen again,' she said, closing her eyes. 'You're a good friend, Fraser.'

Silently, he collected his jacket and the box of ghosts and made his way down the stairs. As he closed the front door and filled his lungs with the cool night air, he pictured Maura as he'd left her, at peace for a short while at least.

He'd meant it when he said he would be there for her whenever she needed him, as a friend as well as a business partner. It was probably wisest not to examine the ripple of regret clouding his thoughts. He'd been as good as his word – he'd tried his best not to make things worse, although he'd be a liar if he didn't admit he'd teetered on the brink for a heartbeat or two. But at least he would be able to look Kirsty in the eye the next time he saw her, as well as his own reflection in the mirror tomorrow morning, and that was what really mattered. Not the faint whisper in his head that something had been lost.

Thrusting the thought away, Fraser jammed his hands into his pockets and set off for home.

PART FOUR

PROLOGUE

The last thing Fraser expected to see on the concourse of Euston station was a face from school.

It was a week before Christmas, the Met Office had issued a weather warning for imminent snow, and there was a feverish buzz hanging over the jostling crowds scanning the departure boards. Some trains had been cancelled, others were delayed, and it seemed to Fraser as though half of London was trying to escape the city before the blizzard began. Judging from the tense expressions of those around him, there would be a stampede when the whirring boards eventually revealed the platform of the Edinburgh train. Elbows would be deployed. Every upturned face was grim with the expectation of battle.

The only person not staring upwards was a dark-haired girl of around Fraser's age, who stood a few metres away with her nose in a book, seemingly oblivious to the simmering tension among her fellow travellers. He recognised her instantly – until the summer, they'd attended the same school. How many times had he seen her through the window of the art block, as he'd passed by on his way to the drama studio? They'd shared some classes too, before study choices had sent them in different directions. And now here she was, out of place but with the same otherworldly serenity that had so often caught his eye at school, her head bowed as she read. Her stillness stood out even more among the grumbling and muttering of the Euston crowd.

Fraser guessed she must be waiting for the same train he was, probably heading back to Edinburgh for Christmas after her first term at uni. He hadn't known she was in London.

He was just debating whether to disturb her when the departures board began to rattle. An expectant rustling joined the clickety-clack, like the soft hiss of a brush on the snare beneath the louder percussion in an orchestra, as the assembled travellers got ready to move. For a second or two, everyone held their breath. Fraser's own attention switched momentarily upwards. And then the whirring stopped and the spell broke. Several hundred people seemed to sigh, moving as one towards platform fifteen.

Fraser went with them, glancing over his shoulder to see if the girl was near, but there was no sign of her. By the time he located the correct carriage and settled into his seat, he was beginning to wonder whether he'd imagined her. It had often been that way at school – a fleeting glimpse that had ensnared him for a heartbeat or two and then let go. If the train hadn't been so busy, he could have tried to find her, but he knew the aisles would be too full to allow that. He might run into her at Waverley station, once the train reached Edinburgh, but he didn't hold much hope. She was a will-o'-the-wisp, there one moment and vanished the next, a glimmering girl always tantalisingly beyond his reach, even when they'd shared the same classroom. And who was to say she'd have known him, had she looked up from her book to see him among the crowd? He suspected she would simply have frowned, wondering at this vaguely familiar stranger with the tentative smile, before returning to her book with the same gentle indifference she'd shown throughout their school years.

As the train jolted and rumbled out of London, Fraser pulled out his battered study copy of *Henry V*, determined to force the encounter from his thoughts. He was heading home for Christmas, where the old St Ignatius crowd would be waiting to catch up and celebrate the festive season. There was a faint possibility she would be there, he realised, although he couldn't recall her hanging out at the Strawberry in the past.

With a sigh, he turned his attention to the highlighted passage of the text and silently ran through the lines for next term's assignment.

By the time the train reached Watford, the dark-haired girl had slipped away once more.

CHAPTER TWENTY-ONE

Eighteen Years Later

'Maura, come in.' Ewan McRae ushered her into his wood-panelled office. 'Good to see you again. Can I offer you a tea or coffee?'

Maura gave a polite smile. 'No, thanks,' she said, and tapped the bag slung over her shoulder. 'I have a bottle of water.'

'Excellent,' Ewan said. He turned his attention to the young woman who had met Maura at Edinburgh Castle's imposing gatehouse and guided her through the maze of corridors. 'Thanks, Catriona. I'll show Maura out when we're finished.'

'No problem,' she said. 'Lovely to meet you again.'

The door closed softly behind her as she left, and Maura had to fight the sudden wave of nervousness that was threatening to engulf her.

Now that she was here, she was starting to regret turning down Fraser's offer to accompany her to this meeting with the castle's head of visitor engagement. But, strictly speaking, it was about her own work rather than the ghosts she produced for Fraser's walking tour, Dead Famous. She wanted to show him she was capable of doing this without someone to hold her hand.

Ewan indicated one of two empty chairs standing sentry beside a grand but unlit fireplace. 'Have a seat,' he said, settling into one of the chairs.

Maura perched on the other, surreptitiously wiping her palms on her skirt, relieved he hadn't offered to shake hands. She did her best to appear composed. 'Thanks for inviting me here. Your workplace is a lot more impressive than mine.'

'There's a tad less clay, I imagine,' he said, returning her smile. 'But it's not bad, as long as you don't mind the odd ghost.'

Maura felt some of her tension ease. She knew all about the castle's unearthly inhabitants from Fraser's ghost tour of the vaults the previous month. 'Of course.'

'But it's the human visitors I wanted to discuss with you today,' Ewan went on. 'The castle welcomes around two million people each year and we're always looking for fresh ways to engage with them. Sometimes, that takes the form of special tours, like the one Fraser performed for us, and on other occasions it might be an exhibition of items we think our visitors might find interesting or educational.'

She nodded. During her last visit, there had been a display of maps and photographs relating to the Second World War curated by the grandson of a captain in the Royal Scots regiment, and she thought she recalled an exhibition on traditional tartans linked to the castle.

'When Fraser showed me the wee ghosts you'd produced for him, I took the liberty of looking you up,' Ewan went on. 'And of course I liked what I saw, particularly the bowls inspired by the sea and pieces reflecting Edinburgh's volcanic past. Which leads me to the reason I invited you here. As an Edinburgh artist, how would you feel about a month-long exhibition of your work?'

It wasn't exactly a surprise – he'd mentioned a possible exhibition when they'd chatted after Fraser's press night tour of the castle – but a month was more than she'd anticipated.

'I'd be honoured,' she said truthfully, and then doubt began to creep in. 'How big is the space? A few pieces spring to mind but I'm not sure I've got anything impressive enough to do the castle justice.'

He raised a hand. 'I thought one of the guards' barracks,' he said. 'There's some armour and weaponry in there that could easily be redistributed. As to what you include, you'll liaise with Catriona but the curation is entirely in your hands. All I ask is that you include one or two pieces that reflect the castle in some way, as well as the wider city.'

Maura sat back, her mind whirling. How long had it been since she'd had an exhibition of her own? Three or four years, at least. The biggest had been sponsored by the bank Jamie had worked for; she'd sold a lot of pieces and it had led to a number of interesting commissions, as well as a bumpy five-year relationship with Jamie himself. But did she have anything already made that met the brief Ewan described? She wasn't sure. 'When did you have in mind?' she asked, running through her existing workload.

'I thought perhaps the beginning of September,' he suggested. 'Once the madness of August has died down.'

She blinked. That gave her around two months – less time than she'd like, once she factored in the ongoing ghost order from Fraser. But a message from Lisa, the last of her Thursday morning students, was still fresh in her mind.

The first cancellation had arrived from Nina a few days earlier. All three of the Thursday group had been known to take
breaks from the studio, dipping in and out as their commitments allowed, but Nina had been the most openly disgruntled
about the length of time it had taken to fire recent pieces. Maura
wanted to point out that she'd never made any promises – the
kiln ran when she had enough to fill the different types of
firings and there was an unspoken agreement among all of her
students that her own work sometimes took priority.

The unexpected success of Fraser's ghosts meant pressure on
the kiln had increased and, after the initial sting of Nina's message had subsided, Maura had consoled herself that a temporary
drop in the number of students she worked with might not be
a bad thing. Jude's message arrived a few hours after Nina's,
citing an increase in working hours, and Lisa's had dropped
that morning, which left Thursdays mornings clear in Maura's
diary. She still had her Tuesday morning students, thankfully,
but she was beginning to wonder if the universe was trying to
tell her something. No pieces to fire from Nina, Jude or Lisa
meant more space in the kiln, which would allow Maura to
experiment with fresh ideas.

'I'd need to see the room,' she said slowly, aware she'd been
lost in her own thoughts for longer than was socially acceptable.

Ewan spread his hands. 'I can take you there now. And it goes
without saying that we'll be paying you. I thought we might
negotiate a flat fee, with the potential to mark items as reserved
on a commission basis if someone takes a fancy to them.'

Again, Maura's thoughts flew to the trio of messages on her
phone, and the corresponding hole in her income. Breaking up
with Jamie might not have left her worrying about keeping a

roof over her head, but she still had bills to pay. 'That sounds perfect,' she said, hoping she didn't sound too grateful.

'Excellent,' he said, rubbing his hands together in brisk satisfaction. 'Why don't I show you the space and then you can have a think about it before you make a final decision?'

The barracks were a series of low-ceilinged stone rooms. As Ewan had said, they were currently housing an intimidating display of sixteenth-century armour, but even so, Maura could see the potential of the space. The windows were small, a handful of diamond-shaped panes split by lead that didn't allow much daylight in, but spotlights had been fitted overhead, illuminating the displays with clean, bright brilliance.

Standing in the centre of the room, Maura turned in a slow, deliberate circle, taking care not to rattle the nearest suit of armour. Narrow tables could line the walls and a series of islands at differing heights in the middle would make an arresting focal point, she thought, with sculptures to represent the volcanic foundations of Castle Rock, the stone magnificence of the man-made structure that sat on top of it and the nearby North Sea that had made the site such a logical choice for a stronghold. She might even try to capture a flavour of the challenges the city had borne as it evolved into the thriving capital it was now.

'What do you think?' Ewan asked.

Maura took a deep breath. 'I've got one or two ideas,' she said cautiously. 'Leave it with me.'

The first person she wanted to call, once Ewan had escorted her through the gatehouse and left her on the esplanade, was Fraser. It was thanks to him that she had this opportunity in the first place, and she knew he would be delighted for her. But she kept her phone resolutely in her pocket, resisting the urge to dial his number.

While she had no doubt he'd forgotten the moment she'd all but thrown herself at him, in the early days after breaking up with Jamie, Maura herself had not. Fraser had been far too kind to mention it – had been his usual friendly, concerned self – and Maura would rather gargle with glass than raise the subject. But she'd be lying if she said the impulse to ask him to stay had been a fleeting thought.

It had grown over the weeks that followed, nurtured by the care he took to check in with her, making sure she was eating and sleeping rather than spending half the night working. On one occasion, he'd turned up with a bag filled with all the foods he knew she liked. She'd almost burst into tears – how long had it been since she'd been looked after like this? And yet she knew he was acting as a friend. He'd told her so when he'd turned her down. It hadn't been a flat, horrified rejection, but one couched in understanding; what she'd needed then was an ally, not a one-night stand that would ruin their business relationship as well as their friendship. And he had been tempted to say yes. Maura hugged that admission to herself whenever mortification threatened to overwhelm her. Could she dare to hope that he was being a friend to her now, when she was getting over the break-up with Jamie, so that he could be more in the future? She didn't know, and the thought of testing the boundaries of friendship again made her feel hot and cold with anticipation and dread.

She would call Kirsty first, she decided, as she began to make her way towards Castlehill. Her sister's no-nonsense attitude would ensure Maura wasn't getting swept away by the enticing prospect of an exhibition of her own at such a prestigious venue. Kirsty would demand to know how Maura planned to fit the work in, as well as offer an opinion on the fee she could reasonably negotiate.

And then, once Kirsty's pragmatism had brought her back down to earth, she might allow herself to call Fraser.

'I've got a proposition for you.'

Sharon had arrived at the studio early on Tuesday morning, her expression both set and hopeful as she took off her coat.

'Have you?' Maura said, somewhat warily. She knew that look. Mostly she'd seen it when Sharon first started classes, when she had been determined to ignore Maura's advice with regard to a technique or glaze. It meant she had already made her mind up and it had generally ended badly, at least where her pottery was concerned.

The other woman nodded. 'You need help with the ghosts. I like helping you. So why don't I come in one day a week and, well, help you properly?' She fired an appealing look at Maura before hurrying on. 'That way, I can make my own things on Tuesdays, and still do the ghosts another day. You wouldn't have to pay me – it would be a privilege to do it and I'd be learning a lot. I thought maybe Thursdays, since you don't have any students now.' She stopped talking and stared at Maura, wide-eyed and slightly breathless.

Maura's first instinct was to say no – she didn't need an assistant, or an apprentice, or whatever it was Sharon was suggesting. But the prospect of the exhibition made her pause. The truth was that Sharon had been an enormous help over the past weeks, along with Effie and Cordelia, and it was quite likely

Maura would need to rely on her again as she began working on the new project. Perhaps the idea wasn't as bad as it seemed. It might even be a way of saying thank you. She held up a hand. 'First of all, I'd absolutely pay you. It wouldn't be much but that's non-negotiable.'

Sharon opened her mouth to object but Maura shook her head. 'No, don't argue. Apart from that . . .' She took a deep breath and let it out again as a smile crept across her face. 'Apart from that, I think it's a great idea and I'd be over the moon to work with you. When can you start?'

Sharon beamed at her. 'Is this week too soon?'

CHAPTER TWENTY-TWO

It was no good, Fraser thought as Sam's number flashed up on the screen of his phone for the second time that morning. After weeks of hitting mute, he was going to have to speak to his agent.

'Finally!' Sam's voice exploded from the speaker the moment the call connected. 'I was beginning to think you'd lost both your hands in some terrible supernatural accident.'

Fraser perched on the edge of his sofa. 'I've replied to your emails,' he said defensively. 'Some of your emails.'

'Two,' Sam said. 'And that was months ago. Where have you been, Fraser? Under a tombstone?'

That caused the corners of Fraser's mouth to twitch. 'You know where I've been,' he said after a moment. 'In Edinburgh, running walking tours. I'm not acting anymore, remember?'

'Of course I remember,' Sam huffed. 'But I have Marco Minelli's people breathing down my neck. He wants you for his new blockbuster and he won't take no for an answer.'

The name made Fraser pause. Marco Minelli was film industry royalty – everything he directed turned to box office gold and he was used to getting whatever, or whomever, he wanted. No wonder Sam had been so desperate to get hold of him. But the news raised more questions than it answered. While Fraser had achieved some notable success throughout his acting career, he couldn't imagine any of the roles he'd played catching the eye of someone like Minelli. 'Are you sure it's me he wants?' he asked doubtfully. 'There isn't another Fraser Bell he's confusing me with?'

Sam's tone was dry. 'Credit me with some sense, Fraser. They linked to your IMDb profile – it's definitely you he wants.' He paused. 'To be honest, I was as surprised as you at first. But a director like Marco Minelli does not come calling every day. When he does, you don't ask if he's confused you with someone else.'

Fraser couldn't argue. There'd been a time when he would have crawled over hot coals to work with such a stellar director. But that had been before he'd made the decision to change career. 'Is this a wind-up, Sam? Something to suck me back in before you hit me with another fast food audition?'

'Would I do that?' Sam said, now sounding wounded. 'Look, I know you said you're out of the game but seriously, Fraser, you don't need me to tell you this could change your life. Marco. Minelli. You'd be an overnight superstar.'

Fraser's mouth twisted wryly. 'An overnight superstar who actually took twenty years to go supernova.'

'Never mind that now,' Sam dismissed. 'He wants to talk to you – get the measure of you before he offers you the role.'

There was no doubt it was flattering, but Fraser had known his agent a long time. He still wasn't convinced Sam hadn't made the whole thing up to reel him back in for the kind of smaller role he'd left acting to escape. 'Even if I was interested,

I've got commitments here in Edinburgh,' he said, shaking his head. 'I can't just take off to London at a moment's notice.'

'You don't need to. He's going to be in Glasgow. He'll meet you there.'

Fraser laughed. The thought of Minelli hanging out in Glasgow was possibly the most unbelievable moment of the conversation so far. 'Doesn't he live in LA?'

'Yes.' Sam drew the word out with exaggerated patience. 'But we have these things called aeroplanes; they move people from one place to another. Apparently, he needs to check out some locations so he'll be in Glasgow next month.'

That was interesting, Fraser thought, his interest piqued in spite of himself. 'So the film is set in Scotland?'

'I don't have all the details,' Sam said. 'But it was pitched to me as *Trainspotting* meets *Ocean's Eleven*.'

Fraser considered what he knew of both films. It was hard to imagine two plots with less in common. 'Right.'

Sam seemed to sense he was losing him. 'Okay, I know it's not exactly your thing but think of all the roles it would lead to. You could be the next Gerard Butler – the next Clooney.' He hesitated, then went for broke. 'The next Connery.'

Fraser laughed again. Just when he thought things couldn't get any more preposterous. 'Seriously? I thought Nick Borrowdale was all set to be the next Bond.'

'Okay, you might have to wait a few years for that,' Sam replied expansively. 'But it definitely won't happen if you don't take a chance. All you have to do is meet Marco. What have you got to lose?'

When he put it like that, it was harder for Fraser to argue. 'When?'

'Obviously, I don't have a date right now,' Sam said. 'I wasn't sure you were still alive, for a start. But I'll speak to Minelli's assistant and get back to you. Watch this space.'

Fraser closed his eyes. It would be like the bad old days, when his life had revolved around last-minute dashes to auditions and inevitable disappointment when they came to nothing. 'Sam—'

'I know, I know,' Sam said soothingly. 'But it will all be worth it when he offers you the part.'

Would it? Fraser wondered, but he could already feel the pull of temptation. He needed to remember all the times Sam had made similar proclamations, only for his hopes to be crushed. It was a rollercoaster he hadn't missed since moving to Edinburgh, that was for sure. 'I'll think about it. No promises.'

'Good man,' Sam said. 'I'll be in touch as soon as I know more. You won't regret this.'

'I already do,' Fraser said, before realising he was talking to himself. Sam had rung off.

He spent a moment or two staring out of the window, watching the clouds scud across the pale blue sky. The world Marco Minelli inhabited was a million miles away from anything Fraser had experienced, even when he'd been doing well enough to attend glamorous London parties or pose on the red carpet, and the revelation that the director was inexplicably interested in Fraser was starting to feel like a dream.

Even so, he picked up his phone and tapped out a message to an old friend. It wouldn't hurt to get the lie of the land, would it? And if anyone had their finger on the pulse of who was hot and who wasn't in the film business, it was Nick Borrowdale.

*

'I can't believe you did this.'

Fraser stared across the table of Edinburgh's most exclusive restaurant, taking in the grin of his old drama school friend. Only a celebrity of Nick Borrowdale's calibre could sail into Wallace's without a reservation and be ushered to a prime lunch spot without a murmur, and Fraser was happy to travel in his wake.

Nick was one of the happy few whose career had taken off after he'd landed the lead in a BBC adaptation when he was in his mid-twenties, and it had shown no signs of slowing down since. When Hollywood had come calling, he'd taken the elevation in his stride, while somehow managing to remember his roots and remain one of the nicest people in the business. If he wasn't his friend, Fraser would probably hate him.

'I'm between jobs,' Nick said, his trademark Irish brogue as undimmed as the day Fraser had first met him. 'It only takes an hour or so to fly from London to Edinburgh and this felt like a conversation we needed to have in person. And since you never come south of the border these days, I had to come to you.' He glanced around the restaurant, catching the eye of the starstruck waitress and flashing her a charming smile. 'Besides, I love Edinburgh. I was glad of the excuse to hop on the plane.'

'You've changed,' Fraser said, with mock reproof. 'I still remember when you had to scrape together the train fare to go from London to Elstree.'

'Me too,' Nick said cheerfully. 'But luckily for you, I've got a bit more change down the back of the sofa these days.' Sinking his fork into a buttery new potato, he fixed Fraser with a look. 'So, the big time is knocking at your door, is it? I can't say I'm surprised.'

Fraser chewed ruminatively on a mouthful of steak. 'Is it, though? I've only got Sam's word for it.'

Nick shrugged. 'There's definitely a script and Minelli is on board. Rumour has it the Oscars are being engraved already.'

That gave Fraser a moment's pause. Hearing it from Nick gave things a solidity, and the mention of the Oscars sent a thrill chasing along his spine, even though he knew any awards would be for Minelli. 'If it's such a stellar role, why aren't you up for it?'

'A schedule clash,' Nick said, lifting his glass of red. 'There's only one of me, sadly, and even I can't be on two continents at the same time.'

Fraser raised his eyebrows. 'Not even for an Oscar? What's the other role?'

'I'm sworn to secrecy,' Nick replied, dropping an exaggerated wink. 'But even if I was available, the truth is that I'm not right for the part – I can't do a Scottish accent to save my life, for a start. It's perfect for you, though. Are you sure you're not tempted?'

'We wouldn't be having this conversation if I wasn't tempted,' Fraser pointed out. 'But you know what acting is like – the audience can smell it a mile off when your heart isn't in the role. And it's been a long time since I felt the love for telling a story.'

It wasn't strictly true – he loved doing the ghost tours, watching the audience fall under his spell and live every word of the tales he spun. But that wasn't what was on offer here. In the film industry, the audience reaction occurred long after the performance had been captured. If they loved it, he'd only know by reading the critics' reviews.

Nick eyed him closely. 'You'd be working with the best. That can be powerful.'

Fraser tipped his head. 'I know all about the Minelli magic, but that's the other thing. From what Sam said, the concept sounds mad.'

His friend laughed. 'I can't argue with that. But I got the impression that the script is still a work in progress so that might change. And actually, it doesn't matter too much because you've already put your finger on the salient point, which is that Marco is a maestro who can spin straw into gold. Most actors would sell their own mothers to work with him.'

That was certainly true, Fraser thought. 'A few years ago, maybe,' he admitted, and thought guiltily of his mum, who had always been his biggest fan and would probably volunteer to be sold if she thought it would help. 'Not my mother, though. Maybe my dad.'

'You don't have to sell either,' Nick said, pointing his fork at Fraser for emphasis. 'You, my friend, have been chosen.'

'But how?' Fraser asked, repeating the question that had been bothering him ever since his conversation with Sam. 'How does someone like Marco Minelli even know who I am? Surely I can't have been in anything he could have seen.'

Nick fired a mischievous grin across the table. 'Maybe he's a fried chicken man.'

'My point exactly,' Fraser said, trying not to groan.

'You could always ask him,' Nick suggested. 'You know, when you go to meet him.' He gazed at Fraser thoughtfully. 'Unless there's something you're not telling me. Something that's worth more than the glittering opportunity you've dreamt about since drama school.'

For all Nick was his friend, Fraser wasn't sure he could explain why he hadn't immediately leapt at the chance to meet Minelli. The quiet enjoyment he'd found doing the walking tours wasn't anything like the extraordinary career Nick enjoyed. It paid more than enough to meet Fraser's needs, as well as supporting two other storytellers, but it wasn't even close to the status offered by appearing on TV or in a successful movie. It didn't offer the plaudits or gravitas of performing night after night on stage, nor was it going to win him an Oscar or see him invited to A-list parties, but for Fraser, that didn't matter. His audience might be small but they left him having been thoroughly entertained, and that gave him no small amount of job satisfaction. The challenge of finding new ways to grow Dead Famous into a thriving business drove him out of bed each morning and even Edinburgh's notoriously capricious weather couldn't dampen his enthusiasm. Having been at the mercy of casting directors for so long, he liked knowing he was in charge of his own creative endeavours. It was the sense that now, at last, he was enough. How could he explain any of that to Nick, who had probably forgotten what it was like to be rejected?

'I think I'm happy with what I have,' Fraser said at length. 'I know it doesn't look like much, running tours and telling ghost stories every night, but it's steady. Predictable. Enjoyable.'

'The complete opposite of an acting career, in other words,' Nick said dryly.

Fraser dipped his head in acknowledgement. 'I like having the audience so close,' he went on. 'Reading their reactions and judging when to ramp up the drama and when to tone it down so I have them in the palm of my hand the whole time. The stories might be the same but the performances change from night to night. I'm never bored.'

His friend nodded. 'I can see why you don't want to give that up.' He eyed Fraser meditatively. 'Although when I heard you'd broken up with Naomi, I did wonder whether perhaps you'd fallen in love with more than just the city.'

There was no doubt what he was getting at and, unbidden, an image of Maura popped into Fraser's head. He couldn't deny how important she'd become to him, but he wasn't sure he could explain that to Nick either. Apart from anything else, he strongly suspected his protestations that he and Maura were just good friends would be met with raised eyebrows and un-bridled scepticism. It was a conversation he'd rather not have. 'The chance would be a fine thing,' he said, falling back on the time-honoured response to questions of romance. 'I don't have the time.'

Eyeing him over his wine glass, Nick shook his head. 'I think I need to see you perform the role that's making you turn down Marco Minelli. Any chance of a ticket?' A fellow diner passed the table, goggling first at Nick and then eyeballing Fraser, as though checking whether he was equally famous. Nick's mouth twitched. 'I could wear a cap, loiter at the back.'

It would take more than a hat to disguise Nick's identity, Fraser felt, but he wasn't about to say no – not when his friend had dropped everything to listen to his problems. 'I think that can be arranged, although I don't know if you'll be able to get back to London afterwards.'

'Who said anything about that?' Nick asked and winked. 'How do you fancy a flatmate for the night?'

CHAPTER TWENTY-THREE

It wasn't a date, Maura reminded herself for what felt like the hundredth time as she and Fraser took their seats in the Grand Circle of the Lyceum Theatre. Apart from anything else, it was a Saturday afternoon, hardly the most romantic time of day, and the play they were going to watch was *The Merchant of Venice,* which she dimly recalled was about greed and revenge. And since she'd booked the tickets as a thank you to Fraser for his kindness, she was determined to ignore the fizzle of excitement she'd felt when she spotted him waiting outside the theatre. *Friends*, she had told herself sternly as she'd smiled and said hello. *Nothing more.*

'How's the exhibition prep going?' Fraser asked, once they were settled into the red velvet seats. 'Are you coping with the extra work?'

'So far so good,' she said cautiously. 'At one stage I thought I'd made the volcanic lava bowl too big for the kiln, but it just fitted.'

He raised an eyebrow. 'Sounds intriguing. When does the exhibition open?'

'At the start of September,' she answered, forcing down the

familiar stab of anxiety when she considered how quickly time was passing.

Conscious that two months was not long to fill a room with bespoke ceramics, she'd begun sketching out designs almost as soon as she had returned from her meeting with Ewan McRae, before the fee had been negotiated or the agreement signed. Catriona had been delighted with her vision for the exhibition, offering one or two suggestions on layout but bowing to Maura's experience and skill when it came to the work itself. And then Maura had devised a schedule; the larger pieces would take longest to dry and needed to be crafted as a priority. There was more chance that they might crack in the kiln or simply not turn out the way she expected – she needed to allow time to experiment and possibly fail.

There were also the ghosts. She had two designs to produce now and sales showed no signs of dropping off. Having Sharon on board to decorate and glaze them on Thursdays was a big help, and there was no doubt she saw it as a learning experience as well as earning some money, but Maura was still grateful. She seemed happy to help. Effie and Cordelia were keen to do what they could too, but Maura couldn't lean on their goodwill for much longer. Once the pieces for the exhibition were complete, she intended to make sure all three students felt able to focus on making things for themselves once more, at least on Tuesday mornings.

Fraser's gaze was concerned as he regarded her. 'You're not pushing yourself too hard, are you? All work and no play is a famously bad combination.'

She straightened her shoulders, determined to show him she had everything under control. 'That's why we're here. I mean, what could be more playful than an actual play?'

To her relief, he laughed. 'Point taken. Although this particular play isn't overflowing with fun. I played Bassanio for the Royal Shakespeare Company a few years ago and he makes some terrible decisions that almost cost Antonio his life. But Portia steals the show. She's resourceful, strong and clever – a bit like a certain potter I know.'

The unexpected praise caught Maura off guard. She dropped her head to the programme in her hand, flustered and pleased at the same time, hoping the sudden burst of warmth she was experiencing had not transferred to her cheeks. 'Oh, shush,' she said, although she couldn't help smiling as she fired a sideways glance his way.

'It's true,' he said mildly. 'There are a few Shakespearean characters that remind me of you, actually.'

It was too much for Maura, who was still struggling to accept the previous compliment. She held up the programme and hid behind an obvious joke. 'If you say Bottom, I'll hit you with this.'

He smiled. 'I was going to say Ariel, from *The Tempest*. At school, you always had this aura of otherworldliness about you, as though you slipped in and out of lessons when it suited you. I remember catching sight of you once or twice and not being sure whether you were real or a figment of my imagination. You were magical. Mysterious.'

The breath caught in Maura's throat. She'd expected him to suggest Hermia, because one of the few times they had spoken at school had been after an English class where she'd read Hermia's lines against his Lysander. But instead, he'd chosen Ariel, whose superpower was flitting in and out of the shadows, often staying invisible. It was quite a perceptive observation, Maura decided, given how distantly their worlds had orbited each other, although perhaps not as flattering as it first seemed, given that Ariel was male, despite often being played as female. But still – she hadn't realised Fraser had noticed her at school. And he'd used the word 'magical'. That was definitely pleasing, even if he must now have come to realise just how disappointingly ordinary she was.

She was saved from having to address any of it by the sudden dimming of the house lights. An expectant hush settled over the audience as faces turned towards the stage, leaving Maura relieved and discombobulated in equal measure.

'Showtime,' Fraser whispered, sounding so like a child on Christmas morning that she had to smile. It was probably a good thing she hadn't had time to respond to his revelation. At least now she couldn't say anything embarrassing.

Even so, she was acutely aware of him beside her as the characters strode on stage. His shoulder pressed against hers in the narrow seats, his leg mere centimetres from her own in the darkness. If she turned her head a little to the right, she could see his rapt expression. When Bassanio appeared, Fraser's lips silently moved as the actor delivered his lines.

Afraid he would catch her staring, Maura pinned her gaze to the action on stage and before long, the story drew her in. As Shakespeare's brilliance wove its spell, she forgot who sat next to her; she forgot she was in a theatre. By the time the curtain fell for the interval, she was entirely invested in the characters' predicaments. She knew, of course, how the play ended, but it was a testament to the excellent performances that she found herself worrying all the same.

Fraser was full of praise as they sipped their drinks in the bar, surrounded by the excited chatter of their fellow theatregoers. 'Shylock is incredible,' he said, shaking his head in disbelief. 'It's a tough role to get right, with modern sensibilities, but I found myself sympathising with him more than once.'

His face was alight, glowing with the same enthusiasm she had observed as they'd been watching the play. She'd never seen him quite so inspired, not even when he'd been immersed in telling ghost stories during the castle tour. 'You must miss that,' she said. 'Delving into a meaty character, I mean. Really becoming them.'

The glow dimmed a little as he considered her words. 'Yes and no. I don't miss having to memorise hundreds of lines, that's for sure, but it wasn't all hard work. Once or twice I really felt as though I got under the skin of my character, so that it hardly felt like work at all.' He took a pensive sip of his drink. 'I miss that.'

'Maybe you should think about going back to it,' she said, and instantly felt it was the wrong thing to say. He'd confided more than once that acting hadn't made him happy, no matter how much he might miss certain aspects of it.

But Fraser was eyeing her thoughtfully. 'It's funny you should say that.' He puffed out a long breath, as though weighing up his next words. 'An opportunity has come up – a possible film role in an upcoming production.'

A burst of excitement fizzed in the pit of Maura's stomach at the unexpected news. 'Really? But that's amazing.' She took in his neutral tone and tempered her own. 'Isn't it?'

'It's flattering,' he said, shrugging. 'The director is keen for me to do it – I don't even have to audition and it's the kind of offer I dreamed of for years.'

She stared at him, not sure she understood the problem. 'If it's a dream come true, then you should definitely do it. Who's the director? Anyone I've heard of?'

He puffed out his cheeks. 'Marco Minelli.'

'Seriously?' Maura squeaked. Was there a single person alive who couldn't name a Minelli film? Even her dad had heard of him, and he rarely watched anything that didn't involve a ball. 'Bloody hell.'

'You see my dilemma,' Fraser sighed. 'If I say no, I'm always going to wonder what it would have been like. But if I say yes . . .'

He trailed off, but Maura didn't need him to finish the sentence to appreciate the enormity of what would happen if he took the role. He'd have to go on location, for a start, probably to America and for months on end, which would mean handing the ghost tour business over to someone else. And when the film came out, everything would change. He wouldn't be able to walk down the street without being recognised. He'd be propelled into global stardom, with all the highs and lows that came with such fame, hanging out with Hollywood A-listers and other beautiful, talented types.

A hot flush of realisation surged through Maura. He would be whisked far beyond her, no longer only a message away, because he wouldn't have time to worry about pink-tinged ghosts or any of the other inconsequential concerns of his one-time business partner. In the whirl of his long-cherished dreams coming true, she would be forgotten, and her own barely acknowledged dream of a future with Fraser would be lost too.

She took a gulp of her drink, scarcely tasting it. 'You should do it.' Her lips felt numb. She was sure she mumbled the words, barely able to believe she could say them at all, but he still heard.

'You're not the first person to tell me that,' he said, shaking his head. 'And obviously, I'm tempted. It's just . . .'

He broke off, his eyes resting on hers, and for an awful moment, she thought he must see her selfish fears reflected there. But he couldn't know, she reassured herself, forcing her thudding heart to slow. Apart from the night he'd gently turned her down, she'd given no sign she felt anything inappropriate for Fraser. Maura was sure of that. Whatever was holding him back, it had nothing to do with her. But that didn't mean she couldn't understand his reluctance.

At school, he'd seemed so confident, so blessed by talent that success could not fail to follow. And it had – he'd made a career for himself, bagging roles in well-respected television shows and stage productions as well as the fast food adverts he was so quick to poke fun at – but Maura knew ambition could be an exhausting companion. From what Fraser had said, that exhaustion had exacted a heavy toll.

But she also recognised The Fear when she saw it; that insidious voice heard by every creative person she knew. The one that instilled doubt in their abilities and fostered a sometimes insurmountable fear of failure. Perhaps what Fraser needed most was encouragement to take a leap of faith. Wasn't that what a true friend would offer?

'You should go for it,' she repeated, her tone quiet and resolute. 'Yes, your life will probably change beyond all recognition, but think what you'd get in return. The chance to work with the best in the business. An opportunity to find out how incredible you could be. A star with your name on it.'

'Maybe,' he said, but she thought he looked less doubtful.

She pushed on. 'How many people get to live their dreams, Fraser? Not many.'

His gaze held hers and she saw indecision swirling there. He opened his mouth but the speaker over their heads crackled into life.

'Ladies and gentlemen, please take your seats. This afternoon's performance will resume in two minutes.'

The spell broke. Swigging the last of his drink, Fraser squared his shoulders. 'Come on. Let's see if Shylock is going to get his pound of flesh.'

Maura tried her best to focus on the story unfolding on the stage, but it felt as though she saw everything through a veil. The ramifications of Fraser's revelation swirled around her head, muting the performance and dulling her own reaction to it. There was no possibility that Fraser could turn down such an opportunity – not if she had anything to do with it – and yet encouraging him to take it meant letting go of her own hopes.

Her only consolation was that she hadn't made a fool of herself by telling him how she felt – he'd saved her that embarrassment at least. Because there was one thing Maura knew for certain: she cared too much for Fraser to do anything that might hold him back.

She would bury her own emotions deep inside until he was far beyond their reach. No matter how much it hurt, she would not – could not – stand in his way.

CHAPTER TWENTY-FOUR

Fraser had met any number of directors over the years, from those whose domain was a provincial theatre with a shoestring budget, to the ones casting global commercials or long-running, much-loved TV shows. Drama school had taught him to view these gatekeepers with a mixture of terror and respect and, despite an innate confidence in his own ability, it had been a long time before he was able to deliver an audition piece without feeling as though he might vomit at their feet. But he'd eventually learned to ride the adrenaline wave, to make himself heard over the thudding of his own heart and trust in the meticulous preparation he put into each performance. He didn't get every part but he got some, and the failures taught him just as much as the successes.

On the morning he was due to meet Marco Minelli, he had yet to throw up, but the queasiness in his stomach as he waited in the lobby of Glasgow's Grand Gordon Hotel suggested it was a distinct possibility. It was not a sensation he had missed.

'Fraser Bell?'

The question came from an immaculately dressed young woman of around twenty-five. She was smiling at him, and the dazzling whiteness of her teeth would have told him she was an American even if her accent hadn't. Although dentists in other countries were catching on to the trend for perfect smiles, so it wasn't as reliable an indicator as it had been.

'That's right,' he said, standing up.

'I'm Krystal, Mr Minelli's assistant,' she said, offering him her hand. 'Would you like to follow me? We're ready for you now.'

She led him across the black and white marbled lobby to a bank of lifts. Fraser took the opportunity to check his reflection in the smoked glass mirror on the far wall as they waited; whatever came from the meeting, first impressions counted. He'd gone for smart casual – a cashmere jumper beneath his charcoal suit, rather than a shirt and tie. Thankfully, he saw nothing in the mirror to cause him any concern. No suddenly materialising trail of toilet roll attached to his shoe, no stubborn lick of hair standing on end. He suspected there was probably a large dose of rabbit-in-the-headlights around his eyes and forced himself to drop his shoulders. However impressive his achievements, Marco Minelli was only human. And he had asked to see Fraser, not the other way round.

He'd been in eye-wateringly expensive hotel suites before – usually when briefly visiting the paying guest, although he'd once been upgraded in Turin and hadn't believed his luck – but he'd never been in one as luxurious as the one Marco Minelli was occupying. It was on the sixth floor, accessed via a private lift that travelled from the floor below and was attended by a liveried concierge who nodded with old school deference as they entered.

There were only two doors lining the thickly carpeted

corridor, one on each side. Krystal waved a key card at the door on their right and Fraser tried hard not to react as she ushered him into the opulence that lay beyond. A mirrored entrance hall opened into an airy sitting room, where floor to ceiling windows draped with gold brocade curtains framed the view over Glasgow's rooftops. Cream velvet sofas surrounded a marble-topped coffee table and an oversized gilt chandelier hung from the high ceiling. A delicately embroidered Persian rug softened the practicality of the dark wood parquet flooring. An aria soared from unseen speakers – Fraser recognised it as Puccini, although he couldn't identify the soprano singing.

As he followed Krystal into the room, he saw corridors snaking to the right and left, lined with tall windows that offered the same spectacular view. He guessed the suite must cover one half of the entire top floor and didn't want to think how much it cost per night.

Krystal waved a hand at the immaculate sofas. 'Have a seat and I'll let Mr Minelli know you're here,' she said. 'Can I offer you a drink? We have a range of teas, freshly brewed coffee, or I'm sure our private chef can whip you up a juice or smoothie if you prefer. And there's a fully stocked bar if you'd like something stronger.'

Fraser did his best to project an easy confidence, as though he found himself in command of a private chef every day. 'Just coffee, thanks. Black, no sugar.'

She nodded. 'Sure. Make yourself comfortable.'

Perching on the edge of the sofa facing the fireplace, Fraser listened as the aria swelled to a dramatic climax, the soprano's voice aching with sorrow as she delivered the final anguished notes, and then died away. Now that he was alone, he allowed himself a discreet breath in and out to counter the sense of unreality that had come over him on entering the suite. Everything about the situation felt like a scene from a movie, right down to his own ambivalence about meeting Marco Minelli at all; he couldn't shake the feeling he was playing a role. Perhaps that was the best way to get through the next hour, he thought, reaching out to lift the cover of a magazine on the coffee table. He could play the part of an actor keen to land the role of a lifetime. But he strongly suspected Minelli would see through that in an instant. Better to just be himself and see how things played out, he decided.

The opening bars of another aria floated on the air but Fraser thought the volume was more muted, as though lowered to allow conversation. Feeling a prickle of sweat break out on his back, he rose to peel off his suit jacket, wondering if there might be a hanger inside one of the hall cupboards. The last thing he wanted was to be caught rummaging in places he shouldn't be, however, so he laid it over the arm of the sofa, where it looked untidy. Hesitating, he was about to put the jacket back on when the whisper of footsteps from one of the corridors made him sink down into the sofa, easing back against the meticulously placed cushions and hurriedly adopting an air of relaxed curiosity.

'Fraser.'

Glancing around, he saw Marco Minelli striding towards him, looking exactly as he had on every glossy magazine cover and in every interview Fraser had ever seen him give. He wore a navy blue roll-neck jumper and jeans, and his hand was outstretched in greeting.

'It's good to meet you at last.'

'You too,' Fraser said. Up close, Minelli's wavy black hair was threaded with grey and the skin around his eyes was criss-crossed with fine lines as he smiled. His olive tan owed much to his Mediterranean roots, although Fraser knew he'd grown up in America. The handshake was firm but not intimidatingly so. He exuded presence, demanded attention, to the point where Fraser hadn't even noticed Krystal following him into the room. She skirted round the sofa to place two cups on the coffee table, before backtracking to scoop up Fraser's jacket and disappearing into the hall. She returned a moment later and took a seat at the far end of the sofa Marco Minelli had just settled into.

Fraser sat too. The coffee steamed invitingly but he didn't dare reach for it in case his hands shook and caused the cup to rattle against the saucer, which would seriously undermine the chilled out professionalism he was trying to project. Now that he was face to face with Minelli, the armour provided by decades of experience seemed to have fallen away – he might as well be in his first year of drama school for all the quaking anxiety rumbling through him. It didn't help that the director's dark eyes were fixed upon him, his brows drawn together in an assessing frown as though he knew exactly how Fraser was shaking inside. It was hardly Leading Man energy.

'Sam tells me you're taking a break from acting,' Minelli said, without preamble. 'Do you mind if I ask why?'

It was a question Fraser had been expecting. 'I lost the hunger for it,' he said simply. 'I still loved telling stories but the desire to fight a hundred other actors for each role disappeared. I realised I was just going through the motions, so I decided to try something new.'

'Your ghost stories at the castle,' Minelli said, nodding. 'I read about that.'

A hot rush of embarrassment blossomed in the pit of Fraser's stomach. Coming from such an accomplished director, the job he'd abandoned acting for sounded ridiculously trivial. He willed his cheeks not to redden. 'It's reignited my love of performing. The immediacy of the audience reaction has reminded me why I got into acting in the first place.'

The director studied him thoughtfully. 'It's a tough business, that's for sure. Anything that reminds us why we do it is worth pursuing.' He shifted on the sofa, leaning back to contemplate Fraser with an unwavering gaze. 'How much do you know about my work?'

Fraser took a breath. He'd anticipated this question too, had spent several hours reading up on Minelli's past projects and directorial style. 'I know you're a perfectionist,' he began. 'You demand the best from everyone you work with, whether that's your actors, the sound engineers or the post-production colourist. You're prepared to cut entire scenes if they don't come up to scratch and you aren't afraid to take risks. You're innovative, brilliant and uncompromising, which is why your work stands head and shoulders above the competition, and why you win awards. You do things differently.'

Minelli showed no reaction to the glowing praise. He continued to regard Fraser. 'All of that might be true, but at the heart of it, I'm a storyteller like you. It's an ancient instinct. Those who could weave a tale around the fire have always been revered, and with good reason – it's the most powerful magic we have. Which means that for all the awards, we're chasing the same thing, you and I, even if our chosen vehicle is a little different – to make the audience *feel*.'

Fraser sat in silence for a moment. He'd told himself on the way up that Minelli was only human but he hadn't expected him to exude so much warmth and, well, humanity. No one could deny the gulf in status between the two of them but Minelli had taken the trouble to establish them as equals. 'There's nothing quite like that moment of connection,' he agreed.

The director continued to regard him. 'How about you do that now?'

Every one of Fraser's senses jolted at the same time. He fought the panic, striving to appear calm and relaxed, as though Hollywood directors made this kind of demand every day. 'Sorry, I'm not sure I follow.'

'Tell me a story,' he said. 'Make me feel something – laughter, sadness, whatever you like. Anything goes except nothing.'

Fraser swallowed. 'What kind of story?'

'How about one of your ghost tour tales?' Minelli suggested. 'And don't worry, it's not an audition. I decided I wanted you for my next movie long before I met you today.'

Sam had said as much, Fraser recalled, but it still didn't make any sense. There had been plenty of television roles throughout his career – he was quite proud of some – but he still had no idea how any of them had come to the attention of Marco Minelli. Was it simply that he fitted the physical characteristics of the part the director had in mind? Nick Borrowdale had read the script and observed Fraser would be perfect for the role – could that be all it was? However it had happened, he was here now, sitting opposite the most well-connected and influential man he was ever likely to meet. And he wanted to hear a story.

Raising his head, he set himself to address both Minelli and Krystal, and took refuge in familiarity. 'If you've ever been to Edinburgh, you'll know the city has a long and bloody history. So perhaps it isn't a surprise there's no shortage of graveyards tucked within its walls. The dead need somewhere to rest, after all, and the living somewhere to mourn. And for the most part, those departed souls lie undisturbed.' Nerves settling a fraction, Fraser allowed his gaze to flick between them as he let the pause stretch. 'For the most part. Until the body snatchers began their grisly trade.

'No recently buried corpse was safe. Grieving relatives did their best to watch over the graveyards but medical science paid well for fresh bodies and didn't ask too many questions about where they came from. That made the Resurrection Men cunning and resourceful – they hunted on moonless nights to fill their sacks with the dead. And when they were denied their prize by a determined mob, their thoughts turned to how else they might earn the money. Who among their community might not be missed? Who would be easy to murder? Enter William Burke and William Hare – the most infamous body snatchers of them all . . .'

He described how the pair had discovered the body of Old Donald, a lodger in Hare's house on Tanners Close behind Grassmarket. Donald had died of natural causes but he had owed Hare rent, so they settled on selling his body to the eminent city doctor, Robert Knox. The payment more than covered the debt but Burke and Hare were not satisfied with the profit. Another lodger was unwell and it wasn't long before his body was delivered to Dr Knox. Greed took control of the men, who began to lure beggars and prostitutes to Tanners Close, plying them with whisky before smothering them as they slept.

'They murdered seventeen people before suspicions were finally raised and they were caught,' he went on solemnly. 'Hare begged for immunity, turning on Burke and accusing him of killing the victims. It worked – Burke was executed for their crimes, while Hare escaped to London. A change in the law in 1832 meant bodies could no longer be bought for cash, and both the living and the dead could rest a little easier.'

Minelli's expression was unreadable but Krystal was leaning forward. Wide-eyed and rapt, she seemed to have followed the entire tale without breathing.

'But Edinburgh's streets have a long memory and, as Lord Macbeth observed when confronted by the ghost of a murdered friend, "blood will have blood". So take care when wandering the narrow wynds and closes that twist away from the Royal Mile. On a dark and starless night, you might just run into the murderous spirit of William Burke, whisky bottle in one hand and a blood-stained cushion in the other. It's said he sang to his victims as he smothered them. I suggest, if you hear a mournful crooning, you run and don't look back.'

He finished by slamming one of the scatter cushions into his hand, and had the immense satisfaction of seeing both Minelli and his assistant jump. Krystal squeaked, covering her mouth in shock, while Minelli's expression simply split into a wide grin.

'Now that is what I'm talking about.'

'I'm not sure I'm ever going back to Edinburgh,' Krystal said weakly.

Parched, Fraser reached for his now cool coffee, amused to notice his hand was steady as he lifted the cup and saucer. 'Just keep to the main streets and you'll be fine,' he said, then paused to recall the tale of the ghostly piper who played beneath the Royal Mile. 'Mostly fine, at least.'

The assistant jumped to her feet. 'I think we could all use some fresh coffee.'

Minelli nodded. 'Thanks, Krystal.' As she left the room, he eyed Fraser with renewed interest. 'My position hasn't changed – I'd like you to consider a major part in my next film. But today isn't meant to be a hard sell. Why don't I send over the script and you can see what you think? If you're interested, we can meet again and talk details.'

The buzz of performance was starting to ebb away as Fraser weighed up the offer. He couldn't deny that he'd warmed to what he'd seen of Minelli so far, and the opportunity to work with someone of his calibre was something he'd given up on a long time ago. Maura's words echoed in his head. *You should go for it. How many people get to live their dream?* He still wasn't sure she was right, but her resolve lent him strength. Was there any harm in looking at the script?

'Okay,' he said. 'Yes, I'd like to see the script. But I do have one question.'

Eyebrows raised, Minelli seemed amused. 'Only one?'

Fraser took a breath. It was a risk, but he had to know the answer. 'How do you – a directing genius – even know who I am?' The words tumbled out too fast and Fraser resisted the urge to squeeze his eyes shut. If he mentioned Louis the Chicken, he thought he might die.

The other man grinned. 'Ah. Well, it's kind of a funny story but you don't seem like the kind of man who's driven by his ego, so I'll be honest.'

Fraser wanted to groan. It was the adverts. It had to be the adverts.

'My mother is a big murder mystery fan. She loves Agatha Christie and Dorothy L. Sayers and all those Golden Age detectives – the quainter, the better.' He shook his head. 'She even tried to get me to cast Angela Lansbury in a movie once, but it didn't work out. Anyway, she really got into an English TV series called *Death in Dorset*. You probably know where I'm going with this.'

He did, Fraser realised with horrified certainty, although he really wished he didn't. Not trusting himself to speak, he waved the director on.

'She made me watch a few episodes when I was staying with her and of course I saw your glorious death at the hands of the brilliant Penelope Keith.'

Fraser took refuge in a swig of cold coffee. *Death in Dorset* had been years ago – he'd played much more fulsome roles than that since, although none that had ended with him face down in a bowl of soup. 'And that made you want to work with me?' he said incredulously.

Minelli laughed. 'Let's just say you got my attention. And then I looked up some other stuff you'd done and I liked what I saw. So when I agreed to this new project and saw it needed a Scottish actor who could really nail character, I thought of you.'

'Really?' Fraser said, unable to believe what he was hearing. 'It was *Death in Dorset* that brought me here?'

The director nodded. 'Absolutely. The best death in the entire show, bar none. What was it, vegetable soup?'

'Broccoli and Stilton,' he corrected, then winced. 'I think the props department thought it would be funny. It took days to get the green bits out of my nostrils.'

Krystal came back into the room then, bearing two fresh coffees.

Minelli grinned again. 'First rule of acting – make friends with the props team.' He took one of the saucers from his assistant and lifted the cup as though in a toast. 'Here's to *Death in Dorset,* anyway.'

Fraser managed what felt like the world's least convincing smile as he raised his own cup, still not entirely sure he wasn't dreaming. 'And here's to broccoli and Stilton soup.'

CHAPTER TWENTY-FIVE

I took the part.

Maura stared at the message for almost a minute on Wednesday morning, struggling to control her tumbling emotions. On the one hand, Fraser's news was a punch to her torso, stealing the breath from her lungs and causing her stomach to contract as though she was actually absorbing the impact of a blow. And on the other, she was happy for him, knowing how long he had worked for such a moment before finally letting go of the idea that it would ever come, this well-deserved reward for years of dedication. The resulting tumult inside Maura made her feel nauseous. She was glad she hadn't eaten breakfast yet.

Congratulations! she typed back, determined to be supportive. How does it feel to be a superstar in waiting?

The words Fraser is typing ... appeared at the top of the message thread. It hasn't sunk in yet. Lots to do before I actually sign. Need to go to London to meet the producers.

Maura let out a long slow breath as she cast around for the right reply but her brain was still too muddled for anything beyond the obvious. Exciting!

His response was instant. Terrifying, tbh. But I want to celebrate with you – champagne soon, OK? I'm buying!

Maura didn't reply immediately. Instead, she left the message unread and went down to the studio. It wasn't that she didn't want to celebrate Fraser's success, or that she had anything against champagne. It was simply that her heart felt too raw to contemplate either at that moment.

She jabbed her fingers into a lump of clay and carried it to the potter's wheel. But the hypnotic spin didn't soothe her jangling nerves the way it usually did. The clay wobbled and stubbornly refused to obey her instructions, collapsing in on itself before it could become the shape she intended.

After several further attempts, Maura was forced to concede that the clay could feel her restlessness. She cleaned the wheel, reformed the failed pot into a shapeless lump and wrapped it in polythene to keep it moist. She allowed the water to run for a long time as she listlessly scrubbed the grey from under her fingernails.

It wasn't the first time her skill had deserted her, but she supposed it might help if she wasn't shaking from hunger; she hadn't felt like eating after reading Fraser's messages, a realisation that made her feel worse. Hanging her apron on a hook, she went back upstairs to make some toast. Hopefully, it would give her the strength to be a better friend too.

'Can I give you another potato?' Maura's mother was eyeing her anxiously from the end of the dining table, the spoon in her hand hovering beside a tureen of steaming roasted potatoes. 'They'll only go to waste otherwise.'

Maura glanced at her plate, which seemed to contain six

already, as well as a mountain of carrots and parsnips. Around the table, her family were helping themselves, piling their own plates with food. Or at least, her father and brother-in-law were – Kirsty was still expertly picking out the things her children would eat and trying to hide some vegetables underneath. There had never been a surplus of roast potatoes at the end of a Sunday afternoon, as far as Maura could recall, and unless her mother had gone a bit mad with the King Edwards before everyone arrived, she couldn't see that there would be many to waste today. 'Why don't I start with what you've given me and take another if I need it?'

'Are you sure?' her mother asked. 'You look terribly thin.'

So that was it, Maura thought, and flashed a suspicious look at Kirsty, who seemed to be studiously ignoring her. 'I'm fine, Mum. Like I said, I can get more if I need to.'

'All the more for us,' her dad said cheerfully.

She watched as her laden plate was passed down the table. Sundays at her parents' house always followed the same slightly chaotic pattern: too much food as they caught up with each other's news, punctuated by the occasional scream from one or both of the children and the occasional eye-watering smell from Mitzi, the elderly spaniel they had rescued the year before. Since the break-up with Jamie, Maura had become aware of her mother surreptitiously trying to feed her up and she was sure Kirsty was a co-conspirator, but she didn't really mind. Nor did Mitzi, who had settled at her feet in dribbly, wide-eyed expectation.

'How's the exhibition looking?' her mother asked, sitting down with her own plate filled. 'Did you get all the pieces where you wanted them?'

Maura nodded. Catriona had arranged for her to drive into the castle early on Saturday morning to deliver the ceramics for the exhibition and they had spent several hours laying them out on the plinths and tables. Some had display cards explaining how the piece related to the castle, others simple bore the name of the item and Maura's own name as the artist. She'd also provided some information about herself, which Catriona had turned into boards that were dotted around the walls; it had been quite unnerving to see a giant version of her own face whenever she'd turned around in the barracks. The exhibition would open first thing on Monday morning – a fact she was both excited and nervous about. She'd done all she could. Only time would tell if it would be a success.

'It's all done,' she said. 'We had a few problems persuading one of the bowls to stay in place but we got there in the end.'

'I can't wait to visit,' her mother said, a glint of pride in her eyes. 'A display at the castle, no less. And I see your friend Fraser is making headlines. There was a full-page story in the paper about his new film.'

She should have expected as much, Maura thought. Weeks had passed since Fraser had told her he'd accepted the part – long enough for the Tinseltown gossip to filter through to the press. She couldn't actually remember the last time she'd looked at a newspaper but her parents still had one delivered every day. On Sundays it was a bumper edition, accompanied by a magazine, and she could easily imagine a glowing piece about Marco Minelli's latest star gracing its pages. 'Oh?' she said, striving for a casual tone. 'What did it say?'

She saw Kirsty flash their mother a look that appeared to go completely over her head. 'Just that he'd been cast in a

Hollywood blockbuster and that he was tipped to be the next big thing. There was a photo of him leaving a nightclub.'

'Really?' Maura couldn't recall Fraser spending much time amid Edinburgh's club scene but she supposed being seen in the most fashionable places was part of a movie star's job.

'It was a restaurant,' Kirsty corrected. 'Not a club.'

'And there was a gushy comment from his girlfriend,' her mother went on. 'She's an actress too, isn't she? What's her name again?'

Maura felt her appetite wither away. Unless Fraser had fallen into a whirlwind new romance, there was only one person the press would laud as his girlfriend. 'Naomi.'

'That's right. I seem to remember you telling me they'd split up, but I suppose they've got back together, as these celebrity couples seem to do.'

Kirsty frowned as she glanced Maura's way. 'I'm not sure that's the obvious assumption.'

Head spinning, Maura stared at her plate. It wasn't impossible for Fraser to have rekindled things with Naomi. From what he'd said, being based in Edinburgh had been a major source of friction between them and it didn't seem as though that was going to be a problem now. 'It could be true.'

'It calls her his "on-off girlfriend" and says they broke up months ago.' Kirsty shook her head dismissively. 'It's just filler to go with the story. They don't have anything else on him and gossip sells, remember?'

That was definitely true, Maura had to concede. All the same, she wouldn't be surprised if there had been a reconciliation – glamorous Naomi would fit right into the A-lister lifestyle. The mental image caused a needle of irritation to prick at her insides.

Pushing the thought away, she looked up to see Kirsty watching her through slightly narrowed eyes. She forced herself into a carefree shrug. 'I'm pleased for him,' she said stoutly, and decided it was time to change the subject. 'What have you been up to, Mum? Any updates on the new bus shelter in the village?'

It did the trick. Her mother launched into an impassioned tirade about the bureaucracy of the parish council and Fraser was forgotten. Or at least, Maura thought he was.

Her sister cornered her in the garden after the table had been cleared, and Maura knew the expression she wore only too well. 'Everything okay?' Kirsty asked, holding out a mug of tea. 'Only, you seemed a bit out of sorts earlier. When we were talking about Fraser.'

'I'm fine,' Maura replied, trying to sound blasé. 'It's just a bit weird to see him splashed across the papers.'

Kirsty eyed her askance. 'He's been in the papers before, when he did those tours at the castle.'

'That's different,' Maura said, her tone a shade defensive even to her own ears. 'You know it is. It's ... it's like he's another person. Someone who looks like the Fraser I know but isn't actually him.' She shook her head. 'Sorry, that sounds ridiculous.'

'No, I get that,' Kirsty said. 'Have you heard from him much?'

Maura nodded. She couldn't fault him on that score – he'd messaged almost every day, checking in and asking how she was. He hadn't mentioned Minelli or the film much, but she supposed he wasn't allowed to. 'That's what I meant by ridiculous – nothing's really changed. We're still business partners, still friends.' She stopped, uncomfortably aware that Kirsty possessed an uncanny knack of seeing more than Maura wanted her to. 'For now, at least.'

Her sister reached out to touch her cheek. 'You'll be okay. I know it's been a rollercoaster of a year but you've got us. We're not going anywhere.'

The warmth of the gesture kindled a spark of gratitude in Maura's bruised heart. She smiled and took Kirsty's hand. 'I know. Thank you.'

The words came back to her later, when the family was immersed in a chaotic game of Pictionary. The notion she'd had for a while now, that Fraser was slipping away from her, still caused her stomach to clench but she thought she was starting to accept it. Until this year, she'd all but forgotten he existed; she could do that again, although it might be more of a challenge if his face was splashed across buses and billboards all over the city.

But Kirsty was right – she had her family to hold onto. She would be okay.

She would have to be.

'Hello, Maura.'

For a moment, Maura doubted the evidence of her eyes. The last person she'd expected to see when she'd answered the cautious knock on the door of the studio was Jamie. But there he was, as tall and broad as ever, wearing an expression of uncertainty that was most unlike him. She gaped, open-mouthed, then realised how she must look and hurriedly pulled herself together. 'Jamie.'

His air of hesitation grew. 'Am I interrupting? I guessed you'd probably be working, even at this hour.'

In the past, she might have taken it as a dig – it was after eight o'clock, and Jamie had always hated her working so late into the evening – but now she simply glanced down at her clay-caked hands and nodded. 'You know me.' She looked up at him, feeling a frown start to crease her forehead. 'Is there something you need?'

He puffed out a breath. 'In a manner of speaking. Can I come in? I . . . It shouldn't take long.'

She looked over her shoulder, taking in the assortment of ghosts in various stages of production, the half-coiled vase she'd been battling to keep straight, and the potter's wheel she had yet to put away from that afternoon's session. The studio was a mess, but whatever the reason for Jamie's visit, she found she would much rather entertain him here than in the apartment they had once shared. At least he didn't smell as though he'd been drinking. 'Sure,' she said, stepping back to allow him to duck inside. 'Sorry about the mess.'

'No problem,' he said, gazing around with cursory interest. 'I saw you have an exhibition at the castle – I bet you've had a few commissions off the back of it.'

Maura nodded. 'A few.'

'I'm glad. You deserve the success.'

'Um . . . thanks,' Maura said, slightly nonplussed. Was this what he'd come to tell her? But it appeared not, as Jamie cleared his throat.

'I owe you an apology,' he said, holding up a hand to forestall any reply. 'No, I need to say this. There's no excuse for the way I treated you – I was the worst kind of idiot and I'm sorry.'

Maura waited. The man stood before her, eyes fixed on the floor, was so unlike the Jamie she knew that she wondered for a wild second if she might be dreaming. His shoulders were slumped, his hands were clasped as though in prayer and his voice was utterly devoid of his usual bombast. He looked like a man consumed by regret and she was almost tempted to reach out to him. Then he was speaking again and his next words took her breath away.

'But more than that, I was a drunk.' Looking up, he met her gaze with clear-eyed honesty. 'I have a problem with alcohol and I let it affect you. For that, I'm sorry too.'

She watched him with stunned compassion. Even now, after all the pain he had put her through, her heart ached for him. How many times had she wished he would face the truth about his drinking? And how much had it cost him to admit it to her now? 'You don't have to apologise for that,' she said.

'Yes, I do.' He ran an anguished hand through his hair. 'My counsellor says it's important to make amends, once you've decided to stop drinking, so that's what I'm trying to do.'

'You've stopped?' Maura said, but the truth of it was written all over him. Now that he was no longer staring at the ground, she could see his skin had lost its sallow tinge. His hair was no longer lank, but shiny and soft, and his beard was freshly trimmed. The biggest change of all was in his eyes, however; they were clear and bright and direct, not pink-rimmed and bleary, the way they had been most mornings for as long as she could remember.

'Thirty-seven days sober,' Jamie said, and he sounded both proud and surprised at the achievement. 'I'm not out of the woods yet, still taking each day as it comes, but my counsellor is brilliant. And now that I'm not drinking, I can see how bad it was.' He shook his head. 'I'm not asking you to forgive me, Maura. I just want you to know I'm sorry.'

Silence stretched between them while Maura tried to process everything she'd heard. It seemed that the end of their relationship had served as an abrupt wake-up call to Jamie, prompting him to face an uncomfortable truth, and for that she was glad. A small part of her wished he'd come to the realisation earlier, before so much damage had been done, but she'd come to accept a difficult truth of her own in the months since the break-up, which was that she and Jamie hadn't been right for each other from the start. 'It's okay,' she said. 'I do forgive you.'

His eyes brimmed with tears, and that was perhaps the most astonishing thing of all. In the five years they had been together, Maura had never known Jamie to cry. It went against everything he believed – that rugby players didn't admit they were hurt, on or off the pitch, that real men stayed strong and endured, that emotions were to be tightly controlled and wielded as weapons against the opposition. Something cataclysmic had occurred if he was able to set those beliefs aside now.

'Thank you,' he said. 'Everyone has been so kind – my parents, the guys at the club. I had to apologise for letting them down and they insisted I hadn't. Even Liam, although I'm not sure he meant it.'

'That might take time,' Maura allowed, remembering how hurt the younger man had been when he discovered who his girlfriend had been cheating with. She took a deep breath, bracing herself to voice the question she couldn't leave unasked. 'And is Zoe being supportive?'

Jamie's gaze was candid. 'We're not together. We never were, not once I found out she'd told Liam and he'd told you. I didn't move into her place, which is probably a good thing, given how much she likes to party.'

'Oh,' Maura said, caught off guard again. She'd assumed that Jamie and Zoe would be the new golden couple, perfect for each other. But perhaps it wasn't such a surprise, she thought. Hadn't she suspected the affair was a symptom of Jamie's deeper unhappiness, rather than a serious attraction to Zoe herself? 'So where are you staying? Did you rent a place?'

He nodded. 'One of those fancy penthouse apartments someone had bought as an investment. But I'm not living there just now.' A rosy blush suffused his cheeks. 'I'm back with my parents for a while, until I'm strong enough to manage on my own.'

An unexpected surge of pride blossomed inside Maura. 'Good for you,' she said, impulsively closing the distance between them to lay a hand on his arm. 'There's no shame in admitting you need help.'

'That's what my counsellor says,' Jamie said. He took a deep breath. 'Anyway, I've said what I came to say, so I'll leave you to your work. Thank you for understanding.'

She managed a smile. 'How could I not? And thank you for coming. I'm glad you're ... well, I'm glad you're okay.'

Jamie nodded. 'I am.' He fixed her with a sincere look. 'Take care of yourself, Maura. Be happy.'

Now it was Maura's turn to feel tears welling up in her eyes. 'You too,' she said, and watched as he stooped through the door and disappeared. For a moment, she thought the ache in her chest might overwhelm her, but the sadness ebbed away, leaving only a bruised, raw space. With deliberate care, she eased the tension from her shoulders and returned to the workbench, staring down at the uneven, lumpy vase for a moment. With a gentle exhale, she started to roll a fresh coil of clay, muscle memory guiding her hands even as the significance of Jamie's visit sank in. She'd thought they'd said all that needed to be said, and yet he had given her something she hadn't known she needed – an ending. Perhaps it also held the seeds of something else.

Her fingers stilled as she gazed at the length of clay on the workbench, and then at the stubborn vase that was resisting all her efforts to impose symmetry. With a sudden, decisive movement, Maura flattened the walls into the base and squeezed everything together into a ball. As symbolic gestures went, it was as subtle as a brick, but perhaps it was time for a fresh start with more than just this pot.

'Wow,' Kirsty said when Maura told her about Jamie's visit the next evening. 'I did not have that on my Jamie-is-a-bastard bingo card.'

'Me either,' Maura admitted. She shifted the phone from her ear and switched it to speaker phone as she stirred the chilli she was making for dinner. 'But I'm pleased he's getting help. Now that I've come to terms with what happened, I want him to be happy.'

'Hmmm,' Kirsty said, sounding as though the jury was very much still out for her. 'You're more generous than I would be.'

Maura grimaced. Her sister had suggested any number of unpleasant ways to make Jamie's life a misery, none of which she had accepted. 'There's no point in hanging on to negative emotions,' she said in a practical tone. 'Everything worked out for the best.'

'Hmmm,' Kirsty said again, and hesitated. 'Any news from Fraser?'

There it was again, Maura thought with an inward sigh, that sixth sense for subjects she would rather avoid.

After the photo in the newspaper, she'd made a conscious effort to distance herself from Fraser, in part to prevent the ache whenever his name appeared on her screen but also to wean herself off the support she'd come to rely on after breaking up with Jamie. She would always be grateful for the way he had helped her move past the initial hurt, but it was also blindingly obvious she'd mistaken his kindness for something deeper. It wasn't Fraser's fault – he had been very clear that he saw her as a friend, nothing more – but there was no doubt in her mind that she had teetered on the brink of making a fool of herself. Thankfully, his decision to go back to acting had arrived just in time to save her from embarrassing them both again.

'Not really,' she said, deciding not to mention that she'd left Fraser's most recent message unread for two days. 'I've been in the studio and I imagine he's got a lot going on too.'

There was a distinct sniff. 'It doesn't take a moment to say hello. Making these ghosts was his idea and now he's vanished and left you to do all the work.'

'Hardly,' Maura said, uncomfortably reminded of the unread messages. 'I deal with Tom at Dead Famous now. There's no reason for Fraser to be in touch.'

'If you say so,' Kirsty replied. 'Look, I know you think I'm poking my nose in but I'm just worried about you. We all are.'

'You don't need to be,' Maura said, wanting to reassure her without fuelling her concerns. 'I know you think the ghosts are too much work but at least they sell and give me a steady income. And over half the pieces from the exhibition have been reserved and three galleries have been in touch about stock.'

Kirsty gave an impatient sigh. 'Yes, your career is flying, but that's not what I asked. What about you? Are you happy, Maura?'

Feeling very much as though she was under interrogation, Maura took refuge in honesty. 'I wouldn't go that far,' she admitted. 'But I'm better than I was. I'm enjoying my work a lot more, taking time to cook proper meals and sleeping better. Is that enough for now?'

There was a brief pause, in which she pictured her sister fighting the desire to traverse the Firth of Forth to shake her into enforced happiness.

'I suppose it will have to be,' Kirsty said, her tone suggesting she remained a long way from convinced. 'For now.'

CHAPTER TWENTY-SIX

It wasn't that Fraser disliked having to spend more time in London. The city was as bright and bustling as ever, its brash charm beguiling and energising now that he had a concrete reason to be there. And he couldn't complain about the way he'd been looked after. On the day he was due to meet the producers, he'd been picked up from his hotel by a chauffeured car and whisked to an expensive restaurant, where Minelli and Sam were already waiting. The meeting had gone better than he could have dreamed, although he suspected he had Minelli's influence to thank for that, and Sam had been full of praise when they'd caught up the next morning. 'You wowed them,' he said over breakfast. 'It's the start of something big, I can feel it.'

Even so, Fraser had been glad to get back to Edinburgh. No smartly dressed chauffeur had held up a sign bearing his name when he'd made his way through the arrivals gate at the airport, and he'd taken the bus into the city centre before hopping onto the tram to Leith.

There'd been a cluster of photographers outside the restaurant, shouting Minelli's name as their cameras whirred and flashed – Fraser hadn't enjoyed that. A day or two later, one of the tabloids had leaked the news that he'd been cast in Minelli's new blockbuster. But in Edinburgh, no one had the faintest idea who he was, and no one cared. It was a blessed relief after the whirlwind of London.

He'd been glad to slip back into the routine of the walking tours too. Thankfully, it seemed the gossip columnists had yet to find out what Fraser did when he wasn't being wined and dined by Hollywood executives, but he had a sinking feeling it was only a matter of time. In the meantime, he was determined to savour the comfortable familiarity of the stories he'd been telling for more than a year while he still could.

Maura's silence was another thing that had been troubling him. Now that he'd handed over responsibility for the day-to-day ghost production to Tom, he'd missed seeing his phone light up with her name. He suspected she was focused on work; he'd managed to squeeze in a visit to the exhibition at the castle and had been blown away by the talent and skill she'd poured into it. Every piece was unique, but she had somehow managed to create a sense of symbiosis between them all, plunging her audience into the majesty of both the city and its castle. His heart swelled with pride as he listened to the awed comments of those stood near him in the barracks. Several pieces had stickers denoting they had been reserved – he thought the centrepiece must have been snapped up by the same buyer – and he was certain more would be sold before the exhibition closed. He had hoped to see her, that they might share a bottle of champagne to toast each other's success, but she'd replied to his suggestion with an apology that she was up to her elbows in unfinished pots. While he had no doubt that was true, he also had the sense that she was pulling back. The realisation left a leaden feeling in his stomach. After the night she had asked him to stay, he'd relived the moment more than once and each time he had been certain he'd done the right thing. But he was beginning to appreciate that it had come at a cost, one that his own change in fortunes had only increased. His instinct then had been to protect Maura and the friendship they shared, but he couldn't shake the nagging suspicion that he'd accidentally pushed her away.

His phone vibrated and he saw a message pop up on the screen. After the customary stab of disappointment that it wasn't from Maura, he opened it and began to read.

> Hey Fraser, thought I'd give you a heads up that I took a call just now from someone asking if the Fraser Bell who runs the walking tour is the same person as Fraser Bell, the actor. I said I had no idea what they were going on about but I got the feeling it might have been a reporter. Thought you'd want to know.
>   Tom

And so it begins, Fraser thought wearily, closing the message. He'd known this would happen, of course, but he'd hoped he might be able to fly under the radar for a little while longer. It was time to speed up his plan to bring another storyteller on board and step back from Dead Famous as soon as he could.

It took three days for the first journalist to turn up at Fraser's ghost walk.

Over the past year, he'd become an expert at spotting those

who'd purchased tickets for a tour, even when they were hesitant to approach him. He found it saved time to be proactive, greeting them with a cheerful, 'Hullo. Are you here for the Dead Famous tour?'

It also paid to ensure they had booked onto his tour, rather than one of the others that ran from various places along the Royal Mile. And there were always those cheeky few who hadn't paid but who hovered nearby to listen for free; he'd learned how to politely move them along too, suggesting they book on the next evening's tour if they wanted to hear the city's dark stories.

The man watching Fraser from a few metres away didn't look like he was interested in ghost hunting. He looked as though he had other prey in mind.

Fraser focused on checking everyone in, wondering whether he was imagining the fixed stare. When he raised his lantern and greeted his audience, running through the usual pre-tour practicalities, the man stepped nearer. The movement caught Fraser's eye and he saw that he had a companion. A shorter man stood at his shoulder, carrying an expensive-looking camera. Heart sinking, Fraser finished his introduction and broke off to address them. 'Can I help you with something, gents?'

The taller of the two men shrugged. 'We're here for the tour.'

Fraser offered a professional smile. 'I'm afraid it's fully booked. I can recommend a few others that run nearby, if you'd like? You might catch one if you hurry.'

'It's yours we're interested in,' the man said. 'You are Fraser Bell, right?'

'That's right,' Fraser confirmed. 'But as I said, this tour is full. If you check the Dead Famous website, you'll be able to see availability for the next few weeks. Sorry to disappoint you.'

Turning his attention back to his audience, he gathered himself together and began again. 'Be warned that this walking tour is not for the faint-hearted. We will visit some of the city's darkest wynds and traverse her deadliest stairways. Stay close and do not be tempted to stray if an unknown voice whispers your name. Our safety is in numbers. Follow my lantern and do not fall behind.'

At the back of the group, the shorter man raised his camera. It was just after seven-thirty, nowhere near dusk but even so, a series of flashes went off, causing several members of the audience to turn sharply round. The photographer peered down at the camera screen, then lifted it to his face again and clicked.

Blinking the brightness away, Fraser fought to keep his tone level. 'No flash photography, thank you.' He surveyed the group before him, determined to ignore further intrusions. 'But enough talk. It's time to hear our first terrible tale, in the blood drenched alley of Fleshmarket Close.'

The photographer had at least switched the flash off, but Fraser was aware of his continued clicking as he turned to lead the tour attendees down the Royal Mile. His companion hurried to catch up with Fraser. 'I'm sure you know the drill, Fraser. Just a few questions, then we'll be out of your hair.'

His words removed any lingering doubt Fraser had about who he was. 'You're a journalist.'

The man nodded, seemingly unperturbed by the flatness of Fraser's tone. 'Charlie Fleming, *Daily News*. Congratulations on the new film role. You must be delighted.'

A few of the audience members were listening in. Once again, Fraser fought to keep any trace of irritation from showing. 'There'll be a press conference in due course. You can save any questions you have for that.'

Charlie pulled a face. 'Thing is, my questions aren't strictly to do with the film. They're about your relationship with Naomi Dean.' Fraser's head whipped round to stare at him. 'More specifically, the way you cheated on her with your business partner, Maura McKenzie.'

And now Fraser stopped dead, causing squeaks of alarm behind him. A couple of people weren't able to stop themselves from clattering into him but he barely noticed. 'I beg your pardon?'

'Don't get angry. I'm only repeating what my source told me,' Charlie said, smirking. 'They allege that you persuaded Naomi to start a new life in Edinburgh, only to break her heart by falling into bed with your old flame, Maura. Is that how it happened, Fraser?'

Whispers broke out among the cluster of tour attendees behind them. Out of the corner of his eye, Fraser was aware of the photographer clicking away.

Battling for composure, he eyed the journalist coldly. 'That's a lie.'

Charlie cocked his head. 'That's not what my source says. Word is, you and this Maura couldn't keep away from each other, in spite of the fact that you were both in long-term relationships.'

Fraser couldn't believe what he was hearing. 'That's not what happened,' he ground out, even as he wondered where such rubbish could have come from. 'And if you print one word of it, you'll find yourself on the receiving end of a libel suit before the ink is dry. Understand?'

Charlie held his hands up, although the expression on his face was anything but conciliatory. 'I'm only doing my job, mate. You're not the first actor to be a love rat and you won't be the last, but the public have a right to know the truth.'

Taking a deep breath, Fraser stepped towards him. 'You wouldn't know the truth if it punched you in the face. Now get lost before I have you done for harassment.'

Backing away, the journalist glanced at his photographer. 'Come on, Kev. We've got what we need.'

Scowling, Fraser watched the pair scurry away. He knew about the underhand techniques of some members of the press – Nick had plenty of horror stories about their sly tricks – but this was the first time he'd experienced it first hand and it had left him shaken, not least because he had a crawling suspicion that the unnamed source could only be Naomi herself. She'd messaged a few times since the news of the Minelli film had been leaked and he'd been polite but firm in resisting her flirtatious tone. Could she be trying to exact her revenge for his most recent rejection? He had no idea, but he couldn't imagine where the story had come from otherwise. And who else would know about Maura?

'Um . . .' The voice behind Fraser was hesitant. 'So, is this part of the tour?'

Remembering where he was, Fraser slipped automatically back into character. 'I'm afraid not,' he said, turning round with an apologetic smile. 'Tabloid reporters are not actually evil ghouls who prey on the living but, like Edinburgh's ghosts, sometimes there's no escaping them.'

Laughter broke out, much to his relief. Determined to re-store normality, he swept a sombre gaze around the group, pausing to linger at random on a face here and there. 'Now, shall we continue our dark business? Stuart the Slice and his dripping blade await.'

The first message on Sunday morning was from Fraser's agent. It contained a screenshot of the *Daily News* website, which showed a close-up picture of Fraser, his face angry and menac-ing as he loomed over Charlie Fleming. The headline screamed MINELLI'S NEW STAR SHOWS UGLY SIDE.

Heart pounding, Fraser zoomed in and scanned the story beneath it to see if Maura was mentioned. To his utter relief, it seemed Charlie had taken his threat seriously and had merely accused Fraser of threatening to punch him in the face – which was nowhere near the truth, but Fraser could live with that. Sam was less relaxed, accompanying the picture with a terse instruction to call him.

The second message Fraser read was from Nick.

I see you ran into Gnarly Fleming. Don't tell me – he wound you up, you took the bait and his faithful photographer was there to capture the moment.

Fraser sighed. Nick had no way of knowing the journalist had threatened Maura but it was still a shrewd description of what had happened. Pretty much, he replied.

It took a few moments for his phone to buzz again. Don't worry. Everyone will see it's a non-story.

But everyone did not include Fraser's mother, who rang as he was making a much-needed first coffee of the day. 'Oh, Fraser, what have you done?' she said, her tone a mixture of bewilderment, worry and disappointment that instantly made him feel six years old again. 'It's all over the papers that you threatened to punch a journalist. Bessie from next door brought her copy in to show me. Is it true?'

'No, Mum, it's not true,' Fraser said patiently. 'You raised me better than that.'

'Oh,' she said, sounding slightly less panicked. 'So I did. But it's there in the paper and I must say the photo makes you look very angry.'

'That's because I was angry. A reporter interrupted one of my tours and let rip with some fairly nasty accusations. I told him to go away and he did, but not before his sidekick had snapped a picture.'

His mother's voice went up a note or two. 'What kind of accusations?'

Fraser closed his eyes for a moment. He had no intention of repeating Fleming's lies; the mere thought of Maura's name on his lips sent a spike of fury coursing through him and the last thing he wanted was for his mother to pick up on his anger. 'It doesn't matter. None of them were true.'

She was silent for a moment. 'So you didn't threaten to punch him?'

'No, Mum. I threatened to sue him,' Fraser reassured her.

'That's alright, then,' she said, sounding mollified. 'I told Bessie you couldn't have actually hit him. Remember that time at drama school when you broke three bones in your hand pretending to throw a punch?'

He did. The intended recipient of his stage punch had

panicked at the last second and moved, leaving Fraser to connect with the wall behind. 'I've got a bit better at it since then,' he said dryly. 'But don't worry, my hands are fine. It's a story about nothing.'

Once he'd made a coffee, he took it through to the sofa and sat down to call Sam. His agent answered on the second ring. 'Bloody reporters,' he said, when Fraser offered his explanation. 'But it goes with the territory, unfortunately. The important thing is that you're okay.'

The important thing was that the more damaging lies hadn't made the papers, Fraser thought, as a vision of Maura popped into his mind. The thought of her name being dragged through the mud made cold beads of sweat break out on his forehead. 'I'm fine,' he reassured Sam. 'Do you know if Minelli has seen it?'

'He's back in LA, so I doubt it. Which brings me onto something else – they want you to fly out there for on-screen chemistry tests with Priscilla de la Cruz and Juno Crosby.'

Fraser tried not to groan. He'd known there would be demands like this but he'd hoped they might be restricted to London. 'When?' he asked, mentally shuffling through his commitments for the coming weeks.

'Tomorrow,' Sam said.

'Tomorrow?' Fraser echoed in dismay. 'But I've got meetings – tours to run.'

'Cancel them,' his agent said. 'You're booked onto the 6.25am flight from Edinburgh to Heathrow, then on a connecting British Airways plane to LA at ten o'clock. You'll land at 2.30pm local time, where you'll be met and taken to your hotel. Screen tests at the studio the next day.'

Fraser's head whirled with the sudden onslaught of information. He'd done screen tests before, of course, but never anywhere remotely as glamorous or distant as Los Angeles, and never with such famous names. He seized on the most obvious question. 'How long will I be away?'

'As long as it takes,' Sam said pragmatically. 'And it might not be a bad time to get out of the country. Tabloid reporters are like cockroaches – if you can see one, there are another ten scuttling around out of sight. And as you've discovered, when they've got nothing on you, they make something up.'

With some reluctance, Fraser accepted the argument made sense. Like Nick, Sam had no idea how close to the truth he was, but his words reminded Fraser of the need to put some distance between himself and Maura. Leaving the country might well be the best thing for both of them. 'Okay.'

'One other thing. Disney have been in touch – they're casting a new Jilly Cooper adaptation and want to know if you're interested. What shall I tell them?'

Fraser blinked. Sam sounded utterly matter of fact, as though gigantic corporations enquired after his clients every day. Perhaps they did, he thought faintly. 'I don't know. Doesn't it depend on Minelli?'

'Disney won't start filming until next year,' Sam explained. 'But I've seen the script. There's a nude scene.'

Leaning back against the sofa, Fraser puffed out his cheeks. It shouldn't be a surprise – there'd been an adaptation of another Jilly Cooper novel that had been filled with raunchy scenes and it had proved a runaway success. But he'd never had a role that demanded he strip off. He'd have to cut down on the chocolate digestives. 'Let me think about it.'

'No problem,' Sam said. 'I'll send you the flight details. I know it's an early start but Minelli's assistant has booked you into business class so you should be able to sleep on the plane.'

Thank you, Krystal, Fraser thought. He'd never flown anything better than premium economy before. 'Okay. Thanks, Sam.'

'A final piece of advice,' his agent went on. 'It's probably time to step back from the ghost tours. I know you enjoy them but they make you far too easy to find. That's going to be a problem once you become more widely recognised, and not just with the press.'

It wasn't anything Fraser hadn't worked out for himself, but the warning still caused his stomach to clench in resistance. Sam was right – the run in with Fleming had proved that – but it didn't mean he enjoyed hearing it. 'I'll think about that too.'

'Sure,' Sam said. 'Enjoy LA. Oh, and don't take any of the CDs on Venice Beach – it's a scam.'

'CDs?' Fraser repeated, wondering if he'd heard correctly. 'As in, compact discs?'

Sam laughed. 'It'll make sense when you get there. Have a good flight. Speak soon.'

For the second time in his life, Fraser was met at the airport by a chauffeur carrying a sign bearing his name.

The journey had been smooth, if long, and made much more bearable by the champagne he'd been offered as they'd travelled. He hadn't managed to sleep, despite the seat that reclined fully into a bed. Instead, he'd watched several Marco Minelli films and read through the scenes he was due to work on at the studio the following day. By the time he located his driver, he

was feeling the effects of his 4am alarm call. It might be three
o'clock in the afternoon in LA, but his body was telling him
it was bedtime.

He stifled a yawn as the car eased out of the airport and onto
the freeway, which was crawling with traffic even though it
wasn't yet rush hour. Perhaps he'd have a nap once he reached
his hotel. Then again, since Krystal had booked him into the
five-star Beverly Hills Montgomery, he might take a dip in the
luxurious, palm-shaded pool first and marvel at his incredible
good luck.

Mindful of the need to adjust to the time difference as soon
as he could, Fraser lasted until eight o'clock that evening before
he fell into the pristine white bed linen and closed his eyes.

He awoke nine hours later, spent a fruitless hour trying to get
back to sleep and then gave up and got dressed. The doorman
nodded as he crossed the lobby and offered to summon him a
cab, despite the early hour. Fraser declined with a smile. 'I'm
going to watch the sunrise,' he explained.

'An excellent plan, sir,' the doorman said. 'If you turn left
and walk for around ten minutes, you should get a good view
of the hills from the park.'

Even before dawn, the heat hung heavily and Fraser's T-shirt
was stuck to his back within minutes. This was why everyone
drove, he reminded himself, wiping a sheen of sweat from his
forehead. He wouldn't last long doing walking tours around
these streets. But he'd needed to stretch his legs and get some
fresh air – the day ahead would be exhausting and almost certainly spent indoors. And there was something magical about
watching the sun rise in a new place. The palette seemed different, for a start, but perhaps it had more to do with taking the

time to appreciate it – something he rarely managed at home. Finding an empty park bench, Fraser settled down to wait.

At first, it promised to be glorious. A thread of deep crimson laced the horizon, blossoming into oranges and reds as the sun's rays banished the dark. But although the tangerine glow spread as far as Fraser could see, it didn't split into the sumptuous shades of amber, pink and gold he was hoping for. A dull mauve curtain seemed to creep over the sun as it climbed, muting its brilliance and shrouding it in gloom. The overall effect was dramatic, but not as spectacular as Fraser had anticipated. He took a few photos, sending one to his mother and to Sam. Then, after a moment's consideration, he sent it to Maura too, with the words Living the dream. Leaning back, he waited on the bench for another fifteen minutes, until it became obvious there was nothing more to see, then made his way back to the hotel to shower and find some breakfast. His driver was due to collect him at eight o'clock and he wanted to read through the scenes one last time before then.

It was impossible not to be overawed as the car drove through the tall studio gates and onto the lot. Fraser took in the combination of low, rose-pink buildings and vast warehouses, watching the open-topped buggies zipping between locations as they transported everything from employees to background panels. It was exactly how he'd expected it to be, and yet he couldn't shake a sense of unreality. It felt as though he was on the set of a movie – a movie about movies, like *La La Land* or *Singin' in the Rain*. It scrambled his brain if he thought about it too much.

Krystal met him in the reception area of one of the offices.

'I have good news and some not-so-good news,' she said, after checking there had been no problems with his flight or hotel. 'The not-great news is that Priscilla has been held up, so she isn't here yet. The good news is that rather than leave you kicking your heels for a few hours, Mr Minelli has arranged for a studio tour so you can get a sense of how things work.' She regarded him anxiously. 'Does that sound okay?'

'It sounds great,' Fraser said, delighted that he was going to get a coveted glimpse of everything that went on behind the scenes. 'I mean, I'm sorry Priscilla has been held up. I hope she's alright.'

Was it his imagination or was Krystal's smile slightly strained? 'Perfect. If you'd like to take a seat, I'll send someone to pick you up. Oh, and I need to take your lunch order. What would you like?'

Fraser shrugged, assuming there would be a canteen or a catering truck. 'What's on the menu?'

Krystal eyed him with some puzzlement. 'Whatever you'd like. The chef will make you something fresh. All you need to do is tell me what you want to eat. Or we can order in – Priscilla usually gets something delivered from Gordon Ramsay's place.'

Fraser was no stranger to dining in expensive restaurants but he'd never considered that they might do deliveries. His usual on-set experience encompassed overcooked stews or tepid burgers, and it took him a moment to adjust to the new possibilities. 'Uh. I don't know. Pizza, maybe?'

Instantly, he wanted to die. Did Gordon Ramsay even make pizza?

But Krystal simply made a note. 'No problem. And toppings?'

He reeled off his favourites.

Krystal jotted them down. 'And perhaps a green salad? A smoothie of some kind?'

He shouldn't be surprised; this was health-conscious California, after all. At breakfast, he'd overheard the man at a neighbouring table order an egg-white omelette and wondered what possible enjoyment he would get from something so bland. 'Sounds good,' he told Krystal. 'As long as it's not kale.'

She flashed her perfect white teeth. 'Understood.'

Fifteen minutes later, Fraser was sitting in one of the buggies he'd observed on his way in. A blond-haired, tanned young man called Zachary was driving, pointing out the various buildings and explaining their purpose. 'There are fourteen studios in total, of varying sizes. Three of them have green screens and one is set up as a permanent courtroom.' He glanced across at Fraser. 'I don't know if you've ever seen the movie *All Rise* but that was filmed here.'

Fraser smiled politely. He had seen it but hadn't been blown away due to the lacklustre performances. 'Impressive.'

'Standing sets are stored in the warehouses at the back, near the workshops where the carpenters and set painters hang out,' Zachary went on, slowing to allow a forklift truck to cross in front of them. 'We have six wardrobe departments, four make-up rooms and two private lounges for the talent to use.' Seeming to remember who he was talking to, he blushed. 'I mean, for the big-name actors to use.'

'Don't worry,' Fraser said, grinning. 'We're called that in the UK too. I've learned not to take it personally.'

Zachary pulled up next to an enormous roll-up door that led into a vast warehouse space. 'Studio Three,' he said, climbing out of the buggy. 'They filmed *Death Star* in there. Built the whole lost city of Oribi, complete with catacombs and the famous cantina where the final shootout between Lord Ringwald and Endymion takes place. Let's take a look.'

There was so much to see that before long, everything began to merge in Fraser's mind. His most vivid recollection was the bejewelled golden sarcophagus in the centre of a studio laid out as a dusty Egyptian tomb. Maura would love the intricate detail; he could imagine her frowning at the urns and jars in professional appraisal, offering suggestions on size and decoration technique. He took special care to chat with the make-up artists and wardrobe crew, which was something a much more famous actor had recommended early on in his career – it paid to be nice to the people with the power to make him look better in front of the camera.

By the time Zachary deposited him back at reception, the early morning start was catching up with Fraser again. He was in need of a substantial caffeine fix.

'Of course,' Krystal said when he asked her. 'Priscilla is here now – she's in make-up, so there's time for you to refuel before we get you ready too.'

Fraser didn't know much about the two actors vying for the female lead in the film, beyond the usual online gossip and bland PR interviews put out to promote past projects. The characters in this film didn't become romantically involved until the final scenes, but they did need to strike sparks from the first moment they met. He supposed that was why the chemistry screen tests were needed; both actors had a number of high-profile successes behind them but Minelli wanted to see who worked best with Fraser. It was the kind of test that needed to be done face to face and, up until now, he hadn't been nervous. But adrenaline was fluttering in his stomach, despite the fact that the part was already his. Sipping his coffee, he read through the scenes again. He'd done his preparation, he reminded himself. And he didn't need to impress anyone.

When Fraser finally met Priscilla, he was startled to realise she was even more beautiful in real life than on the screen. Her dark hair shimmered under the lights, her wide, full-lashed brown eyes reminded him of Princess Jasmine from *Aladdin* and her skin glowed as though lit from within. Where some actors were washed out by the overbright studio bulbs, Priscilla seemed to blossom under them. He could see why the camera loved her. But her smile upon meeting Fraser had been a disappointment – perfunctory and lacking warmth. Perhaps she was saving its brilliance for the performance, he thought. Or perhaps she simply hadn't liked the look of him. She was used to working with much bigger names, after all.

Minelli was standing behind one of the cameras, muttering instructions to its operator as he peered at the screen. Other studio executives watched from the wings; Fraser had been introduced to the casting director when they'd first entered the studio but he didn't recognise the others. Apparently satisfied, Marco glanced up to nod at Fraser and Priscilla. 'We'll try Act One, Scene Three first. The one where Bash and Delores meet after the bank job goes wrong.'

Fraser nodded, taking his position beside the X marked on the studio floor, summoning up his opening line. Turning discreetly, he checked his breath in his cupped hand. The last thing he wanted to do was breathe coffee fumes over his possible co-star.

But Priscilla hadn't moved. 'I need the script,' she said, her tone flat. 'I can't do this off book.'

Minelli looked surprised. 'You haven't learned the scene?'

She tapped her foot impatiently. 'I haven't had time. And I'm hardly going to learn the lines when I haven't been offered the part. Be reasonable, Marco.'

Fraser fought the urge to stare. Plenty of actors struggled with lines, especially when there were a lot to remember. He'd always been lucky – the words had stuck after one or two read-throughs and reappeared like magic when he needed them. But he wasn't sure he'd ever heard someone admit they hadn't bothered to learn them at all, not least at a studio screen test with Hollywood's biggest director. That took a special level of entitlement.

But Minelli simply nodded. 'Someone get her a script.'

Krystal hurried over, a sheaf of paper in her hand. She gave it to Priscilla, who glared at it as though it was a personal insult.

'It's not open to the scene.'

Fumbling with the pages, the assistant found the right one and handed it back. When she passed Fraser, he saw two spots of colour burning in her cheeks and felt a surge of indignation on her behalf. But this wasn't the time to rock the boat and he suspected Krystal would not thank him for speaking out. Forcing down his misgivings, he replayed the scene in his head and got into character. Bash was confident, maybe a little arrogant, and he thought he didn't need any help. Delores was about to prove him wrong.

After a moment, Priscilla came to stand within view of the camera. She held the script aloft, her gaze scanning the page as she took in her lines. Fraser tried not to let her lack of preparation irritate him further, but it was tough. Had she even read the bloody thing before today?

'Quiet on set,' Minelli called. The noise levels dropped. Someone held a board in front of the camera, whisking it away a second or two later. 'And action!'

'Who the hell are you?' Fraser glowered at Priscilla, his lip curling in disdain. 'Don't tell me you're the cleaner.'

Chin jutting in defiance, she matched his scorn. 'O' course ah am. Here to sweep up your mess.'

The accent was so unexpected, so different from her American drawl, that Fraser had to battle to maintain Bash's trademark scowl. 'You're going to need more than a dustpan and brush to fix this.'

'Then it's a good thing I brung ma team.'

'Cut!' Minelli was gazing at Priscilla, his head cocked. 'Let's lose the accent.'

Priscilla scowled at Fraser. 'Why does he get to do one when I don't? I trained for this, Marco. I can do Scotland.'

Fraser kept his eyes on the floor, determined not to react. If she'd read the script, she'd know Delores was a Londoner. But there was no way he was going to point that out and it seemed the director wasn't going to mention it either.

'Fraser gets to do a Scottish accent because he's from Scotland,' Minelli explained. 'That's his natural voice. So can we go from the top? Quiet on set.'

This time, they managed to complete the scene before Minelli cut them off. Fraser wasn't sure if the humiliation had heightened Priscilla's furious performance but she spat the words at him like bullets and made his ears ring with a slap that had very little stagecraft and a whole lot of venom to it.

His cheek burned where she'd struck him and he suspected he now had a red hand mark imprinted on his skin.

Checking the screen, Minelli nodded with what appeared to be satisfaction. 'Act Four, Scene Four – the elevator scene,' he instructed.

Krystal appeared at Fraser's side, holding a small blue and white square. 'An ice pack,' she murmured. 'For your cheek.'

He took it gratefully and pressed it to his face. 'Thanks.'

'This is the scene where Bash and Delores view each other as equals,' Minelli called. 'Fraser, I want newfound respect and unexpected attraction. Priscilla, you're seeing him as someone you can trust, maybe even admire. I want sparks between you. Let's go.'

It would be easier if she wasn't continually glancing at the script, Fraser thought as he growled his way through the scene. And then she held up a hand.

'Does he have to loom over me like that?' she asked, glancing at Minelli. 'It's distracting.'

Fraser shook his head, wondering if she had ever undertaken a screen test before. 'It's in the stage directions. We're in a lift – an elevator. I'm supposed to stand too close.'

She gave no indication that she had heard. Her extraordinary eyes remained fixed on the director, who eventually inclined his head. 'Give her some room, Fraser. Happy, Priscilla? Then let's try again.'

It took two more attempts to get through it. On the second run-through, Priscilla complained that Fraser wasn't giving her enough eye contact and it took all his patience not to point out that he would stand a better chance if she looked up occasionally. His own performance had grown more sardonic as the interruptions and complaints stacked up; he wasn't sure he was managing to convey respect or attraction.

Minelli called over the studio executives to view something on the camera screen. They nodded as he murmured to them, then looked up to study the two actors. 'Act Five, Scene Twelve,' Minelli said at last. 'Bash and Delores finally admit their feelings. I want passion. I want tenderness. I want to believe. Places, please.'

Fraser squared his shoulders. He'd done plenty of stage kisses before and passion had always been the last thing on his mind. But at least in the past he'd liked his co-stars – had been reassured that they were invested in making the scene work. He was not sure he could say either was true of Priscilla.

Script in hand, she sidled close to him. 'Keep your mouth shut for the kiss,' she hissed.

He couldn't help himself. Widening his eyes, he stared at her in mock astonishment. 'What, no tongues?'

Priscilla leapt away from him, her exquisite features contorted with horror. 'Marco!' she shrieked. 'I cannot – will not – work with this ... this Neanderthal any longer.' She threw the script to the floor. 'Either he goes, or I do.'

The director ran a weary hand over his face. 'It's probably time to take a break,' he said. 'Krystal, why don't you show Priscilla to the green room? Fraser, you stick with me.'

Once the room had cleared, Minelli gave Fraser a long look. 'I know. She's a pain.' He reached for the camera, swinging it round so Fraser could see the viewer. 'But she lights up the screen. And you look great together.'

Fraser did not agree; most of the time, all he could see was the top of Priscilla's glossy head. But as the action progressed, he grudgingly accepted that Minelli was right about one thing. When Priscilla did deign to look up, she looked amazing. 'Obviously, she'll be better once she's off book. She draws energy from being on set.'

Given these pre-requisites for performance, it was astonishing Priscilla had been cast in anything, Fraser thought. But then he glanced at the viewer once more and knew exactly why. What was less certain was whether he could work with her, or she with him. There were plenty of sparks, but he suspected they were the kind that would trigger an explosion.

Minelli appeared to read his mind. 'Just finish the screen test and have some lunch. Juno will be here this afternoon – she's another one who knows how to work the camera. If the two of you hit it off, we might just have your co-star.'

Fraser could only hope Juno was less of a diva than Priscilla, or at least better prepared. And in the meantime, he had a screen test to finish. He was tempted to go and find some garlic to eat so that his breath smelled revolting, but there was an outside chance that he might have to make an entire movie with the wretched woman. Better to grit his teeth and get through it with as little fuss as possible.

With that in mind, he delivered his lines opposite Priscilla, did his best to convince those watching that Bash had fallen for Delores. But as the moment of the kiss approached, Fraser's stomach began to churn. His mouth seemed to be working independently, delivering the words even as his insides roiled. He took a breath, hoped he didn't look as clammy as he felt. The camera was bound to pick up any beads of sweat and even Minelli might lose his enthusiasm for Fraser if he threw up on a potential co-star.

Priscilla had turned towards him now and he could see in her eyes that she loathed the idea of this as much as he did. Briefly, Fraser closed his eyes to gather himself for the task and an image swam unbidden into his thoughts, of Maura raising her face to his, inviting him to kiss her. Of course he had pulled away, even though he'd been tempted. That temptation was long gone now but that didn't mean he couldn't make use of the memory. If he could somehow transport himself back to that moment and channel the fight between doing what was right and giving in to feelings he was trying to suppress, he might just be able to convince the camera that Bash and Delores were perfect for each other. With a Herculean effort, he summoned up Maura's face and reached out a hand to caress her cheek. He closed his eyes, determined to hold on to the illusion as he dipped his head to deliver the kiss. But just as he was sure their lips would meet, he heard Minelli's dispassionate yell.

'Cut!'

The image of Maura vanished as Priscilla pulled rapidly away. He opened his eyes to see she was staring at him, her brow faintly furrowed. 'That was the best performance you've managed so far,' she said, with haughty condescension. 'Who were you thinking about?'

He wasn't about to admit the truth. Apart from anything else, the ache left by the longing to kiss Maura was too acute. But he didn't mind Priscilla knowing that it certainly hadn't been her talent that had inspired him to raise his game. 'No one.'

She offered him a disbelieving stare but whatever she'd been about to say was lost as Minelli strode towards them.

'That's a wrap,' he said. 'Priscilla, thanks for your time. We'll be in touch if we need anything else from you.'

Fraser said nothing as she was escorted from the room by Krystal.

A few minutes later, the assistant returned. She smiled in sympathy as she approached Fraser. 'How's the cheek?'

He touched the skin, which was still a little tender, and gave an exaggerated wince. 'I think we'll ask Juno to hit the other side.'

Krystal laughed. 'I'll be sure to let her know. Are you ready for lunch?'

He was, Fraser realised with surprise. It seemed simmering rage created an appetite. 'More than ready.'

'Come on,' she said. 'Gordon will have my guts for garters if we let that pizza get cold.'

It wasn't until much later, when Fraser was watching the Pacific Ocean lap at white gold sand, that he realised how exhausted he was. Venice Beach was almost deserted; the clusters of skaters, footballers and volleyballers had long since gone, leaving only a handful of people to watch the sun dip below the horizon. He'd laughed earlier when an enthusiastic musician had tried to get him to listen to his music, offering him a special deal if he bought a CD. This is what Sam meant, he'd realised, and moved on quickly, still grinning to himself. It had been good to laugh, after the tension of the day.

Juno Crosby had been blonde-haired and less classically beautiful than Priscilla, but Fraser had liked her more. Their scenes together had been easy; fun, even when she was slapping his cheek and calling him an asshole. He'd tried to ignite the fires of antagonism, mindful that their characters needed to go from dislike to the first stirrings of love over the course of the film, but he wasn't sure how successful he was. Judging from the expression Minelli wore, he hadn't been convinced either. He'd stopped the final scene just short of the kiss, exactly as he had with Priscilla, and Fraser had been relieved again. The image of Maura had floated into his mind at exactly the same moment and he wasn't sure it was healthy to keep imagining what it would be like to actually kiss her.

After the screen tests were over, Krystal had been keen to discuss his fitness routine ahead of the start of filming. She was surprised to learn he didn't belong to a gym and made a note to find him a personal trainer – one who understood the rigours of preparing to star in a Hollywood blockbuster. She also suggested he work with a nutritionist to help him stay in the best shape possible. 'Not that you're overweight,' she said hastily, when his lips had twitched. 'But we're all carrying a little bit more than we'd like, aren't we?'

Privately, Fraser had thought that Krystal could do with eating more than green salads but that was a minefield he knew better than to approach. Would it have been any better than her suggestion that he could lose a few kilograms? He didn't think so. And then it had been time for him to say goodbye to Minelli and Krystal, with firm handshakes and their fulsome thanks for his hard work.

They'd told the driver to escort Fraser back to his hotel but once in the car, he'd asked to head to the beach instead. The driver had baulked at the idea of leaving Fraser there – clearly, he had his instructions – but in the end, Fraser's determination had prevailed. And now here he was, at just after seven o'clock in the evening, somehow both glad to be on Venice Beach and wishing it was Portobello.

Krystal had told him when he'd left that she'd booked an extra day in case one of the potential co-stars didn't turn up, or filming took longer than it should. But as they'd wrapped up on schedule, despite Priscilla's best efforts, he had the following day to himself. 'Let me know if there's anything you need,' Krystal said. 'And of course we'll make sure you're collected on time for your flight tomorrow evening.'

Except that Fraser was overcome by a sudden desire to feel Edinburgh's cobbles beneath his feet instead of golden sand. He knew a lot of successful film actors relocated to California, but he couldn't imagine living here himself. He might acclimatise to the heat, but he'd miss the way Scotland showed off throughout the seasons; snowy in winter, cautiously green in spring, vibrant in summer and spectacular in autumn. He'd miss the dour humour of his fellow Scots – Priscilla aside, he'd found LA to be relentlessly sunny in more ways than one. But most of all, he would miss Maura. The distance between them over recent weeks had troubled him more than he'd realised, and he'd been in the same city. How could he expect the situation to change if he moved to another country?

Pulling out his phone, he checked flights back to London; the last one departed just after ten o'clock that evening, landing him back in Edinburgh at 9.30pm the following day. There appeared to be seats available. The urge to settle his feet on Scottish soil once more was almost tangible, only beaten by the desire to see Maura's smile again. Before he could change his mind, he reached for his credit card. It didn't matter that he had a flight already booked for the following evening. Sometimes, the heart had to have its way.

CHAPTER TWENTY-SEVEN

There had been a pleasing flurry of interest from the press since Maura's exhibition opened at the castle. Some had been simple requests for a quote; a pottery magazine had been in touch about a feature and the *Wild Scotland* website wanted to explore the way she took inspiration from the natural world. But the message from a *Sunday Times* journalist was the biggest she'd received so far. It came through her website, praising the exhibition as it drew to a close, and asking if she would consider an interview about what the future held. He suggested meeting for coffee at a venue of her choice and Maura saw no reason to turn him down.

She arrived at the Copper Kettle ten minutes early, but the reporter was earlier still. He rose from a table opposite the door when she entered the café, waving in a slightly self-conscious way to get her attention. 'Maura, hi,' he said when she approached. 'I recognised you from the photo on the castle website. I'm Charlie Fleming.'

She shook his hand and sat down. 'Lovely to meet you. Thanks for getting in touch.'

'Not at all,' he said warmly. 'Thanks for agreeing to the interview. But first things first, what can I get you to drink?'

She asked for a pot of tea, which he went to the counter to order.

A moment later he was sliding into his chair once more and regarding her with friendly curiosity. 'Down to business, then,' he said, and she was a little surprised to see an old-fashioned notebook and pen on the table. She'd assumed he'd have a laptop or tablet to make notes on. He saw her looking and grimaced. 'I'm a bit old-school. I once lost months of research when a laptop crashed and I hadn't backed it up, so I prefer a pen and paper approach these days. More difficult to hack, too.'

She smiled, although the final comment confused her. Did the arts correspondent at the *Sunday Times* need to worry about being hacked? She had no idea – journalism could certainly be cut-throat. Perhaps there was a thriving dark web trade in stolen articles about regional potters. 'It's refreshing,' she said. 'I'm quite old-school myself.'

Charlie nodded, as though that was exactly what he'd expected her to say. 'So, I've managed to glean a fair bit about your career path from the internet. You went to St Ignatius School here in the city until you were eighteen, then left to study at Saint Martin's college in London, is that right?'

'That's right.'

He glanced down at the notepad. 'St Ignatius seems to be a hotbed of talent. That's the school Fraser Bell went to – the actor who's just been cast in the new Minelli blockbuster.' A faint frown creased his forehead. 'Did you know him?'

Maura felt her shoulders stiffen and forced herself to relax. She'd expected him to segue into her master's course at Glasgow School of Art but she supposed it was only natural that he would ask about Fraser, given his imminent rise to stardom. 'I knew of him,' she said carefully.

The tea arrived, giving her an opportunity to arrange her cup and saucer, and fuss with the pot. When she looked up, she saw Charlie was watching her. 'You must be around the same age,' he said. 'Were you in the same year?'

There was no point in lying, Maura decided. 'Yes, but we weren't friends. I was always in the art block and he was into drama. As you'd expect.'

She watched Charlie jot down a few notes. 'Just background,' he said easily. 'After you graduated from Saint Martin's, you studied in Glasgow, and then came back to Edinburgh, right?'

'Yes.'

'And that's where you met your long-term partner . . .' He paused to flip back to a previous page. 'Jamie.'

She shifted uneasily. It wasn't impossible for him to have gleaned Jamie's name but it would have taken more than a cursory bit of digging to unearth it. She'd never been one for posting personal information on social media and stuck mostly to pots. 'Yes.'

The journalist didn't look up. 'He's a rugby player, isn't he? Plays for Inverleith Warriors?'

And now Maura had a cold prickling sensation between her shoulder blades. 'Sorry, how is this relevant?'

Charlie's eyes widened at the question. 'Oh, just background info. Painting a picture of your everyday life; readers love to peek behind the scenes to see how artists work.' He leaned back in his chair. 'I played a bit of rugby myself, back in my uni days. Big drinkers, as I recall.'

Her palms began to sweat as she fought to keep her

expression neutral. Something wasn't right but she wasn't entirely sure what.

'Not necessarily the brightest, either,' the journalist went on, his tone still nostalgic. 'I suppose that's got something to do with it.'

'I don't see what it has to do with anything,' Maura replied, frowning.

Charlie waved an apologetic hand. 'Thinking out loud. It's an occupational hazard.'

Still suspicious, Maura took a sip of tea. 'Do you think we could move onto the pottery?' she asked. 'That's what you said you were interested in.'

'Absolutely,' he agreed. 'The pottery. So you'll forgive me for saying this, but the exhibition at the castle seems like a leap forward in your career. How did that come about?'

She took another sip of her drink. Ordinarily, she would have credited Fraser and the ghosts with introducing her to Ewan McRae, but she had the definite sense that would cause Charlie's ears to prick up even further. 'The castle is trying new ways to boost visitor engagement,' she said, picking her words carefully. 'They asked me to undertake some work as a local Edinburgh artist and I said yes. But I exhibit my pottery in galleries all over Scotland, including a couple here in the city. It's a step up but it hasn't come out of the blue.'

'Right,' the reporter said, tapping his pen against his notepad. 'So it wasn't a direct result of your affair with Fraser Bell?'

'What?' Maura felt her jaw drop.

Charlie's gaze hardened. 'Your affair with Bell,' he repeated. 'According to my source, the two of you met at a New Year party. Jamie's drinking problem drove you and Fraser to rekindle your romance from your school days, behind his girlfriend's back, while you pretended to be business partners. Isn't that what happened?'

A dull roaring filled Maura's ears. 'No!'

He smiled but there was no humour in his eyes. He reminded Maura of a weasel baring its teeth. 'You might as well admit it. My source has proof. Times, dates, locations of hookups – the works.'

And suddenly, everything clicked into place. This wasn't an interview about her career at all, Maura realised. It was a trap to get dirt on Fraser, and she had walked right into it. Unsteadily, she pushed her chair back. 'Which newspaper do you really work for?' she asked, fighting to control the wobble in her voice. 'Because I don't think it's the *Sunday Times*.'

Charlie shrugged. 'The *Daily News*. You're about to be famous for a whole lot more than crappy pottery, Maura.'

She glared at him, shaking with shock and rage. Ordinarily, she wasn't a violent person, but his sly insinuations had made her want to hurl the sugar bowl at his head. It would be a mistake, she knew, but the thought did give her another idea; perhaps one that would hurt him more. Without a word, she picked up her barely touched cup of tea and splashed the contents onto his open notebook.

'Hey!' He leapt backwards to escape the tide of hot brown liquid flooding the table and snatched at the sodden pages. 'That's my work.'

'I know,' Maura said, watching the ink run on the dripping paper. 'I hope you had a backup.'

Praying her shaking legs would not let her down, she turned on her heel and walked out. For a moment, the bright afternoon sunlight dazzled her, but every instinct was screaming at her to put as much distance between herself and the despicable Fleming as she could. Pausing briefly to get her bearings, she set off at pace along George Street, blinking back furious tears. She wasn't sure who she was angrier with – Fleming, for his lurid accusations and lies, or herself for trusting him in the first place. The email address should have been a red flag – Gmail rather than an official *Sunday Times* account – but so many journalists were freelance these days and it hadn't occurred to her to suspect an ulterior motive.

Snatches of the conversation leapt out as she walked; had she said anything to corroborate his story? She didn't think so, but it was hard to be sure. And she couldn't even call Fraser to explain what had happened, to warn him about the lies that were almost certainly about to be splashed all over the tabloids. He was in Los Angeles, living his lifelong dream – he'd sent her a photo of a glorious sunrise only yesterday. Never mind that the same bloody dream had just tipped Maura's life upside down. While she knew it was unfair to blame him for what had just happened, it was also true that his burgeoning fame had caused it. But even so, she couldn't bear the thought of spelling out the lurid details of her encounter with Fleming – the idea was simply too mortifying.

Instead, she pulled out her phone and rang her sister. 'I think I've just done something really stupid,' she said, when Kirsty answered. 'And I don't know what to do next.'

'That utter toe-rag!' Kirsty exploded when Maura poured out the awful story. 'And pretending to be from a broadsheet so you'd talk to him – that's low.'

Beside her on the sofa, Maura hung her head. 'I know. I feel like such an idiot.'

'It's not your fault. How were you supposed to know you'd be targeted by tabloid journalists?'

The unspoken suggestion that the blame somehow lay with Fraser made Maura's defensive hackles rise. She forced the instinct down, knowing that wasn't what her sister had meant. 'What am I going to do?'

Kirsty folded her arms. 'There's only one thing you can do – tell Fraser. Let him sort it out.'

The mere thought made Maura want to throw up. She shook her head. 'He's five thousand miles away – what is he going to do?'

'I don't know, maybe instruct his lawyers?' Kirsty replied, exasperated. 'Last time I checked, it was illegal to print things that aren't true. It's defamation or libel or something.'

'But they haven't printed it,' Maura cried. 'Or at least, not yet.'

'This journalist said they intend to,' Kirsty pointed out. 'A well-timed intervention from an expensive lawyer might make them think twice.'

Maura gnawed at her lip. 'I don't know if Fraser has an expensive lawyer.'

'I bet he does,' Kirsty said firmly. 'Or at the very least, his agent does. You have to tell him what's going on, Maura. Once the story goes to print, it will be too late.'

With a heart that felt like a stone, Maura grudgingly accepted she was right. This didn't just affect her and Fraser – Jamie was going to be dragged into it too, and that was the last thing he needed. Reluctantly, she reached for her phone and tapped out a terse message to Fraser giving the bare bones of what had happened. Pressing send, she waited for the single tick to become a pair. It did not. She did a quick mental calculation; it was mid-morning in LA and Fraser was unlikely to be asleep, unless he'd been out partying. She shook that thought away and stared down at her phone, willing it to change, for the ticks to multiply and turn blue, telling her Fraser had read the message.

'Give it time,' Kirsty said, seeing her frustration. 'He might have no signal – you know what roaming is like. And try not to beat yourself up. You didn't do anything wrong.'

Logically, Maura knew that was true. So why did it feel as though she'd been unforgivably naive?

Maura tried not to constantly refresh her messages in the hours that followed but anxiety made it hard to resist. Kirsty had left her just before eight o'clock, with strict instructions to tell Fraser the whole story as soon as he responded, followed by a promise to keep her in the loop with any developments.

Unable to bear the silence of the apartment once her sister had gone, Maura had taken refuge in the studio. She'd known better than to attempt to make anything; the clay would undoubtedly pick up on her jitters. Instead, she'd set about sweeping every dusty corner of the room and scrubbing the floor by hand. Her arms ached, her knees were numb and her hair was damp with sweat, but it felt good to be doing something – anything – rather than staring at her phone.

A muffled knock at the door made her jump. She checked the time – almost nine-thirty, far too late for anyone she knew to be knocking. Whoever it was seemed to be waiting. They knocked again and she realised they weren't at the door of the studio but outside the front door of her apartment. Her puzzlement deepened – who on earth could have a legitimate reason to disturb her so late in the day? It wouldn't be Kirsty; she would be at home by now and, in any case, she had a key. It might be one of her neighbours, and that thought made her pause. Several were elderly – what if one of them needed her help? And then an equally unsettling possibility occurred to her: it could be someone she absolutely did not want to see. Charlie Fleming was a journalist, with access to all kinds of databases and records. If he wanted to know where Maura lived, she thought he could probably find out. But just as she decided to go and see who it was, they tapped on the door of the studio.

Not Fleming, she decided with a faint shiver of relief. To the uninitiated, the doors of the studio looked like all the others along the street – the entrance to a garage. Only those who knew Maura were aware that it was the entrance to her pottery studio. Wincing at the stiffness in her knees, she got to her feet and rinsed her hands in the sink before moving quickly to open the studio door.

The sight of Fraser took her breath away. 'But you're – how—' She gripped the doorframe to steady herself against a wild burst of disbelief. 'I thought you were in California.'

'I was,' he said, his expression uncharacteristically sombre. 'But I came back early. Judging from your message, it's a good thing I did.'

Maura hadn't truly known how tightly wound she was until then. The shock of seeing him standing there, tired and grey-looking but solid and real, seemed to have loosened something inside her, allowing her to breathe properly for the first time since her hideous encounter with Fleming in the café. Tears bloomed at the back of her eyes but she dug her fingernails into her palms, determined not to cry. Stepping back, she opened the door wide. 'You'd better come in.'

As she closed the door, it belatedly occurred to her that she must look an absolute mess. With horrified speed, she dragged her wayward curls back into their scrunchie, hoping her face wasn't as flushed as it felt.

Fraser, meanwhile, was taking in the wet floor and the abandoned brush in the middle of the studio. 'Have you been cleaning?' He didn't point out how late it was to be scrubbing the floor, but he didn't need to.

'Displacement activity,' she offered. 'I wasn't sure if or when you'd see my message and I needed something to do while I waited.'

'I was on a plane from Heathrow,' he said. 'I didn't know what had happened until I reached Edinburgh . . . I landed just after eight.'

The news generated a squirm of guilt. He must have come straight from the airport, after flying through the night from LA. No wonder he looked so rumpled and exhausted. 'I didn't mean to speak to Fleming,' she burst out miserably. 'He pretended to work for the *Times*, said he wanted to talk about my pottery. It was only when he started asking about you that I realised what he was really after.'

Fraser shook his head. 'It's my fault. He accosted me last week, at one of my ghost walks. Things got a bit heated. He mentioned the same rubbish then but I told him I'd sue if he ever published the story.' He ran a hand across his face. 'I thought the threat would make him see sense. Obviously, I was wrong.'

Maura stared at him. 'You knew about his accusations already? Why didn't you tell me?'

'I thought I'd handled it,' Fraser said. 'And then I had to go to LA at short notice, which was a gigantic pain.'·He hesitated. 'And you've been a bit ... well, a bit distant over the past few weeks. I didn't want to bother you.'

And yet it had all blown up in her face anyway, she wanted to point out, but that seemed unkind. None of this was really Fraser's fault and she couldn't deny that she'd been harder to reach. Deliberately so, in fact. 'You still should have told me.'

'I know,' Fraser said, his gaze wretched. 'But I genuinely thought Fleming would drop it. I was horrified when I read your message – it never occurred to me that he'd contact you.'

And yet that was exactly what had happened, Maura thought, rubbing both hands over her too-hot face. 'So now what?'

He puffed out his cheeks. 'I spoke to a friend who's been through this kind of thing. He recommended an urgent letter from my lawyer to the *Daily News* legal department, denying the accusations and warning them what will happen if they're stupid enough to go to print with their lies. That letter is being drafted now.'

It was the same course of action Kirsty had suggested, but Maura could still remember the anger in Fleming's eyes when she'd thrown her tea over his notebook; he had a score to settle and she wasn't sure a letter would make any difference. 'Will that be enough?'

'My lawyer thinks so,' Fraser said. 'The paper would need to have evidence of an affair, or at least something to show they had good reason to believe it was true, and we know they can't have anything like that because it didn't happen.'

'But Fleming mentioned a source—'

His smile was a grim line. 'Naomi. She's the only possible suspect.'

It made sense, Maura realised, although she wasn't sure what Naomi stood to gain. Perhaps there was more to their break-up than Fraser had told her. 'Fleming knew a lot of detail. He knew about the New Year party, mentioned Jamie's drinking.' She glanced at Fraser. 'I did wonder if it might have been Zoe, but it didn't seem like her style. She was never vindictive.'

'No,' he said with flat certainty. 'Naomi isn't great at handling rejection. I'm afraid this has her sticky prints all over it. But I don't really care about that.' His expression softened as he regarded her. 'What I want to know is whether you're okay.'

Wrapping her arms around herself, Maura slowly nodded. 'I think so. Shaken up and worried, but otherwise fine.'

'That's good,' he said, although the doubtful look in his eyes suggested he was far from convinced. 'And I know it won't make anything better, but I'm sorry.'

Maura closed her eyes briefly. Her heart had leapt to find Fraser on her doorstep and she was glad he'd taken such prompt action to stop Fleming from causing more damage. But it didn't change the fundamental problem. Fleming had approached her because of her friendship with Fraser, and it was something that would probably only get worse the more successful he became. Who was to say this wouldn't be a recurring theme – that other journalists wouldn't pick up the scent and follow it back to her? Could they target her again in the future?

'Thank you,' she said at length. 'I know it's not your fault. It's just the price of fame, isn't it? People want to know everything about you. Scandal sells newspapers and when there's no scandal, they make one up.' Glancing up, she saw he was utterly still, watching her with an air of wary expectation, as though he knew what she was going to say next. 'I can't live that way, Fraser,' she said softly. 'I don't want to be looking over my shoulder every time I go out, or wondering if the messages that come through my website are genuine. I'm happy you're living your dream but I don't want to be caught in the crossfire.' She took a breath. 'I don't think we can be friends anymore. I'm sorry.'

He eyed her silently, his expression unreadable. 'I can't say I blame you,' he said. 'But I've come to a realisation of my own over the last few days. I don't think this *is* my dream. Not anymore.'

Confused, she blinked. 'What do you mean?'

'I mean the whole movie star thing,' he said. 'Fending off journalists, flying thousands of miles at a moment's notice, working opposite actors who are rude and entitled when there are more talented alternatives who don't get a look-in because they don't know the right people. Being away from home and living in hotels . . .' He dragged a hand through his hair and sighed. 'I don't think it's for me.'

'You're jetlagged,' she countered, because he couldn't mean any of this. 'You'll feel better in the morning.'

He took a step towards her. 'That's the thing – I don't think I will. I sat on Venice Beach, telling myself how lucky I was to be there, how incredible it was going to be to star in a Marco Minelli film, and I felt – nothing. No excitement, no happiness. I couldn't wait to leave.'

Maura frowned. 'But that's just homesickness. Everyone gets that when they're outside their comfort zone.'

'Maybe, but I think it was more than that.' He hesitated, uncertainty etched across his face. 'Sitting on the plane, waiting for it to take off, all I could think about was you.'

'Me?' she echoed, her forehead crumpling in dismay. 'Please tell me you didn't come back early because of my run-in with Fleming.'

'No.' Fraser shook his head. 'I didn't know about that until I landed.' He let out a slow breath and fixed her with steady eyes. 'The truth is, you were on my mind long before that. When I was watching the sun come up in Beverly Hills, on a tour of the studio and even when I was supposed to be kissing Priscilla de la Cruz. That's when I realised the only woman I wanted to kiss was you.'

The admission caused Maura to gasp. She goggled at him in wide-eyed astonishment, certain she must have misheard. 'What?'

His gaze didn't waver. 'I'm not sure how long I've wanted that. Maybe for months, although I convinced myself I was mistaking friendship for something else. And then you broke up with Jamie and you were so lost – so fragile – that it felt wrong to even think of you as anything more than a friend. I was scared to do anything that might hurt you or frighten you off.' He puffed out a sigh. 'I still am.'

Head reeling, Maura let out a shaky laugh. All this time she'd been holding back, worried that admitting she wanted more than friendship would drive Fraser away, and it seemed he'd been doing the same. But fear hadn't been the only thing holding her back. His return to acting had given her another good reason to say nothing, and that hadn't changed. The hesitation Fraser was experiencing now would undoubtedly pass, and

Maura would be left nursing more disappointment – perhaps even a broken heart.

'Why are you telling me this?' she asked, anguish colouring the words. 'You're about to become world famous, Fraser. I don't want to be part of that.'

Shaking his head, he kept his eyes fixed on hers. 'But that's what I'm trying to tell you. I'm not going to be famous. I pulled out of the movie.'

'You did what?' The calmness with which he had uttered the words only bewildered her more. 'Are you insane?'

Fraser grimaced. 'I know that's how it looks but I'm actually thinking rationally for the first time in months. Or as rationally as a man who's lost his heart can ever think.'

It was too much for Maura. Did he mean he'd lost heart in acting? She took a breath. 'I don't understand. What exactly are you saying?'

He took three steps forward to close the distance between them and gently took her hands. 'I'm saying that I love you, Maura.' He gazed steadily down at her, a smile curving the corners of his mouth. 'I think I always have, right from the first time I saw you. I just didn't appreciate it until yesterday.'

'Me?' she whispered, certain she had misunderstood once again. 'You *love* me?'

Fraser nodded. 'Do you remember that Christmas years ago? When we bumped into each other outside the pub and you stopped me from landing face down on the pavement?'

She felt her eyes widen. 'Yes, but I didn't think you did.'

'How could I forget?' he said. 'You looked like an angel, sent to save me from myself. But no sooner had I got you in my arms than you vanished, and it took me eighteen years to find you again.' Smiling once more, he reached out to brush a curl from her forehead. 'I fell in love with the idea of you then. It's taken me until now to realise I love the woman you've become.'

Tears pressed at Maura's eyes but this time she didn't fight them. How often had she dreamed of him saying these words? Could she trust that it was real now? 'Do you mean that?'

He nodded. 'I do. And I hope with all my heart you love me too.'

The dam broke inside Maura. All her fears and objections were washed away, leaving only the shimmering glow of happiness. 'I do,' she cried, turning her face towards his. 'I do love you. I think I always have.'

Afterwards, she would marvel at the way time seemed to stop. The breath caught in her throat as she stared up at him, this man who had danced in and out of her life for so long. She took in the long lashes that still framed the oceans of his eyes, the fine cheekbones and firm chin, now partly softened by the ticklish brush of his beard. He'd called her an angel but he was the beautiful one, and somehow, he was hers to kiss; not for a single stolen moment, but slowly and lengthily. With infinite wonder, she reached up to caress the curve of his cheek and drew him towards her. The touch of his lips was tentative, feather light and all too brief, making her skin catch fire. But less than a heartbeat later, his mouth was on hers again, pressing with a gentle insistence that sent her thoughts spinning, before pulling away once more. When at last he kissed her fully, she lost all sense of anything except him. Her arms tightened around him as the embrace deepened, and she never wanted to let go. It had been so long since that first kiss, too short to do much more than teach her what a kiss could be. But even that was nothing compared to what she felt now. Joy mingled with rightness to create an intense sense of belonging – the feeling that she was exactly where she ought to be, that at long last she was home. Warmth blossomed in every part of her and, for a time, that was all she knew. Then, before she was entirely lost, the kiss slowed. Finally, they broke apart to gaze at each other in dazed wonder.

'Wow,' Fraser murmured, sounding more than a little breathless. 'That's what I call a kiss.'

Maura nodded, trying to gather her scattered thoughts. 'Were we that good at it last time?'

'I don't think so,' he said. 'I'd never have let you get away if we were. But maybe we'll just keep getting better and better with age. What do you think?'

The look in his eyes lit an answering flame in Maura. 'Only one way to find out.'

It seemed to her that their third kiss lasted the longest but felt different again. She was aware of the studio around her but somehow she sensed the stars glittering above them and the nip of December's frost in the air. And then she gave up trying to make sense of anything and allowed herself to float away on the blissfulness of being held by him.

'I should probably tell you that my agent is furious with me,' Fraser said cheerfully, once they finally parted. 'Does it bother you that I'm a washed-up has-been who can't hold down a job?'

Wrapping her arms around him, Maura nestled into his chest. 'Not in the least.' She stayed there for a moment, hardly able to believe he was hers at last, then pulled back to gaze up at him. 'If I ask you to stay, will you?'

Fraser's eyes glittered. 'Forever, if you'll let me.'

And then he kissed her again.

ACKNOWLEDGEMENTS

First thanks go, as ever, to Jo Williamson of Antony Harwood Ltd, for her unwavering support and kindness. Second in line is my perfect editor, Molly Crawford – patient (oh so patient), insightful and unceasingly funny. I am glad to have you – thanks for everything. I am so honoured to be published by Simon and Schuster UK – the team always go the extra mile. Many thanks to everyone on the Books and the City team but a special mention to Pip Watkins for her wonderful cover designs, Misha Manani for extra editorial/admin support, and of course to SJ Virtue for being a wonderful cheerleader.

Many people contributed to the creation of Maura and Fraser's story – with ideas, advice and support, and occasionally with cups of tea or a long phone call about entirely unrelated things (looking at you, Charlotte Dennis). Top of the list here is the incredible Elly Wall – ceramic artist, potter and all round brilliant human being. I have borrowed so much of her expertise, knowledge and career to write Maura, while also absorbing everything she could teach me about making my own pottery.

I first went along to her studio with an idea that I would take a couple of classes to get a feel for clay, and work out how to make an Edinburgh Ghost. More than two years later, I am still going to her studio, although I think I've finally nailed my ghost. Thanks for your patience and generosity, Elly, and for explaining how clay traps work! In addition, a huge thank you to the members of the Tuesday morning pot club – no names, as agreed, but you know who you are. I am so grateful to you for sharing the ups and downs of pottery with me. I tried really hard to get the details right but it goes without saying that any mistakes are entirely my own.

It wouldn't feel right if I didn't tap up Clare Watson for book-related assistance and, on this occasion, she was my go-to gal for advice about Edinburgh. Thank you once again – cocktails soon, yes? I also need to thank the most excellent Keris Fox, who gave me invaluable tips about LA and Venice Beach – you're a gem and much appreciated.

I'm massively indebted to Tania Noble, who helped with a number of sticky plot points and encouraged me to see the story through fresh eyes. Thank you for putting up with my random demands for your razor-sharp insights.

My final thanks go to the loves of my life – T and E, who are my heart, and Luna the Labrador, who seems to be growing more resigned to sleeping at my side while I tappy-tappy-tap but also wants to go for a walk right now, please. And finally, thank you to my gorgeous readers – I hope you enjoy your visit to beautiful Edinburgh. I'll meet you by the Mercat Cross on the Royal Mile for a Dead Famous ghost tour sometime. Don't fall behind, now – Stuart the Slice isn't far away . . .

Discover more from Holly Hepburn

Available Now